Betrayed in the Dark

The Alarie Heirs: Book Two

Ashley Elizabeth

For every woman who has worn a practiced smile while walking around with a broken heart.

This one is for you.

A note from the author

Betrayed in the Dark occurs right after *Broken in the Dark*.
Although it is highly recommended that you read the Alarie Heirs series
in chronological order to fully appreciate the story, it is not a requirement.

Book 1 – *Broken in the Dark* (Leo and Scarlett's story)
Book 2 – *Betrayed in the Dark* (Madeleine and Eli's story)

During Eli's time in the military, he and Madeleine exchanged letters over
the course of several years, beginning when she was seventeen and he was
nineteen. She wrote to him when she felt lonely, had things she wanted
to share, or simply missed him. He wrote to her because he loved her.

Throughout their book, I thought it would be fun to include some of
these letters (not all of them) to show you a tiny glimpse into how their
love unfolded.

I hope you enjoy their story.
Xoxo, Ashley Elizabeth

Content Warnings

This book contains references to assault, gun violence, kidnapping, losing a parent (years prior), miscarriage, panic attacks, PTSD, violence, and other topics that may be sensitive to some readers, as well as sexually explicit scenes.

Reading is an escape for many of us, so if you feel that the mention of any of the above will upset you, please put this book down.

Your mental health matters.

Prologue

MADELEINE

The letter slips between my fingers, descending to the snow-covered dock as my heart splinters down the middle into two jagged beating pieces.

Tears fill my eyes, my vision blurring as I stare across the frozen lake, snow falling heavily around me, dusting my hair. The tips of my fingers transition into a light shade of blue, but I don't feel the bitter cold that tries desperately to sweep over me.

Not when I'm numb.

Lost inside my head.

The only thing I focus on is the four words I just read aloud. Four words that are sure to haunt my dreams and plague my remaining days on this Earth. They repeat themselves over and over again, cruelly suffocating me by binding my lungs in an iron grip.

With a trembling hand, I rub my palm over my sternum, the tenderness in my chest intensifying. I haven't experienced pain like this in years—a pain so strong it feels like I'm on the cusp of dying.

Tears glide down my cheeks, one after another, while my throat tightens and burns, fighting the inevitable sob that wants to escape like a caged animal seeking freedom.

A strong tremor crashes throughout me, sending my knees to the icy layer beneath me. Wind whips past me, and before it can steal from me, my hand shoots out, seizing the letter between my fingers and bringing it before my eyes.

I read it again.

And again.

And again.

The four words engrave themselves onto my fragmented heart, the pain becoming too much to bear.

Before I can stop it, a blood-curdling scream rips from my throat, echoing across the ominous night. I clutch the letter to my chest, hunched over as sob after sob wracks my body.

"Why?" The word forces its way between my lips, thunderous amidst the giant oak trees that sway fiercely back and forth.

There's no response.

No other sound except for the relentless howl of the winds.

How could he do this to me?

After everything we've shared. After the years, the memories, the letters...

I shake my head, my mind unable to understand.

Unable to accept that this is my reality.

Because he wouldn't do this to me.

But when I hold out the letter again, feeling the thin piece of paper between my fingers, I know it's as real as a goddamn nightmare.

The urge to shred it overcomes me.

I try to hold it steady between both wavering hands, prepared to tear it right down the middle—to do to it what it did to my heart. Yet, as the seconds tick by and the snowfall slows, I can't bring myself to destroy it.

One last agonizing scream echoes across the lands, and all the hurt residing inside me releases into the darkness.

I fold the letter, tucking it inside my coat pocket.

Eventually, I stand, wiping every single tear from my face as I retreat into the safety of my home, ensuring no one ever finds out about this moment of weakness.

A moment where I let love blind me.

I let it lead me straight into its venomous trap.

But never again will I be so naïve to the dangers of its power.

Never again will I be betrayed in the dark.

CHAPTER ONE

Madeleine

TEN MONTHS LATER

Who the fuck invented mascara that isn't waterproof?

Oh, I know. Probably a goddamn man who didn't think about the consequences of what would happen if one might cry while wearing it.

Because men don't cry.

No, no. God forbid they ever display their true feelings openly for others to see.

Not when they leave that job for us women to perform.

And when we do show our emotions, well, then we're labeled as crazy and overly emotional.

But not me.

Nope. In our world, I'm known as a cold, heartless bitch who takes mercy on no one.

So, why would I need to worry about mascara that isn't waterproof when I never cry?

I'm an Alarie, for God's sake, the most feared and idolized family in the northeast, reining over those around us.

And we definitely didn't achieve this reputation by showing weakness with tears.

But as I stare at my reflection in the gold antique-framed mirror, watching black tears crawl down my cheeks, I can't help but feel like a complete failure.

Unworthy of the Alarie last name.

What have I done?

I hold my left hand before my eyes, noting the glint and sparkle of the extravagant diamond ring. It's gaudy. Not at all something I would have picked out for myself.

But it seems that recently, I haven't had much say in anything that goes on in my life.

Knock. Knock.

Shit.

I hastily wipe the mascara smears off my skin as best as possible to hide all evidence of my mini-breakdown. "Be right there." Just as I finish swiping a tissue beneath my bottom lashes, the door swings open, slamming against the wall and leaving a noticeable dent.

What the fuck?

"I said I'd be right—"

My words die on my lips as I glance into the mirror and catch sight of a pair of familiar dark irises resembling storm clouds, ready to unleash terror.

It's him.

Eli Lyon.

A man I grew up with.

The one who gave me my first kiss while playing spin the bottle as kids.

The one who wrapped me in his arms after my father's death, providing a sense of safety I've never felt before in this dark world.

The one who traveled across countries and oceans to be with me in secret.

And the one I wish I could hate.

I knew I'd see him eventually. It was inevitable, given that he's now playing the role of bodyguard to my brother's wife and my best friend.

But in a sense of delusion, I had hoped that by some chance, some miracle, our paths would never cross again.

Merely because I knew it would hurt too much.

And I was right. It does.

Not wanting to give him the satisfaction of seeing me in a moment of weakness, I quickly throw on a faux smile and toss the tissue into the barrel beside me, my fingers gripping the marble counter for support.

"Eli," I say evenly, hoping and praying he doesn't see through my confident façade.

"Madeleine," he replies, watching my every move with intense eyes like a predator on the hunt as his gaze travels down my ivory satin dress. His voice is the same—smooth and gravelly, extra velvety when he says my name, which sends a pleasant shiver down my spine. The English accent he bears only adds to his appeal.

Because he couldn't just be graced with good looks. No. He was also gifted a voice that would instantly make any woman drop to her knees.

I should know.

With a raised brow, I tilt my head to the side. "I didn't know you'd be making an appearance tonight. Did you come to my engagement party to congratulate me?" I purposely wipe an imaginary piece of lint from my right shoulder, giving him an unobstructed view of the monstrosity displayed on my ring finger.

His eyes narrow in on the diamond, his jaw clenching forcefully. If I didn't know any better, I'd say he was giving the look of a jealous man.

He steps inside the room, closing and locking the door behind him.

My heart rate picks up as I straighten my shoulders.

Stay strong.

He stands behind me, his large tattooed-clad hands gripping the counter on both sides of me, caging me in. I watch, frozen, as he leans forward to brush his soft lips against my ear, sending a raging swirl of heat throughout my entire body. If I weren't grasping the counter so tightly, I'd probably crash to the floor, embarrassing myself before him.

"No," he breathes. "I didn't come here to congratulate you. Because your engagement is not something to celebrate."

"That's a little cruel, don't you think?"

He shakes his head. "What would be cruel is watching you walk down an aisle toward that prick and not doing a goddamn thing about it." His hand comes forward, grasping the front of my neck, his thumb resting on my erratic pulse. A wicked smile stretches across his handsome face as his thumb glides back and forth over my skin. "It's nice to know I still affect you."

"The only thing you affect is my heartburn," I bite back.

His smile falls, his solid chest pushing up against my exposed back. Tension sweeps over me as he glowers down at me, his eyes desperately trying to see right through me. "What game are you playing, Princess?"

Princess.

My lips part, a silent breath fleeing.

That nickname once made me feel special as if I meant something to him. Maybe even everything to him. But now, it lacks any of the same power over me that it once held. "You can't..." I say far too softly for my liking. I clear my throat, desperately trying to sound poised like his presence isn't chiseling away at the stone walls I constructed around my heart. "You can't call me that anymore."

His grip tightens, igniting a fire low in my belly. One that needs to be quickly extinguished. "Why the hell not?"

"Because I'm engaged. My fiancé would not take kindly to know another man—

"Fuck your fiancé." His eyes darken, chaos brewing beneath the surface. The tiny flecks of gold that I used to count swirl delicately with the deep brown until they vanish entirely.

With his eyes locked on mine, his fingers clutching my neck, and his comforting scent—cedar with a hint of spice—wrapped around me, a familiar ache blooms in my chest. It's a deep, unsettling pain that tries to drag me under the surface. It's the reminder I need to douse the flames brewing between us.

"I can't do this." I push away from him, his hand falling as I slip past.

He's letting me go.

It shouldn't surprise me.

And I shouldn't want him to fight for me.

To prove to me that he was wrong.

That the letter was just a momentarily lapse of judgment.

One he wrote in the heat of the moment and never should have followed through with by sending to me.

I shouldn't want any of that.

But I do.

A brief sting of disappointment washes over me as I step away. That is, until his fingers wrap around my shoulder, spinning me and pushing my back against the door. My breaths come out rapidly as he bends down, bringing his face merely a few inches from mine.

I know this face.

I know the hard edges of his chiseled jaw.

I know the way his stubble feels when he rests his cheek against my palm.

And I know how those soft lips taste.

God, do I remember.

I've been cursed during these months apart, unable to forget.

Even when I've tried so desperately to.

"What are you doing?" I ask, my voice unsteady as his chest brushes against mine. Every nerve ending in my body comes alive, waiting for what happens next. The anticipation of it alters my mind, temporarily causing me to forget why I should hate this man.

His palms rest on each side of my head, his body covering mine like a fortress I could never escape.

"Answer my question first."

I stare at him, forgetting what he asked of me. Forgetting what fucking year it is as his lips slide across my cheek to my ear.

"What. Game. Are you playing?" His nose travels down my neck, stopping at my collarbone before his eyes meet mine under those dark lashes. "The Madeleine I know wouldn't be doing this." Softly, his lips press against my skin, leaving heat in their wake. "This isn't you."

This isn't you.

The words bring me right back to reality.

Back to a world where knights in shining armor don't exist.

And men don't actually mean it when they say those three words.

My hands at my sides clench into fists, my blood boiling with liquid rage.

"This isn't me?" I repeat, a sardonic smile splashing across my face. "Who are you to pretend like you know me?"

His shoulders tense as he rises to his full height. "I know—"

"You know nothing!" I cut him off, shoving at his muscular chest. "You think because we shared some measly letters or a few forgettable nights together that you know me, but you don't." I walk to the other side of the room, fury overtaking me. "You don't fucking know me." I shake my head, getting lost in my memories. "Not since…"

My words trail off as my mind relives a moment that has continually haunted me.

Four words echo across my skull.

Back and forth.

Up and down.

One sentence that changed everything between him and me.

My heart thunders violently beneath my rib cage, a tremble tumbling through me, shaking me to my core.

I pinch my eyes shut, my fingers digging into my scalp. "Make it stop," I plead.

Eli's large hands cup my cheeks. "Make what stop?"

I open my eyes, blinking back tears I won't let escape, especially not in front of him. I take in his worried features, his eyes softening with concern.

He's the man I dreamed of spending forever with.

But that's all it ever was—only a dream.

"Nothing." I swallow down every emotion and straighten my shoulders, placing a smile back on my face. "Now, if you'll excuse me, I have a fiancé waiting for me." I shove past him and turn, my knuckles wrapping around the doorknob.

"When was the exact moment you stopped waiting?"

His words slice through my icy heart, stopping me in my tracks. "That's not fair," I whisper, peeking over my shoulder.

"Fair?" Anger unleashes in his voice. "Did you forget about the damn promises we made to each other?"

I stare at him, completely bewildered by his accusation.

How dare he?

I've spent the past ten months crying in the shadows because of him, mending a broken heart in silence, never letting anyone witness my daily agony: the nightmares, the panic attacks, the guilt, and the insomnia—all because of him.

I face him, crossing my arms over my chest. "Clearly, we made promises to each other that neither one of us could keep."

"Oh? And how did I break mine? Because if I remember correctly, you were engaged to another man when I came home. It was you who broke your promise to me. So, please, enlighten me: which promise did I break?"

"You promised to never hurt me." My words settle in the space between us. His features contort with either confusion or understanding; I'm not entirely sure which one. But either way, I can't stay this close to him any longer.

My walls are cracking with every passing second.

And I refuse to break in front of him.

He opens his lips, a sorry-ass excuse probably sitting on the tip of his tongue, but it's too late. The damage has been done.

Holding up a hand, I stop him. "Let's get one thing clear right now. You're my brother's best friend and, unfortunately for me, a part of my family. But that does not give you the right to storm into my engagement party—one of the happiest nights of my life, I might add—and be mad at me for moving on with my life." I twist the doorknob, opening it a few inches. "Oh, and do not ever refer to me as 'Princess' again. That name died along with the girl who once believed in fairy tales and happily ever afters. Now, I know the only person who will ever rescue me is my goddamn self." Locking eyes with him, my heart beats wildly beneath my rib cage. "I once made the mistake of loving you, Eli. But I promise you, I will never make that same mistake again."

Slamming the door behind me, I straighten my shoulders and stride confidently back into my engagement party toward the man across the room, flirting with a blonde by his side.

Alastor Manacorda.

My fiancé.

And the villain of my story.

November 28th

Dear Eli,

I bet you're surprised to receive a letter from me. But I figured I should admit something. And you should know that this is very difficult for me to say. But the truth is that it feels strange not seeing you at the Alarie Estate almost every day. It's weird not hearing that perfectly annoyingly posh English accent. It's weird not knowing when I'll ever see you again.

It's just really weird. And I don't like it.

Anyway, how's life in the military treating you?

It snowed today. The estate always looks so beautiful when it's covered in a blanket of white. It's my favorite time of the year.

Please don't mention this letter to my brothers.

Stay safe,
Madeleine

P.S. Is it weird that I wrote to you?

Chapter Two

Eli

I don't know the exact day it happened—the day I fell in love with Madeleine Alarie.

Maybe it was when she sent her first letter to me, subtly trying to let me know she missed me without directly saying she did.

Maybe it was when she kissed me during spin the bottle, her heart beating as fast as mine was.

Or maybe it was the day she felt safe enough to break in my arms, letting me see a side to her that she never showed anyone else, in fear of appearing weak.

Like I said, I don't know the exact day it happened, but that's only because I can't think of a single day when I didn't love her.

"So, what do you think?"

Leo's voice cuts through my thoughts, and I internally shake my head, looking at my best friend as he waits for my answer. If only I weren't daydreaming over here about his fucking sister, then I might have a bloody clue what the hell he just asked of me. "Think about what?"

He crosses his arms over his chest, his dark eyes focusing on me. "Reassigning you to Madeleine."

My cold, beating heart picks up speed for the first time in a long time, thundering violently as if awakening from hibernation.

"You promised to never hurt me."

The words she hurled at me at her engagement party awaken. Thundering across my skull. Invoking a restlessness that slinks across my chest.

And every day since that night, I've wondered, what the hell did she mean?

How did I hurt her when I wasn't even here?

I'm the one who came back from the Middle East to find out that the woman I've been in love with for my entire life is engaged to another man.

I'm the one who had his heart brutally ripped from his chest, shredded into a million fucking pieces.

So, how could she accuse me of hurting her when she's the source of the pain that emits over the center of my chest, day and night?

"Eli?"

I drag my fingers through my hair, exhaling. "Sorry. Didn't sleep well." *Not a total lie.* I lean against the counter as I process his question. "You want me to be Madeleine's bodyguard?"

Leo reaches for the bottle of whiskey on the counter beside him and pours it into two glasses, handing me one. His gaze turns to the back of the kitchen, toward the commotion.

A few caterers dash around the space in a tizzy, preparing the final touches on the desserts for his celebratory engagement dinner with his wife. Yeah, I didn't say that wrong.

A pan falls to the floor, dishes crash in the sink, and someone shouts out orders to others.

"Signore, concedeteci un momento," Leo instructs the staff, who nod and step out of the room, giving us privacy. He picks up his glass of amber liquid on the counter, swirling the contents before taking a sip. "Actually, it was my mother's idea. She thinks it will be good for Madeleine to have you nearby. Someone she's known her whole life."

Fuck, none of them have any clue as to how well we know each other. If they did, well, I probably wouldn't be standing here before Leo breathing air into my lungs.

That's for bloody sure.

Not to mention, he'd probably regret the day in primary school when he beat up the kid for making fun of my accent, instantly making us best friends.

"And what about Scarlett?" I ask before taking a hefty taste of my drink. Scarlett, his wife and a woman I grew up with, is who I've currently been assigned to these past few months while they were hunting down her kidnapper.

Leo hesitated to call me about the job offer, waiting until it was essential for my presence, understanding the challenges I had recently faced. He was giving me time to heal—both physically and mentally. However, he didn't realize that his need for me in such an important matter made me feel like I had a purpose in life for the first time in too long.

Let's just say that right after that phone call, I didn't hesitate to pack a bag and hop on the first flight from England to New York.

Back to a place that always felt like my second home.

The Alarie Estate.

"I'm assigning Asher to her," Leo answers, placing his empty glass on the counter beside him. "He's ready for the new assignment and has proven himself worthy of this position through his years of loyal service. Besides, it's not like he hasn't already been keeping an eye on Scarlett for me while she was living off the estate, even if she didn't know it."

I nod. Asher's a good guy and highly qualified to keep Scarlett safe. I can't argue with that, and I don't see any problems with the reassignment except for one thing...

"What does Madeleine have to say about this?" I saw her just a little while ago on the beach with the others, and she didn't seem upset. Maybe she's okay with—

"We haven't told her yet."

Dread coils in my stomach. Heavy and impenetrable.

I bring my drink to my lips, downing the rest of it. The slight burn from the liquid slithers down my throat, temporarily distracting me from the uneasiness that begins to simmer within me.

"She's waiting for us in the office," Leo tells me. "Vin will be the one to inform her." He squeezes the back of his neck. "I'm not exactly sure how she'll take the news, but you did take a bullet for her, so that's got to count for something, right?"

"Right," I solemnly answer, remembering that day like it was yesterday and not almost a month ago.

The Alarie Estate was overtaken by men who coveted two things: power and revenge.

And they were dumb enough to think they would achieve it.

But the scariest moment of that night wasn't when the explosions went off or when the power went out.

It was when we circled the cottage, where we knew Scarlett was being held captive, and I looked through the window, finding Madeleine unconscious. I didn't know if she was alive or dead. I didn't know up from down. Left from right. Or even how to fucking breathe.

But the second I saw the perpetrator raise his gun and aim directly at Madeleine, I acted on pure instinct. Everything around me blurred as I jumped through the window, shards of glass flying all around me. My body flew before hers, the bullet piercing me in the shoulder.

Me and not her.

That's all that mattered to me.

That she lived even if that meant I died.

Fortunately, I didn't.

But the impact of the bullet, plus the loss of blood, had me going in and out of consciousness.

When Madeleine came to, learning what I did for her, she gripped my shirt as she sat in the ambulance beside me, quietly pleading, "Please don't do this to me! Don't you dare leave me, Eli Lyon! I can't live in this world without you!"

Maybe she thought I was dying.

She certainly didn't know I could hear her every word.

However, when I came back to the Alarie Estate, she returned to being her distant self, keeping as far from me as she possibly could. Acting as if the two of us were merely strangers.

When that's far from the truth.

"Why now?" I ask.

"Things are tense," Leo replies. "Vin's concerned others in our world view us as weak after what happened, and in case anyone gets brazen enough to pull anything, we want to ensure that every security precaution is taken both on and off the estate. Madeleine should have always had a bodyguard, and she did when she was younger. But we've been lenient with her over the years. Too lenient. And it's time to step up safety protocols. It would destroy this family if anything ever happened to her. So, as furious as she is going to be, it will be worth it knowing she'll be in good hands."

Furious is probably an understatement of how Madeleine will be, but I don't dare mention that to him.

Footsteps approach, and Leo and I both turn to see his brothers Vincenzo, Alessandro, and Mauro entering the space. Three intimidating motherfuckers who've always treated me as one of their own.

"I'm assuming you've told him," Vin states, glancing at Leo. He rolls up his shirt sleeves as he approaches before crossing his arms over his chest. With his imposing size and presence, it's clear why he became the head of the family after his father's death; not only is he the oldest of the five siblings, but he also exudes authority.

Leo nods.

Vin's eyes land on me. "And what do you think?"

I release a deep breath as I rub the back of my neck. "I'll guard her with my life."

None of them realize the extent of my words. That I'd willingly sacrifice my life for hers if need be. Or that I'd burn this fucking world to ash for her if that's what she asked of me.

I'd do anything for that woman.

Well, anything except watch her walk down the aisle to marry another man.

Yeah, that's not happening.

Mauro grunts in approval before pouring himself a glass of whiskey and downing it in one go. His stature matches that of Vin's: burly and muscular. His shoulder-length hair is held back with a black leather strap while a few loose strands escape, framing his face. My eyes catch on the scar across his neck, a reminder of one of the worst days this family has endured, before quickly looking away.

We all bear scars.

Some that can be seen, and others that can't.

I should know.

"Good," Alex answers, grabbing a paper towel to wipe away a few drops of liquid on the counter. "That's what we wanted to hear."

"Jesus Christ, can you go one day without fucking cleaning something?" Vin pinches the bridge of his nose.

"If this falls to the hardwood floors, it will stain." Alex tosses the napkin in the trash and then adjusts his glasses before pushing back his light brown hair.

"Oh, in that case, you missed a spot," Vin informs him.

"Where?" Alex scans the counter, grabbing the roll of paper towels.

"Made you look," Vin chimes back in amusement.

Alex rolls his grey eyes. "Fuck you." He whips the roll of paper towels at Vin's head, who ducks out of the way.

"It's too easy." Vin smooths out his dark hair, laughing.

"You're giving me a headache." Leo rocks his neck from side to side. "Don't forget why we're meeting."

"Of course." Vin turns his attention to his Rolex. "Well, let's not keep her waiting. If I know our sister, she won't take the news very well. She's used to a certain level of freedom, which she'll still have, but...with a shadow nearby."

"I take it I'm the shadow." I squeeze the back of my neck, every muscle in my body tensing with apprehension.

Vin's finger taps on the counter beside him as he watches me with trepidation in his eyes.

"What?" I ask.

"We know this has been a challenging year for you. And we don't want to force your hand in this assignment or risk setting back any progress you've made." He sighs, his fingers gripping the counter behind him as he looks down. "I can only assume the unfortunate incident at the Alarie Estate last month might have caused some...unease." His eyes meet mine. "So, if you'd rather take some time off, we understand. We can find someone else to guard Madeleine if—"

"I can handle this," I interject. There's no way in hell I'm trusting anyone else with her safety. "I'm fully prepared to be her bodyguard."

Vin takes a moment to digest my answer, determining if I'm being truthful. "Okay then," he answers as he steps away, walking out of the room. "Let's get this over with."

Mauro clasps my shoulder before turning and walking out of the room, his other brothers trailing behind him.

I follow after, my heart rate accelerating with each step I take.

Right before I step into the office, I take a deep breath and pray that agreeing to this doesn't make things worse between us.

But then again, she's engaged to another man.

How much worse could it get?

January 16th

Princess,

Is it really that hard for you to admit that you miss me?

Life is…different? Not bad, but not great either.

Some days are harder than others. Like when I found out I couldn't go home for Christmas. I missed my mom's famous Christmas pudding, but she promised to make me some the next time I visit.

I'm not quite sure when that will be, though.

I can't disclose my location, but unfortunately, there's no snow here, which is a shame. I know how much you love the snow. You always have that twinkle in your eye during the first snowstorm. I'm sorry that I missed it.

Yours,
Eli

P.S. Not weird at all. Your letter came right when I needed it.

CHAPTER THREE

Madeleine

S trumming my polished nails on the arm of the leather chair, I let my eyes travel around the office as I continue to wait for my brother, Leo, to make his grand appearance. He told me we had an urgent matter to discuss, which has now put my nerves on edge, as I'm unsure what could be so pressing. Especially since this weekend is supposed to be a special getaway to our Hamptons house to celebrate his engagement to his wife, my best friend, Scarlett.

Yeah, they did things a little out of order.

But the point is, this weekend isn't for work.

It's for relaxing.

Something my family clearly doesn't know how to do well.

I check the slim gold watch on my wrist. He's ten minutes late. Is this part of his tactic? Is he purposely making me sweat it out?

What could be so important that—

Fuck. My chest tightens, and anxiety crawls over my skin.

He must know.

That's the only plausible reason why I'm here right now.

He knows about me and Alastor.

I press my fingers to my temple, massaging the pressure points where a headache begins to form.

Have I been too careless over this past year?

Did I let something slip?

I reach for my glass of champagne, needing to calm my nerves. Throwing back the drink, I close my eyes and enjoy the fizz from the bubbles sliding down my throat.

There's no way he could know. Not when I've played my part so perfectly.

Standing, I make my way to the closest window, observing the waves crashing along the shoreline as the sun sets over the horizon—a picturesque view that my family paid millions upon millions to enjoy.

It's a home that offers elegance and all the comforts one could want in life. Twelve bedrooms, fourteen bathrooms, a ten-car garage, a private beach, and an indoor pool, just to name a few of the amenities. But it doesn't give me the same calm I experience when I'm home.

My real home.

At the Alarie Estate in Upstate New York.

A place that outsiders find to be intimidating and know better than to venture to in fear of what may await them.

Like death.

It's a fortress unparalleled to any other in the world, surrounded by thick stone walls that have recently doubled in height and width. A place where I, my mother, my siblings, and the many loyal workers of my family reside.

It's been my sanctuary since the day I was born.

A home where I truly feel at peace.

Even from things I can no longer avoid.

Like my impending wedding.

I glance down at my watch. Twelve minutes.

This is ridiculous. I wait for no—

The click of the doorknob unlatching and steady footsteps approaching let me know he's here without even having to turn around. But what has me pausing is the additional footsteps.

Shit. This isn't good.

Staying strong, I keep my composure, turning as my four brothers all make their way before me, followed by... My throat goes dry as my eyes freeze on Eli.

The man I so badly wish I could hate.

Because then everything would be so much easier.

Not to mention, less painful.

"Madeleine," Vincenzo, aka Vin, my oldest brother and the head of this family, greets me with a kiss on my cheek before making his way behind the mahogany desk. He took on this role over seven years ago after our father was murdered, and I hate to admit it, but he's done a pretty damn good job over the years keeping our family safe, considering all the enemies who would love to stab a knife in our backs. With his dark black hair and bright blue eyes resembling mine, we look more like twins than siblings, even with a seven-year age gap. As he takes a seat, his eyes hold mine, a silent apology flashing over them.

Unease settles inside me.

"Take a seat," he tells me.

"I'll stand." I defiantly cross my arms over my chest, jutting out my hip. It might be a man's world, but I'll be damned if I ever let one tell me what to do.

Even my own brother.

"Of course you will." He tips his chin, knowing me better than anyone in this room—well, maybe not everyone—and he recognizes that this is not the battle he wants to fight me on.

Not when a bigger one is brewing.

The others take their places around the room, all eyes landing on me.

"Thank you for speaking with us," Leo says too formally for my liking. He stands behind Vin with his tattooed-covered arms crossed over his chest, his dark brown eyes never wavering on me as he appears very much the part of the deadly predator that he is. He's the one responsible for hunting down those in the streets of New York who are past due on payments to our businesses or dare to attempt harm to our family.

I'll never understand why the bastards run. Not when he always finds them.

The others in the room remain silent. There's a current of tension stifling the air between us.

What the hell is going on?

Clearing my throat, I stand a little straighter. My spine turns into a steel rod as I plaster on my famous Madeleine Alarie smile. The one I've perfected over the years. The one no one can see through.

"Brothers and...Eli." I spare him a glance, unable to make eye contact with him. "What is so important that you had to step away from the celebration to speak with me so formally?" I question with my gaze directed at Leo. It is his big night, after all. "Is there a problem with the casino?"

Over the years, I've become the unofficial financier of my family. Always good with numbers, I welcomed the responsibility and took pride in my ability to keep the family's investments...*clean*. Or as clean on the books as I allow anyone ever to see.

Not that our investments have ever been a problem, seeing that half the police force in this state is willingly on our payroll.

But the casino, referred to by guests as Luxe, is one of our family's most profitable streams of revenue.

And most importantly, it's mine.

"No problem with the casino," Vin states. He steeples his fingers before him. "With everything that has occurred recently, we think it would be wise to take some extra precautions."

"Of course," I answer, my eyes bouncing to each brother. "But what does this have to do with me? Do you need access to funds for more improvements to the estate?"

Maybe that's all this is about. My shoulders relax a fraction at this notion.

"No." Vin shakes his head. "This is more of a family matter." His eyes move to Leo before he gives a quick jerk of his chin.

Leo runs his fingers through his dark hair, briefly eyeing Eli before his gaze lands back on me.

No. No. No. Something doesn't feel right.

If this is a family matter, then why is Eli even here?

"It's imperative to us that you're safe," Vin starts. "You have always been our top priority, but recently, we've been too lenient in a world with so much darkness. So much cruelty." He pauses, looking deep in thought as he stares at his desk, and then slowly, he nods. "So, with that said, we have asked—"

"No!" I spit out, my hands falling to my sides, transforming into fists. "No fucking way in hell." My heart races beneath my chest, panic swirling throughout me. This can't be fucking happening.

"Madeleine," Vin states, his voice laced with authority. "Eli is the best one for the job. He will keep you safe and—"

I take two steps, my palms landing on the desk with a loud thud as I lean closer to Vin. Fury radiates through my veins. "I am quite capable of taking care of myself. I don't need a bodyguard. I don't need him!" My chest heaves with each breath I take as my eyes dart to Eli, who sits there calmly. All six-foot-five of his muscular body. His gorgeous, deep brown eyes hold mine, causing my breath to catch in my throat. His thick, brown hair is tousled as if he had run his fingers through it a hundred times. Something he does when he's nervous.

Am I making him nervous?

I quickly look away, my eyes connecting with Vin's, who stares me down, an eerie calm surrounding him. "Eli," he says, his eyes still on me. "Do you mind giving us a moment?"

I don't dare look away from my brother, not wanting him to win this one. I won't back down from this fight.

After hearing the door close, I stand straight, crossing my arms over my chest, my eyes drilling holes into Vin's face.

God, I wish he didn't look so much like me, or I'd call him ugly.

"I'm only going to ask you this once," Vin says calmly. "Did something happen between you two that, as your brother, I should know about?"

My lips part but then close just as quickly. I scoff, turning to face the wall of books behind me before suddenly saying, "No. Don't be ridiculous."

It isn't totally a lie.

As my brother, he definitely doesn't want to know the details about what happened between us.

"Then why do you hate him so much?" Leo asks.

My shoulders drop, my hands dwindling to my sides. "I don't...hate him."

I've tried.

Believe me, I have, but never with any success.

"Well, you sure fooled us," Alex notes, making me roll my eyes. Sometimes, I really despise how smart Alex is. He's the brains of our family. The one you go to when you need security footage retrieved, a computer hacked, a new identity created, etc. But he's also the one you go to when you spill a glass of red wine on your white carpet at two a.m. in a drunken panic.

Yeah, he wasn't too fond of that wake-up call.

I turn to face the four of them.

None of them believe me.

They're all looking at me like I'm the problem.

A clearing of a throat causes me to look at Mauro, whose dark eyes say more than he'll ever be able to after sustaining injuries from the same explosion that killed our father. There's not much I can hide from him. He's the most perceptive of all of my brothers. And probably the deadliest.

However, this is one secret that he and the others can never discover.

"Alastor won't like this," I utter, my voice steady, hoping the threat of him might cause them to reconsider their ludicrous plan.

"Let me deal with him." Vin pulls at his tie, loosening it until it falls apart. "Although, it's not like your safety seems to be of any concern to him." He cocks an eyebrow, waiting for me to protest.

To tell him he's wrong.

But why would I?

Alastor is a monster who feeds on the weak.

One I am soon going to be tied to for the rest of my life.

I shake my head. "Eli is not going to be my body—"

"He fucking will be!" Vin snaps, standing to his full height, his burly body leaning over the desk. He takes a deep breath, staring down at the dark, stained wood. I can count on one hand the number of times my brother has raised his voice at me. And this moment just made that list. "Do you have any idea what it felt like when I stormed inside the cottage, seeing not just Scarlett in danger but you too? Finding you tied to a chair, practically unconscious with bruises and a gun being pointed at you." His bright blue eyes dart up, meeting my identical pair. There's so much regret in his eyes. So much pain I've never seen him display before. "I won't make the same mistake again by leaving you unprotected. I'm sorry, but this is how things are going to be. And if it's not him, then it will just be someone else. Figured this would be the lesser of two evils for you."

The lesser of two evils? I internally laugh. If only he knew.

I shrug as my throat burns with the overwhelming urge to cry in defeat. But I won't. Not in front of them or anyone. Because no one deserves my tears. "Well, it looks like I have no choice then."

Vin sighs, rubbing a hand down his face. "We all have to make sacrifices sometimes, Madeleine."

"And pray tell, what sacrifices have you had to endure?"

If his stare could kill, I would be nothing more than a corpse at this very instance.

"Don't make things tough for Eli." Leo leans against the wall, glaring at me.

"Tough for Eli," I repeat with a mocking laugh, anger igniting within me.

"He's had a rough year. He doesn't need more shit from you. Just let him do his job."

My blood boils. Eli's had a rough year? I pinch my eyes closed, taking a deep breath.

What about me?

"Are we done here?" I ask calmly, glaring at my four brothers.

"Yes," Vin answers. "You may leave. We have a few more things to discuss, and then we'll meet you out there."

I nod, taking my leave.

As I briskly stride out the door and into the hall with my eyes focused on the floor, my mind is in a fog when I walk into someone.

Hands grip my upper arms as I begin to fall back, holding me steady and bringing me right up against his chest.

I look up under my lashes to see Eli's eyes locking with mine.

Seconds tick by with my chest pressed against his and his warmth caressing me like a lover's gentle touch before he removes his hold and takes a step back.

The spots on my skin where his touch occurred go cold.

"Madeleine, I..." He turns his head to the side and stares off down the hall.

"Don't." I shake my head, gazing down. "Nothing you say will make this any easier for me. I'm just a woman living in a man's world doing what I'm told every goddamn day."

His head whips in my direction. "That's not what this is, and you know that."

"Isn't it?"

His hands transform into fists at his side as he takes a deep breath. "You were taken against your will by a bloody psychopath. Tied to a goddamn chair with bruises covering your skin. You were—"

"I can handle myself! I was taken because I had a momentary lapse of judgment and wasn't prepared, but I don't need a bodyguard! Especially not—"

"You were fucking shot at!" His chest heaves violently, his eyes wide and dark. "You were seconds away from being killed right in front of my eyes." His eyes soften, his tattooed-covered hands running frantically through his thick dark hair. The same hair that I used to run my fingers through as his head rested against my chest, and he would fall asleep. "Don't you understand the severity of what could have happened?"

Of course, I understand.

My chest tightens as visions from that night float before me.

I was getting ready at my house for the annual Halloween party, looking in my mirror, when a figure moved behind me. I quickly reached for the gun hidden in my nightstand, but I was too late. An arm wrapped around my chest, binding me to the perpetrator, and the moment my eyes looked up to see who it was, he pressed a cloth to my lips. One that, I'm assuming, was soaked in chloroform as I woke up later, bound to a chair with Scarlett hysterically entering the door before me.

And that's when chaos ensued.

The moment the gun fired, I saw my life flash before my eyes.

And it made me mad.

No, it made me pissed off.

Pissed off that I was dying engaged to a man I despised.

Pissed off that I had let everything spiral so far out of my control.

But then, a body flew before me, shielding me. Protecting me from death as it took the bullet for me.

Eli's.

And for the first time in months, my heart slowly started to beat for a man I used to love with everything inside of me.

Eli's eyes bore into mine as if trying to read my thoughts. Trying to place all the puzzle pieces together, forming a perfect picture of the chaos inside my mind.

But before he has a chance to say anything else...

Before he drags me back into his orb...

Before I unravel in front of him...

I turn and walk away.

With my head held high and my heels clacking against the marble floor, I escape to the safety of my room, where I can shatter into pieces. I lock the door behind me and slide against the wall until my ass hits the floor, and I have my knees wrapped in a tight hug.

Slowly, I drop to my side, curling into the fetal position as sobs take over my body. And as I let the tears fall, there's only one thought invading my mind.

How will I survive being so close to the man who has my heart, whether he knows it or not?

April 7th

Dear Eli,

Well, it's official. My dad and I have started working on the plans for my house. We found the perfect spot right on the lake, where I'll have an unobstructed view of every sunset and sunrise. I'm so excited to see everything come together and to finally have a place of my own.

My dad keeps saying I have expensive taste, but I just tell him I know what I like! He can't blame me for that.

Maybe when it's finished, you could visit? I mean, no pressure or anything. It's not like it will be completed for a while anyway, but just know that you have an open invitation.

Stay safe,
Madeleine

P.S. I miss you. There, I admitted it. Happy?

Chapter Four

Eli

Sweat trickles down my temple, my muscles ache, and my chest burns from exertion. But no matter how long I spend sparring in the ring with Mauro, I can't shake the unease surging aggressively through my veins.

Mauro catches me off guard, landing a hook to my left side that sends me tumbling back against the ropes. I shake off the pain and step toward the center, where he waits, bouncing on the balls of his feet, anticipating my next move.

He tilts his head to the side, his eyes observing me as he relaxes on his feet and raises a hand to signal for a break.

Fucking finally.

A harsh breath escapes my lips as I look up at the ceiling, my taped-up fingers kneading the back of my shoulder.

Mauro grabs our water bottles and hands me mine.

"Thanks," I say, guzzling down a few sips before soaking my face with the cool liquid.

He grabs his phone and then turns it toward me.

What's wrong?

I arch a brow. "What makes you think something's wrong?"

He quickly types on his phone before showing me the screen.

Because your head's not in it. You're distracted, thinking about something else.

A sudden silence fills the training center, and I turn to see Leo and Vin heading our way. All the men in the facility nod in greeting as they pass, showing their respect.

Vin approaches, rolling up his shirt sleeves. He wraps his fingers around one of the ropes and leans forward. "You ready for the big move?"

And there it is—the reason I can't focus. The reason I can't sleep, eat, or even fucking breathe. In just a few hours, I'm expected to move in with Madeleine and act like her personal bodyguard. Nothing more.

I'm supposed to pretend like I don't know every square foot of her home. That I didn't fuck her in almost every room or fall asleep in her bed with her soundly wrapped up in my arms.

That's what's bloody wrong.

I feel like I've been dropped in an alternate universe where the past never happened, and I'm supposed to be fucking okay with it when I'm not.

I shrug, feigning indifference as I squeeze the back of my neck. "Ready as I'll ever be."

Vin removes his tie and tosses it over his shoulder. "We need to talk to you."

I reach for my towel and drag it across my face. "What's going on?"

Leo jumps into the ring and leans against the corner pole. "We're not letting Madeleine and Alastor's wedding happen," he tells me.

Relief washes over me.

I mean, I wasn't going to let this fucking wedding happen either, but hearing that we're on the same page feels reassuring.

"And how do you plan on doing that?" I ask.

"With your assistance," Vin answers. He pushes himself away from the ropes, crossing his arms over his chest. "Madeleine hasn't been herself this past year. And I think there's only one person to blame for my sister's unhappiness."

A muscle tics in my jaw. "Alastor," I grind out. That fucking twat leaves a bitter taste on my tongue every time I have to say his damn name.

"That's why we came to talk to you." Leo nods, shoving his hands into his pockets. "As far as we can tell, Alastor and Madeleine barely communicate. Barely see each other, for that matter." He shrugs. "I don't consider myself an expert on love, but this seems more like an arrangement than two people madly in love like she's trying to make us all believe."

Arrangement?

"But why would she agree..." My words die off as I look between them. "You think he's blackmailing her?" It would make sense, but she's a fucking Alarie. What could he have on her that she can't come to her brothers about?

Or even me, for that matter?

"Most likely." Vin nods, deep in thought.

Mauro grunts in agreement, crossing his arms over his chest.

"Can't we just ask her?"

Vin laughs. "She's stubborn—maybe even more so than I am. Asking her if she's being blackmailed will only make her retreat further into herself, and I won't risk pushing her away." He rakes a hand through his hair. "Her house is her sanctuary. I won't break her trust by spying on her with cameras, but having you move into her house will give us a chance to observe her without intruding."

I nod, understanding more than most how much she loves her home and why. "So, you don't just want me to be her bodyguard but a spy as well?"

"Yes," Vin answers as if it should have been obvious.

I take another gulp of water as I mull over his request. "I'll do what I can."

"Good." He scratches at his facial hair. "I've arranged a meeting for you and Leo with Alastor's stepbrother, Enzio, at his club in the city tonight."

My brows cinch in confusion. "And why would we meet with an enemy in his territory?"

"Because Enzio has been cast aside by Alastor and their father, Adolfo. He was always set to become the CEO of Manacorda Enterprises, but after Alastor announced his engagement to Madeleine, there were some changes in the family business structure."

"You think Alastor's using her as a pawn in his family's schemes?"

"Possibly. But I think you'll gain better insight after speaking with Enzio. Face to face."

"And you trust him?"

"We are not privileged to trust others in our world, but he wants what we want. To bring his stepbrother down."

I toss my water to the side and then lean against a pole, stretching my arms across the top of the rope. "I might be stating the obvious here, but instead of wasting time uncovering everything, can't we just make him disappear?" That's how we usually resolve issues with this family. Why should this matter be any different?

"If only it were that simple," Leo answers, giving Vin a pointed glare.

Vin rolls his eyes. "If we kill him, we risk going to war with the Russians. The Vasiliev family, to be more precise. And seeing that we recently killed the head of their family and have a...future arrangement with them to uphold..." He tugs on his collar. "We need to try to stay level-headed in this situation. Or at least for as long as possible until we're left with no choice but to kill him. If it comes to that, I will take full responsibility for it. But it needs to be our last resort."

"Not that any of the Vasiliev sons seemed too upset about the loss of dear old daddy Igor," Leo remarks. "Although, as far as I'm aware, they're still under the impression that his death was caused by the explosion and not by me."

"Wait…" I process Vin's words. "Future arrangement?"

"You don't want to know." Leo shakes his head. "Let's just say when we needed a favor from our cousins, the Marchettis, well—"

"I'd prefer not to discuss that right now. My sister's safety is more important than any favor owed," Vin states firmly.

"Okay…" I glance between them. "But how are the Manacorda and Vasiliev families connected? What am I missing?"

Vin lets out a heavy sigh. "Not only are the Manacorda and Vasiliev families related by blood, but they are also business partners. They have worked closely together for years, dealing in oil in the Middle East, specifically in Iraq." The mention of that country churns my stomach. A cold sweat breaks out on the back of my neck, and I clench my teeth as I fight back the nausea, swallowing the lump in my throat. "It's common knowledge in our world that because of their connections and land ownership in Iraq, the Vasiliev family has enabled the Manacorda family to transport oil directly from the country without going through the proper channels. In return, the Vasilievs receive a significant profit for each barrel sold. The more oil that is transported, the wealthier both families become," Vin explains. "Basically, they scratch each other's backs, and if we decide to kill Alastor for no good reason except that he's engaged to our sister…"

"Then you risk creating an enemy of the Alarie family," I respond, understanding the implications. "A rather powerful one."

"Exactly." Vin nods. "We must start taking extra precautions whenever necessary, which is something we should have been doing from the beginning. The women in this family are our top priority, and we need to do everything possible to ensure their safety. So, yes, your primary job is to keep Madeleine safe, but we also need you to be our eyes and ears in the hopes of finding out what's really going on between these two."

"Of course."

"Madeleine is used to doing whatever she pleases," Leo adds. "She hasn't had a bodyguard in years—not since our father's death—so having someone around her all the time will be difficult for her."

"I can handle her."

He nods. "We'll need this problem resolved before the wedding day."

My stomach plummets. *The wedding day.* Fuck, I don't like hearing that. "Is there a date yet?"

Leo sighs, looking at Vin. "New Year's Eve."

My heart thuds heavily beneath my rib cage as every muscle in my body tenses. *She chose a date.* A date that is just over a month away.

I stretch my neck to the side. "How often do they see each other?"

"As far as we can tell, not often. He's been to the estate only a handful of times. His primary residence is in Italy, where he spends most of his time, only visiting the States when required for business. When he does, he stays in his penthouse in the city," Leo answers.

Good. The fewer times I have to deal with Alastor, the better. The thought of seeing them together sends a burning rage through me. It was hard enough to restrain myself at their engagement party, where I nearly threw her over my shoulder and took her away from all this bullshit like some caveman.

Vin's eyes narrow in on me. "We consider you a part of this family, Eli, which is not something that should be taken lightly. But I'll ask you what I asked Madeleine." He pauses before saying, "Did something happen between the two of you that should be brought to my attention before proceeding with this arrangement?"

I've never been more grateful for my military training than I am at this moment.

"No." Confidence echoes in my words as I hold Vin's gaze. One blink, and he'll know I'm lying. "Nothing happened between us."

Leo runs his fingers through his hair. "Then why the hell does she hate you so much?"

"Your guess is as good as mine."

I wish I knew.

Maybe then I could fix everything between us.

But from the moment I landed back on U.S. soil, she's despised me, wanting nothing to do with me.

And if I'm being honest, it fucking hurts.

Absent-mindedly, I rub a hand over my sternum. I've spent so much time trying to figure out what could have happened between the last time I saw her and my return, but nothing makes any goddamn sense to me.

"Promise me one thing, Eli." Madeleine's soft lips press against mine, her fingers tangling in my hair, pulling me closer toward her.

"Anything, Princess."

"Promise me you won't hurt me." Her eyes soften as her body relaxes against mine. "When I love, I love with everything in me, and I don't know if I could survive a broken heart." She rests her head on my shoulder. "Don't make me regret this."

My arms tighten around her. "I'll never hurt you, Madeleine, I promise. This is it. It's you and me." I brush my lips lightly over the top of her head. "But now I want you to promise me something in return."

"What?"

"Promise you'll wait for me." Her eyes look up into mine. "I don't know how long I'll be gone or where my next mission will take me. But if I know you're here for me, it'll keep me going. It'll help push me through each day, knowing I'm that much closer to being with you."

Tears blur her eyes, but a small smile tugs at her lips. "There's no one else for me but you, Eli." She kisses me one last time before saying, "I promise I'll wait for you."

Vin's authoritative voice interrupts my memory. "Don't make me regret this, Eli." He scrapes a hand over his jaw, glancing at the ceiling before returning his gaze to me. "She's everything to us, and I can't risk her safety. Figure out what the fuck is going on with Alastor and keep our sister safe. That's all I'm asking."

"I won't let you down."

He glances at his watch. "I have to go. I have a meeting with the Hajdari family soon, but keep me informed on your meeting with Enzio." He turns, making his way for the door.

Leo slips out of the ring and looks over his shoulder as he says, "I'll see you tonight."

Mauro holds his phone before me.

Let's call it.

I grasp his shoulder and grin. "About fucking time."

An hour later, I shower and pack the rest of my belongings from my cottage. I don't have much, so it doesn't take long. Just as I zip up my bag, I feel an inexplicable pull toward the nightstand. I glance at the drawer, my heart racing.

With cautious steps, I approach. An invisible tether pulls at my chest, growing tighter with each movement. Carefully, I reach inside and wrap my fingers around the small black box, holding it before me. As I open it for the first time in months, I'm hit with the familiar ache in my chest that accompanies every glimpse of its contents.

The pear-shaped diamond stands securely between six prongs, with a thin platinum band running beneath it and smaller diamonds spaced evenly around it.

It's nothing extravagant—nothing that demands attention.

"Timeless" is the word the jeweler used to describe it.

Yet, it's the simple, elegant design that reminds me of Madeleine, which is why I purchased it on the damn spot when I saw it.

I bought it for her right before I left for my last deployment, planning on giving it to her after seeking approval from her mother and brothers, of course.

But when I returned, reality hit me like a sledgehammer.

And everything I dreamed of and longed for came crashing down around me.

I should return it, maybe even toss it into the bloody ocean.

But every time I try to rid myself of its presence, I cave and hide it beneath my things, keeping it close. Never too far out of reach.

It's a weakness brought on by the most dangerous thing a man can store inside his heart.

Hope.

My phone vibrates in my pocket, and when I pull it out and see the name flashing across the screen, I immediately tuck the ring in my bag, keeping it safe. Keeping it hidden.

Answering the call, I'm instantly greeted by a familiar, sweet voice.

"Eli?"

"Hey, Angel. I'm here."

July 10th

Princess,

Of course, I'll visit. It's only fair that I get to see what your expensive taste comes up with. Knowing you, I'm picturing gold everywhere. I'm talking about the floors, the banisters, the windows, the counters… You'll probably put the Golden Pavilion to shame. Kidding, of course, as you've always had a way of making everything you touch look beautiful.

I'm hoping to get some time off soon so that I can visit. How's everyone? Enjoying the summer in New York? I bet you're soaking up the sun by that lake every damn day.

God, I miss those days.

Yours,
Eli

P.S. Very happy.

Chapter Five

Madeleine

Sitting on the dock behind my house, I look up at the ominous sky, pinching my eyes closed as I take a deep breath. My beige quilted jacket offers little protection from the elements, so I wrap my arms around my middle a bit tighter.

As I open my eyes, I take in the frozen lake before me. The snow-covered mountains in the background create a charming view as big, fluffy snowflakes slowly fall from the sky.

This is my home: the Alarie Estate.

And I will miss it more than I can put into words.

"I miss you, Daddy," I whisper, a puff of smoke escaping into the cold air in front of me. "Although I don't think you'd be too proud of me right now. Or maybe you would be. I'm not really sure anymore." My throat burns, and the tip of my nose stings. "I wish you were here to tell me what to do."

As my eyes blur with unshed tears, an alert on my phone chimes. I pull it out of my pocket and glance at the screen. I bring up my surveillance camera and see a black Land Rover descending my long, winding driveway.

Of course, he's right on time.

With a heavy sigh, I uncross my legs and stand up, pushing my hair behind my ears and wiping under my eyes in case any tears have managed to somehow escape.

Entering through the back of the house, my boots squeak slightly against the marble flooring as I walk toward the front and approach the larger-than-life black iron door of my entryway. Momentarily hesitating, I press my hand to the scanner and step back. As the door slowly swings open, my eyes catch on the man standing on the other side. A black T-shirt molds to his muscular chest, and his defined biceps, which are covered in intricate designs, are on display as he drags one hand through his thick brown hair and lifts his duffel bag onto his shoulder.

My eyes quickly scan his body, taking in every hard line and perfectly sculpted muscle. This is not a body built from steroids or countless hours spent in the gym. It was created from manual labor. Put through a level of physical hell that the average person could never understand.

There was a time when I was privileged enough to appreciate every inch of it as it deserved.

A sudden warmth rushes over me, a small fire igniting in my lower belly as old memories come to the surface to play.

"Hey, roomie." Eli smirks, his words instantly dousing the fire within me.

"We are not roommates," I deadpan.

He casually shrugs. "Roommates. Flatmates. Whatever you want to call us works for me." He winks, and that annoying warmth within me returns tenfold.

"We are neither," I grind out, crossing my arms over my chest. "No coat? It's thirty degrees out and snowing."

One corner of his mouth lifts in a playful grin. "You worried about me?"

"Not in the slightest."

He laughs, the sound sending a swarm of wild butterflies to my stomach. "I like the cold. After spending so much of my life in the Middle East, I find this weather to be my favorite."

The Middle East. My stomach churns, the butterflies dying one by one as I'm suddenly hit with guilt, knowing what he's been through.

Or actually, not knowing. Not really.

"Well, are you going to let me in, or is your real plan to let me freeze to death?" A puff of air forms before his lips, proving just how cold it is.

I step to the side and let him enter, closing the door behind him, leaving us completely alone for the first time since...

"New painting?" he asks as he steps into the living room and approaches the canvas hanging above the roaring fire.

It's an abstract piece I found while visiting family in the south of France. The image is split down the middle, with one side engulfed in darkness and the other in light. Two figures stand at the bottom, back-to-back, staring off into their respective sides, longing for the other, but the worlds they live in keep them apart. Separating them from the one thing they both desire most in this world—each other.

The artist I bought it from didn't tell me this story.

It was just something I felt deep within my bones.

"Yes," I say, waving a dismissive hand. "It was a gift from an artist overseas." *Lie.* I bought it the moment I saw it, drawn to it like a moth to a flame. But I won't admit that to him—he'll read too much into it.

His eyes skim the canvas, taking in every detail before he turns to look at me.

He knows.

Of course, he knows.

It shouldn't surprise me that he would see the same story I do.

There used to be a time when I felt so in sync with him.

Like no matter what, we would always have each other's backs. That we would always be on the same page as each other.

That is...until we weren't.

Four words.

Back and forth.

Up and down.

I press my fingers into the side of my scalp, where an ache forms, and take a few steps toward the kitchen. "All right, well, would you like a tour?"

He adjusts his bag on his shoulder, gazing off into the distance. "I'm pretty sure I remember my way around the place," he states coolly.

A slight stab of irritation from how casual he's being hits me in the center of my chest.

Did none of it mean anything to him?

"Of course." I turn, making my way to the stairs. "Well, if you'll follow me, I can show you to your room."

Awkwardness instills as silence reigns over us.

It's not that I've never had a bodyguard before. There have been times in my life when tensions were high between rival families, especially right after my father's death, when I was forced to have a bodyguard with me at all times. I didn't particularly mind it, but I didn't love it either.

So, this isn't new to me.

It's just that none of my bodyguards have ever been...him.

As we approach the guest room that I've arranged for him, I point to the scanner on the wall. "Alex had your handprint programmed, so you'll be able to use this."

Eli extends his arm and presses his palm against the scanner. I'm immediately drawn into the tattoos swirling over his skin, the ones I used to trace with my fingers—and sometimes even with my tongue. I get lost in thought until the scanner chimes and the door opens.

Eli gestures for me to go ahead of him, and I do.

It's a lovely bedroom, if I do say so myself. It's large yet simple, expensive but classy. The walls were painted with a fresh coat of grey just last week, while the dark wood beams were left untouched. The exposed bulb fixtures have been hung to provide a soft glow. The weathered wood and steel furniture that was recently delivered gives the space an almost industrial look.

"There's an en-suite bathroom, and the mattress was just delivered a few days ago, so it will probably take some time to...break in." My cheeks flush as I face the balcony doors overlooking the terrace. What the hell is wrong with me? I step closer to the balcony, trying to avoid looking at him as I open the door, enjoying the arctic air that cools my overheated skin. Once I feel sufficiently cooled down, I close the door and turn to find Eli starting to unpack. "If there's anything you may need, just let me know."

I step for the door, but Eli takes a larger step between me and the exit, blocking my path. "You placed me in the room directly across from yours," he notes.

I swallow hard and manage a small smile. "I hope my close proximity to your room won't be an issue, but all the other rooms are currently packed up as I will be expected to move after the wedding."

His brows furrow. "Alastor isn't moving here?"

I run my fingers through my long hair, pushing it over my shoulder. "No. He thinks it would be better for us to move to Italy. That's where most of his business is conducted."

His eyes darken. "I see."

"Yes, well." I sidestep him, positioning my foot to step out into the hall, but my boot heel falls awkwardly and makes me lose my balance. Just as I'm about to face plant, strong hands grip my arms, spinning me and pulling me against Eli's chest. My breaths come out hot and fast as I look up, finding his face far too close to mine. His lips part, and I swear the look in his eyes tells me he's about to go in for a kiss, but just as suddenly, he shakes his head and releases me, allowing me to stand upright.

Good. I didn't want him to kiss me anyway.

Definitely did not want that.

Nope. Not one bit...

"Well, I'd better unpack." He turns away from me, bending down to retrieve items from his bag.

Standing in the doorway, my lips part, ready to say the words that have been on my tongue for weeks. But I lose my courage and slightly close the door before walking away. I take a few steps down the hallway and come to a stop.

I am Madeleine fucking Alarie.

I can say these simple words and then be on my way.

He's going to be living with me, for God's sake.

It would be even more awkward if I didn't say anything.

Quickly returning to Eli's room, I push the door open and walk inside. "Eli, I—"

My words die in my throat.

He looks over his shoulder, our eyes connecting, but I lose all train of thought when my gaze lands on his exposed back.

His very red, scarred back.

Burns.

A small gasp escapes me as my chest tightens.

What happened to him?

Without missing a beat, he quickly faces me and throws on his shirt. "Sorry, I was just going to take a quick shower."

I stare at the carpet, shaking my head. "No. That was my mistake. I shouldn't have just walked in like that."

Silence envelops us, and I'm unsure how long we stand there before he asks, "Did you need something?"

"Huh?"

"You came in here saying my name."

"Oh. Right." I tuck my hair behind my ear. "Yes, I just wanted to, umm, well, see, I never properly thanked you for jumping in front of that bullet for me. I don't even want to think about what could have happened if you didn't, so...thank you."

He nods but looks down at his bag, continuing to put his clothes away. "It was nothing."

"It was something to me." The words slip from my lips so quickly and softly that I'm not even sure I actually said them.

But the look in his eyes, reflected in the dresser mirror, tells me he heard them.

I avoid his gaze. "I'll give you some privacy. Sorry about just barging in. It won't happen again." Clearing my throat, I add, "My...bridal shower is tomorrow. We'll need to be there at one."

I don't wait for his response as I quickly march across the hall, never once looking back. I enter my bedroom, shutting the door behind me.

Grabbing my phone off my dresser, I call Scarlett.

She answers on the first ring. "Hey, what's up?"

"Any chance you feel like coming over and splitting a pint of ice cream with me?"

I crouch down beside my bed, pulling out an old shoebox.

The shoebox that every girl keeps under her bed.

"Eli moving in is going that bad, huh?" she asks sympathetically.

I throw off the lid and reach inside for a specific envelope. Pulling out the piece of paper, I bring it before my eyes, reading the words over and over again to remind myself why I need to keep my distance from him.

The four words send a fresh stab of pain through my chest, doing precisely what I hoped they would.

"Let's just say it's a whole bottle of wine kind of night."

"I'll be there in ten minutes," she says before hanging up.

As the words from the paper sink into my soul, causing fury to boil inside me, I drop the letter back into the box and flop down on my duvet, staring up at the ceiling.

A tear crawls down my skin, soaking into the pillow beneath me. My heart thunders, my pulse racing as my eyes pinch shut, determined not to let another one escape.

Does he even think about our last moment together?

THIRTEEN MONTHS AGO

As I shove a handful of chocolate-covered popcorn into my mouth, my eyes glued to the TV before me, an alert on my phone lets me know that someone has entered past the gate at my driveway. I tap the screen and zoom in on the unfamiliar black vehicle, which is slowly approaching my house.

The tinted windows make it impossible to see the driver clearly.

It could be one of my brothers.

Or maybe even my mother.

But something in my gut tells me it's none of them.

Pieces of popcorn fall from my lap as I rise from the sofa, wrapping a blanket around my shoulders. I walk toward the front door, my gaze fixed on the decorative painting next to it. I take the painting down from the wall and press my hand against the scanner until I hear the metal door of the safe unlatch. Slowly, it swings open.

Reaching inside, I grab my gun and turn off the safety before facing the door. I glance down at myself, wondering if I have time to change. It's probably frowned upon to meet an enemy in a black silk nightie, but I don't seem to have a choice, as the sound of tires crunching over gravel echoes just outside.

Standing on my tiptoes, I peek through the peephole and watch as the vehicle comes to a stop about fifty feet from my front steps. My heart races as the driver's door opens.

Thanks to my brothers, I've been trained on how to handle situations like this. However, being trained in a simulated scenario versus participating in a real-life scenario are two completely different things.

A man stands with his back to me as he straightens, adjusting a bag over his shoulder. A dusting of snow begins to cover his shoulders, his body covered in a dark winter coat, most likely hiding his actual size.

Fuck, he's a big guy.

But I can handle him.

I'm a goddamn Alarie.

Adrenaline courses through me as I open the door and aim with both hands. "I will kill you if you take one step toward—"

All the words die on my tongue as the man turns to face me.

Dropping my gun onto the side table, I step outside, my body humming to life for the first time in months. My bare feet barely register the cold as his eyes land on me, a fire within them scorching a path across my skin.

"Eli," I breathe.

The corners of his lips curve up. "Princess."

The blanket falls from my shoulders as my body moves of its own accord, rushing toward him with a burning need like I've never experienced before.

He's here. For me.

He meets me in the middle, dropping his bag and lifting me into the air as I leap for him. My thighs wrap tightly around his torso while my arms cling to his neck, tugging him closer.

His lips connect with mine, his invigorating taste awakening every part of me. Every fragment of my goddamn soul.

This isn't a gentle kiss.

It's not slow or soft.

It's urgent and volatile.

Hungry and desperate.

It says everything we haven't been able to tell each other while apart.

I've missed you.

You're all I've thought about.

I love you.

My fingers slide up the back of his neck, gripping the ends of his hair. Reluctantly, I pull away to get some much-needed air and bury my face in the crook of his neck, breathing in his familiar, comforting scent. "This doesn't feel real." I dig my fingers into his shoulders, my chest heaving as I pull back to look at him, our eyes locking. "Is this real?"

He grins and sweeps his nose against mine. "It's real."

"What are you doing here? I didn't think I'd see you until after the New Year."

"In your last letter, you said you needed me, so I'm here, love. I'll always be here when you need me." He softly brushes his lips over mine. "I have three days of leave before my next deployment, and there was only one person I wanted to spend them with."

I bite my bottom lip as heat creeps up my neck. "Me?"

He presses a kiss to my temple. "You, Princess." His hand cradles my cheek, his thumb gently stroking my skin. The warmth of his minty breath dances across my face, his lips only inches from mine.

"Then what are we standing out here for?" I brush my lips over his ear. "Take me to bed."

He doesn't hesitate as he strides through my front door, his arms securing me to his body. Our lips find each other as he kicks the door shut behind us and walks through my house, knowing every part of it like it were his own, never breaking the kiss as we ascend the stairs.

With every step he takes, my urgency grows, my core throbbing with anticipation for what's to come.

It's not our first time together.

Not by a long shot.

But every time we're together, it feels like it is.

I suppose that's what happens when we only see each other fewer than a handful of times in a year.

As we walk through the bedroom, he lays me down on my black satin sheets, his body hovering over mine. My hands slide down his back, my fingers tugging at the hem of his shirt and dragging it over his muscled body before flinging it to the floor. I stare in admiration at his perfectly sculpted torso, dragging a finger along every ridge across his abdomen.

"My turn," he whispers, reaching for the bottom of my nightie. The fabric glides effortlessly up my stomach, over my breasts, and around my head before being tossed to the floor, leaving me in nothing but a pair of black lace panties. His eyes rake over me, growing darker by the second as his head shakes in disbelief. "I've traveled all over the world, witnessing some of the most famous sights and breathtaking landscapes that this world offers, but you... You are my favorite view." He leans down, pressing a kiss between my breasts. "So soft." Kiss. "So beautiful." Kiss. "So perfect."

I revel in his every touch. Every kiss. Every caress.

I've waited months for this moment.

And now that I finally have him back in my arms, I can't wait a second longer.

I rock my hips up, searching for friction.

"Someone's impatient," he teases, taking one of my nipples into his mouth. He sucks and nips, sending a bolt of pleasure straight to my core as his hand kneads my ass.

"It's been so long without you," I complain, my fingernails scraping down his shoulders. "Too long."

"I know, love. I'm sorry." His smile falls as he sits up and moves his hands to my thighs, pushing my legs farther apart. "I won't make you wait any longer." The palm of his hand glides over my core, rubbing softly against my clit. "Is this what you want? For me to take care of you?"

"Mmm, yes," I moan, biting down on my bottom lip.

He lowers himself, positioning his head between my legs. "These need to go." He tugs my underwear down my legs, revealing all of me to him. "Bloody hell," he whispers in awe as he bites down on his fist. He glances up at me as he presses a kiss to my center, inhaling my scent. The act alone makes me wetter than I care to admit. His fingers grip my thighs. "Spread your legs for me, love. I've been dreaming about this pussy for months, and I want nothing in the way of what I'm about to do to you."

I do as he says with no shame, a pure carnal need taking over me.

Gently, he leans forward, leisurely dragging his flattened tongue up my slit all the way to my clit.

"Fuck," I breathe, my fingers curling into the sheet.

"You're the most delectable thing I've ever tasted," he says right before going in for more. But this time, he's not gentle or slow. He's ravenous. Like a starved man who just had a taste of his favorite meal. His tongue thrashes against me better than any vibrator ever could. I scream out as his lips wrap around my clit, sending me closer and closer to the impending orgasm.

"God, I've missed you," he breathes against me. "Your taste. Your sounds. Every single part of you."

My fingers twist into his hair, keeping him exactly where I need him to focus. "I'm almost... I'm so...close..."

One of his hands holds down my thigh as his other hand teams up with his tongue. Two fingers swirl above my soaked entrance, relentlessly teasing me.

"Please," I plead. "I need more."

He plunges both fingers inside me, coaxing a throaty moan out of me as my face turns into my pillow. My walls tighten around his fingers as he rubs the right spot, creating the perfect amount of friction as his tongue remains focused on my most sensitive part.

It's the combination of his fingers and tongue, the way he gives me his full, undivided attention, not stopping until he leaves me completely satisfied, that is my ultimate undoing.

The orgasm crashes over me, my back arching as inaudible sounds leave my lips. The only time I experience this intense bout of pleasure is with him. Only with him.

He continues to lap up every last drop as I lie in a state of euphoria, my heart thrashing against my rib cage, my mind in a pleasurable haze as the orgasm slowly fades away into the horizon.

He gently pulls his fingers out from me and kisses his way up my body, rekindling the desire in me for more.

I need all of him.

"Eli, please," I say softly, as he wraps his lips around my nipple, sucking hard just the way I like as his fingers intertwine with my own, providing me with the right mix of rough and gentle.

Because he knows exactly what my body wants and needs.

He's the only man with that privilege.

"Tell me what you want, love. I need to hear you say it."

"Fuck me," I say in a breathy whisper.

He licks his bottom lip, his eyes darkening with lust. "Every second of every day, for the past eighty-three days, I've dreamed of hearing you say that."

I grin playfully. "I gave you an order and expect you to follow through with it, soldier."

In the next second, I'm thrown over his shoulder, squealing in excitement as he smacks my ass, a delicious burst of pleasure spreading to my core.

The French doors open, and a cool breeze skates around me, causing goose bumps to erupt over my flesh.

He places my feet on the ground and then just as swiftly spins me around. I lean against the stone banister, overlooking the lake.

He bends down, his warm breath ghosting over my ear. "Hold the railing, love."

My knuckles grasp the edge, holding on tight as his hand skims down my back, pushing me over the edge. Blood rushes to my head as I hang forward, my breath catching in my throat when I realize how high up we are.

I hear him speedily unfasten his pants, letting them fall to his ankles before kicking them away. "I won't let anything happen to you," he promises me as he positions himself behind me, dragging his thick cock through my release. "You're always safe with me."

I gasp as he nudges inside my entrance, the pressure almost unbearable. My body tenses, waiting for him to slide further inside me, which only adds to the discomfort.

"Relax and let me in." His hand snakes around my hip, cupping my center, his fingers rubbing gently over my clit. "You can take it."

My muscles loosen with each stroke, my body melting into his tender touch.

"That's my girl," he groans as he inches inside me. "You take my cock so well, love. You always do."

The praise sends a flutter of warmth through me.

Once he's entirely inside, he stills, giving my body a moment to adjust to his size. His hands grip my hips, anchoring me to him, and my eagerness intensifies.

Then, slowly, he pulls out, and my body quickly feels lost without him until he thrusts back inside.

"Oh, fuck," I exhale sharply. Desire washes over me when he hits that special spot, the one that truly makes me see not only stars but the whole goddamn universe.

"You were made for me," he says just before he picks up speed, his cock plunging harder and rougher. A delicious sting of pleasure surges through me, igniting with each thrust as he fucks me senseless. "I've been away too long." His hand comes down hard on my ass, eliciting a whimper as wetness runs down my thighs. "And it's time to remind you who you belong to."

"More," I beg, sounding desperate and needy. "I need more."

In one swift move, he pulls out of me, spins me around, and lifts me in the air, his cock impaling me as I wrap my legs around him.

"Yes," I yell, the new angle allowing him to thrust further within me.

His fingers dig into my ass, lifting me up and down with the rhythm of his thrusts. Our foreheads press together, our pants mixing around us. A familiar tremble travels through my thighs, a fire emitting in my belly. My hands skim his biceps, wrapping around his neck as I hold on for dear life.

"Come for me, Princess."

And I do.

Like a storm of fireworks taking off into the night sky, my body convulses as the orgasm wracks through me, sending me over the edge of ecstasy.

Eli's release follows soon after, a guttural groan leaving his lips as he clasps his arms around me, securing me to his body.

The two of us catch our breath while the cool night air caresses our sweat-soaked skin.

His lips sweep over mine. "I could spend forever like this with you."

My heart flutters, the corners of my lips tugging up. "I'd be okay with that."

"Yeah?"

"Yeah." I tilt back, staring into his eyes, wishing forever could start right now.

August 28th

Dear Eli,

He's gone.

-Madeleine

CHAPTER SIX

Eli

Quietly, I walk past Madeleine's bedroom door, make my way down the stairs, and out the front door, where Mauro and Leo are waiting for me by their cars.

"You ready?" Leo asks, a puff of white smoke escaping his lips into the cold night air. He rubs his palms together and holds them in front of his mouth, exhaling against them for warmth.

"I'm ready." We don't want Madeleine to know what lengths we're going to in order to stop this wedding, so we waited until after Scarlett left and Madeleine fell asleep before embarking on this mission. I glance at Mauro. "We'll be back in the morning. If she wakes up, notify me, and I'll return right away."

He gives a two-finger salute as we turn and depart.

I look at Leo. "Scarlett's secure?" He raises an eyebrow, and I chuckle. "I know, dumb question."

"Asher's on duty now," he replies. "I let Scarlett know I had some business to take care of in the city. I won't lie to her, but I don't want her to know more than she needs to. There's no reason to add any additional stress to her life."

I nod as I open the driver's side door to my SUV. Leo slides into the passenger seat and adjusts his gun inside his jacket.

I start the car, and the gentle purr of the engine vibrates through the cabin. Unease fills me as we leave the estate and head toward the city, not knowing if we might be walking straight into a goddamn trap.

But I trust that Vin knows what he's doing.

After entering the club with a guard escort, I find myself on high alert as we navigate through the crowd.

I hate fucking crowds.

Too many faces to read.

Too many movements to watch for.

My chest tightens as my heart rate begins to accelerate.

Every square inch of this place is packed to the brim like a can of sardines.

The strobe lights dance around the room, heightening my sense of impending doom.

And the noise...

There's so much goddamn noise.

If a bomb went off right now, we'd be—

"This way," the guard says, leading us down a quiet hallway toward an open elevator that seems to be waiting for us. I step inside with Leo beside me and immediately notice that there are no buttons on the walls.

"Floor three." The guard's deep voice echoes in the enclosed space, prompting the doors to close before the elevator ascends.

"Neat trick," I remark, clasping my hands behind my back.

After a brief moment, the elevator comes to a stop, and the doors slide open, revealing an office. The guard gestures for us to enter, and we step cautiously into the room, alert to our surroundings.

"Welcome, gentlemen."

My eyes lock with none other than Enzio Manacorda, Alastor's stepbrother, who sits in his wheelchair behind his desk. He motions toward the empty chairs across from him. "Please take a seat."

Leo and I exchange glances before both of us settle into our chairs.

"You may leave now, George," Enzio instructs the guard behind us. "We have business to discuss, and I won't require your assistance."

"Of course, sir." George steps back into the elevator right before the doors close behind him.

For the first time since entering the club, we're immersed in deafening silence.

"Well, I must say, I'm a bit disappointed that your brothers didn't join you," Enzio remarks, leaning back in his chair and scratching at the stubble over his chin. "It's been quite some time since I've seen them."

"We didn't want things to become too...boisterous," Leo replies.

"Boisterous?" He glances between us, steepling his fingers. "Well, color me intrigued. Why have you come to see me? Vincenzo didn't give me much information except that it was an urgent matter."

"It is," Leo states. "It's a pressing family matter that we can't put off any longer."

Enzio eyes the gold rings on his fingers. "And when you say a family matter, you mean—"

"The wedding's not happening," I interject, getting straight to the point.

Enzio freezes for a moment before cautiously placing his hands on the arms of his chair. "I see."

"As you can imagine," Leo continues, "my brothers and I are not pleased with the upcoming nuptials. Alastor is not exactly who we would choose for our dear sister, which is why we intend to put a stop to this."

Enzio nods in understanding. "He is not someone any brother would want their sister to marry." He glances at me. "And how do you fit into this?"

I offer a sly smirk. "I'm merely the bodyguard."

Enzio raises an eyebrow, clearly perceiving more behind my remark. "And what's stopping me from going straight to Alastor with your plans?"

"You could," Leo says. "I mean, you could pick up the phone right now and call him, but you won't."

"What makes you so certain?"

Leo offers a half shrug. "Because it seems we both have something to gain from working together instead of against each other."

"Perhaps." Enzio taps a finger on the arm of his chair, deep in thought. "I'm just trying to decide if I can trust you."

"The feeling's mutual," I voice.

Enzio's eyes narrow. "And if I help you with this matter, what's in it for me?"

Leaning forward, I rest my elbows on my knees. "Look, we're stopping this wedding from happening one way or another—whether you help us or not. But we're men of our word, so if you help us with our problem, we'll vow to help you with yours."

Enzio's brow raises, curiosity flashing over his eyes. "By helping me with my problem, you mean..."

"Doing whatever it takes to get you back on your precious throne."

His gaze drifts between me and Leo, letting a moment of silence pass before he lets out a heavy sigh. "Fine. Not like there's much left for me to lose at this point."

"All right." I drag my fingers through my hair. "Now that we have that out of the way, let's start by you telling us what we need to know. Preferably from the beginning. We don't want any details left out."

He nods, adjusting the sleeves of his jacket. "As most know, I am—or should be—the rightful heir to the Manacorda Empire. But about a year ago, that all changed. On the day Alastor and Madeleine's engagement was announced, I was, how should I say, dethroned from my rightful place in this family. No longer in the running for CEO." He sighs. "It was a position I had spent my whole life preparing for, and just like that, it was taken from me."

"Why?"

"That's what I need to figure out. By traditional standards, I am of pure Manacorda blood, while Alastor has none. He's not truly one of us. But after I sustained my injury many years ago..." He stares down at his lap, his fingers tightening on the arms of the chair. "I've only been seen as a weakness by my father." He peers out the window and then back at us. "My mother, may God rest her soul, died when I was just a boy. Soon after, my father remarried my stepmother, Mila, as he felt it made him look weak to be viewed as a widower. With her came Alastor and Cressida."

"Cressida?" The name doesn't ring a bell.

"Yes, Alastor has a twin sister," he says, arching an eyebrow. "Have you not met her?"

I shake my head, trying to recall this piece of information, but Leo interrupts my thoughts.

"She'll be at the bridal shower tomorrow. You won't miss her; she looks just like Alastor."

"She's a sweet girl. Mostly keeps to herself. Can't say I blame her, knowing who she grew up with," Enzio comments, his eyes bouncing between the two of us. "Alastor is a snake in disguise. A true psychopath, if you ask me. But because of his...tendencies, my father was drawn to him."

"Tendencies?" I ask.

"Let's just say that as a kid, he took pleasure in making my pets go missing. And as we grew older, it only got worse from there."

My blood boils with rage thinking of this monster anywhere near Madeleine.

Especially alone.

"Alastor, well, he worships my father. Wants to be just like him. Actually, no." Enzio shakes his head. "He wants to be more powerful, more influential than he is. He'd take over the world if he could."

"And my sister," Leo says, looking deep in thought. "You think she comes into play because a marriage with her secures a connection to our family—the most powerful family in the northeast."

Enzio points a finger. "Bingo."

Why the fuck would Madeleine agree to marry this lunatic?

I tug at my collar; the room suddenly feels too warm.

The fact that Alastor has her in his clutches doesn't sit well with me.

Not one goddamn bit.

"He's blackmailing her," I state. "It's the only plausible reason behind their engagement."

"It wouldn't surprise me," Enzio answers. "Alastor will do whatever he needs to do to get what he wants."

"But what could he possibly have to blackmail her with?" I grit out, trepidation spreading throughout my chest.

Enzio shrugs. "We all have monsters in our closets. What are hers?"

Leo shakes his head in disbelief. "She's never even killed a man."

I arch a brow.

"As far as we know..." He scratches the back of his head.

"Sometimes we think we know someone when we truly don't," Enzio says matter-of-factly.

"Isn't that the truth?" Leo's eyes darken, lost in a memory.

I squeeze the back of my neck in frustration. "None of this makes any sense. Madeleine doesn't take crap from anyone. She's always been strong and independent. And then, suddenly, she's engaged to Alastor, who, no offense," I say, glancing at Enzio, "is about as attractive as a naked mole rat."

He lifts a shoulder. "No offense taken."

"And on top of all that, he's a raging psychopath. We need to find out what he's holding over her, and we need to do it quickly. I won't let her walk down that aisle toward that prick. It will be a cold, bloody day in hell before she ever gets to call him her husband." Out of the corner of my eye, I notice Leo's gaze shifting to me, his eyes narrowing in suspicion.

His body tightens as he leans closer, opening his mouth as if he's about to say something. *Shit.* "The Alaries are my family, and I will not let your arsehole of a stepbrother cause any one of them harm."

Leo shifts in his seat, leaning back in his chair as he nods in agreement. Enzio considers this for a moment, then opens his desk drawer. Leo and I instinctively reach for our guns, but we quickly pull our hands back when Enzio retrieves a manila folder.

"When Vincenzo called to arrange this meeting, I had my suspicions about what it was regarding." He holds out the folder for me. "This contains everything I've gathered over the past few months concerning Alastor. Every loyal person in his life, every financial transaction concerning Manacorda Enterprises, every flight taken on our family's private jet—even his goddamn tee time. You name it, it's all here. Maybe some fresh eyes can help find something worth noting."

I take the folder and skim through the contents. "Who would you say is closest to Alastor?"

He scoffs. "That would be his guard, Tony Amante. Wherever Alastor goes, he goes. If anyone knows something, it would be him."

"Have you tried questioning him?" Leo asks.

"Unfortunately, in my position, I'm not at liberty for that kind of activity anymore."

"Leave it to us then." A malicious grin spreads across Leo's face. "Our specialty is interrogation."

"I figured you'd be up for the challenge." Enzio smirks in amusement. "If you can get him alone, I'm confident you can get something out of him."

Leo rubs his chin. "And if he goes missing..."

Enzio waves a dismissive hand. "People go missing all the time. It's no skin off my back."

"Tell me something," I say as I continue skimming through the documents. "How close are you to your cousins, the Vasilievs?"

His head tilts to the side, his brows furrowing. "You know them?"

"We've had dealings with them," Leo answers. "Mostly with their father."

"Heard he died."

"He did." Leo leans forward. "I killed him."

Enzio sits back, waiting a minute before he speaks. "I never cared for my uncle. Never cared for anyone in that family, to be honest. The way they conduct business is not up to my standards, but my brother and father show no disapproval of their methods. As long as they bring in money, they don't care how things get done. Oil is my family's legacy. It's what we're known for. But the Vasilievs always seem to have a way of obtaining it where others can't. Probably through force or other barbaric methods. But over the years, they formed a partnership with my father and Alastor where they secure the lands, and Alastor and my father send a team out there to produce as many barrels as they can, ensuring very profitable margins from countries like Russia, Saudia Arabia, Iraq, Brazil... Just to name a few."

He taps his index finger thoughtfully against his desk. "I'm not sure this will be of any use, but the oldest brother, Mikhail, has had several private meetings with Alastor over the past year. For what? I'm not quite sure. Maybe scheduling a meeting with him and his brothers isn't such a bad idea for you to consider."

I close the folder and look at Leo. Meeting with the Vasilievs is dangerous and, quite frankly, the last fucking thing we want to have to do, but if it ensures putting an end to this wedding, then we'll do what needs to be done. "We'll look into that."

Enzio sits up straight, his expression turning grave. "But I must warn you: the Vasiliev family is not one you want to make enemies with. They steal, kidnap, torture... They don't leave any survivors in their path of destruction." He glances at Leo. "You may have had dealings with their father, but the five brothers are an entirely different story. If they discover you've interfered with any of their business or family matters, they will bring a war to your front door when you least expect it."

Leo nods. "Let them."

I check the time on my phone and stand, suddenly anxious about returning to Madeleine's house. I've been away for too long. "Keep us informed of any new information, and we'll do the same for you."

Enzio dips his chin. "I'll be in touch."

August 31st

Princess,

When you open this letter, I'll be on a plane, headed back to base where I'm expected to be. As much as my heart and every part of me wishes I could have stayed by your side and with your family during this time, I can't. And that kills me.

For the first time, I've questioned whether being in the military is worth it when I can't be with the ones I love. It's really made me think about things.

There's nothing I can say to ease the pain in your heart. There's nothing I can do to bring him back or turn back time. Because if I could, I would.

I would do anything to make your tears stop.

Your father loved you, Madeleine. So very much. I know this won't be easy for you. Grieving will be a long and hard journey to navigate, but always remember that I'm here for you. Even thousands of miles away.

Yours,
Eli

Chapter Seven

Madeleine

Someone just kill me and take me out of my misery.

As my eyes scan the opulent room at Le Noir, one of my family's many restaurants, I take in the horror before me.

Scarlett appears by my side, her blue eyes trailing over the space. The scrutiny on her face matches my own as she tucks her long blonde hair behind her ear. "It looks…"

"Like Pepto-Bismol threw up in here," I finish for her.

Pink flowers. Pink tablecloths. Pink banners. Pink centerpieces.

Pink. Pink. Pink.

Scarlett grimaces. "I tried to suggest she tone down the pink, but she thought you would like it."

I roll my eyes and scoff. "Anyone who knows me knows pink is not on my color palette. I'm all about neutrals, gold, black—"

"Hi, Madeleine."

I jump, placing a hand on my chest. Turning around, I find Cressida, the mastermind responsible for today's festivities, standing behind me. *Oh, fuck me.*

Her long, platinum-blonde hair cascades over her shoulders, gliding across the pink fabric of her knee-length dress. Her brown, wide doe eyes only enhance the princess image she portrays. She's petite, quiet, and normal—completely the opposite of her twin brother, that's for damn sure.

"Do you not like it?" she asks softly, her eyes glistening. Shit, is she about to cry?

"Of course I do!" I quickly reply, catching Scarlett's eye.

"It's just so...beautiful," Scarlett adds as she peers around, feigning awe.

I place my hand on Cressida's shoulder. "I appreciate this, really." Yeah, her brother is a goddamn asshole, but she doesn't deserve the hatred I feel toward him.

"You're sure? Because I can change things before anyone else arrives. Maybe I could—"

"Oh my God." Alina approaches my other side, her deep brown eyes wide as she takes in this atrocity. "Who decorated this—"

"Cressida designed everything," I swiftly interject. "Isn't it lovely?"

Alina looks too stunned to speak, so I lightly elbow her in her side. "Ow... Oh yes. Yes! It's just so...elegant."

Cressida beams at the compliment, dabbing at her eyes. "I'm just so happy you're marrying my brother. I wanted to help in any way I could." Her pink glossed lips widen. "After all, we'll be sisters soon enough."

The floor feels like it just opened beneath me, sending my stomach free-falling.

I've always wanted a sister. Scarlett and Alina, my two best friends for as long as I can remember, have always been the closest I've had to sister figures in my life. But Cressida? She seems nice enough, but anyone who shared a womb with Alastor for nine months isn't someone I can ever fully trust.

I muster a tight smile.

"Oh, I see the caterer sneaking out the back," she says. "I need to catch him before he leaves! I'll be right back!" She hurriedly strides after him in her six-inch heels, calling out his name.

I sigh. "She means well."

Alina interlocks her arm through mine, pressing the side of our heads together. Her long brown strands blend with my black ones. "At least I spotted a chocolate fountain in the corner; we can totally ambush it later."

I frown. "I'm not sure chocolate will lift my spirits right now."

A gasp escapes Scarlett, and she abruptly places her hand on my forehead. "Oh my God, are you sick?"

I laugh, waving her hand away. But just as quickly, my smile fades. Sick? No.

Depressed? Most definitely.

"Hello, ladies."

The deep timbre of Eli's voice rushes over me, sending a pleasant shiver down my spine.

"Eli, thank God you're here." Alina laughs as she adjusts her glasses. "Madeleine just told us she didn't want chocolate. We think she might be sick."

I roll my eyes, tugging my arm from Alina's. "I'm not—"

The palm of Eli's hand presses against my forehead, and my whole body stills as words escape me. *He's touching me.* And yeah, it's not in a sexy way since he's merely checking my temperature, but his touch alone does something funny to me. Leaving me momentarily incoherent and disoriented. His brows furrow as he looks me over. A flush spreads across my skin, heat coursing through me.

"You're a little warm," he notes with concern in his tone. "Should I take you home?"

"I..." I blink a few times and clear my throat, taking a step away from his touch as I internally shake my head. "I'm fine. Alina"—I point a glare in her direction—"was just teasing."

His eyes don't leave me, and I feel a honeyed warmth course through my veins under his attention. I scratch my arm, dropping his gaze as I look off into the distance.

"I'm surprised you're not still sleeping," Scarlett says to Eli, causing his eyes to travel to her. "You and Leo got home pretty late last night. Or should I say early this morning?" She laughs.

Excuse me?

"I'm used to having to stay up for long hours. Part of the perks of military life," he jokes with a slight grin.

I turn my attention to him. "I didn't know you were out last night."

He nods. "Just taking care of some business."

"Anything I should know about?"

"Nothing for you to be concerned with."

I cross my arms over my chest. "You're my bodyguard. You are my business."

He arches an eyebrow, challenging me to continue. "Is that so?"

"Yes." I uncross my arms, placing a hand on my hip. "The first night you're on duty, and you leave me alone, unprotected. This is going as poorly as I imagined it would."

His eyes darken as he steps closer, lowering his head to my level. "You think I would ever leave you unprotected?"

"Well, clearly you—"

"Mauro was standing post until I got back."

My lips part in surprise. "Oh."

He leans in closer, his breath warm against my ear as he speaks soft enough so only I can hear him. "Your safety is my top priority. Always has been and always will be. So, you will do well not to question my methods." He stands straight, towering over me as he glares down at me. "Your brothers asked me to keep you safe, and I promised them I would. Some of us know what it means to keep a promise."

My hands clench into fists at my sides, my blood pressure on the precipice of boiling over. "How dare—"

"Hey!" Alina squeezes herself between us. "Let's go visit that chocolate fountain. I think I saw chunks of brownies we can dip in it!"

I lock my gaze on Eli, waiting for him to look away first. Surprisingly, he does. I smile in victory until I notice who has caught his attention—Cressida.

Looking back at him, I see that he can't tear his eyes away from her, and suddenly, my chest tightens.

"Who's that?" Eli asks.

Scarlett looks across the room. "Oh, that's Cressida. Alastor's twin sister."

"Huh."

Seriously?

Taking a step toward him, I give him a playful pat on the chest. "Be careful, Eli. You have drool running down your chin." I toss my hair over my shoulder and turn to walk away, giving him something to really stare at when a voice suddenly stops me in my tracks.

"There you are, darling." A sudden chill slithers over my skin, every muscle in my body locking up. "I've been looking all over for you."

I take a deep breath and turn, facing the man who haunts my nightmares almost every night.

"Alastor." I feign a smile as he approaches. His blond hair is slicked back, and he's wearing a soft blue three-piece suit that appears straight off the runway, perfectly fitting his lean frame. He unbuttons his jacket, positioning himself in front of Eli. "I thought you were in Milan for business."

"I was. But I decided to surprise my fiancée." His sinister smile grows, revealing everything I need to know.

He's not here to check on my well-being or because he misses my presence. That's for damn sure.

He's here to ensure I haven't run away.

That I haven't called the whole thing off.

And by the way his eyes dart over his shoulder at Eli, it's clear he's also here to claim his territory.

"Don't you have a kiss for your future husband?" he asks, a menacing gleam in his beady eyes.

I swallow hard, trying to force down the lump in my throat.

So far, I've managed to keep a physical distance from Alastor as much as possible in these circumstances. Merely holding hands or standing by his side while in public.

But now, he knows I can't deny him. Not with all eyes on us.

"Oh." I wave a hand around. "Unfortunately, my throat has been a little sore. I would hate to get you sick—"

"Nonsense." I'm taken aback when one of his hands slips around my waist, pulling me closer to his chest, while his other hand sneaks to the back of my neck. His fingers dig into my skin, holding me in place and ensuring I can't escape. "You're worth getting sick for."

That's the only warning I'm given before his lips crash down on mine.

Bile rises in my stomach as he kisses me, devouring me in front of everyone. I keep my lips pressed tightly together, breathing through my nose and enduring every excruciating second.

Finally, he releases me, a look of arrogance spreading across his ugly features. His rancid taste lingers on my lips, and I have to fight the urge to wipe my mouth with my forearm.

I glance to my side and see Scarlett and Alina with their eyes wide open, unsure how to react.

Humiliation washes over me.

Alastor then turns to his side. "Oh, I didn't see you there." He releases his grip on my neck and extends his hand toward Eli. "I don't think we've officially met. I'm Alastor, the fiancé." He emphasizes the last word, ensuring everyone hears it loud and clear.

Eli stares at Alastor's outstretched hand, his jaw clenching forcefully. I know he wants to break it. He wants to twist each finger until he hears the bones snap, and Alastor screams out in agony. But when his darkened orbs look up, entrapping mine, I'm hit with an overwhelming surge of guilt.

This is my fault.

He looks ready to assassinate Alastor on the spot.

Anxiety skates across my body as tension forces its way between us, grasping its talons into me.

"Eli." Eli takes Alastor's hand, his knuckles turning stark white. His eyes never leave mine. "I'm the bodyguard."

"Yes." Alastor winces slightly before releasing Eli's hand and shaking it out. "Vincenzo told me all about you. Ex-military, correct?"

"Yes." Finally, his gaze leaves mine, moving to Alastor. "I'm prepared to kill anyone who dares to cause any kind of harm to Madeleine."

His words produce a not-so-subtle flutter in my heart.

Alastor's left eye twitches. "Well, good thing we have you to keep my future wife safe, then. Right, darling?" He glances down at me and pulls me closer to his side. His fingers ram painfully into my waist, likely leaving a bruise.

"Yes." I nod. "Eli's everything I need...to keep me safe."

⸻

"Madeleine." Cressida's soft voice drifts closer to my side as I take a generous sip of champagne, hoping that a little buzz will help me get through the rest of the day. At least Alastor left shortly after staking his claim on me to take care of some business in the city...or sleep with a hooker. Who knows? It's not like I give a flying fuck which of the two he plans on doing.

"Mm-hmm?" I turn to my side as Cressida takes the empty seat beside me. *Ugh.* Where the fuck did Alina and Scarlett go?

Her big, soft eyes stare at me as if waiting for permission to speak. I arch an eyebrow, silently urging her to continue.

"Is Eli single?"

I slightly choke on the champagne, quickly slapping a hand against my chest as a few drops travel down the wrong pipe.

"Oh my God. Are you okay?" Cressida frantically pats my back.

I raise a hand to signal her to stop. "I'm fine." I grab my napkin and gently blot it over the stain on the front of my ivory dress. Clearing my throat, I say, "What did you ask?"

Her cheeks turn a light shade of pink as she pushes a lock of her hair behind her ear. "I was just wondering if Eli is single."

"Oh, single? Eli?" I let out a slight scoff. "As far as I know, he is. But I'm sure his definition of single might differ from yours and mine. Why?"

"Well, I mean, look at him." Her eyes dart over to the corner of the room where Eli hovers by the door, his gaze directed at me. "He's gorgeous." She sighs wistfully. "I wonder if he'd ever consider... someone like me."

Does she mean someone blonde, tiny, and with perky boobs? Last I checked, Cressida looked like a man's wet fantasy. Add to the fact that her family is loaded, and what man could resist her?

Looking away from Eli, I grind my teeth and cross my arms over my chest. "Beats me. I've never seen him with a girl, so it's hard to say what his type is."

Well, no girl except me.

"So, you would be okay if I went over and talked to him?"

My chest tightens. It feels like a claw is wrapping forcefully around my lungs, constricting my airways. But I shake off the feeling as I say, "Why wouldn't I be okay with that? I'm engaged to your brother. Not to Eli."

That's for damn fucking sure.

Her lips part, and her hands intertwine in her lap as she adjusts nervously. "I'm sorry. I didn't mean to insinuate anything. I know you and my brother are very happy together. But with Eli being your bodyguard,

I just wanted to make sure it wouldn't make things uncomfortable for you." Her shoulders curl in, and an apologetic smile appears on her face.

With a heavy sigh, I turn on my Madeleine Alarie charm and place my hand on her shoulder. "It wouldn't make things uncomfortable for me," I lie.

"Really?" She beams. "Oh, wonderful!" She stands, pushing back her chair and smoothing out her dress. Reaching into her clutch, she pulls out a tube of soft pink lipstick and applies a generous amount to her lips. "Well, wish me luck."

I give a tight smile as she saunters off, her hips swaying eagerly as she approaches Eli. His attention turns to her, and one of his stupid, handsome smiles graces his face as she no doubt bats her long lashes.

He laughs at whatever she says, and suddenly, a sharp pain hits me right in the center of my chest. I rub at it, but as the two of them continue to talk, my throat tightens, and the tip of my nose begins to sting.

For just a second, Eli glances my way.

His beautiful brown eyes lock with mine.

Everyone around me disappears.

And then, just as quickly, he looks back at her.

Blinking back tears that I refuse to let fall, I pause to look at the monstrosity on my ring finger. How many times have I thought about hurling this ring into the lake beside my home? How many nights have I spent tossing and turning, scared of what's to come? Yet, I don't regret anything I've done to reach this point.

Taking one last look at Eli, I see the same smile he used to have when we were together.

And it takes everything in me not to stand and scream at the top of my lungs, *I did all of this for you!*

"What's wrong, dear?" My mother sits beside me, reaching for my hand on the table. Her blue eyes, identical to mine, are filled with concern, creating tight knots in my stomach. "You look like a bride who just saw a ghost."

I smile softly. "It's nothing. I think I just got some dust in my eye."

She frowns. "I'm your mother." Her hand cups my cheek. "I like to think I know my only daughter pretty well. Not to mention, I would never allow a speck of dust in one of our family's establishments."

I look down at the table, wishing I could crawl into a hole and hide.

"If you don't want to do this, you don't have to."

Her words hit me like a punch to the gut.

But I do have to, I want to tell her.

Instead, I merely shake my head. "The wedding is happening. And everything will be fine."

"Are you trying to convince me or yourself of that?"

"Alastor will provide for me."

"But will he love you?"

We both know the answer to that question.

I look away, biting my bottom lip. "Can't you just be happy for me?" I ask softly, feeling my emotional restraint ready to shatter.

"I would be if you were marrying the right man."

My head snaps her way. "And who would that be?"

Her shoulder-length black hair sways as she tilts her head to the side. "The only man your father ever approved of for you."

"Don't." Tears threaten to spill like a dam ready to break, knowing the only man he ever approved of for me was...

"Dad," I whine. "I'm not a little kid anymore. I'm seventeen, and eventually, you have to let me date. Every other girl in my class has a boyfriend. I'm the only single one left!" I throw my hands up in the air, exasperated. "Don't you want grandkids?"

He chuckles, shaking his head. "Oh, Madeleine, you will always be my little girl." He leans down and presses a kiss to my temple. "But when the time comes for you to date, there's only one man I will approve of, and it certainly isn't going to be some boy who doesn't know how to treat my daughter well."

I roll my eyes, crossing my arms over my chest. "And who, may I ask, is this mystery man?"

His gaze travels to my brothers and Eli as they play a card game around my mother's dining room table, laughing as they catch up with one another.

He doesn't say anything.

Because he doesn't have to.

I swallow the lump in my throat as I look across the room at Eli, who's still caught up in a conversation with Cressida. Still smiling and still laughing. Still the man my heart belongs to.

"Don't bring Dad into this. Please," I say as I stand, smoothing out my dress. "I love you, Mom. But I need you to trust me on this. The wedding between Alastor and me needs to happen. Everything will be fine, you'll see."

She offers a sad smile as I bend down to kiss her cheek. I walk away, deliberately heading in the opposite direction of Eli, my eyes focused on the bathroom door where I can hide from the world and let myself break in private.

After closing the door behind me, I check each stall before I lock the main door and let out a heavy breath.

Standing before the sink, I grip the counter's edge, my knuckles aching from the force to hold me upright. My chest heaves violently as a wild tremble rushes through me, causing every part of my body to shake in rage. I stare at my reflection, not recognizing the woman I see.

She's weak and scared.

Certainly not the image of strength and beauty I've managed to uphold over the years.

And to top it all off, she's currently letting a man control her life.

A man.

Fury builds inside me as tears cloud my vision.

Without a second thought, my fist flies forward, sending shards of glass into the sink and across the counter.

A stream of blood rushes over the back of my hand, trailing across my knuckles.

"Great." I sigh as I turn on the sink and let the cold water coat my skin, watching as the water transforms into a shade of pink. After drying my hands, I spot a first aid kit on the wall and open it to find some bandages, which I use to wrap tightly across my fingers.

Closing my eyes, I lean against the wall and slide down, allowing the tears to cascade over my cheeks. My arms wrap around my legs, and I press the side of my face into my knees.

"Everything will be fine," I whisper, rocking back and forth, knowing deep down in my heart it's a lie.

November 22nd

Dear Eli,

Life has been too quiet.

My brothers have been busy adding extra security around the estate while they try to find the person responsible for my father's murder. My mother has been spending a lot of time overseas with her sister. I think being here is too much for her heart to bear right now.

As for me, I now have a security guard. An older man named Peter, who seems nice, just doesn't say much. I'm sure he's bored since I don't really go anywhere. I'm not sure if you heard, but Scarlett is gone. Her father moved her off the estate the night everything happened, and her number is no longer in service, which I suspect is also his doing. I just wish I knew where she was.

Alina's father announced his retirement. I'm happy for him; he deserves it. But he wants to move off the estate to be closer to his family. Thankfully, it won't be too far, but it'll be weird having no friends on the estate.

My house is completed, but I don't feel ready to move in yet. Maybe someday, but right now it reminds me too much of my dad.

Stay safe,
Madeleine

CHAPTER EIGHT

Eli

"**I** need to go shopping."

Those are the first words I've heard from Madeleine in two days, and she doesn't even have the decency to look at me as she crosses the kitchen to grab her iced coffee from the fridge.

Two days ago, when we returned from her bridal shower, she immediately went to her room with a pint of ice cream, slamming the door behind her. Then, just yesterday, when she finally ventured out, I told her I had made some iced coffee and put it in the fridge for her, but she merely narrowed her eyes at me, grabbed an orange, and retreated to her room, where she spent the rest of the day holed up.

And for the past two days, while she's been avoiding me, I've been replaying that fucking kiss between her and Alastor that I had to witness with a front-row seat. I tried to take out my fury in her gym basement, but no amount of time spent punching the boxing bags or lifting weights has managed to ease the wrath coursing through my veins when that image keeps resurfacing, taunting me.

Fucking with my head.

The only thing that gives me a semblance of solace is knowing that one day, that bloody wanker will regret ever touching what is mine.

Mark my words.

I lower my coffee mug to the table and observe Madeleine as she pours cream into her drink, either completely oblivious to my presence or pretending that my existence doesn't faze her in the slightest. Her knee-length black sweater dress hugs her curves, making me wish I could peel it from her skin, inch by inch until it lies tossed on the floor. Her long raven hair falls to the middle of her back, causing me to imagine wrapping it around my fist as I—

She slams the fridge closed, pulling me out of my thoughts. I internally shake my head and adjust my seat.

Glancing at my watch, I note that I have some time to kill.

So, I'll play along.

I stand and walk over to the sink, rinsing my mug. I hear the impatient clacking of Madeleine's heels on the floor as she waits for me, so I decide to take my time. And after hearing an impatient sigh, I finally turn to face her and grin.

I gesture toward the front door. "Lead the way, Princess."

She takes a breath, closing her eyes as her spine straightens. "I told you not to call me that."

I give a half-shrug as I pass her. "Old habit."

As we step outside, her driver, Reginald, pulls up in front of the steps. Just as her hand reaches for the handle, I beat her to it and open the door for her. She shakes her head and steps inside, sliding across the leather seat. I follow her in, taking the seat beside her.

"What are you doing?" she asks incredulously.

"Sitting."

"You're supposed to sit up front with Reginald."

"Nah. I think I like it better back here." I place a hand on my stomach. "The front seat makes me car sick," I lie.

Her face scrunches in annoyance, which I find adorable. "You don't get car sick."

"I do."

"You don't."

"I—"

"Fine," she snaps, turning her body toward the window and as far away from me as the car accelerates. She reaches for the side of her head to tuck her long, dark strands behind her ear, and I notice her hand.

I grip her wrist, and she quickly turns to face me, her eyes wide.

"What do you think you're—"

"What happened to your hand?" I ask, running my thumb over the bandage as I try to remain calm. But the sight of her injured stirs something powerful inside me.

She sighs, looking away. "Nothing."

"It doesn't look like nothing."

She shakes her head, trying to pull her hand from my grip, but I don't release it. "It was a cooking accident."

"Cooking?" I arch a brow.

"Yes. I was cutting...an onion."

"You don't know how to cook."

She scowls. "I can cook."

The air becomes stifling as the lie settles between us. "For all the years I've known you, I've never seen you cook one damn thing."

She looks out her window, unable to maintain eye contact. "I'm fine. Why are you making a big deal out of this?"

Because your safety means everything to me.

"Why are you lying?"

She tugs her hand out of my grip and then rubs her temple. "Just drop it, Eli. Please. I have a lot going on, and the last thing I need is to be interrogated by you."

Is that so?

I lean toward her, purposefully brushing my lips over her silky hair. "Don't forget who you're speaking to. I spent years training in the art of interrogation. I know how to use pain to make a man spill his deepest darkest secrets in a matter of minutes."

She turns toward me, her face only inches from mine. Her tongue pokes out and swipes across her plush bottom lip as she swallows hard. "But you...you would never hurt me to get information out of me."

I reach out, brushing her hair over her shoulder. "I would never hurt you. But I do know *other ways* to make you talk." I move closer, pressing my lips against her ear to whisper, "Other ways to make you scream."

A small gasp escapes her lips as I pull back and relax against my seat, facing forward. I watch in amusement as she crosses her legs and turns away from me, trying to appear as if I don't affect her in the slightest.

A grin pulls at my lips.

Oh, this is going to be so much fun.

"I'll take one in every color."

The saleswoman, Lisa's, eyes grow wide as Madeleine continues scanning the rack of coats, pointing out different styles she likes. "But this coat comes in twenty-five colors..."

Madeleine arches a brow as if to say, *And the problem is?*

"Of course," Lisa answers, hurrying off. "I'll go grab them from the back!"

"Wait!" Madeleine calls after her. "I'd also like each one paired with a matching hat, mittens, and scarf. Oh, and some fluffy socks!"

I drag my hand down my face. I know she enjoys occasional shopping sprees, but this seems a bit excessive, even for her.

As Lisa walks off to retrieve everything, I turn to Madeleine. "Don't you think twenty-five coats is a bit extreme? People are starving in this world, and you're buying the same coat in every color just to make a damn fashion statement."

She pauses, her fingers stilling on a cashmere sweater. The corners of her lips lift as she faces me with one of the most lethal stares I've ever seen. "One can never have too many coats. Besides, I don't recall asking your opinion on the matter." She shifts her attention back to the sweater. "You're here to do your job, which does not require speaking to me."

I narrow my eyes on her as I step toward her, crowding her space.

Out of the corner of my eye, I see Lisa enter the room. Without breaking my gaze from Madeleine, I say, "Do you mind giving us a moment? We have some things to discuss."

"Ah...umm," Lisa stutters. "Of course, sir. I'll go look for more matching accessories!"

Poor Lisa scurries out of the room, leaving just the two of us. Forgetting all reason, I grab her uninjured hand and haul her into the closest dressing room, locking the door behind us.

She tugs her hand out from mine, quickly crossing her arms over her chest as her face mirrors disbelief. "What in the hell do you think—"

"What the fuck has your knickers in a twist?" There's an edge of authority in my voice, one she doesn't miss as she juts out her chin in defiance.

Her lips tighten. "You can't speak to me that way."

"I can speak to you however bloody well I please. Especially when you insist on being a royal twat."

A gasp escapes her lips. "You did not just call me that."

I give a slight shrug. "Seems fitting."

Her hands clench into fists at her side. "Jesus Christ, Eli. Just do your job and let me out of here."

I stand tall, crossing my arms over my chest. "Not until you tell me what the fuck is going on. You've been even more distant than usual these past couple of days, giving me the damn silent treatment like a child as you hide away in your room with your pints of ice cream to cure whatever the hell is going on inside your head. And now we're here, shopping for twenty-five goddamn winter coats. So tell me, what the fuck is going on?"

"Nothing is going on."

"Madeleine.

"Eli."

"What's going on?"

"Nothing that concerns you."

"So, there is something."

"No. Nothing! Just let me out of here."

"No can do. Not until—"

"Cressida!" she shouts in exasperation, her hands flying up toward the ceiling. Silence descends upon us as her eyes suddenly widen with regret. "Shit," she says softly, her eyes pinching shut as her arms drop to her sides.

My brows knit together. "What about Cressida? Is she bothering you?"

She shakes her head, raking her fingers through her hair, her eyes looking anywhere but at me. "Forget I said her name."

Why the fuck would she be upset about Cressida—*Oh.*

I can't help it.

One corner of my lip lifts, warmth filling my cold, beating heart.

She actually thinks I would be interested in Cressida? I had only been staring at her at the party because I noticed an uncanny resemblance to Alastor, finally putting two and two together. And sure, I chatted the girl up when she came over to talk to me to be polite, but apparently, Madeleine must think there's more to it than that.

I mean, Cressida seemed nice enough, sure.

But there's one problem.

She's not *my* Madeleine.

I lean down to her eye level, waiting for her to meet my gaze. The moment she does, I ask, "Are you jealous, Princess?"

Her plush lips slightly part as she glares at me.

Fuck, she's beautiful when she's jealous.

And I realize I like this side of her.

I like this side of her a lot.

"Jealous?" She scoffs. "Why the fuck would I be jealous?"

"I don't know." I shrug. "You tell me." I take a step toward her, watching as she takes one back, pressing herself against the wall. "Is it because she asked to go out with me?"

Her mouth is agape. "She did—I mean." She clears her throat, appearing flustered, which I know from experience is not something that happens to her easily. "I don't care what you do in your spare time as long as it doesn't impact your work."

She's lying. I see it in the tiny tremor in her hands clenched at her sides. And by the way she can't hold my gaze.

Lying 101: Never break eye contact.

"Hmm." I reach out and touch a lock of her dark hair, twirling it around my finger. "So you don't mind if I take her to dinner then?"

She audibly swallows. "Not one bit."

"Good to know." I drop her hair, tracing my index finger along the collar of her dress. "There's a new Italian restaurant that just opened in the city. Maybe I'll take her there."

"Maybe you should."

"And maybe if all goes well, I'll take her home after." Her whole body suddenly tenses beneath my touch. "You wouldn't mind, right?" I ask, feeling her pulse accelerate beneath the pad of my finger.

She shakes her head with too much force. "Of course not."

I nod, grazing her collarbone before dragging my finger leisurely upward, my hand cradling her neck as my thumb brushes against her plush bottom lip. A low gasp escapes her.

"I wonder how she likes it," I say, leaning forward, allowing my lips to hover over her ear as I soften my voice. "Fast? Rough? Gentle? Maybe a mixture of all three? What do you think?"

"A-all three, I mean…" She clears her throat. "How would I know? What happens between you two is none of my business."

She pushes against my chest, but I don't budge. Not one centimeter. Her half-hearted effort would usually make me laugh, but not right now, not when I'm this close to her for the first time in too long.

I can't help myself as I abruptly grip her wrists and place them against the wall above her head. She seems ready to protest, to argue, but the moment I tilt my head forward, my lips just inches from hers, she does something that takes me by surprise.

She melts.

Slowly.

Softly.

Almost unnoticeably.

So much so that I don't even think she's aware of what she's doing. But as her wrists go slack in my grip and her body loses all trace of a fight, I realize something that ignites a fire within me.

She wants this.

She wants me.

And she can pretend all that she wants, that she doesn't.

She can lie to my damn face for all I care.

Because the proof is right before me.

The subtle, rosy flush on her cheeks.

The dilation in her bright blue eyes.

The speed of every warm breath she takes.

She wants me as much as I want her.

I glide my nose across her cheek, inhaling her heavenly floral scent. "The best part is the anticipation, don't you think? The buildup for the inevitable that's about to occur."

"Y-yes," she breathes, her eyes closing.

My lips skim across her neck, and she tips her chin up, exposing more of her bare skin for me to taste.

"Should I start slow, savoring every inch of her body?"

Her pulse beats frantically beneath my lips, where I press a tender kiss. "Yes."

Taking one last step, I fill the space between us, pressing my body against hers, my hard cock shifting over her stomach. I place my left knee between her legs, opening her stance as her dress bunches around her hips. My thigh meets her center, and her eyes open, securing onto mine.

I don't move.

I'm letting her decide for us.

Letting her choose whether she wants to admit to wanting this.

Confusion flashes over her irises as she waits for me to make the next move.

But instead, I shake my head, grazing my lips over her ear. "It's your move, Princess."

Honestly, I'm not sure how this will play out.

If she pushes me off her, I'll move.

I'll give her the space she wants.

But if—

Gradually, she rocks her hips forward.

I look down to where my leg meets her pussy and watch as she finds a slow, sensual rhythm. A soft moan breaks free from between her lips, and when I look up, I freeze.

Because the look she's giving me is the same beautiful, vulnerable expression I haven't seen on her face in over a year.

The one that said everything to me that she was thinking without using any words—*I trust you, I miss you... I need you.*

Dropping one of her wrists, I cup her cheek, running my thumb over her smooth skin. Her body continues moving against mine, seeking pleasure, as she bites her bottom lip, her eyes never leaving mine.

Not even for one second.

God, I've missed this.

I've missed her.

Leaning forward, I watch as she closes her eyes, waiting for our lips to meet in what I know will be a kiss that brings her back to me.

That makes her mine again.

And fuck, I feel like I've waited so long for this moment.

Knock. Knock. "Hi, I have everything wrapped up front whenever you're ready!"

Lisa's voice sends a large bucket of ice water over Madeleine as, within only seconds, she completely removes herself from me, quickly smoothing out her dress and hair.

"Thank you, Lisa. We'll be right there. Just wrapping up!" she tells her.

"Great," Lisa replies, her heels clacking against the floor as she walks away.

Madeleine turns her back to me, hiding her face in her hands. "Fuck," she breathes, the regret in her voice punching me right in the center of my chest.

"Madeleine—"

"No." She shakes her head, her black hair dancing across her shoulders. "We shouldn't have done that. I..." She clears her throat, straightening her shoulders. "I won't be making that mistake again." Without looking back, she unlocks the door and exits the dressing room, swiftly getting as far away from me as she possibly can.

It takes five salespeople to help us carry all the bags to the Escalade, where we manage to fill every last inch of trunk space.

Absolutely daft, if you ask me.

I slide onto the seat next to Madeleine. She tucks her phone into her purse and scoots a bit closer forward toward Reginald.

"We'll be doing a drop-off today before heading home," she tells him.

"Of course," he answers.

She sits back beside me, folding her hands on her lap, and looks straight ahead. I check the time on my watch, noting I still have an hour before my call.

"A drop-off where?" I ask.

She turns to look out her window, giving me the silent treatment.

I clench my jaw. "As your bodyguard, it's my job to know where we're going."

"And if we were going somewhere dangerous, I would inform you."

I roll my neck, my muscles bunching with tension. "I think we should talk about what happened back there."

"Nothing happened."

"Really? Because the way you moaned makes me think—"

She spins in her seat, clasping her hands over my mouth. Her eyes dart to Reginald, panic on her face at the thought that he might have heard me, and it almost makes me laugh. She reaches over me and presses a button, causing the privacy screen between us and Reginald to lift into place.

Once it's sealed, she drops her hands and turns in her seat, sitting forward. She reaches up, pressing her fingers into her temple. "Let's get something straight. The only thing that happened was a lapse of judgment on my part. And it won't happen again."

I lean closer to her. "Tell me you weren't wet."

A flush spreads up her neck, providing the only answer I need. "I wasn't wet."

"You're a bad liar. Your body gives away every secret."

She shakes her head. "I'm not lying."

"So, if I check now, I'd find you as dry as the Sahara Desert?"

She quickly crosses her legs. "Even drier."

I laugh, slapping my leg.

"What's so funny?"

"You." I shake my head. "You're too damn stubborn to admit you want me."

"I do not—"

"And there you go, lying again."

She scoffs as she looks me up and down. "You think you're so damn special, don't you?"

I wink. "I know I am."

A mocking laugh bursts from between her lips. "You are nothing to me, Eli Lyon. Nothing. In fact, you are the most selfish, self-centered, bloody wan—"

I clasp a hand over her lips, pressing her into the leather seat. "Most people would take what you're saying to heart because they think that's who you are—a spoiled, self-entitled brat. But I know you're not. You're not even close to being one, for that matter. You put on this act when you're cornered and scared of showing your true feelings. You lash out, fight back, and hit them where it hurts because you want to remind them who you are. But I know who you are. Always have." She drops her gaze, her features softening. "So, I will do us both a favor and stop you before you say something you'll regret. You don't want to admit you want me. But I'll admit it. I'll tell you to your face how fucking badly I want you. And when you're ready to tell me you need me, you know where to find me."

Dropping my hand, I sit back in my seat and face forward.

"Miss Alarie?" Reginald's voice comes through the speaker beside our heads.

She takes a steady breath, tucking her hair behind her ear. "Yes?"

"We're here."

"Great. Thank you."

The car comes to a stop, and I look out the window beside me, instantly recognizing the building as I made frequent visits here with Scarlett while I was her bodyguard.

"Why are we here?"

She sighs, her hand gripping the handle. "Because it helps me." She steps out of the car, and I quickly follow her to the trunk, where she begins unloading bags. "Well, don't just stand there." She gives me a pointed glare. "Take a bag or two. Put those muscles to actual use." She walks around me, heading toward the door where a welcome sign for the St. Elizabeth Jean's Center for Women and Children is displayed.

And as I look back at the trunk filled with winter coats, mittens, scarves, and socks, it dawns on me...

Fuck...*I am a bloody wanker.*

With my arms filled with bags, I take off after her. I watch as she enters the building, letting the door close behind her.

"She does this quite often," Reginald comments, catching up to me, carrying more bags in his hands.

"She does?"

"Yes. Usually, when she's stressed, but lately...well, let's just say we've been making this a frequent stop." A slight frown appears on his face as he walks ahead to open the door.

"Wait, are we allowed to go inside?" I ask, peering around. I've never entered the building before, in fear of intimidating any of the women who come here for help. A guy my size is probably the last thing they want to come face-to-face with.

Reginald nods. "We'll be quick."

As we enter, a woman with a friendly smile appears. "Well, if it isn't our most loyal shopper."

"Betty." Madeleine grins. "It's the least I can do. I heard we were expecting a big storm next week, and I just wanted to ensure there were plenty of coats to go around."

"Well, judging by the number of bags in everyone's hands, I'd say we have more than enough." Betty's eyes travel over to me. "And who do we have here?" She looks at Madeleine and waggles her brows. "Is this your handsome fiancé?"

"No!" Madeleine answers with force, aggressively shaking her head. "Definitely not."

My chest tightens, feeling offended by her abrupt response. And before I take a second to stop myself and think, the question, "Would that be such a bad thing?" rushes out of my mouth, taking Madeleine by surprise.

Her lips part in shock, and it takes a moment before she mutters, "Well...it's just..." She glances between me and Betty, completely dumbfounded.

I don't know what I expected her to say, but her silence only adds to the growing ache across my chest.

"Where would you like everything?" Reginald asks, coming up around me, rescuing us from the escalating awkwardness.

Betty gestures a hand toward her side. "Follow me. We can bring them to my office to sort through."

The two of them walk away, leaving Madeleine and me standing in silence.

She appears to be having an internal war in her head as she stares at the ground. "I didn't mean for it to sound the way it did."

"Yeah? And how did you mean it?"

"Eli..." Her eyes lift, meeting mine. "I didn't mean to upset you. I was just—"

"Why would I be upset?" I lift a shoulder, trying to appear unbothered. "You're right. We're not engaged. It's not my ring on your finger."

She instantly covers her ring with her other hand, biting down on her bottom lip. "But you don't understand. I didn't have a—"

"I understand everything just fine." I sidestep her and head down the hall, hearing her heels clack on the floor behind me, maintaining a safe distance between us.

Thirty minutes later, the three of us exit the building and make our way toward the car.

Tension hangs heavily between us, so just as Madeleine reaches for the door handle, I stop her, positioning myself between her and the car. She arches an eyebrow, waiting for me to speak.

"I wanted to apologize for thinking you were merely frivolously spending your money today. Not that I have any say or opinion on how you should spend your money, but I judged you, and I shouldn't have."

She lets out a sigh as she puts on her black leather gloves. "I like to shop when I'm stressed. It gives me a dopamine hit and helps keep my mind off...things. But recently, I don't know, shopping for myself wasn't doing anything for me, and I realized I felt a whole hell of a lot better when I was shopping for others who actually need these things. It makes me feel like I'm doing something good in my life for once." She adjusts the beige scarf around her neck, her eyes meeting mine. "In fairness, I didn't exactly tell you what was going on, and I let you come to your own conclusions about me."

"Which was wrong of me."

She shrugs. "It's what everyone thinks of me. Why would you think any differently?"

"Because I know you and I shouldn't have—"

"Correction." She throws her gloved hand in the air, raising her index finger. "You knew me. Past tense." Her eyes narrow in on me, a chill in the air spreading between us, not from the frigid temperatures surrounding us. "Now, can you please move to the side so I can get inside the warm car?"

Reluctantly, I move, opening the door for her. She slides across the smooth leather seats, quickly turning her attention to her phone.

Just as I take a step up, my phone rings.

Bollocks.

I lost track of time.

Taking my phone out of my pocket, I see the name on the screen and know I can't ignore this call.

"I have to take this. It'll only be a moment," I tell her.

Hitting the green circle, I press the phone to my ear. "Hey, Angel. I miss you." I shut the door behind me, taking a few steps away from the vehicle, watching snow fall around me.

January 3rd

Princess,

On a scale of one to ten, how much did you enjoy my Christmas visit?

Was your favorite part when I kept you up all night to binge-watch a marathon of the Great British Bake Off while we ate way too many Christmas cookies? (You gotta love Prue!) Or was it the drunken sledding contest we had down your mother's stairs with your siblings?

She might not have been too happy about that one, but I think the smile on your face made it all worth it.

I know it's been bothering you that you haven't moved into your house yet, but when the time is right, you'll know. Don't rush yourself.

Hopefully, I'll be able to come back soon. But, unfortunately, no promises this time. Things have been a little chaotic around here. This is the first moment I've had to myself in quite a while, and I just wanted to take the time to let you know I'm thinking of you.

Yours,
Eli

P.S. Happy New Year, Princess.

CHAPTER NINE

Madeleine

Alastor

Don't forget. Friday night at 8 pm sharp. Don't be late!

Alastor

Answer me!

Alastor

You can't ignore me!

Alastor

If you think this is some kind of fucking game then I will be sure to remind you what's at stake. You won't make a fool out of me!

Fuck.

I stare at the latest text messages from Alastor, filled with dread.

A splitting headache pounds against my skull as I lean back, resting my head on the cushioned headrest while I shut my eyes.

I'd literally rather do anything else than sit at a confined dining table with Alastor and his family, feeling completely imprisoned.

Like lie on a train track...

Drive off a cliff...

Jump out of a plane without a parachute...

The list could go on and on.

"Are you okay?"

Eli's rough yet soothing voice floats over to me as he slides closer across the leather seat and closes the door behind him.

"Hey, Angel. I miss you."

A slight, uncomfortable pressure forms inside my chest. Why? Well, I don't very much care to look into that. It's probably just heartburn from that chocolate cake I ate last night.

"Madeleine?"

I turn toward the window. "I'm fine. Just have a slight migraine coming on."

"Do you get those a lot?"

Just for the past year.

"Now and then."

"Anything I can do to help?"

Kill Alastor.

"No. Just need some pain meds and to keep my eyes closed."

I reach for my bag, searching for my bottle of pain relievers, but when I take off the cap and tip the bottle, I discover it's empty. I internally groan as the car begins to move, and I'm suddenly hit with a wave of nausea.

Oh great.

The last thing I need is to vomit in front of Eli, completely embarrassing myself in the process.

Taking a deep breath, I turn into my seat, wrapping my arms across my stomach as I close my eyes.

"Would that be such a bad thing?"

Eli's question from earlier pounds back and forth between my skull. I internally scold myself for being so careless after almost letting it slip out that I didn't have a choice in this marriage.

How could I be so reckless?

So weak?

If the truth were to escape, it would ruin everything.

"Would that be such a bad thing?"

No! I wanted to scream in his face.

Not when that's all I've ever wanted.

We hit a bump in the road, intensifying my churning stomach. My arms wrap tighter around me.

"Do you need us to pull over?" Eli asks.

I know he's only trying to help, but every sound vibrates throughout my skull like a jackhammer.

"No," I whisper. "Home." I take another long, deep breath. "I just need to go home."

Thirty minutes later, we pull through the gate of the Alarie Estate, and a weight lifts from my chest.

"We're almost there," Eli tells me, and I can't help but note an edge of concern in his voice.

I feel the car navigate the familiar twists and turns of my driveway deep in the woods, and I count the seconds until I can get out of this car and safely throw up in the privacy of my bathroom.

"Whose car is that?" Eli asks.

I don't have the energy to look. "Vin was car shopping recently. If you don't recognize it, maybe it's his," I murmur.

Once the car comes to a stop, I put on my sunglasses and unwind before stepping out. Within seconds, Eli is by my side, his strong arm wrapped around my back and his hand gripping my waist to support me.

"I've got you," Eli voices.

As we take the last step up the stairs, a figure appears to the side, catching us both by surprise. Eli jumps in front of me, positioning himself to keep me behind him, protecting me from danger.

"What the fuck are you doing here?" Eli growls.

Definitely not Vin's car, then.

I peek around him, finding the devil standing before us.

"Alastor?" I manage to get out as I take a step around Eli. I look toward my driveway, spotting a bright orange hideous sports car. "Is that your car?"

Alastor looks over proudly. "Ah, yes. Just got it for a small two million." He chuckles, brushing a hand down his shirt. "She's one of the fastest cars in the world. They only produced a few hundred of them, and now, well, she's all mine."

She?

I grimace as I internally shake my head. I felt my phone vibrate in the car on the way here, probably with notifications alerting me to a security breach, but I was in too much pain to look. Now I wish I had.

What the fuck is he doing here?

Unfortunately, I don't have time to analyze this predicament because, at this exact instant, the chocolate cake from last night decides to make a reappearance.

I lean over the railing and vomit straight into the snow-covered bushes. A strong hand gently caresses my back while the other holds my hair away from my face.

With nothing left inside me, I take a deep breath and stand, turning to find that it was Eli who took care of me in my moment of weakness.

My bodyguard.

Not my fiancé.

Why am I not surprised?

Eli's hand slides protectively down my spine, his body staying right beside mine. I swipe my forearm across my mouth, unsure of how much time I have left before I get sick again. So, I need to figure out what the hell is going on since Alastor's never made an unannounced visit.

Alastor stands there, horrified, with his hand covering his mouth. "Please tell me you're not contagious."

I roll my eyes, instantly regretting the motion. "Migraines are not contagious."

"Oh." He laughs while lowering his hand. "Thank God, it's just a migraine."

Just a migraine? The pressure returns to my temple, and I pinch the bridge of my nose, massaging the area with my fingers. Eli's hand moves in slow, gentle circles, calming me. "What are you doing here? I didn't think I was seeing you until Friday night."

His eyes bounce between me and Eli, taking in the proximity between us, I'm sure. But I don't have the energy to move away from him, nor do I want to. Not when he's the only thing keeping me up. "Well, I was worried for you, *darling*. You never returned my messages, and I just wanted to ensure you would actually be joining us."

"For what?" Eli asks, staring down at me.

Alastor beams. "Dinner with her future in-laws. They're so looking forward to seeing you since it's been a while. Not to mention, there will be a few photographers there as well to capture the moment."

What he really means is that he wants to showcase an Alarie on his arm so the whole world can see his new powerful accessory.

I squint beneath the sun's glare, which feels too bright even behind my sunglasses. I just want to retreat into darkness by getting under my covers and calling it a day.

"Madeleine's not well—" Eli starts to say before I cut him off.

"Yes, of course. I'll be there."

"Great." Alastor's beady eyes move from me and then to Eli. "Well, I'll be out of your way so you can rest. Wouldn't want anything to cause you to miss such an important night, now would we, darling?"

"Of course not," I answer quickly.

He hesitates for a moment, as if he might want to lean in for a kiss, but then stops himself, likely reconsidering since I just threw up—thank God. After a short pause, he nods and walks toward his obnoxiously bright-colored car, where I notice his guard, Tony, waiting for him. Looking up, I find Eli's gaze fixed on him.

"Who's that?" he asks, his free hand resting on the gun inside his holster.

"Tony. His right-hand man."

I wait until Alastor disappears down the driveway before stepping inside my home, slipping out of my heels, and trudging up the stairs to my room.

I'm so lost in my thoughts that I don't notice Eli behind me until he steps around me and closes all my drapes, shrouding my room in shadows.

He turns to look at me and takes a step closer. His hands reach out, slowly and carefully unbuttoning my jacket. It falls to the floor around me, and then, without taking a moment to overthink it, I reach for the zipper on the back of my dress and tug it down, letting the material pool at my feet.

It's not like he hasn't seen me like this before.

His eyes darken, and his gaze travels leisurely over my body, leaving a scorched path from my head to my toes.

I swallow hard. If I weren't in so much pain, I might do something I'll regret.

Or would I?

"I might get sick again," I say.

"I'll be here if you do," he answers automatically.

Of course, he will be.

He's always here.

I press my fingers into the side of my temple. "It hurts so much."

My head. My heart... Yeah, especially that one.

Eli turns, removes his shoes, and makes himself comfortable on my bed, leaning against the headboard. "Come here." He pushes my blankets aside, making room for me to join him.

Not wanting to overthink things, I get into bed and wrap the covers around me. He places a pillow on his thigh, and I instantly lie down, resting my head on his lap. His fingers gently begin to massage my scalp.

It feels heavenly.

"How is this?" he asks softly.

"This... This feels great. Thank you."

A few minutes pass, and I feel myself starting to doze off when Eli's voice awakens me.

"Madeleine?"

"Mm-hmm?"

"Do you hate me?"

The vulnerability in his words squeezes my heart a little harder than I can handle, leaving me defenseless.

I could lie to him.

I could tell him yes and hope he never asks me again.

It would make things easier.

It would keep him away from me, guaranteeing nothing comes between Alastor and my wedding.

But instead, I tell him the truth. "No, Eli. I don't hate you," I breathe. "I wanted to. I tried to. But I never could."

"And do you, Madeleine Alarie, take Alastor Manacorda as your lawfully wedded husband? To obey until death do you part?"

My heart pounds beneath my rib cage as I absorb the priest's words. "Obey?" I shake my head. "These aren't the vows I agreed to—"

Alastor's fingers wrap forcefully around my neck, cutting off my air supply. I claw at his hands, trying and failing to pull them away from me as he sneers down at me, a sinister smile spreading across his face as he watches me suffer under his touch.

My eyes dart to the audience in panic as I struggle to break free from his grip. Every face watches me, appearing unaffected by what's happening.

"H-help," I try to scream, but my voice comes out hoarse and practically inaudible. I look at my brothers, who view the scene with boredom in their eyes.

Is no one going to save me?

Tears streak down my cheeks as I feel my last breaths on the cusp of vanishing. My eyes close as I wait for death to take me before suddenly, the doors at the back of the church crash against the wall. My eyelids flutter open as I turn to look and see Eli striding through the entrance.

"Get your hands off of her!" he roars, every person in the church turning their attention to him.

Alastor laughs cruelly, his grip tightening, his fingers digging agonizingly into my flesh. "No. In fact, I think I'll kill her." He squeezes harder, completely closing my airways when—

I jump up, clasping a hand to my heaving chest, my breaths coming out labored and heavy. My eyelids flutter frantically as I look around the space, immediately recognizing my bedroom.

I'm safe.

"It was just a nightmare," I whisper, brushing my hair back from my damp forehead before I bend my knees and hug my legs against my chest, rocking back and forth.

This isn't the first time I've had this recurring nightmare. One where I feel entirely helpless, immobilized under Alastor's touch and power. But it was the first time that someone actually tried to save me.

When Eli tried to save me.

It takes a moment for my breathing to even out and for my heart rate to return to an acceptable pace. But when it finally does, I slide my legs over the side of the bed, and that's when I find some pain relievers and water on my nightstand and a paper bag on the floor.

Warmth cascades through me.

It might seem like nothing more than a little gesture, but I know the man who put them there.

He's the same man who had my mom's freezer filled with ice cream after I had my tonsils removed.

The same man who showed up at my prom after somehow knowing my date would be a no-show.

The one who's always taken care of me.

Whether I deserve it or not.

Stepping out of bed, I'm relieved to note that my migraine is gone, but just in case, I swallow a couple of the pain relievers with water. I head to the bathroom, where I take a quick hot shower and then throw on a blue silk nightie, feeling refreshed.

My stomach rumbles, reminding me that I missed dinner. When I glance at the clock and see it's just after midnight, I wonder if I should wait until morning, but after my stomach rumbles a second time, I decide to head downstairs.

Standing in the kitchen and staring at the contents of the fridge, words from earlier float across my mind.

"Hey, Angel. I miss you."

My appetite unexpectedly vanishes, and I close the fridge, pressing my forehead against the cold metal. A frustrated groan slips from my lips.

What is wrong with me?

Hearing him say those words to another woman shouldn't upset me.

I'm engaged to another man, after all.

Not by choice, but still.

And what the fuck happened in that dressing room?

Did I dream that all up?

I take a step back, shaking my head. I can't think about it—not about the way his body felt against mine, nor about how my heart raced in my chest with each rock of my hips against his muscular leg. And definitely not about how we were just seconds away from kissing.

I cover my face with my hands.

I can't do this.

I can't mess this up.

There's too much at stake.

As I walk out of the kitchen and up the stairs toward my room, I feel anxiety simmer inside me.

Everything was simple before Eli got here.

Everything was moving according to plan.

And now...I don't fucking know what to do.

Restlessly, I play with my hideous engagement ring on my finger until it slips off, rolling across the hall and straight into...

Oh no.

I swallow as I stand before Eli's room and lightly knock on the slightly ajar door. "Eli, my ring rolled into your room. Can I come in to get it?" There's no answer, so I knock again while poking my head inside. "Eli?"

My eyes scan the space, noting no Eli in sight. Strange. I step inside and spot the gaudy ring directly in front of the bathroom door.

"Found you," I say triumphantly as I crouch to pick it up.

"Fuck." A moan from inside the bathroom causes me to freeze, my eyes darting to the narrow gap between the door and the frame. The sound of rushing water from the rain showerhead seems amplified as my body tenses.

Eli's...in the shower.

I can't stop my eyes from spotting his form in the mirror reflection. I can't help the way my body reacts to seeing him, every nerve ending buzzing with need. And I definitely can't stop myself from moving closer, pushing the door further open by just a smidge, and seeing every solid inch of him as he stands in the shower with his fist wrapped tightly around his hard cock.

I swallow as my throat goes dry. My body thrums to life as I continue to watch in awe while getting lost in his smooth movements.

His back muscles tighten as his bicep bulges from the exertion, his hand moving faster and harder. His left-hand presses against the tile above his head, the water raining down his back and over his perfectly sculpted...

Holy ass.

"Madeleine," he groans in pleasure, and I still, panicked that he sees me, but then I realize...

He's thinking about me.

He's thinking about me while getting off in the shower.

I'm suddenly turned on more than I've ever been in my life, a pulsing need thundering between my legs.

Without thinking about it, my hand moves on its own, sliding down my silk nightie and inching under the lace trim to reach my satin panties.

Biting down on my bottom lip, I let my fingers slip inside the fabric, gliding over my wet slit.

My eyes never leave Eli as his thrusts increase, his shoulder and back muscles bunching in desperation.

Suddenly, he lets out a guttural groan as white ropes of cum shoot out against the tiled floor. His breathing comes out rough and wild as his head falls back, his whole body appearing relaxed like that release was everything he ever needed.

"Did you enjoy the show, Princess?"

I freeze as my heart thunders in my ears.

He turns toward me with a devilish smirk on his chiseled face, proud of himself for catching me in a moment of complete and utter weakness.

But the moment his eyes travel down to where my hand resides, frozen between my legs, his smirk falls, and his eyes darken, his stare intensifying.

Oh, fuck.

Heat engulfs me, a violent pink flush covering every square inch of my body.

What am I doing? I should be dashing out of here in embarrassment. I should be looking away from his perfectly sculpted naked body. I should be moving my damn hand. I should be doing literally anything other than standing here like a deer caught in fucking headlights!

Eli shuts the water off and reaches for the glass door, the movement finally stirring me out of my fright.

Like prey that has just come face to face with its predator, I run like hell and don't stop until I'm in the safety of my room with my back against my door, panting and mortified.

So *unbelievably* mortified.

My hands cover my face in shame. "What the hell is wrong with me?" I whisper-yell at myself.

There's no way this could get any worse—

Knock. Knock.

"Madeleine. Open the door."

CHAPTER TEN

Eli

S he doesn't get to fucking run from me.

Not this bloody time.

Hastily, I wrap a towel around my hips and march through my room, stepping into the hall. Droplets of water fall from my bare skin onto the floor as I stand in front of Madeleine's closed bedroom door.

My knuckles rasp against the wood. "Madeleine. Open the door."

Seconds tick by, and I'm about to either knock again or kick the damn thing down when, surprisingly, it opens.

She stands before me, appearing exactly the way I imagine her in every one of my fantasies.

Hair tousled, falling to her waist.

Wearing the sexiest little piece of material that she considers to be a nightgown.

Her breaths come out in short, quick pants, her chest heaving.

Bright blue eyes look up at me under those long, dark lashes, waiting for me. Needing me.

I note the pretty pink flush that spreads up her neck and over her cheeks.

Her body is wound up, edging with tension.

She needs a release.

"Did you like watching?" I ask her, stepping inside and closing the door behind me. "Did you like knowing it was you I was thinking of while I was fucking my hand?"

Her lips part as she gives a tiny nod, her eyes never leaving me. I step toward her, eliminating the space between us. Gripping her hips, I pull her flush against me. A small gasp escapes between her lips, but she doesn't fight my hold; if anything, she gives in to it, melting into my touch.

I lean down, my lips sweeping over her ear. "Say it, Princess." My thumbs stroke over the soft fabric as I lower my lips, scraping my teeth down her neck. Her chest heaves faster as her hands reach out, grasping my arms for support, probably thinking she'll fall.

But I'll never let that happen.

She bites her bottom lip, fighting to say the words I need to hear. She's too stubborn to admit how much she wants this, but her body tells me everything I already know.

"Say it," I repeat softly. "Tell me what I need to hear, and I'll take care of that ache between your legs."

She looks at me, swallowing hard. For a few seconds, she hesitates before finally saying, "I need you."

That's the only permission I need for what I'm about to do to her.

Clutching her waist, I lift her in the air, eliciting a squeal out of her as I spin her around and drop her feet to the floor, pressing her back against the door.

I drop to my knees, my fingers digging into her hips as my lips caress her bare thighs.

I've never felt such an animalistic need in my life.

It's like I can't get close enough to her.

I need to taste her. Touch her. Devour her.

She stands on her tiptoes, arching forward, trying desperately to direct my lips where she wants them most.

"Don't worry, love. I won't make you wait for this. Not when we've both waited long enough." A whimper escapes her as my hand runs up the inside of her left thigh, sending goose bumps over her soft skin. "Place this over my shoulder."

She swallows nervously but does as she's told, giving me a front-row view of the wet spot soaking her panties. Leaning forward, I inhale her intoxicating scent. "Goddamn." I drag my lips over the fabric, peppering her with kisses.

"Eli," she breathes, tilting her head back and tangling her fingers in my hair.

With two fingers, I yank the fabric to the side, revealing her to me. My cock hardens painfully at the sight of her pretty pink pussy, her clit swollen with need. "Fuck, I've missed this view," I say roughly against her core. I drag my tongue down her slit, her taste hitting me like an aphrodisiac I can't resist. Her whole body shudders in my grip, causing my restraint to snap.

With an unbridled need, I tear her underwear from her body, tossing the shredded fabric to the side before I push her thighs farther apart and shove my face between her legs, feasting on her pussy like a starving man.

"Oh my God," she moans as my tongue flicks at her clit over and over again, providing her with the perfect amount of friction.

She trembles, thrashing against the door. Her fingers tug on the ends of my hair as she greedily grinds her pussy over my lips. I slide my hand between her legs, my index finger coming to a stop above her entrance. I swirl the pad of my fingers over her tight opening, pressing further against her walls.

She whimpers in pleasure as I plunge all the way inside and begin to thrust in and out, quickly adding a second finger to the mix for more pressure. My tongue glides to her clit, where I press it flat, repeatedly rolling it against her nerves.

"Oh, fuck," she breathes desperately.

I glance up, finding her hooded eyes unable to look away from what I'm doing to her.

Abruptly leaning back, I lick my lips, savoring her sweetness, and say, "Hold on tight."

"What—"

Grabbing the back of her right thigh, I throw it over my shoulder and bury my head between her legs as I place both of my hands beneath each one of her round ass cheeks to keep her secure in the air. Her hands frantically grip the side of my head, her fingers pulling on the strands of my hair.

It doesn't take much longer before her legs start to shake, vibrating against me as her body begs for the release I'm about to give it.

My lips wrap around her clit, and she screams out in ecstasy as the orgasm rolls through her, her thighs squeezing around my head as every muscle in her body coils up tightly before eventually falling slack against the door.

Glancing up, I admire her post-orgasm glow spreading over her porcelain skin. Especially because I'm the reason it's there. My eyes catch on a little smile tugging at the corners of her lips, one I'm not even sure she realizes she's showing.

It's an image I try to engrave into my memory.

To hold on to for rainy days.

Carefully, I drop her feet to the floor, ensuring she's sturdy before I stand before her. I gently grip her chin, angling her face toward me. Her eyelids flutter open, a flurry of emotions sweeping over her glossy irises as that slight smile completely vanishes.

Lust. Panic. Satisfaction. Regret. And something else I can't entirely decipher.

Leaning forward, I press a kiss to her temple. "Sweet dreams, Princess." She holds on to the wall for support as she looks down and steps out of the way, saying nothing as she opens the door, and I step through it.

However, just as I enter my room, ready to shut the door behind me, she calls for me.

"Eli."

I glance over my shoulder, watching as she fidgets nervously, adjusting the straps on her nightie. "I..." Her eyes meet mine, the watery reflection taking me aback and causing me to turn, facing her head on. They're not glossed over from the orgasm but from tears. Tears she's desperately holding back.

My chest tightens at the sight, my throat burning.

This girl doesn't cry in front of anyone. Not even me, except the one and only time years ago after her father's death.

But there are monsters in her eyes that she's scared of.

Ones that she shouldn't fear because I'm here.

And I won't let them harm her.

I want to run to her.

Hold her in my arms and tell her everything will be okay.

To tell her...

"I'm sorry," she whispers right before turning around and stepping farther into her room, closing the door behind her.

I stand there, wondering what she could possibly be apologizing for. Doesn't she know that she could stomp on my heart a thousand times, rip it clean down the middle, and shatter it into a million pieces, and I would never need an apology?

Not from her.

CHAPTER ELEVEN

Madeleine

"**M**iss Alarie, welcome to Taste This." Elena, the CEO of this luxury bakery, extends her hand for me to shake. Her long, dark hair falls in waves, meeting the pastel pink apron tied around her slender waist.

"Thank you for fitting me into your busy schedule." I remove my coat, offering it over to her assistant's outstretched hands.

Elena smiles. "I must say, I was quite surprised to receive a request for a cake tasting so close to your big day. However, it would be an absolute honor to have one of my cakes at your wedding." Her warm, brown eyes trail behind me. "And you must be Alastor."

Chills dance up my spine as Eli's dominating presence approaches from behind.

Delicious memories from a few nights ago flash in my mind.

I tighten my thighs together, trying but failing to ease the pulse blooming in my core.

I haven't spoken to him since then and didn't have the nerve to say more than four words to him this morning—*I have an appoint-*

ment—before I walked out the door and threw myself in the back of my waiting car.

What we did shouldn't have happened.

Purely because it left my body desperately searching for another orgasm that it would never find.

But now that I've had a taste of it, a delicious reminder of what we used to be like together, I can't help but crave more.

"This is my bodyguard, Eli," I answer before he can correct her.

He extends a hand around my waist, and I suck in a breath, his closeness sending me over the edge of any sanity I might have left.

"Lovely to meet you," he says, his hand enveloping hers.

"Do I detect a hint of an English accent?" Elena asks, her cheeks tinting a soft shade of pink.

I internally scoff. *Oh, please.*

"Yes." Eli grins. "I'm from Surrey."

"Ah! I thought it sounded familiar—"

"I'm here!" Alina rushes inside, brushing snow off her shoulders. She quickly unwraps her scarf and takes off her gloves before sliding her coat down her arms. "Sorry. I couldn't find any parking nearby." The same assistant from earlier takes her things, glancing down at the wet mess around her boots with dismay.

I quickly embrace her. "I told you we could have picked you up."

She waves a dismissive hand. "Don't worry. I'm out of the way anyway." She smiles and greets Eli before looking around at everyone. "So, what did I miss?"

"Nothing yet," I reply, taking a step back and accidentally bumping into Eli. He steadies me by gripping both of my arms. "Sorry," I say, jumping out of his touch as I smooth a hand down my white blouse.

He looks at me with one eyebrow raised. "Someone's a little on edge."

I lift a shoulder. "I haven't really been sleeping well."

"Really?" He grins. "I've been sleeping like a baby. Best nights of sleep I've had in a while, actually."

My cheeks flush as I quickly look away.

Elena gestures toward the back room. "I have everything prepared in the back if you'd like to follow me."

The three of us trail behind with the scent of chocolate wafting through the air. Taste This has won countless awards over the years, establishing itself as the best bakery in the northeast. And while I may not be particularly looking forward to my wedding, I knew that if Taste This made my wedding cake, I could at least be guaranteed a piece of delicious cake to help ease the pain that day would bring me.

"I think I might be in heaven," I murmur as we settle around a circular white table.

An employee approaches with a tray of samples and places them on the center of the table.

"In order, we have our vanilla cake, dark chocolate cake, carrot cake, lemon cake, red velvet cake, spice cake, and our signature ginger chai." Another server appears, placing a second tray before us. "And here, we have the lemon curd, vanilla buttercream, vanilla buttercream with a hint of lavender, raspberry preserves, a salted caramel filling, a ganache, and an apricot filling."

Three glasses of water are positioned in front of each of us.

"Wow." My eyes travel across each sample. "This is going to be a difficult decision."

"If you have any questions," Elena begins, "please don't hesitate to let me know. I'll be back shortly to check on you." She exits gracefully, disappearing around the corner.

After several minutes of consuming more calories in one sitting than I think I ever have in my life, I lean back in my seat, placing a hand on my stomach. "I don't think I can look at another piece of cake for as long as I live."

"Well, good thing we all know what flavor you're probably leaning toward," Alina teases, bumping my shoulder. She takes her fork, digging it into the decadent chocolate cake.

And she would be correct if Alastor hadn't explicitly told me *no chocolate*. Normally, I wouldn't ever let a man tell me what to do, but with Alastor, I need to learn which battles to fight.

And having a chocolate wedding cake isn't at the top of that list.

"Actually, I thought the vanilla cake with the buttercream would be nice."

Alina chuckles, licking her fork. "Right."

I give a slight shrug.

"Wait." She drops her fork, her eyes blinking. "You're serious?" She looks at Eli. "Is she serious?" Her phone on the table in front of her vibrates, stealing her attention.

He leans back in his chair, crossing his arms over his chest as he regards me. "You're not going with chocolate?"

"Is that a problem?"

"Not at all. It's just that for as long as I've known you, chocolate has been its own food category." He smirks, placing his hands behind his head. "I never took you for someone who liked vanilla."

He winks at me, rekindling that pulse between my legs that I thought I had managed to extinguish. I quickly cross my legs, which doesn't go unnoticed by him. His grin grows wider, his eyes darker, and I'm thankful that Alina is too busy staring at her phone to notice.

She abruptly stands from her chair, glancing down at her phone in her hands with furrowed brows. "Sorry, I have to take this. I'll be right back." She heads toward the entrance, leaving Eli and me behind.

Alone.

Silence fills the room. The only noise I hear is the clock ticking above the giant oven.

Where's Elena? Shouldn't she be checking on us by now?

I tap a steady finger on the table, my leg bouncing in rhythm.

"Something on your mind?" Eli asks, crossing his arms over his chest.

"Actually, yes." I clear my throat and say, "I think we should talk about what happened the other night."

He leans forward, rubbing his jaw as he gazes down at the table. "Yeah, you're right. Let's talk about it." His eyes meet mine. "Which part did you want to talk about, though? The part where you watched me jerk off to the thought of you? Or the part where I had my face buried in your—"

I jump across the table, slamming my hand over his mouth. My eyes dart around the room to ensure no one is nearby. I look him dead in the eye. "I meant," I say calmly, "we need to talk about how that can never happen again."

He mumbles against my palm, so I let my hand fall as I sink into my seat.

"Tell me you didn't enjoy yourself," he says, arching a brow and waiting for me to defy him.

"I didn't," I grit out.

He *tsks*. "Look at you. Lying again."

"I'm not—"

"I still taste your orgasm on my tongue."

Heat creeps up my neck as I look away, biting the inside of my cheek. "We shouldn't have done that," I say softly. I glance back at him. "You have no idea…" I stop myself from finishing that thought, shaking my head.

He truly has no clue as to what we're risking.

"No idea about what?" He sits up straight, his attention focused entirely on me.

"Nothing." I scan the room, brushing an irritated hand through my hair. "Where is Elena?"

Eli picks up the sample of the chocolate ganache and swipes his finger through the rich filling, coating the tip of his finger in the decadence. He eyes me like a predator, a coy smile spreading on his face as he holds it toward me and says, "Taste."

I swallow hard. "I already tried it."

He shakes his head. "Don't think you did. In fact, I believe this is the only one you haven't tried, which is odd considering how much you love chocolate."

I groan internally. He's right, of course. But I purposely didn't try it because I didn't want to know what I would be missing out on.

Coincidentally, it's the exact same reason why we shouldn't have fooled around a few nights ago.

He arches a brow, challenging me.

And because I've clearly lost my mind and all sense of reason, I lean forward and part my lips. His chocolate-coated finger rests on my tongue as I suck off the contents, my eyes closing. A moan flees me as the decadent flavor erupts over my taste buds.

"Fuck, Princess," Eli breathes harshly.

My eyes open, finding him staring at me like I'm the most important thing in his world.

But that can't be right.

Can it?

"Hey, Angel. I miss you."

One letter—Four words.

"Would that be such a bad thing?"

Abruptly, I pull back and grab the closest napkin, patting it against the corners of my lips. Warmth blooms across my cheeks as I tuck a lock of hair behind my ear, staring down at the table.

What the hell am I doing?

Nothing can happen between me and Eli.

Not anymore.

Two fingers hook under my chin, tilting my head up until my eyes meet his.

"You feel it, too," he says. "I know you do."

It *doesn't matter what I feel.*

My lips part, a lie sitting on the tip of my tongue.

"Don't," he insists, shaking his head. "Don't say anything." His hand glides along my skin, gently covering my cheek. "I know you still feel it—that thing between us. I've never been able to explain it. But there was always something there, like a magnetic pull I could never see. It's a force bigger than either of us could ever comprehend, and you're fighting it with everything you have. I just can't figure out why." A sad smile pulls at his lips. "But I'll be here when you're ready to stop fighting it. I'll always be here."

He drops his hand, a chill coating my skin.

It feels like he just chiseled away a considerable chunk of the stone that surrounds my heart.

And for the first time in a long while, it beats not because it has to but because it wants to.

Which leads to a dangerous thing... *Hope.*

Because for the first time, I look at him and think that maybe I should tell him. Maybe I should explain everything and hope that he'll be able to save me. Save himself. *Save us.*

So, without thinking, I part my lips. "Eli, I—"

"So, what do we think?" Elena enters the room with a bright smile, oblivious to the tension swirling in the air between us.

Her interference at the exact moment I would have confessed is the only sign I need to keep my damn lips closed.

I show a smile and abruptly stand. "Everything was delicious. I think my top choice would be the vanilla cake with the vanilla buttercream."

She claps her hands together. "Lovely! I'll have the contract prepared and sent to you later today with all the details." She extends her hand, and I take it. "Don't hesitate to reach out at any time." Her beautiful smile widens. "I'm so excited for your wedding."

At least that makes one of us.

April 19th

Dear Eli,

I did it. I'm all moved into my home. And surprisingly, it doesn't feel as weird as I thought it might. If anything, it makes me feel closer to my dad, knowing he had a hand in all of this.

I only have a few weeks left of school before graduation. I can't wait to spend my days by the lake, soaking up every minute of freedom before college starts in the fall.

It's scary thinking about leaving the estate. It's the only place I've ever known as home. The place where I've always felt the safest. And a place with so many memories. Especially ones that I'm scared of losing. But maybe a change of scenery will be good for me. At least, that's what I'm trying to tell myself.

Stay safe,
Madeleine

P.S. I think about you too. A lot. Maybe more than I should.

CHAPTER TWELVE

Eli

S omething isn't right.

Madeleine, usually poised with her chin held high and her back straight as a rod, has been a nervous wreck since we left the house.

"Care to explain what has you in a tizzy?" I ask, stretching my arm across the back of our seats.

She stops biting her thumbnail—her biggest giveaway to her anxiety—and instantly adjusts her posture beside me.

"I'm not in a..." She makes air quotes. "'Tizzy.'"

"Really? Well, you've fooled me." I arch a brow, watching as she rolls her eyes and looks out her window.

"I can handle them," she says softly, almost too quietly for me to hear.

"Handle who?" I ask, but before she can respond, the car pulls to a stop beside the restaurant.

She quickly scurries out of the car, stepping up the stairs in her six-inch heels toward the front entrance. The black dress she's wearing hugs every delicious curve of her body, and unfortunately, I'm not the only one who notices as the doorman holds the door open for her with his gaze lingering on her ass.

Fucking wanker.

Taking two steps at a time until I stand right before the man, I grab his collar and shove him against the glass wall.

"Do you have any idea who you were just eye-fucking?" I demand. He shakes his head vigorously as fear radiates off him in waves. "Madeleine Alarie." He pales as recognition washes over his face.

"I had no idea! I swear!" he exclaims, his eyes widening in panic. He glances in her direction, and I shake him again.

"Don't fucking look at her!"

"Okay! Okay! I won't!"

"The next time I catch you admiring what isn't yours, I'll ensure that you never get the chance to see anything ever again." I push him aside and quickly approach an unimpressed Madeleine, who stands with her arms crossed and her hip jutting out to the side.

"Do you feel better?" she asks, attempting to sound annoyed, but I notice a hint of amusement in her eyes.

I roll my neck and grin. "Very much so."

Facing the main room, she sighs and says, "That makes one of us."

She takes a step just as I reach out and grasp her elbow, stopping her. She stills, looking up at me with those captivating blue eyes I want to get lost in.

"You don't have to go in there," I tell her. "I can say you weren't feeling well and arrange for a bottle of the most expensive champagne to be sent to their table as an apology."

She smiles, but the corners of her lips barely reach her eyes. Her hand lands on mine, giving it a reassuring pat. "I do have to, but thank you." She takes a step away but then stops, glancing over her shoulder. "Just...don't leave my side, okay?"

"Never," I answer.

The moment she resumes her steps, her smile fades, and she pulls her shoulders back, striding confidently through the space. An aura of authority and power surrounds her. I closely follow behind, maintaining only a few inches between us.

The room is filled with posh socialites dressed to the nines, here to be seen and heard. They laugh as they shove their forks into their overpriced caviar and drink a bottle of champagne worth the price of someone's car. Servers stand at the ready nearby, prepared to be called upon for whatever these snobs desire. The lights are dim, casting an ambient glow over the expansive space—a space that, the more I look around, I realize is designed to resemble the Palace of Versailles.

"Madeleine, darling."

Alastor's unpleasant voice causes my eyes to snap in his direction just as he leans forward, pressing a kiss to each of her cheeks. He snakes an arm around her waist, pulling her against his side.

"Smile!" A photographer appears before them, capturing a picture of the supposed happy couple. Onlookers nearby watch in admiration... If only they knew.

My hands, clenched at my sides, tremble with fury as I stare at the place on Madeleine's hip where Alastor's hand comfortably rests. That is until she manages to slip out of his grip, sneaking between a chair and positioning herself closer to me.

Alastor narrows his eyes, focusing on the small distance that separates us.

Can't say he looks too pleased.

Subtly, I scan him from head to toe, mentally noting any places he may be storing a hidden weapon.

Should I be surprised to find him dressed in a custom-tailored white suit, looking like the goddamn Easter Bunny? No. What does catch me off guard is the presence of an older man standing beside him, both of them wearing almost identical ridiculous attire.

We step toward the table with four pairs of eyes on us.

"Hi, Eli." Cressida tucks her hair behind her ear, looking up at me. "It's lovely to see you again."

I tilt my chin politely. "Always lovely to see you, Cressida." I wasn't lying to Madeleine when I told her she asked me out. The girl has balls; I'll give her that. However, when she asked me if I'd like to join her for dinner, I gently declined, explaining that work was my primary focus at the moment. Not a lie, given that Madeleine is my work and, consequently, my primary focus.

"Madeleine, dear. I swear you get lovelier every time we see you," the older man, who I assume is Alastor's stepfather, Adolfo, says. She forces a smile as he reaches for her hand, but Madeleine pretends not to notice and sits down, sipping the wine before her.

Alastor and I stare off momentarily before he says, "Sorry, chap. Must have forgotten you'd be accompanying my darling girl here tonight. Don't seem to have an extra chair for you." He smiles wickedly as if he had just won a war.

But if there's one thing he should know about me…

I never lose in a battle.

I grin. "Don't think it will be a problem. In fact…" I turn to quickly scan the room and spot an empty seat two tables away. Hurrying over, I grab the chair and then place it between Madeleine and Cressida. As I sit down, my knee brushes against Madeleine's. "Perfect fit."

Alastor appears to want to say something, but instead, he tugs at his collar and takes the seat on the other side of Madeleine.

"Eli," Madeleine voices as she subtly shifts away from Alastor. "This is Adolfo and Mila, Alastor's parents."

Adolfo leans back in his chair, his eyes taking me in. "You must be the new bodyguard we've heard so much about."

"Yes, sir. The one and only."

"And you're equipped to handle Madeleine?"

Handle? This senile dickhead knows what century we're in, right?

"If you mean to ask, am I equipped to keep Madeleine safe? Then yes. I would take a bullet for her and have. But handle?" I shake my head. "One doesn't *handle* a queen in her own kingdom."

Madeleine glances up at me with parted lips, her eyes holding mine as they shine radiantly. The tiny flame from the candle at the center of the table reflects across them, making her appear divine.

"Women are to be tamed," Adolfo mutters, raising his amber drink to his lips. "You'll learn that soon enough."

Tamed? This son of a—

"Will Enzio be joining us tonight?" Madeleine asks, smoothing a napkin over her lap.

Alastor scoffs. "Let's hope not. The sight of him will make my appetite vanish."

"So, Eli," Cressida begins. Is it just my imagination, or did her chair move closer to mine? "I heard you were in the military. That must have been very scary."

I nod. "It can be, yes. Depends on the assignment and the location, but overall, I enjoyed my time in the service." *Up until the very end.* "I ended my career as a Navy SEAL and would like to think I became the man I am today because of it."

Adolfo waves a dismissive hand. "Technology provides most of the legwork in the field. Not the soldiers."

My fist curls on the table. "That's not—"

"But how were you able to join the American military if you're British?" Cressida asks, her wide eyes appearing curious.

I take a sip of water to rein in my anger. "The Alarie Estate is my primary address. It's where I grew up while attending school in the States. I've always considered it my home."

Out of the corner of my eye, I see Madeleine fight back a soft smile before she brings her glass of red wine to her lips.

"Well, if you enjoyed it so much, then why aren't you still doing it?" Cressida tilts her head to the side, batting her lashes as she waits for my answer.

"Well, I umm." I clear my throat, trying not to think about that day. My hand slides across the back of my neck, squeezing my tight muscles. "I was kidnapped and then...tortured." I swallow hard. "And according to the government's standards, my injuries sustained were too severe for me to perform my job adequately anymore."

"You were injured?" Madeleine asks softly, her brows furrowing together. "No one told—" Her bright blue eyes widen, staring up at me. She connects the pieces, remembering the burns across my back. The ones she saw when I moved into her home. And the same ones that are a constant reminder of a time in my life I wish I could forget.

"Finally, we're practically starving over here!" Alastor scolds the waiter who appears beside me, placing salads in front of all of us.

I'm just about to cut into mine when I hear Mila speak for the first time tonight. "Don't you think that dress is a little too revealing for a place like this, dear?"

Who is she talking about— My knife clatters onto my plate, silencing everyone around the table as I realize her eyes are fixated on Madeleine's outfit.

It takes everything in me to control my temper as I watch Madeleine fidget with her dress, her skin turning a soft shade of pink.

"I thought it was suitable for tonight," she says defensively.

"It looks very lovely to me," Cressida adds.

"Hmm." Mila purses her lips in clear disapproval. "It's not very classy. I think it's a bit too tight."

"She's right." Alastor stares at Madeleine with disdain. "My fiancée shouldn't be traipsing around like some common whore."

My vision blurs with rage, my fingers curling into a fist on the table before me. "You think it's appropriate to speak to your fiancée that way?"

Alastor narrows his eyes. "I will speak to my fiancée any damn way I please." His line of sight turns to Madeleine. "Next time, check with me first on what you're allowed to wear."

Ha! As if Madeleine would ever—

"Okay," she responds, taking a bite of her salad and chewing extra aggressively.

I blink once. Twice. Three times.

Am I fucking dreaming right now?

Living in some fictional world?

I glance down at Madeleine beside me, and she suddenly seems smaller than when we arrived. Her shoulders are hunched in, her chin is lowered, and her eyes are downcast.

I glare at Alastor, who looks far too pleased with himself.

What the fuck does he have on her?

"How's the McLaren W1 treating you, son?" Adolfo asks Alastor. "Worth every penny?"

"If you mean, was it worth the over two million I paid for it? Then yes." Alastor grins arrogantly. "You'll have to come over to see it sometime. A photographer from the magazine *Business Century* will be visiting next week to shoot it for their cover with me inside. They'll be featuring a whole spread on my success in the oil industry."

"That's wonderful, dear," Mila offers proudly.

"Maybe some time," Cressida starts, "I could drive it?"

"Ha!" Alastor feigns laughter. "That car is the most important thing in the world to me. No one but me will drive it, touch it, or breathe near it."

As the Manacorda family converse over cars, stocks, and other bullshit, I feel a storm brewing inside me. The belittling of the most significant person in my life doesn't sit right with me. Not one fucking bit.

My fist slams down on the table, rattling the silverware and glasses. I'm fuming, feeling ready to unleash violence—

My body freezes as Madeleine's hand slides over my thigh. She looks up at me with pleading eyes. Her slender fingers gently squeeze my leg as she mouths, *Please don't.*

My cock swells as blood rushes to my groin. Her hand is only an inch from where I want it to be. From where I dream of her touching me.

I'm paralyzed by her closeness.

The way her thumb glides back and forth only adds to my longing for her.

A voice clears, and we both turn to see Alastor watching us. By some miracle, he can't see Madeleine's hand placement from the angle he's sitting at.

"Darling, how did the cake tasting go?" he asks, bringing his drink to his lips.

Madeleine's hand slides further up my leg, making her intentions clear. I spread my legs farther apart, careful not to bump into Cressida.

"It was great. They offer so many flavor combinations; it was hard to choose," she responds, taking a sip of her drink. A few drops of the red liquid fall onto the top of her dress. "Oh, how clumsy of me." She removes her hand from my leg and reaches for her napkin to dab at the wine stain, which only seems to grow.

"You should be more careful," Mila says, frowning. "That won't come out. You should at least blot it with some cold water."

Madeleine smiles, but I note the hidden venom in her gaze. "You're right. I should take care of this in the restroom. I'll be right back."

She stands, and I follow her lead as we make our way toward the bathroom. Just as I say, "I'll wait right here," she reaches for my hand, intertwining our fingers and tugging me into the room with her.

She closes and locks the door behind us, pressing her forehead to the door while she takes a deep breath and then turns to face me.

I cross my arms over my chest and lean against the wall. "That wine spill was no accident, was it?"

She shakes her head, her hair falling in waves over her shoulders. "No. I needed to get out of there." She leans against the door and looks at me, like really looks at me, as if seeing me for the first time. She mirrors my stance, crossing her arms over her chest, which draws my attention to her cleavage.

"What's going on inside your head?" I ask.

She swallows. "I'm confused."

"About what?"

"You."

"Me?"

"You...you stood up for me out there."

My brows furrow. "Of course."

"But why?"

I tilt my head to the side. "Because you're the most important person in my life and I won't let those bloody wankers talk badly about you. It doesn't sit right with me. Not one fucking bit."

She blinks a few times, her chest heaving a little faster.

"Why the fuck do you let him treat you like that?" I shake my head, dragging a frustrated hand through my hair. "Why do you let any of them treat you like that? Like you're less than them when you're a goddamn—"

"Don't." She shakes her head, dropping her hands to her side. Her eyelids flutter shut for a quick moment as she takes a deep breath. "I didn't bring you in here to argue with you."

I arch a brow. "Then why am I here?"

She hesitates before taking a few steps toward me, sauntering forward, not stopping until she stands directly before me. She places her index finger on my chest, and gradually slides it down my torso, slowing when she reaches my abs. Her eyes lock with mine as a playful little grin appears on her face. "So I can properly thank you."

She starts to lower her body, but I stop her by gripping her chin. "You never have to thank me for having your back."

Her smile grows as she leans forward, her soft lips brushing my ear. "I know, Eli, and that's why I want to. So, shut up and let me suck your cock."

She drops to her knees, and my cock hardens painfully from being restrained.

Her fingers make quick work of unhooking my belt and unzipping my pants. She shoves the material down, my cock noticeably erect beneath the thin fabric of my boxer briefs. Her eyes widen in appreciation as she reaches up and pulls the fabric down. My cock springs before her, and she doesn't hesitate as she grips the length between her fingers. Leaning forward, she sticks out her tongue and glides it over the tip, licking the precum.

"Fuck," I groan, watching her with rapt fascination.

"I always did enjoy this part," she murmurs, kissing the tip.

I tangle my fingers in her hair, wrapping the ends around my fist. "What part?"

She gazes up at me under her dark lashes. "Making you feel good."

Her mouth opens wide as she leans forward, sliding my cock between her luscious lips as far as she can go. When I'm almost all the way in, she starts to gag but quickly shakes it off and pushes through. Her eyes well with tears as she creates a rhythm, thrusting my dick in and out. Her tongue swirls over my tip as her hand sneaks under, cradling my balls.

"Bloody hell," I moan, tipping my head back. "You're doing so well, love."

She reaches for my hand and places it on the back of her head, pressing it down.

Well, fuck me.

"You want me to fuck your mouth?" I ask, my grip tightening.

She nods, never stopping her movements.

"Fuck, you are perfect." I reach down, cupping her cheek. I can't help but admire her as she takes almost every inch of me. "You look so beautiful on your knees with my cock between your lips, Princess."

She moans around me, the vibration making my dick pulse.

I grab her hand and bring it to my thigh. "Tap out if you want me to stop. Okay?"

She nods, her fingers curling around my leg.

My length hits the back of her throat, and my restraint snaps.

My fingers press into her scalp, and I thrust with urgency, her warm, wet mouth wrapped firmly around my dick. Her bright blue eyes pool with tears, her fingers gripping my thighs as she takes everything I give her.

It doesn't take long for my balls to tighten, given that my cock hasn't had any attention like this in over a year, except from my goddamn hand.

I stare down at her, my grip loosening. "I'm going to come. Are you going to show me how much you've missed my cock and swallow every last drop?"

She nods frantically as she moans around me.

The orgasm rips through me, pleasure surging through every cell of my body. A guttural groan escapes between my lips, my whole body straining as I hit my peak. White, hot ropes of cum shoot down Madeleine's throat, and she greedily swallows all of it.

My dick slides out of her mouth, saliva leaking from the corner of her swollen lips. Her chest heaves, and her cheeks are flushed as she stares up at me with a proud grin.

"Fuck, that was brilliant." I tuck myself back into my pants and lean forward to grip her at the waist, bringing her back to a standing position. Reaching a hand toward the counter, I grab a few tissues and gently wipe under her eyes and then around her mouth.

"On a scale of one to ten, by looking at me, how obvious is it that I just gave you a blow job?" she asks with a chuckle.

"Ehh." I shrug. "Probably an eleven."

She swats my chest, and we both laugh. "At least I invested in waterproof mascara." Her fingers pull at the hem of her dress. "Honestly, how bad do I look?"

I shake my head. "I'm not the right person to ask, love." I extend a hand, smoothing down her hair and tucking it behind her ear before I snake an arm around her waist and pull her before me. Her hands rest on my chest as she gazes up at me. "You could wear a goddamn potato sack and still look beautiful in my eyes."

Her eyes soften, and she bites her bottom lip. "Well, we'd better get back out there before they come looking for us."

I cradle her cheek, my thumb gliding over her smooth skin.

I want to kiss her.

I need to kiss her.

But just as I lean down, she pats my chest and turns toward the sink, soaking a paper towel under the cold water before pressing it to the wine stain on her dress. She manages to get most of it cleaned up before turning toward the door to unlock and open it, disappearing through the other side.

Disappointment flashes over me, but I quickly shake it off as I follow after her. I run my fingers through my hair and tuck my shirt back inside my pants, trying to appear like I didn't just get the best blow job of my life in the bathroom.

Everyone in the Manacorda family is engaged in conversation as we approach the table, not giving us a second glance.

Madeleine takes her seat, which now has her main course before her, and looks up at me with a secret smile. Her hand finds my leg as I take my seat beside her.

"Madeleine," Alastor says, his tone stern. "Can I have a word with you?" He crumples the cloth napkin on his lap and tosses it onto the table as he stands.

I cross my arms over my chest, glaring at him. "Why don't you give her a chance to eat her goddamn—"

"Of course," Madeleine interjects, swiftly removing her hand from my leg and standing.

I immediately follow suit, standing beside her, ready to go wherever she goes. *"Just...don't leave my side, okay?"*

"If you don't mind, my *fiancée* and I would like a moment of privacy," Alastor states, emphasizing the word fiancée, which has officially become my least favorite word in the dictionary. He snakes an arm around Madeleine's waist and hauls her into his side.

She looks at me. "It's okay. I'll be right back."

Adolfo laughs. "Can't wait until the wedding night, huh? You're more like me than my actual son."

Madeleine's cheeks flame with embarrassment as she pulls out of Alastor's grip and storms away, heading out of the main room.

Alastor adjusts his tie and smirks. "We'll be back shortly." He leans closer so only I can hear him. "Just need a few minutes to remind her who she belongs to." A wicked grin spreads over his face before he turns and walks away, leaving me seeing red as I fight with myself on what to do.

On the one hand, she can take care of herself. I know she can. But what I've been witnessing over the course of the night has me questioning everything I've ever known.

My Madeleine wouldn't take this shit.

She wouldn't cower under their stares or cruel words.

She'd fight back.

With her sharp tongue and lethal gaze.

She'd come out victorious with some witty remark or insult.

But the woman I just witnessed being berated by almost every member of that family left my chest feeling tight, my head confused, and my heart heavy.

My Madeleine wouldn't be engaged to the world's biggest arsehole.

But she's not yours.

Not anymore.

I stare at the spot where she disappeared around the corner out of sight, and all I can think is...

Like hell, she isn't mine.

Pushing the chair out of my way a little harder than necessary, I step in that direction when the sudden vibration of my phone in my pocket catches my attention. Pulling it out, I see Enzio's name on the screen.

"Excuse me," I say, looking around at everyone as I back away, place the phone to my ear, and walk toward the back of the room. "Yes?"

"You ready to kill someone yet at this dinner?"

"How'd you know about it?"

"Cressida always tries to get me to come to them."

I shake my head. "I can't decide which of them I want to kill first."

"My money's on my father. Although that Mila is a feisty one." He laughs. "I'm calling because, with Alastor in town for the week, it gives you an opportunity to *question* Tony."

"Where is he?"

"He has an apartment in the same building as Alastor's."

"And how do you plan on us getting him alone?"

"I happen to know he despises our parents, which is why he's not at the dinner tonight." He chuckles. "On Thursday, my parents are hosting a gala in the city. Alastor will be in attendance to show his face, and Tony will most likely stay behind, giving you the opportunity for some one-on-one time."

"Okay…" I process his words. "But if it's Alastor's building, how do you expect us to enter unseen?"

"Alex can hack into the security system, correct?"

I pause, considering. "Shouldn't be a problem."

"Good. Let me know what you find out. It may be nothing, but it doesn't hurt to confirm."

"We will," I answer.

"How much longer will this dinner be?"

I glance over at the table where Madeleine and Alastor are taking their seats. Madeleine frowns, pressing her fingers into her temple, while

Mila talks animatedly about something, and Alastor and Adolfo laugh boisterously.

"We're leaving now. Text me with the details."

I quickly end the call, place an order for food on my phone, and then shove my phone into my pocket as I walk over to the table. Resting a hand on the back of Madeleine's chair, I state, "I'm sorry, but we have to leave. That was Vin on the phone, and he mentioned a family emergency that he would like you to come home for."

Madeleine's eyes widen as she stands without a second thought.

"Oh my, I hope everything is all right," Mila offers before taking a large gulp of her champagne.

Alastor stands as well. "I'll accompany you home."

"No," both Madeleine and I reply in unison.

She quickly places her hand on his chest, looking up at him. "I'll be fine. Besides, you don't want to leave your family's dinner so early." She looks at his parents. "Apologies, but I must go. We should do this again soon."

Alastor bends down to kiss her, but Madeleine quickly spins on her heels and turns out of his reach. I don't give the rest of the family a chance to continue their polite exchanges, placing my hand on her lower back to gently guide her away from the table. Over my shoulder, I notice Alastor's eyes fixed on where my hand rests, which gives me a small sense of satisfaction.

We walk side by side out the front door into the frigid air. I stop her, gently pulling on her hand, and then take off my jacket, placing it around her shoulders just as Reginald brings the car to a stop at the entrance. She wraps the material around her waist, swimming in its length.

I reach out, placing two fingers under her chin to guide her gaze up to mine. "Did he hurt you?"

She shakes her head.

"And you'd tell me if he did?"

She nods.

"Good."

Opening the back passenger door for her, she places her hand on the inside panel before stilling and turning to face me.

"There is no family emergency, is there?"

"No. And I just put in an order for pizza to be delivered to the front gate."

She smiles—a true, genuine, Madeleine heart-stopping smile. "Thank you, Eli." She leans forward and presses a tender kiss against my cheek before stepping inside the vehicle and sliding across the leather seat.

I don't know what I did to deserve that smile, but fuck, I want to memorize it so it's the last thing I see before I take my dying breath.

June 16th

Princess,

I was just staring up at the night sky, thinking about how we might both be looking up, but you'll see the sun, whereas I'll see the moon. I usually can handle being so far away from home, but for whatever reason, it's hitting me extra hard today.

Yours,
Eli

CHAPTER THIRTEEN

Madeleine

As I step out of the Escalade, I lift my sunglasses to my eyes and adjust the belt around my jacket before heading into the private back entrance of My Something White, an exclusive bridal boutique owned by the talented Star Bamford, with Eli closely following behind me.

"I told you that you could wait in the car. This will only take a moment," I say, turning to face him as the door swings open at our arrival. One of Star's assistants stands there, holding the door open with a bright smile.

"No can do. Where you go, I go. You know the rules, Princess," Eli replies, clasping his hands behind his back and staring straight ahead at the door like an obedient soldier.

He doesn't understand.

Me standing in my wedding dress isn't going to be an easy thing to witness—for either of us.

Not when we used to dream of a future together.

One where I would be walking down the aisle to meet him.

Not Alastor.

I internally shake my head and take a deep breath before I turn and step inside the warm space.

"Madeleine!" Star greets me with her arms wide open. "We're so excited to see the final product on you." She embraces me, kissing both of my cheeks before her eyes shift to Eli.

"And you must be the—"

"My bodyguard," I answer quickly. How many times are people going to assume he's my fiancé?

"Of course." She gives him a once-over before facing me, her smile widening. "I'm so glad we could finish in time for your big day."

I give a heartfelt smile, knowing it's not this woman's fault for the predicament I find myself in. I had been postponing dress shopping for as long as I could until I finally had no choice. Had I waited one more day, I would have had to settle for a dress off the rack. "I appreciate your time. I'm honored to wear one of your designs on my...special day." I internally cringe.

"It's my pleasure. Having you in one of my gowns, well..." She waves her hands around animatedly. "It will be one of the highlights of my career." She gestures for us to follow her. "I have your dress all steamed and hanging in a dressing room waiting for you."

Eli's hand rests on my lower back as we follow behind, and for a fleeting moment, everything feels like it might be okay.

That is until we reach the room, and he removes his touch to stand outside of the space as I enter through the threshold with Star. The dressing room is the size of my bedroom, featuring sofas and chairs, scenic paintings covering the cream-colored walls, and a presentation of chilled champagne and hors d'oeuvres to cater to every guest's needs. It's certainly an establishment that goes all out for their brides.

As I look around, my eyes catch on the wedding gown displayed in the back.

Anxiety slithers over my skin as I consider what this dress truly represents—a symbol of my loss of freedom.

"Isn't it stunning?" Star asks, running her hand over the lace bodice.

I swallow the lump in my throat. "It sure is."

"Would you like some assistance with putting it on?"

"No." I remove my jacket, placing it over the back of a chair. "That's all right. I'll manage."

"Excellent! Well, I'll give you some space, but I'll be back to check on you shortly. Let me know if you need anything." Star beams as she closes the door behind her, her heels clacking against the tiled floor, disappearing toward the front of the store.

Hesitantly, I step toward the dress, examining the embedded diamonds and noticing the considerable effort that went into creating this gown.

It's beautiful.

But I'm not standing here with butterflies in my stomach.

I'm not envisioning myself walking down an aisle in it.

I'm wondering how fast this material will burn.

As I reach for the dress, my sleeve slides up my arm, revealing the new bruise on my wrist I received just last night.

Alastor's hand tightens around my wrist, yanking me down the empty hallway. There's no one nearby. No one to hear or see anything that might transpire between us. I peek over my shoulder, hoping desperately that maybe Eli did follow us.

But he's nowhere to be seen.

I truly am alone.

"Let go of me!" I whisper-yell, not wanting to cause a scene, as I use my free hand to try to pull his hand off me.

To my surprise, he releases me, but only to shove me against the wall. I stand straight, taking a deep breath. I cross my arms over my chest, trying to hide the slight tremble in my hands.

He paces, smoothing his gelled-back hair with both hands. His shoulders rise and fall with each furious breath he takes. "You won't back out of this marriage, Madeleine. I won't allow it. You won't make me look like a goddamn fool in front of my family. In front of the whole fucking world!"

I roll my eyes. "I'm not—"

"I see the way you're looking at him! Do you think I'm stupid? You two probably fucked in the bathroom." He sneers down at me. "Let me remind you that as soon as you say I do, you belong to me. No one else. Just me. Your brothers may have assigned him to you now, but I promise you he will not be joining us in Italy. Mark my words."

Anxiety spreads over me at the thought of truly being alone with Alastor in another country. But I won't back down without a fight. Squaring my shoulders and raising my chin, I say, "I belong to no—"

He lunges for me, his hands tightening around my throat, pushing me against the wall. "Do I need to refresh your memory and tell you what's at stake here? What you risk losing should you not follow through with this wedding?"

I shake my head, clawing at his hands.

I know what's at stake.

Everything.

"Good." He releases his grip, and I fall to the floor, gulping down air and savoring every breath I can take. "You're the one who came crawling on your hands and knees to me, looking for my help. It wasn't the other way around." He leans down, crouching over me. "I followed through on my end of the bargain. Now it's time for you to do the same."

With trembling hands, I remove my clothes and mentally prepare for what I'm about to put on.

After struggling for several minutes to wrestle myself into the dress, sweat coats my forehead, adding to the sense of impending doom in my stomach.

Rotating in the room, I realize there's no mirror in here and groan in frustration, knowing what I have to do.

Opening the door, I see Eli a few feet away, facing the wall as he speaks on his phone. It's probably that supposed *"Angel"* he misses so damn much while he's stuck babysitting me. *Blah...* I roll my eyes in irritation, shaking my head.

Maybe if I'm quiet, he won't even notice me.

Quickly, I gather the tulle and hurry toward the black podium, which is surrounded by a three-way mirror.

Stepping up, I brace my shoulders and put on the smile I've been practicing for my wedding day, but as my eyes catch my reflection in the mirror, my smile instantly fades.

I tilt my head to the side, taking in the sight before me: the enormous tulle gown engulfs my lower half, making me look like the top of a cupcake while an itchy lace fabric covers my upper body. Red splotches appear across my chest as the itching intensifies, and a bead of sweat trickles down my back.

From the other side of the wall, I can hear women laughing blissfully amongst themselves.

"I can't wait for John to see me in this dress when I walk down the aisle," one woman says.

"You're so lucky you found someone who loves you like he does. That man would do anything for you," another woman replies.

"Anything," a third woman adds with a chuckle.

"I love him so much. My wedding day can't come soon enough," the bride remarks, and I can hear the love and longing oozing from every word.

Love... Who needs it anyway? Who wants to be with someone who would do anything for them? Who looks at them as if they hung the moon? Who puts the other person's needs before their own? Who holds them when they cry? Who promises forever and means it?

I do.

My breathing quickens, and my chest feels strained against the tightness of the fabric. My trembling fingers reach hastily for the zipper while tears threaten to spill from my eyes.

I can't breathe.

"Come on, please don't do this to me," I plead with the dress, my fingers fumbling as I struggle to reach the clasp. "Please," I beg, letting out a low sob.

"Madeleine." My eyes dart to the mirror, finding Eli behind me. "What's wrong?"

"Off." I let out a shaky breath. "Get this off of me," I practically beg, my voice cracking.

He doesn't hesitate as he pulls down on the hidden zipper, loosening the top of my gown. I remove my arms from the sleeves and push the fabric down, gathering it at my waist, leaving me in just my strapless bra.

Suddenly, my knees give out, and I drop to the floor. But before I completely fall, Eli catches me. He allows me to sink to the carpet, the tulle surrounding me like a cocoon, as he sits beside me and pulls me against his chest.

"Breathe, Princess," he commands in his authoritative tone.

I press my hands to my chest, my lips parting as I try to speak, but I feel like a fish out of water.

It's too much.

Everything.

All of it.

I can't do this.

But I have to.

I don't have a choice.

"Breathe," he repeats.

"C-can't," I gasp as black dots start to cloud my vision.

Oh my God, I'm going to pass out.

Suddenly, his hands grip my waist, lifting me out of the tangled tulle and into the air. My bare legs wrap around his torso as I bury my face in the crook of his neck. He adjusts one hand firmly against my back while the other finds the underside of my thigh. With strong strides, he carries us back into the dressing room, shuts the door behind us, and then reaches for something on the table before sitting on the couch with me straddling his lap.

"Take a sip," he says, lifting a bottle of water to my lips. The cool liquid falls on my tongue, and I swallow every drop greedily. His left hand reaches up toward my neck, and I squeal. "Relax. It's just ice," he assures me, his voice softening. He glides the ice down my neck and across my chest, instantly cooling my overheated body. I close my eyes, feeling the lightheadedness dissipate with each gentle stroke. "You're okay," he affirms. But it sounds like he's trying to convince himself more than me. "You're okay," he repeats softly, his eyes absorbing every inch of me. "I won't ever let anything happen to you."

I lean forward, pressing my head to his shoulder, exhaustion engulfing me. Inhaling his familiar scent eases my racing mind. He wraps his arms tighter around me, his tenderness soothing every tense muscle within me.

As his hands gently glide up and down my back, he asks, "What brought this on?"

How do I answer that? How do I tell him I don't want to marry Alastor? How do I explain to him that I signed my life away to the devil? I can't. So instead, I reply, "Everything."

We sit in silence for a few minutes. I'm too scared to move or say anything because I don't want this moment to end.

I just want to be in Eli's arms for the rest of my life.

Because that's where I've always felt safest.

His lips move next to my ear. "You don't need to do this."

I shake my head, fighting back tears. "I don't have a choice."

His hand stills on my bare skin. "What do you mean you don't have a choice?"

I pinch my eyes closed. *Shit.*

"I just mean…" I sit up, looking him in the eye. "Everything is booked—the caterer, the venue, the florist. It's in a matter of weeks and is happening now, whether I want it to or…"

Not.

I let the last word die on my tongue, knowing it lingers in the air, heavy between us.

"Don't marry him."

It's a plea.

One that slices right through my beating heart.

A single tear slides down my cheek. "You don't understand."

"Then tell me. I'm right here. I'm listening." He reaches for my face, his thumb brushing away the tear. "I can fix this for you. Just tell me, love. Tell me what happened."

You, I want to say. *You are what happened.*

But I don't.

Because he never asked me to do what I did.

He never asked me to save him.

But I did what had to be done.

And I don't regret doing it.

Not one bit.

Taking a deep breath, I sit up straight, placing a hand on his cheek. "I need you not to interfere with my wedding. It's happening. It needs to happen. And I'll be okay, I promise."

"You can't seriously expect me to sit back and let you marry that—"

"I do, Eli." I try my best to show a small smile, but it's a struggle.

He runs his hand through his hair, glaring up at the ceiling. "I'll do anything for you, Madeleine. You know that." He shakes his head. "But this is one thing I can't do."

"Eli, please—"

"What about us?" he asks, pain laced in his words.

"There is no us," I answer softly, looking down.

His fingers hook under my chin, tilting my face up. "There is always an *us*." His eyes hold mine, and I feel seconds from shattering—from telling him everything. His lips part, ready to say more, until his eyes shift to my arm, narrowing in on the blue skin.

Oh no.

I try to quickly pull my hand away, but he's faster. His fingers wrap around my wrist, holding me in place—gentle yet firm. He flips my arm over to examine it closely.

I should have done a better job of hiding it.

I shouldn't have let him see.

Because the wrath swirling around his dark irises is unlike anything I've ever witnessed as they fixate on the black and blue fingerprints imprinted on my skin.

This isn't the first time Alastor has manhandled me, leaving evidence behind. But it's the first time I wasn't careful enough to conceal it.

"He hurt you," he states slowly. One might think he's calm if it weren't for the calculated anger charging the air between us.

Anger, not directed at me.

But at Alastor.

I shake my head. "It doesn't hurt. It was my fault. He didn't mean—"

"When he spoke to you privately," he whispers, deep in thought. His thumb glides tenderly over my skin. "When I left you alone with him."

"It's not what it looks—"

"This is my fault. I never should have left your side last night." He drops his hand, his face growing more fearsome with each passing second. "We're leaving. Now." He picks me up, placing me on the couch beside him.

"Wait... What?" I stand, suddenly realizing I'm only in my underwear, and reach for my clothes. "We can't leave. I still need to—"

"He hurt you!" he roars, spinning toward me. His chest heaves with each breath, and his eyes are wild with a desire for vengeance—a need to punish.

I take a step toward him and place a hand on his chest. The rapid beat of his heart beneath my touch terrifies me. "You cannot hurt him. You cannot touch a hair on his head. If you do..." I swallow hard. "Just please promise me you won't hurt him."

He takes a deep breath and closes his eyes.

For a moment, I think he's calmed down.

I think that this whole thing will be forgotten.

But as soon as his eyes open, my relief is short-lived.

Leaning forward, he presses a kiss to my temple. "He hurt what's mine. And he will learn to never do that again."

What's his? But I'm not—

I don't get the chance to say another word to him as he turns away and strides outside, seeming like a soldier on the most crucial mission of his life.

After getting dressed and impatiently waiting for my gown to be bagged appropriately, I head outside, expecting to see Eli waiting by the car for me. Instead, I'm met by Reginald.

And only Reginald.

My stomach plummets.

"Where's Eli?" I glance around the parking lot, hoping to spot him nearby.

"He left," Reginald replies, taking my dress from me and placing it securely in the back of the car. "He said there was something urgent he needed to take care of and had a car come pick him up. He told me to tell you that he would see you tonight."

I nod, my mind racing through every worst-case scenario.

"Are you all right?" Reginald asks with concern etched into his fatherly face. "You seem a bit pale."

I smile, waving a dismissive hand. "I'm fine. It's just been a long day." He opens the door for me, and I slide onto my seat, closing the privacy screen while waiting for him to shut the door behind me. The moment he does, I grab my phone from my bag and press it to my ear.

"Pick up. Pick up. Pick up."
It's Eli.
"Eli, please don't—"
Leave a message.
My heart sinks.
There's no way this will end well for either of us.

August 27th

Dear Eli,

It's been one year without my dad. One year spent navigating grief while trying to live in a world without him.

Some days are easier than others, but today, it felt a little harder to get out of bed. So, I'm here, sitting on the dock at my house while I write this to you. I've found that this is my favorite spot, a place where I can truly feel peace.

Mom wants to take me to Paris before I leave for school. I'm excited to load up on carbs and champagne, but is it weird that what I'm most excited about is being closer to you on the map?

Stay safe,
Madeleine

CHAPTER FOURTEEN

Eli

All I see is red—a bright, bloody crimson that blurs my vision.

He hurt her.

He hurt my princess.

I should have never left them alone together.

But I know one damn thing for sure.

It will never happen again.

Not on my watch.

Because I'm never letting her out of my fucking sight for as long as I live.

I pace in the dark alley, waiting for the all-clear.

My phone buzzes in my grip, and I peer down at the screen.

Alex

> Security system is down. Care to tell me what's going on?

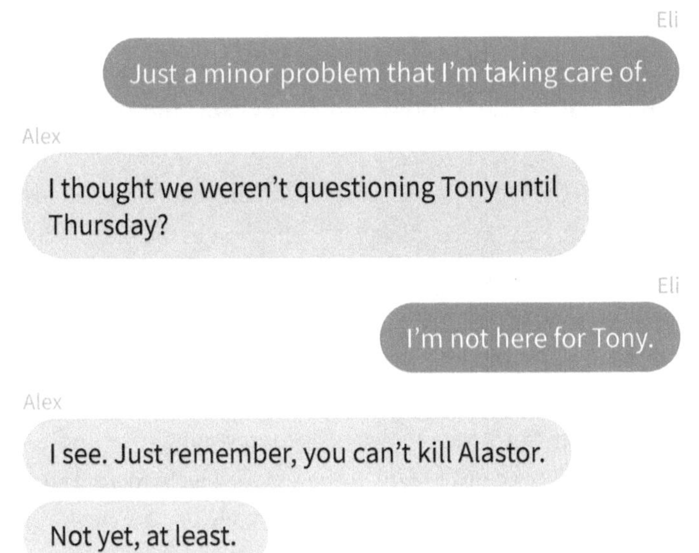

I shove my phone into my coat pocket and step onto the road, striding across the pavement with my knuckles shaking in rage. As I walk through the lobby, I spot the elevator directly ahead and approach it. But just as I reach out to press the call button, I'm stopped by security.

The arsehole daringly places his hand on my chest. "This is a private residence, sir," he states with an air of cockiness that I intend to diminish. He looks me up and down disapprovingly. "An occupying resident must accompany any guest to access the elevator."

I glare down at the man, who stands about a foot shorter than me. He's muscular, I'll give him that, but he has nothing on me. "I'm here on behalf of my employer," I state coldly, pausing for effect before adding, "the Alaries."

The man's eyes widen, a ghostly complexion covering his skin. All traces of his false bravado disappear. "S-sorry, sir. I didn't know." He steps aside, gesturing toward the elevator. "What floor, sir?" He holds out his key card with a shaking hand as he presses the button.

Fucking wanker.

As the doors open, I step inside, turning to face the man. "The garage."

He nods vigorously before scanning his card, and the doors close before me.

Standing in the center of the space, I clasp my hands behind my back and stare ahead, barely recognizing my reflection in the metal walls.

I look murderous, like a man seeking vengeance for the one he loves.

Maybe because that's exactly what I'm doing.

And if I'm not allowed to let my rage out on the monster who dared to hurt my princess, then I'll take the next best option.

After coming to a stop, the doors open, revealing rows and rows of some of the most expensive cars in the world. I walk toward the front of the lot and scan the space. No surprise to anyone, I spot the ghastly bright orange vehicle within seconds.

A triumphant smirk takes over my face as I approach the vehicle that is parked farthest away from all the other cars.

"Two million for this piece of shit," I muse. "I wonder how much you'll be worth when I'm done with you." I reach into my pocket and pull out my phone, pressing it to my ear.

"What now?" Alex asks.

"Can you unlock a vehicle?" I ask, dragging my finger along the smooth exterior.

He scoffs. "Of course I can." I hear him type on a keyboard. "This is Alastor's car, I'm assuming?"

"You assume correct."

It only takes a few seconds before I hear the familiar click of the vehicle unlocking. I step back as the door slowly swings upward like a butterfly wing.

"I'm going to assume you'll need me to start it, too?" Alex asks with a note of amusement in his voice.

"Yeah. And probably disable any and all location features."

"On it," he answers.

The smoothest and gentlest purr sounds from the car, indicating it's turned on.

"Thanks, Alex."

"Enjoy the ride," he muses with a deep chuckle before hanging up.

I slip my phone into my pocket and try to get comfortable behind the wheel of the car, but that's easier said than done given my size.

I shut the door and strap myself in as I glance over the sleek brown and black interior.

"You're a lot prettier on the inside," I note. I wrap my knuckles around the steering wheel, gliding my fingers smoothly from top to bottom. "But it's time to teach your bloody owner a little lesson he'll never forget."

Throwing the car in reverse, I slowly back out of the space. Observing the clear path to the garage door, I look up to find the garage door opener. After pressing it, the door opens, and I grin.

"This was too fucking easy."

I step on the gas, flooring it out of here in seconds. The car's tires squeal as I turn out onto the main road, maneuvering gracefully between other vehicles until I hit the highway.

"Now, let's see how fast you can really go."

I take off down the open road, heading further north. Once I hit the back roads, I take my foot off the gas and let the car coast.

Reaching in my pocket, I pull out my phone and place it on the dashboard before saying, "Call Alastor."

The phone rings, and the fucker immediately picks up.

"Alastor speaking."

God, his voice is like nails on a chalkboard. I roll my neck as my back molars grind together. "You thought you could hurt her and get away with it."

There's silence before he says, "Who the fuck is this?"

"The only man you should fear right now."

He sighs. "What do you want, Eli? I'm quite busy running an empire and don't have time for your little word games."

I press harder on the gas, finding it almost impossible to control my temper. "You are never to touch what's mine again."

"What the hell are you—"

"If you ever touch Madeleine again, I will kill you," I state, my voice becoming deeper and rougher. "And it won't be fast or painless. It will be slow. It will be dragged out for days. Weeks if I'm lucky. And you will suffer like no man has ever suffered."

He laughs as if finding my threat humorous. "Oh, Eli. Do you have any idea what you're risking by doing this?"

"Do you think I care? She's mine! She's under my protection, and I will do whatever it takes to keep her safe! I know you're holding something over her head, and I will find out what that is. I will do everything possible to get to the fucking bottom of it!" He chuckles, the high pitch grating on my last fucking nerve. "Is something funny about that?"

"Not in the slightest," he remarks. "It's just that..." Silence passes before he says, "You claim she's yours, yet it's my ring on her finger. My last name she'll be taking. And most importantly, my cock she'll be coming around every fucking night like the good girl she is for the rest of her miserable life."

Black dots line my sight, my pounding heart echoing in my ears. I've lost all semblance of time as I get lost in the dark space in my head.

"She will never be yours," I growl. "This isn't a threat. And this isn't a warning. It's a fucking promise. If you ever leave a mark on Madeleine's body again, I will kill you."

I end the call, turning off the main road and down a dirt one through the woods, driving until I reach a drop-off and stopping just before it. I place the car in park and step outside, peering down at the vast space, the moon highlighting the dangers that anyone should have if they were ever to find themselves pushed over the side.

This will do just fine.

Turning back toward the car, I reach inside and transition it into neutral. I close the door and head for the back of the car, placing my hands on the bumper. With all my strength, I push.

I force the vehicle forward until the front tires slip over the edge, and I stand there and watch two million dollars disappear down the side of the hill. I step to the edge and view the totaled vehicle sitting at the bottom, smoke billowing from the engine. A fire erupts, and within seconds, the whole car becomes lifeless, completely engulfed.

Representing everything I wish and crave to do to Alastor.

"You claim she's yours, yet it's my ring on her finger. My last name she'll be taking. And most importantly, my cock she'll be coming around every fucking night like the good girl she is for the rest of her miserable life."

Alastor's words echo deafeningly in my mind.

Taunting me.

Tormenting me.

Torturing me.

I look up at the star-filled sky, releasing a pent-up roar into the darkness. A thunderous howl rips across the lands, unleashing my vehemence into the ominous night.

But the words never stop hurling themselves at me. They keep playing over and over as I walk through the woods, heading toward the Alarie Estate. They don't cease until I find myself directly outside of Madeleine's home.

I stare at her door, a deep longing building inside me.

Madeleine's forgotten who she belongs to.

Who she has always belonged to.

And the only person to blame for that is me.

For not doing something sooner about it.

But now it's time to remind her.

I slam my hand on the scanner and impatiently wait for the door to swing open. The second it does, I forcefully shove it the rest of the way until I'm standing in the entryway, finding Madeleine sitting on the bottom step of her staircase with her head in her hands, her knees bouncing nervously.

Her head jerks up as I stride toward her, her eyes scanning me. She stands, shaking her head with tears coating her blue eyes. I spot a slight shiver in her hands as she runs them frantically through her hair.

"What did you do?" she asks, dread laced in her voice.

I stop a foot away from her. "I taught him a lesson he won't soon forget."

"You shouldn't have done that," she breathes, staring toward the painting above her fireplace. The one I know she lied to me about being a gift, when in fact, she bought it. She bought it because when she looked at it, she saw us. She saw our story and our struggles. But above all, she saw our love. "You have no idea what you've done. He'll retaliate. He'll—"

"He'll never touch what's mine again." I reach out with both hands, embracing her cheeks, forcing her eyes onto me as I lean down, ghosting my lips over hers.

"What are you doing?" she whispers.

"Something I should have done the second I was back."

I capture her lips in an urgent kiss as my hand wraps around her waist, drawing her against me. My other hand threads through her hair, cradling the back of her head. *Her taste*—her sweet, heavenly taste—sweeps over me, reviving every part of my damaged soul.

Fuck, it's been too goddamn long since I've tasted her like this. And all I can think is that I need more.

I need all of her.

Her hands push at my chest with no real force as she tries to fight this inevitable need between us.

She pulls back, and I let her, pressing our foreheads together.

"But I..." She looks up at me from beneath her dark lashes, her eyes displaying so many emotions. "I'm supposed to hate you," she breathes against my lips, her chest heaving. Her fingers curl into my shirt, and her eyes well up with tears she won't allow to fall. "Everything would be so much easier if I could just hate you."

"You can hate me all you want, love. As long as you feel something for me, I'm okay with that."

I'll still love you.

I'll always love you.

She hesitates, her breaths quickening with each passing second. She swallows hard, shaking her head. "I'm engaged."

"Do you love him?"

Her breath catches, her wide eyes locking onto mine.

I brush my lips over hers. "Tell me you love him, and I'll stop. I'll never touch you again. I'll leave and try with everything inside me to pretend that there was never anything between us. It will break my fucking heart to pieces, but I'll do it. I'll do anything for you."

She doesn't say a word, not a single one.

And she doesn't have to.

Because I know.

I've always known.

With an unrestrained need, she presses her lips to mine, demanding entry with her tongue. Her hands slide up my chest, wrapping around my neck and hauling me into her.

We're two bodies merging as one. Two bodies meant for each other, fitting together perfectly like puzzle pieces.

There's a fervent yearning between us that will never be extinguished.

One that has only strengthened over the years rather than diminishing.

I pull away, but only to let my lips glide down her silky skin.

I'm ready to worship every inch of her.

"Eli…" she pants, baring her neck for me.

And that's all I need to hear before gripping her hips and lifting her into my arms. Her thighs squeeze around my waist as I step up the stairs, our lips fused. She loops her fingers through my hair, tugging the strands at the base of my neck. The slight pain sends an agonizing need to my groin as my cock hardens uncomfortably against my zipper.

My boot connects with her door as I kick it open, stepping inside her room.

Crossing the space, I lay her on the bed, only separating to stand and toe off my shoes while reaching a hand behind my back to yank at the collar of my shirt and pull it over my head, tossing it to the floor.

Her eyes drink in my body, her hands reaching out to touch. To explore.

I don't make her wait as I hold myself over her, my lips returning to hers.

She grips the hem of her dress, scrunching the fabric between her fingers. I break the kiss to pull back and watch as she slides it up her smooth skin, not stopping until it's completely removed from her and tossed to the floor beside us.

My gaze traces over her body, only covered by small pieces of black lace.

A primal need takes over me.

A need to make her mine again.

A need to make her come over and over again until she's completely spent beneath me.

"Tell me you want this," I breathe against her chest, letting my tongue snake between the valley of her breasts. "Tell me you need this as much as I do."

"I need..." She gasps as my hand slides between her legs, two fingers gliding up and down her slit. "I need this." She grips my bicep as my fingers slip between the fabric, her wetness coating the pads of my fingers. "I need you."

I stop, my eyes locking with hers, fixating on the desire glossed over them.

She needs me.

Our eyes never break contact as my fingers slip inside her, thrusting slowly in and out before working up to a rhythmic speed. One I know will have her coming apart in no time.

She whimpers, holding on to my shoulders as I use my other hand to pull down on the cup of her bra, exposing her full breast. My lips latch onto her nipple, sucking and tasting her while using my tongue to flick the tip the way she likes.

"Oh, that feels so good," she moans, pressing the side of her face into the pillow.

"You ready to show me how well you take my cock, Princess?" I ask, gazing up at her while I swirl my tongue over her. I press my palm against her clit, rubbing gently over her sensitive flesh as I continue to plunge in and out of her, getting her as close to an orgasm as I can before giving her my cock to come around.

"Y-yes." She nods, biting down on her bottom lip as she watches me.

Fuck, she's so beautiful like this.

"Please." She clasps her hands over my cheeks, pulling my face toward her. She kisses me with so much urgency before she bites down on my bottom lip, tugging at it. "Fuck me, Eli."

Blood surges to my pulsing cock, an inferno of desire clouding me.

She reaches inside her nightstand, pulling out a foil wrapper. I arch a brow in surprise. Not because I won't respect her wishes but because we've never used a condom before.

She never wanted anything between us.

Grabbing the condom from her, I stand and quickly remove my pants and boxer briefs. Her eyes trail over my hard length as I fist it, pumping just once.

God, I feel like I've waited forever for this.

Forever for her.

And now that it's finally happening, it doesn't feel real.

My eyes graze over every inch of her, imprinting this moment to my memories, hopefully overtaking the dark ones that lie in wait.

Her hand reaches out for me, and that's when I stop, my chest tightening at the sight before me.

"Take it off," I rush out.

She arches a brow. "Take what—"

"Take. Off. The. Ring."

She doesn't hesitate to pull it off her finger and place it inside her nightstand drawer.

With the ring out of sight, the tightness in my chest slightly evaporates.

"Good girl," I praise. "Now flip over for me."

She does as she's told, giving me her backside in the air as she plants her forearms on the mattress before her.

I slide my hands up the back of her thighs, curving around her pert ass and squeezing a handful. She moans, arching her back as she pushes against my touch. I slant forward to unclasp her bra, the straps gracefully falling down her arms, exposing her ample breasts. My hand slides around her front, finding a pebbled nipple to play with. She whimpers and squirms, her body reacting to my touch exactly how it always has.

I stare down at her in awe. She's too bloody perfect to put into words.

Sitting back on my haunches, I glide a hand over her panty-covered ass. "These need to go." The tear of the lace fabric sounds between us as I rip her panties down the middle, letting the scraps fall to her knees. An aching need fills me as I take in the sight of her soaking wet pussy, glistening with her arousal. "So goddamn pretty." Taking my cock in one hand, I cover it in the latex and then glide it through her slit, coating it. My other hand grips her hips, holding her against me and not letting her move one damn inch away from me.

"Please, Eli," she begs so beautifully.

As slowly and as gently as I can manage, I slide inside, one excruciating inch at a time. I feel her tense beneath me, her walls clamping down.

"You're too big," she groans into the pillow, her fingers clawing at the sheets.

I smirk. "I thought that was your favorite thing about me."

She laughs, the sound shooting straight through my chest until she winces uncomfortably.

I slide a hand around her, bringing my palm right over her clit, and begin to rub in a circular motion, giving her just enough pressure to let her body relax beneath me. "Relax, love. I only want to make you feel good."

She moans as my hand moves faster, her body eagerly accepting each inch of my cock.

I groan, stilling once my whole length resides inside her and pausing not only for her benefit but for mine. She feels too much like a place I haven't been in a very long time. And I want to savor every second of this. Every second of her. "You feel like..." *Home.* "You feel so fucking good." I begin to move, finding a rhythm that appeases her body. One that gets her meeting me thrust for thrust. Demanding more from me.

I gaze down where we meet, loving how perfectly we fit together. "You take my cock so well, Princess." I skim my hand over the back of her thigh and then smack her ass. She whimpers, pushing harder against me. "You're so needy for my cock, aren't you, love?"

She nods, her whole body flushing a beautiful shade of pink. "Please, I need... I need..."

"I know what you need." I grip her hips and fuck her the way she wants and needs in order to see stars.

Rougher, harder, and faster.

"Oh my God," she screams, her body showing all the signs of an impending orgasm on the horizon.

I slam into her ruthlessly, making up for every lost night together. Nights we should have spent exactly like this wrapped up in heated passion, but instead, spent apart.

"I'm so... I'm right..." Her words drift off her tongue.

Snaking my arm around her stomach, I haul her up, my chest and her back flush together. She looks over her shoulder, her hooded eyes meeting mine. "Kiss me."

Our lips merge in a fiery desire like two magnets, unable to pull away.

One of my hands cups her breast, my fingers twisting and teasing her hardened nipple. My other hand reaches between her legs, rubbing two fingers over her swollen clit.

Her flushed body shakes in my hands, and I know it's only a matter of seconds until she unravels.

I break the kiss, watching her features contort in pleasure. "Come for me, Princess," I whisper against her parted lips.

She screams out as she falls apart in my arms, a beautiful sight my eyes will never forget.

My own release soon follows, and I groan as I empty out every last drop, remembering the only other times I've ever felt this euphoric were with her.

Only her.

The calmness to my madness.

Collapsing against the mattress, I pull her against my chest, my lips brushing over her hair. Her fingers intertwine with mine, and she sighs as she snuggles her face into the pillow. Her breathing evens out, and eventually, she falls asleep in my arms.

And for the first time in a long time, everything feels right in the world.

Because for the first time in a long time...*she's mine.*

January 7th

Princess,

I'm sorry it's been so long. A lot is going on I can't fully disclose, but rest assured that you've crossed my mind once or twice... Okay, you caught me...maybe a few more times than that.

How's school going? Is it an all-girls school? If there are boys, I recommend staying away from them. They'll only distract you from your studies.

I'll be getting some much-needed time off soon and will be staying in one of the cottages on the estate, but unfortunately, you'll be at school when that happens.

Talk about bad timing.

By the way, happy belated Christmas. I hope you got everything you wanted and more.

Yours,
Eli

CHAPTER FIFTEEN

Madeleine

"**A**re you listening to me?"

"Huh?" I promptly stop biting my thumbnail and spin on my heel to face Scarlett, accidentally knocking over a mannequin in the process. "Shit. Sorry." I bend down to pick it up, and Scarlett helps me as we adjust it back onto its stand.

"Are you okay?" she asks with a slight frown. "You've seemed a little distracted today."

Me? Distracted?

Pshh.

It's not like I've been spending every second of today replaying the best sex of my life with my bodyguard and not my fiancé.

Nope. Not one single second.

And I definitely haven't been overanalyzing how I felt when I woke up in his arms as if I could finally breathe again for the first time in a long time.

Or the disappointment that followed as he kissed my temple and then slipped out of my room to help Vin and Alex with something.

Fuck. I drag a hand down my face, knowing things just got so much more complicated.

Not to mention that on top of all that, today is—

"Madeleine?"

Shit. "Sorry," I reply, forcing a smile as I take a seat on the bench beside us, leaning my back against the wall. "I guess I'm not really in the mood to shop." I had hoped that spending the day with Scarlett and Alina would help me forget what today is, but I realize there's only one person who can do that for me. And he's not here. I glance toward the store entrance and spot Asher standing guard, alert and ready for any potential danger.

"Honestly, I'm not either." She returns the pink sweater to the rack and joins me on the bench.

"Did I just hear you say you're not in the mood to shop?" Alina walks up to us, bags hanging from both arms. "Since when?"

I sigh. "Just didn't get much sleep last night."

Probably cause I was too busy getting fucked into oblivion.

"Yeah, me neither," she responds, sitting on the free space beside me and yawning.

"Did you buy out the store?" I ask, glancing at her bags.

She laughs, giving a slight shrug. "I might have gone a little overboard. I just want this Christmas to be...perfect." Her eyes appear a little lost, and she quickly shakes her head.

"Is everything okay between you and Eli?" Scarlett asks, catching me off guard.

I tuck my hair behind my ear and furrow my brows. "Why wouldn't everything be okay?"

She casually lifts her shoulders. "I don't know. You just haven't complained much about him recently. Thought you might have had a change of heart..."

"About Eli?" I scoff. "No way."

She grins. "You know, once upon a time, when he entered a room, it was like he was the only one you had eyes for."

I tilt my head back, staring at the ceiling. "I probably just needed glasses."

"Oh, please." Alina nudges my shoulder with hers. "The man worships the ground you walk on. What girl wouldn't be enamored by a man like that? And did you forget about the part where he saved your life not too long ago?" She dramatically places the back of her hand across her forehead. "So romantic."

"I'm taking away all your romance novels. They're clearly a bad influence on you," I tease.

"Don't you dare!" She laughs. "Besides..." She waggles her brows. "I'm pretty sure that at the cake tasting, Eli would have preferred a sample of you instead. He couldn't take his eyes off you."

A flush creeps up my neck, and I quickly look away, turning my attention to my manicure.

Scarlett sits up straight. "Wait, what did I miss?" Her eyes bounce between me and Alina. "I knew I should have skipped my weekend getaway with Leo so I could have gone!"

"You didn't miss anything," I tell her, waving a dismissive hand. "Besides, Leo would have actually murdered me if you did that."

"But something did happen between you two," Scarlett insists, her eyes reading me like an open book.

My lips part. Then close. Part. Then close.

"I knew it!" she exclaims, pointing a finger at me and beaming with excitement.

Heat engulfs me, and I cover my face with my hands.

"Oh my God, this is amazing!" Alina practically squeals in delight. "You and your bodyguard. Well, technically, it's your childhood crush. Or would we consider this your brother's best friend?"

I shush both of them, peering around the store before quietly saying, "Yes, something—well, I guess some things—have happened." They both look ready to cheer, so I quickly cover their mouths with my hands. "But nothing can come of it. I'm engaged to another man." I lift a shoulder, dropping my hands. "It was just...a little fun to get out of my system before the wedding." I feel the bitter lie roll off my tongue as I watch them deflate. "Nothing more than that. Now, can we please talk about something else? Like anything else?"

Scarlett doesn't appear to believe me, but for my own sake, she nods and rests her head on my shoulder.

Alina relaxes against the wall, crossing her arms over her chest. "What should we do now?"

"I'm game for anything," I reply.

Anything to keep my mind distracted from everything else that is currently taking over my thoughts.

A moment passes before Scarlett's voice cuts through the silence. "I know what we can do." She pulls out her phone and starts typing a message.

"What?" Alina and I ask at the same time.

Scarlett's phone vibrates, and a smile spreads across her face. "He's ready for us."

Alina and I share a look.

"Who's ready for us?" I ask.

An hour later, I find myself standing in the center of a sparring ring, with Alina and Scarlett beside me and Mauro in front of us.

I groan as I glance around the space. The place reeks of sweaty men, mostly guards, who come here to get their daily workouts. It's disgusting. "When I said I was game for anything, I probably should have clarified that I meant anything except this."

Scarlett grabs my arm and drags me toward the dummy in the center. "Come on. It'll be fun." She gestures to Mauro. "Mauro's a great teacher."

He smiles proudly, crossing his arms over his chest.

I roll my eyes.

Mauro has spent the past few months with Scarlett, helping her learn self-defense. More importantly, he has helped her come out of her shell by showing her how strong she truly is, whether she realizes it or not. She may never be quite the same after everything that happened to her, but it makes my heart happy to see how far she's come.

He points to me.

"Oh no." I step back, nudging Alina forward. "She volunteers as tribute."

Hey, he may be my brother, but he still intimidates me.

Alina swallows nervously, her big brown eyes appearing like a deer in headlights. "W-what do you want me to do?"

He gives her a come-hither motion with his index finger, and she takes a few steps until she stands directly in front of him. "Now what?"

He tilts his head and slowly reaches around her, locking his hands behind her back. And because Alina is Alina, she wraps her arms around Mauro and rests her head on his chest. He stiffens, his neck transforming into a deep shade of red.

"Like this?" she asks, closing her eyes.

Scarlett and I exchange glances, doing our best to contain our laughter, but eventually, it slips out.

Mauro shakes his head, drops his hands, and steps back. He points to Scarlett, who walks over. She lets Mauro attempt to wrap his arms around her, but before he can clasp his hands together, she thrusts her hands forward, making a fist in front of her pelvis and lifting her knee directly toward Mauro's groin.

He quickly places his hand on her knee, stopping her before any damage can be done.

"You want to hit them where it hurts," Scarlett says, smiling. "You can also use your forehead to hit the attacker's nose if you're tall enough."

Mauro places a hand on her shoulder and then looks back at Alina.

"Ah. So, you didn't want a hug. Got it." She laughs nervously, adjusting her glasses. "Sorry, I don't know what I was thinking," she murmurs, looking down at the floor and shuffling her feet.

Mauro approaches her and reaches out his hand, using two fingers to tilt her head up. She bites her bottom lip as he points to her eyes and then gestures back to himself.

"Eyes on you," she whispers.

He nods in response.

I look at Scarlett, who returns my look with a face that clearly says, *what the hell was that?*

No idea, I mouth.

Just then, a phone rings, snapping Alina out of her daze. She jumps backward and pulls her phone out of her pocket, her expression falling as she checks the screen.

"I have to take this," she says without looking back, leaving the ring and heading out the front door.

Mauro's eyes never leave her.

"So, should we call it a day or..." Just as I lift my leg to step between the ropes, I'm suddenly lifted into the air and placed firmly on my feet. "Jesus, Mauro! You can't manhandle me in front of the men here. They'll think they can walk all over me."

Scarlett bends over, laughing, gripping the rope for support.

One side of Mauro's lips lifts in a grin as he motions for me to meet him in the center of the ring.

"Fine," I huff, rolling up my sleeves.

He stands before me, looking triumphant, but that's probably because he's forgotten what I'm capable of. Maybe it's time to remind him—and everyone else—who I am.

A small group of men gathers at the side, eager to see how this will unfold.

"You all might want to watch and take notes," I tell the onlookers, who chuckle, likely thinking it's a joke.

"Ready?" I ask, locking eyes with Mauro. He nods and reaches out for me.

But I'm too fast for him.

As I spin around, I wait until his chest presses against my back, his arms wrapping around my waist. I bend backward, knowing I won't be able to reach his nose, but it gives me the leverage I need, causing Mauro to stick out one of his legs for balance. The moment he does that, I quickly bend forward, grab his leg by the knee, and pull it up with me, making him lose his balance.

A collective gasp escapes from the onlookers as Mauro's back hits the mat.

Could Mauro have stopped me?

Most likely.

But he didn't.

Because he knows the men in here won't respect me if they think I'm weak.

So he did what any big brother would do.

He swallowed his pride and let me claim victory.

He grins, looking up at me, and I reach out to help him up.

"Umm, since when did you learn how to kick someone's ass?" Scarlett asks, visibly impressed.

"I grew up with four older brothers." I shrug. "Vin taught me to lead. Leo taught me to hunt. Alex taught me to shoot. And Mauro taught me to fight." I raise an eyebrow. "You know that I never liked playing with dolls. I preferred this instead." I glance over at the group of men. "Let this be a reminder: don't ever think about fucking messing with me."

"Yes, ma'am." One of them salutes as they all walk off, heading back to the gym equipment.

Scarlett laughs and leans against the corner pole. "Does Eli know he's the bodyguard to a skilled assassin?"

My smile falls at the mention of his name, my heart constricting as I bend down, reaching for my gym bag.

"There you are," Leo's voice calls out as he approaches, stepping into the ring. He wraps his arms around Scarlett, pressing a kiss on her forehead. "How much longer do you think you'll be? Brutus misses you."

She chuckles softly. "And what about my husband?"

"Oh, Firefly." He cups her cheek, brushing his lips over hers. "Let's go home, and I'll show you just how much your husband misses you."

I glance at Mauro, pretending to gag as he silently laughs.

"Well, not that I don't love being part of this grotesque display of affection, but I should get going." I lift my bag and slide it over my shoulder.

"Are you sure?" A small frown forms on Scarlett's face as she slips out of Leo's hold and steps toward me. "We could have a takeout and movie night."

Leo scowls at the suggestion.

"I think my brother might murder me if I borrow you any longer."

"No, he won't," Scarlett replies.

"Yes, he will." Leo's arm slips around her waist, pulling her to his side. *God, I need to get out of here.*

"It's fine, really. I have to go through the books for the casino anyway. I've been neglecting them for too long. I'll catch up with you later."

"Fine, but don't work too hard. It's almost Christmas," Scarlett reminds me.

As if I could forget.

It'll be the last one with my family.

My throat tightens at the thought.

"Umm, Leo, do you know when Eli will be back?" I ask.

He checks his watch. "Probably not until late. He had to take care of something in the city with Vin and Alex." He eyes me curiously. "Why?"

"No reason." *Just didn't really feel like being alone today.* "I didn't know if I should order enough food for two or just myself tonight." I manage a small smile. "Guess it's just me."

Scarlett appears ready to stop me, but I don't feel like being the third wheel today. Not when I have so much on my mind. So, instead, I turn and yell over my shoulder, "Meet you outside, Mauro!"

He grunts in response, and I catch a glimpse of him packing his things in a nearby mirror.

As I walk out of the building, my phone rings, and when I look down and see Alastor's name, dread squeezes around my chest.

There's no avoiding this.

Pressing it to my ear, I ask, "What do you want—"

"Where is it?"

My movements pause, my heart quickening.

"Where's what?"

"Don't play games with me!" he roars.

"I don't know what you're—"

"My two-million-dollar McLaren is missing!" he screams so loud I have to pull the phone away from my ear.

So, that's how Eli got his revenge. I bite down on my bottom lip to suppress a laugh.

"Well, where did you have it last?" I ask, amusement laced in my words.

"Madeleine! Do you think this is funny? I know it was Eli who did this!"

Fuck. "Do you have proof?"

"No," he grits out. "Because conveniently for whoever stole my car, the security system in my building was down at the same time."

"Gee, that really is unfortunate."

"You fucking bitch! Just tell me where he put it!"

"I have no idea. Besides, it's just a car." I sigh. Today, of all days, I'm not in the mood for this, him, or anything. "Why don't you just go buy another one?"

"There were only a certain amount made, and they were all allocated to exclusive customers! There aren't any more available in the whole goddamn world!" His heavy breathing fills the line. "He will regret this!"

No. No. No.

"Alastor, you're being ridiculous. You don't even know if it was him who took it. I'll just give you the money to buy—"

The call goes dead, and panic floods my heart.

I pinch the bridge of my nose as a sudden headache forms between my eyes.

This isn't good.

A hand lands on my shoulder, and I scream before quickly realizing it's just Mauro.

"Shit, sorry." I laugh, trying to play it off.

His brows furrow, concern etched in his eyes. His fingers move quickly over his phone screen before he turns it toward me.

Are you okay?

I smile. "Aren't I the one who should be asking you that? I mean, I did hand you your ass in front of all your men in there."

He stares me down, trying to read my thoughts, but I won't let him see them—at least not all of them.

"You know what today is?" I ask solemnly.

He nods without hesitation.

"It never gets any easier," I admit, lifting a shoulder as I look away. "I keep hoping that one of these years it will, but it just doesn't."

He types on his phone.

Let's get some ice cream. He would have wanted us to. He always said it made everything better.

"He was right." I clear my throat, buttoning my coat. "But you're paying."

He grins and wraps his arm around my shoulders, leading me to his car.

September 7th

Dear Eli,

It's your birthday today. And I'm sitting on the dock, wishing you were here so we could celebrate. I'm not really sure if they celebrate those things in the military. I'm assuming not, but I hope you at least had a piece of birthday cake and got to make a wish. If you did, what did you wish for?

I'll watch an episode of the Great British Bake Off tonight in your honor.

I have a confession. I sort of, kind of... dropped out of school. I mean, I'll be taking online courses, so technically I'll still be in school, but I was struggling being so far from home. Guess I haven't told you because I didn't want to feel like a failure in your eyes the next time you see me.

Stay safe,
Madeleine

CHAPTER SIXTEEN

Eli

"Three... Two... One." Alex stares down at his phone and then looks up at Vin and me with a grin just as the power shuts off. We turn on our flashlights and enter the stairwell.

"Fuck, how many floors do we have to climb?" Vin asks, leaning over the railing while pointing his beam of light upward to gauge how many steps we need to ascend.

"Thirty-two," I answer, taking the lead. "Tony lives on the floor below the penthouse."

"Maybe we should have shut off the power after we had taken the elevator up," Vin complains, following closely behind.

"Now, where's the fun in that?" Alex responds. "Besides, even if I shut the cameras down, we would have had to walk through the lobby, and too many faces would have recognized us."

"But that's what you did for Eli when he decided to steal the asshole's car," Vin grumbles.

Alex chuckles, grasping my shoulder. "No offense, Eli, but your face isn't as recognizable as mine or Vin's. I didn't see any harm in letting you walk carefree through the lobby."

"No offense taken."

Vin grins smugly, rubbing the palm of his hand over his scruff. "The burden of having such a pretty face." He looks back over the railing and releases a heavy sigh before taking the first step up. "Let's get this fucking over with." When we reach the door to the thirty-second floor, Vin presses his hand against the wall, his chest heaving. "I'm getting too old for this shit."

Alex laughs. "You're not even two years older than me."

Vin shakes his head, turning to me. "You don't even look out of breath."

"That's cause I'm not." I grin and tap his chest. "It's called cardio, buddy. You should try it sometime."

"I do," he huffs. "I just prefer the horizontal kind—not the kind that could give me a heart attack."

"You're just as likely to have a heart attack while having sex as you are while climbing stairs," Alex notes, adjusting his glasses.

"Maybe so, but at least I'll be doing something I love," Vin replies, clasping Alex's shoulder before standing up straight. "All right, let's find out exactly what Tony knows and get out of here before they manage to turn the power back on and Alastor gets home."

I nod and turn toward the door, wrapping my hand around the knob. Slowly, I open it, using my flashlight to peek down the corridor and ensure no one is nearby.

"Coast is clear." I step out with Alex and Vin behind me. We head to the end of the hall, my eyes scanning the number above each door until we reach the last one. "Sixteen." I jerk my head toward the door. "This is the one."

Alex steps up to the door and presses his phone against the scanner. "The door locks operate on battery power due to situations like this," he explains quietly.

The tiny red light at the top of the scanner turns green, followed by a click as the door unlocks itself. Alex hands us our night-vision goggles before we turn off our flashlights, throw on our gloves, and cautiously open the door to enter the entryway. We're enveloped in complete darkness as we close the door behind us. I turn on my goggles, waiting for the lenses to adjust before stepping into the living space.

We freeze as a raised voice echoes to our right. With stealth, we move in that direction, approaching a closed door. I press my ear against the wood.

"I don't care what the fuck happened, just do your job and fix it! I don't pay all this goddamn money to live in darkness!" Tony screams. I assume he's on the phone with maintenance, giving them an earful. "You better hope you have this resolved before Alastor gets home, or it will be your ass on the line!"

After a moment of silence indicating the call has ended, I look to Vin, who nods and mouths, *Now.*

We grip our guns and aim as I step back and use all my strength to kick the door open. Tony nearly falls out of his seat as he tries to open his top drawer, probably to retrieve his gun, but I beat him to the punch. Literally.

"Who's there?" he yells right before I whack my gun across the back of his skull, rendering him unconscious.

Vin turns on his flashlight and removes his goggles. "Well, that was anticlimactic."

I shrug. "Sorry it wasn't more dramatic for you."

We get busy tying Tony to his chair and then wait for the motherfucker to wake up. Alex, feeling impatient, leaves the room and soon returns with a glass of water. He throws it at Tony's face, glass and all. Tony wakes up violently, sputtering and spitting out water as the shards of broken glass fall into his lap.

His eyes blink rapidly as they adjust to the bright light aimed directly at him. There's fabric wrapped around his mouth so tightly that it's preventing him from saying one word. He mumbles furiously around it, his face transforming as red as a tomato, with veins bulging in his neck.

He's pissed.

Can't say I blame the guy.

"Tony," I say, taking a seat on the other side of the desk. My legs spread out wide as I lean forward, resting my elbows on my knees, my eyes directly on the bloody wanker. He looks around the room, his eyes squinting and then suddenly widening when recognition crosses his features. "You don't look so happy to see us."

Alex unties the fabric around Tony's mouth, and the second it falls, well...

"You fucking motherfuckers! I'm going to kill you all! Just wait until Alastor finds out about this. He's going to destroy you! You cock-sucking—"

The barrel of a gun presses into the side of Tony's head, quickly shutting him up as he peers up at Vin. "Now, now, Tony. I might have to wash your mouth out if you keep speaking to us like that, but I should warn you." He bends down to his eye level. "It won't be with soap."

Tony swallows, looking around at all of us. "What the fuck do you want?"

"Simple. We want to know why Madeleine and Alastor are getting married," I reply.

He scoffs. "Because they're in love—"

A shot pierces the floor beside Tony, causing him to scream like a little girl.

All eyes land on Alex as he places his gun on his lap. "We want the truth. Don't waste our time with bullshit."

Tony shakes his head. "It is the truth." A bead of sweat rolls down the side of his head, and I'm not the only one who notices.

"Let me explain something to you, and I'll do it slowly so it gets through your thick skull," Vin states. "Madeleine is an Alarie. She is one of us, which means every man in this room is prepared to rip out each organ in your body, one by one, until he feels satisfied with your death. So unless you start speaking, Eli here will go first."

I stand and reach for the switchblade in my back pocket, grinning as I pop it open and hold it before Tony. He squirms in his seat, looking frantically between us for someone to save him.

But no one will.

I press the tip of the blade into the bottom of his throat, and he screams out in agony as I slice across his collarbone.

After maybe only ten seconds, Tony throws in the towel.

"Okay. Okay! I'll talk," he rushes out.

I remove the blade from his skin, wipe it off on his shirt, and then close it up before tucking it back into my pocket.

"Talk," Vin orders as he slides a chair over and makes himself comfortable. He looks at his watch. "The quicker you tell us what you know, the quicker we'll leave."

Tony clears his throat and looks at the floor. "All I know is that she needed Alastor's help."

Alex scoffs. "Alastor's help? What the fuck could he do for her that her own brothers couldn't?"

Tony shakes his head. "I don't know. I wasn't allowed in the room when they met. She called to arrange a meeting with him, saying it was urgent. She arrived within a few hours and was in his office for only a short time before she left."

We all exchange confused glances. "When was this?" I question.

"About a year ago."

"Be more specific," Alex insists. "We need a date to work with."

"I don't know. There was snow on the ground and..." He furrows his brows, deep in thought. "Wait. It was New Year's Day. Yeah, I know it was because Alastor was in the city for a meeting with..."

"A meeting with who?" Alex prompts.

He swallows nervously. "Mikhail and Kazimir Vasiliev."

"Fuck." Vin runs his fingers through his hair and stands, pacing. "What was the meeting for?"

"I don't know. He made me wait outside."

"You expect me to believe that, as Alastor's right-hand man, you don't know what the meeting entailed?" Vin asks, frustration lacing his voice.

"Listen, I might be his right-hand man, but there are certain things Alastor has always kept to himself. Something Adolfo taught him to do. The Manacorda and Vasiliev families always work together in secrecy. No one is ever privy to their plans."

"And when did this meeting take place exactly?" Alex asks.

"In the morning," he answers. "A few hours later, Madeleine arrived."

"That can't be a coincidence," I note, looking directly at Vin.

"No, I'm afraid not." Vin crosses his arms over his chest. "Anything else you're forgetting to mention?"

"No. That's everything. Well, actually..."

"What?" Alex abruptly stands, glaring at Tony. "What the fuck else happened?"

"Well, umm..." Tony stutters, glancing nervously between us. "The next day, Alastor's father held an impromptu board meeting where he announced a change in his empire. Told everyone that Alastor would be taking over for him after his retirement instead of his older brother, Enzio. And..."

"And?" I grit my teeth.

He swallows nervously. "And that Alastor was engaged to Madeleine Alarie."

I drag a hand through my hair, trying to piece everything together. "And that's everything? You're sure?"

"Positive. I've told you everything I know." He looks at Vin, an unpleasant smirk forming on his face. "Now, will you make good on your word and leave? If Alastor catches you here, we're all dead."

Vin raises his gun, and fear coats Tony's face as he aims straight at his temple and pulls the trigger. "Don't worry, we're leaving."

Boom. Blood splatters the back wall as Tony's head slumps to the side, his vacant eyes staring straight ahead.

"You got the letter?" Vin asks Alex as he reaches his glove-covered hand inside Tony's drawer to retrieve his gun. He places it in Tony's hand, wrapping his fingers around it before dropping his hand and letting them fall haphazardously over the desk.

Alex reaches inside his pocket and retrieves the fabricated suicide note. "Got it." He places it beneath Tony's other hand and steps back, inspecting the scene for anything that might indicate this wasn't a suicide.

My mind races a hundred miles a minute. "Vin?" He glances my way. "We need to speak with the Vasiliev brothers."

He sighs. "I know." He takes a seat, dragging a hand down his face. "I was hoping to avoid them, but it seems like it's time we meet with them. I'll reach out to Enzio when we leave here to arrange a meeting."

I nod, staring at the floor as my mind races with questions. "What the fuck did she get herself into?" Reaching for my phone, I check the last text I sent Madeleine an hour ago, only to see that it hasn't been delivered. My chest tightens, and panic sets in. "Something's wrong. My texts aren't going through to Madeleine's phone."

Alex shakes his head. "Nothing's wrong." He glances at Vin. "She probably just wants to be alone now."

"Why?" I ask.

"Because of what day it is." Vin leans forward, resting his elbows on his knees, his head hanging low. "This day never gets any easier for her. For any of us, really."

I look between them, frustrated that I'm missing something. "Will someone tell me what fucking day it is?"

Vin looks up, his eyes catching mine. "It's our father's birthday."

***

As I walk through the doorway of Madeleine's house, an eerie calm greets me through the darkened space. I climb the stairs, taking two steps at a time, feeling a growing unease as I approach her bedroom. The door is ajar, and when I step inside, I look around and find it empty.

I pull my phone from my back pocket, prepared to call her for what feels like the hundredth time, when movement outside her window catches my attention. Stepping closer to the partially frosted glass, I see her standing at the end of the dock. Her arms are wrapped around herself as she gazes up at the sky, small snowflakes dusting the ground around her.

I grab a blanket from her bed and quickly head downstairs, walking through her backyard and down to the dock. I approach her carefully like I would an injured animal, afraid of startling her.

She doesn't acknowledge me as I stand behind her; she merely continues to stare at the night sky.

And I find myself wishing I could know every thought flashing through her mind.

Seconds or perhaps minutes pass before she finally speaks, her voice soft against the wind whipping past us.

"It's his birthday today." She looks down, her arms wrapping a little tighter around her abdomen. "He would have been sixty."

I take a step closer, my chest only inches from her back. She turns slowly to face me, and my heart breaks at what I see. Her usually bright blue eyes are red and downcast, filled with fresh tears ready to spill. The tip of her nose and her cheeks are flushed, and her entire demeanor is somber.

I place the blanket around her, wrapping it over her shoulders.

"Thank you." She grips the edge with her slender fingers, giving me a tiny smile, but it quickly fades as her gaze returns to the lake. "He always took me out on the lake in his boat when he sensed that something was bothering me or when he needed a break from work." She gives a slight shrug. "I feel like he's with me when I'm here."

"He is," I affirm, reaching out to rest my hand on her cold cheek, my thumb brushing away the last traces of her tears. She exhales softly, her eyes closing as she leans into my touch.

"Did you know we designed my house together? It was one of the last things we did before he died." Her eyes open, and a sad smile appears on her lips.

"I know. You mentioned in one of your letters how you two were working on the plans." My lips attempt to curve up. "I think he mentioned something about his daughter having expensive taste."

She looks up, a single tear escaping down her cheek. "You remember that?"

"I remember every one of your letters," I answer.

She rolls in her bottom lip, gazing off to the side. "I miss him so much it hurts," she whispers.

I can't stop myself from wrapping my arms around her and pulling her against my chest. Holding her like this feels like everything I've been missing in my life—everything I've needed since the day I returned home.

She buries her head into my chest, and for the second time since I've known her, she breaks in my arms. A violent sob wracks her body as she lets her tears flow freely. My hold on her tightens as I keep her steady, never letting her fall.

Minutes pass, and the tremor in her body slowly fades before she finally speaks.

"I always wanted to get married here so that it felt like he would be with me on my wedding day," she says softly, her voice a little hoarse.

I pull back to look down at her. "Then why aren't you getting married here?"

She bites her bottom lip as her gaze drifts down. "Because my father would never approve of Alastor." She shakes her head, appearing lost in thought. "He wasn't the one he wanted me to end up with."

"Then who is?" I ask, my heart quickening with each passing second.

Her lips part, and I can see her walls crumbling. But just as quickly, she shakes her head dismissively, clears her throat, and steps out of my hold.

"I'm pretty cold. I'm going to head inside. Thanks for the blanket," she voices as she sidesteps me and walks down the dock, the blanket dragging behind her, creating a trail in the snow.

And as I watch her enter her house, I'm hit with a memory from the day that everything changed between us. A day when she was no longer just my best friend's little sister but the woman I would protect with my last breath.

The day of her father's funeral.

I nod to the guard on duty as I drive through the Alarie Estate, noticing an increased presence of security—more than usual. But given the recent death of the head of the Alarie family, it seems that life on the estate will never feel the same again.

I stop at the private cemetery and park at the end of a long line of opulent cars. As I step out into the dry, humid air and adjust my suit sleeves, I scan the massive crowd for my second family, immediately spotting them at the top of the hill: Cecilia, Vin, Alex, Mauro, Leo, and Madeleine.

They all stand strong and resilient in the face of death as the casket is carried from the back of a vehicle, making its way to its final resting place. My throat tightens with emotion at the sight of the black casket, knowing who resides inside.

A man I was lucky enough to look up to as a second father figure in my life while studying in the States, thousands of miles away from my actual family overseas. It was Leo who introduced me to his family, but it was Charles Alarie who welcomed me with open arms.

I approach the family as the priest begins to speak, positioning myself behind Madeleine. The brothers all nod in a polite greeting, their eyes telling me how lost they feel.

As the casket is lowered, Cecilia's cries echo across the vast expanse of land. Vin wraps a supportive arm around her, and she clings to him like a lifeline while he appears unaffected by the events happening around us.

But as the new head of the Alarie family, it's his job not to display fear or sadness in front of others, even as his father's remains are being laid to rest.

Nearby, other women let out soft sobs and dab at their faces with tissues. However, when I glance down at Madeleine, who fixates coldly on her father's casket, there's no trace of a single tear. Her face appears uninterested. Cold. Unnerving.

Always wearing her mask for the world to see.

After the burial, everyone heads to Charles's, or rather, Cecilia's home. So many powerful yet unfamiliar faces who will try to get a glimpse into the Alarie world.

In the open living room, I find the brothers and step toward them, but I don't see a girl walking before me, and I clumsily knock right into her. Quickly, I grab her by her arms to keep her standing upright. "Apologies. I wasn't looking where I was going. Are you okay?"

The girl nods, appearing a little startled. I offer her a slight smile as I release her.

"Eli," Leo calls from the other side of the room, gaining my attention.

I dip my chin to the girl and apologize again before moving around her to approach him.

"I'm so sorry, Leo," I say, gripping his shoulder as he clasps mine in return. "I should have been here."

He shakes his head. "You've been off saving the world." One side of his lips slightly lift before altogether falling. "Besides, there's nothing you could have done. It all happened so fast." His eyes glaze over as he clears his throat, running his fingers through his hair.

"Thank you for coming, Eli," Vin greets me, patting a strong hand on my back. "We appreciate your support during this time."

Alex shakes hands with a couple nearby before turning to us. His hand rests on my shoulder. "How long did they allow you?"

"Two days," I respond. "Took most of that time for traveling, so I'll be heading back on a flight tomorrow morning."

They look downcast at my words, and I wish there were a way I could stay longer, but when you're in the military, your life is no longer in your own hands.

"How's Mauro doing?" I ask, hoping for good news.

"Better," Alex replies. "He's out of the hospital and just resting now at his place. The doctors..." He squeezes the back of his neck before pushing up his glasses. "They don't think he'll be able to speak again."

"Shit," I breathe, feeling the weight of that news.

"Yeah." Vin lets out a deep sigh. "It will be an adjustment, that's for sure. But he's alive, and that's all we could ask for."

Leo looks out the window beside us, appearing lost in his head.

"Where's Scarlett?" I ask, scanning the room for her and her father, who is Charles's right-hand man.

"She's gone," Leo answers matter-of-factly.

"Gone?"

Leo turns his gaze toward me, and the look in his eyes conveys more than words ever could.

He's hurting. Not just from losing his father but from losing his heart as well.

"Her father didn't want to risk her safety by staying here, so he took her away." He tugs a finger on the collar of his shirt. "It's for the best. She'll be safer away from here."

I narrow my eyes at him. "Safer away from here? The Alarie Estate is the safest place in the whole goddamn world."

"Clearly, it's not!" he shouts, causing a few heads to turn in our direction. He places his hands on his hips, lowers his head, and takes a deep breath. Shaking his head, he adds, "Sorry. I just... I can't think about..."

I rest a hand on his shoulder. "I know, Leo."

His eyes meet mine, and an understanding passes through us.

"Gentlemen." A woman approaches, displaying a sad smile. "Mr. Fowler would like to see you in the study, please."

They nod in acknowledgment.

"We'll be there shortly." Vin straightens his tie before fixing his attention on me. "We'll see you tomorrow before you leave."

The three of them stride down the hall, and just as they turn out of sight, I catch a glimpse of hair as black as night swaying over Madeleine's shoulders as she walks up the stairs and disappears from view.

Taking a calming breath, I follow her, navigating through the crowd until I reach the stairs. My fingers wrap around the banister, and with each step upward, my heart pounds a little faster beneath my rib cage.

When I finally reach the top, I turn left and walk to the end of the hall, passing by all the other rooms until I arrive at hers. The door is slightly ajar, and as I step inside, I find her standing at the balcony entrance, her arms wrapped around her middle as her body shivers.

She turns to face me, tears pouring from her vibrant blue eyes, coating her porcelain cheeks. "I couldn't hold it in any longer."

I quickly close the distance between us, reaching her in a few strides before wrapping my arms around her and pulling her close to my chest.

And the girl who has always hidden her tears from the world, fearing that she might appear weak...breaks in my arms.

A sob escapes her as her body trembles against me, her tears soaking my shirt. Her slender fingers clutch my jacket tightly as every overwhelming emotion washes over her.

Unrelenting and unyielding.

"It hurts...so much," she chokes out, her chest heaving with so much force.

"I know, and I'm so fucking sorry that I can't make it stop." I cup a hand on the back of her head, my thumb tracing back and forth. I've never seen her this vulnerable before, and it's making me wish I could take her pain away—all of it. Every single fucking piece of it. "Let it out, love."

"I d-didn't t-think you'd be here... I didn't know...if I'd see you. But I..." She rubs her forehead against my chest as a tremor rushes through her. *"I needed you."*

I needed you. *Her admission makes my chest tighten. If I could have been here days ago, I would have, but there were protocols keeping me in place—time zones working against me and three different planes to board that could only get me here so fast.*

"I'll always be wherever you need me to be." I smooth the palm of my hand down her back, up and down. My lips press against the top of her head as my arm locks around her, securing her to my body.

Hours pass as we stand in this embrace, neither of us able to let go. Eventually, the tears all but dry up from Madeleine's eyes. As her eyelids begin to close, I carefully scoop her into my arms and tuck her into her four-poster bed, ensuring she's properly covered beneath her blankets.

Looking down at her, it breaks my heart to know that I have only hours remaining to be in the same time zone as her. Not long after I board my first flight, we'll be on entirely different continents, and it pains me to think that I won't be there to keep her safe—to protect her.

But I know her brothers will.

They'll do everything they can to keep their baby sister out of harm's way.

This thought eases some of the tension coiling inside me.

Leaning forward, I press a kiss to her forehead, inhaling her scent one last time.

And as I stand straight, I retrieve a letter from my jacket pocket and leave it on her nightstand for her to find in the morning.

CHAPTER SEVENTEEN

Madeleine

My eyes flutter open, still partially lost in the haze of my dreams when suddenly, a roar echoes through the room. Shooting up in a panic, I clutch my blanket tightly to my chest, scanning the space around me. The moon, high in the sky, casts the only light through my window for my eyes to see.

But there's nobody here.

After waiting another moment, I begin to slide down the satin sheets when I hear the same blood-curdling shout again, causing me to bolt upright.

Eli.

I reach inside my nightstand and grab my gun before jumping out of bed and swinging my bedroom door open. The sounds of distress continue from the other side of his door, growing louder as I approach.

Taking a deep breath, I cautiously push open the door, peeking inside while keeping my gun steady in front of me. His room is darker than mine, with the curtains closed, but I can just make out his figure on the bed. He's thrashing violently, and the blankets and pillows have been tossed to the floor. There's a sheet twisted around his leg that he's struggling against.

He's having a nightmare.

Relief causes my tense shoulders to drop slightly, realizing that there's no one here causing him physical harm. However, as I watch him suffer from his visions, I know I can't leave him like this. Lowering my gun to my side, I step inside. The plush carpet allows me to enter silently as I approach his bed and place my gun on the nightstand.

"Szhech' yego," he mumbles into the pillow.

I freeze, my ears catching unfamiliar words. It's been a few years since my last Russian class, but I'm almost certain he said, "Burn him."

A knot twists in my stomach.

With a slight tremble, I reach out for him. His handsome face is scrunched in agony, his fingers clawing at the sheets. His chest heaves as he continues rolling around, unable to find peace.

Knowing how much agony he's in causes a heaviness to spread through my beating heart.

Just as my fingers brush against his cheek, Eli's eyes suddenly open wide, appearing unfocused.

"Hey," I whisper. "You were having—"

In an instant, I'm thrown onto the bed, his fingers wrapping tightly around my neck, holding me firmly in place.

"Eli," I breathe. "It's just me."

He doesn't hear me. He's lost in whatever depths his mind has dragged him to—a place I'm sure is his own version of hell.

His beautiful brown eyes lock onto me like a target, but they aren't seeing me.

They're seeing the monsters that haunt his nightmares.

His grip tightens around me, allowing just enough airflow for shallow breaths.

"Eli," I say calmly. "It's Madeleine. You're safe. You're at the Alarie Estate. *You're home.*"

He blinks, and a flicker of realization crosses his face. His grip loosens, and with his next breath, his eyes finally focus on me, clouded with immense regret.

"Madeleine?" He scans me from my eyes down to my neck, where his fingers still rest. "Fuck!" He jolts back, his chest panting as the reality of what just happened sinks in. Horrors dance across his eyes, refusing to leave him. "You need to get out of here," he states, staring at the sweat-stained sheets.

I sit up, reaching a hand toward his face. "Are you okay? I heard you scream, and when I—" He grips my wrist, holding it in midair. Our eyes lock; his are darkening by the second.

"I need you to promise me that you won't come in here again," he pleads, pain twisting his features. "Especially when you hear me scream."

"You were having a nightmare. I only wanted to—"

"You can't help me," he rushes out, dropping my hand. "Don't you realize that I almost fucking hurt you, or worse?" His shoulders slump as he lowers his head, looking lost and maybe ashamed.

"You could never hurt me," I whisper.

He scoffs. "You don't bloody know that." He wipes his arm across his forehead, where sweat lines his temple. "If I ever hurt you, Madeleine…" He swallows hard. "I could never forgive myself."

My heart breaks at the sight of his pain—pain I've never experienced and can never truly understand.

Carefully, I slide out of bed and retreat to the en-suite bathroom. I grab a washcloth, hold it under cold water, and wring it out. As I walk back into the room, I find Eli in the same position I left him.

I approach slowly, and his eyes look up at me as I do. I don't wait for him to tell me to leave again; instead, I lift the washcloth toward his temple and press it against his overheated skin. His eyes close, and his body slightly relaxes at my touch.

I hesitate before I softly ask, "What did you dream about?"

He stills beneath me, the muscles in his shoulders tightening.

A moment passes before he says, "When I was taken in Iraq."

My heart races as anxiety courses through my veins. I remember every second of fear that overwhelmed me during those few days—days that felt like a lifetime of uncertainty. Days when, for the first time in my life, I felt powerless.

It was almost exactly a year ago when I was told that Eli had been captured and taken to an unknown location. It was almost exactly a year ago when my life changed forever.

And not for the better.

"Do you want to talk about it?" I ask.

He sighs, pulling back the blankets and resting against the headboard, his eyes closing.

Disappointment fills me at his reluctance to share this part of his life with me—a part I know I have no right to pry into. I try not to let it affect me as I bite my lip and step toward the door. If he wants to be alone with his thoughts, I will respect that and walk away.

Suddenly, I'm stopped as he wraps his fingers around my wrist. I glance over my shoulder, and my heart cracks at the anguish I see in his eyes.

"Stay," he pleads, spreading his legs to make room for me. I place the washcloth on the nightstand and climb onto the bed, fitting myself against his body as he pulls the blankets around us, cocooning us in warmth. His arms wrap around my waist. "I need to have you in my arms to tell this story."

I find one of his hands and intertwine our fingers, gently squeezing to reassure him that I'm here.

He exhales, his chest rising and falling steadily beneath me. "I was deployed to Iraq with my unit. A country where I had been stationed several times before. We had been there for weeks, assisting the Iraqi forces specializing in security measures and operations such as countert- errorism and targeted strikes." He pauses, taking a deep breath. "One day, we were returning to our base when our vehicle got stuck in some mud. At the time, we didn't think much of it, but now I'm positive it was a trap set for us."

He looks down at our joined hands and brings them to his lips, pressing a kiss to my knuckles before exhaling slowly.

"The three men I was with were the bravest individuals I knew—funny, smart, and just all-around great guys. Harry was married with three kids and a fourth on the way. John was a single bachelor who loved to travel. And Steve couldn't wait to propose to his girlfriend when he returned home." A tiny smile appears on his face. "He carried that ring with him everywhere we went. No matter the mission, that ring was always by his side. It was his special item."

"His special item?"

"We had a little tradition. Each of us kept one item with us at all times—something that helped remind us of home and why we were there, fighting. Harry had one of his children's favorite stuffed animals. John had his favorite player's football jersey. And Steve had that ring."

I turn closer to him, assessing his downcast features. It doesn't escape me that he's been talking about these men in the past tense. "What was your item?"

His lips part, and he pauses a moment before saying, "Just an old watch from my dad." He looks to the side, dragging his fingers through his hair. "Anyway, after our vehicle got stuck, we played Rock-Paper-Scissors to see who would sit behind the wheel while the other three pushed the back of the truck out of the mud. I won." A solemn laugh escapes his lips. "Although it feels a lot more like I lost everything that day. I, umm..." Clearing his throat, he continues, "I was behind the wheel, stepping on the gas while Harry, John, and Steve used all their strength trying to get our vehicle out of the mud. We were too exposed and needed to get out of there quickly before being spotted. Eventually, the car moved forward, and I drove a good distance away from them, ensuring we were out of the worst of it. I looked in my rearview mirror and watched as the three of them were jumping up, quietly pumping their fists in the air, excited for us to finally be on our way back to base. And then…"

His eyes blur as if he's no longer here with me but reliving that moment with them. I tighten my grip around his hand, and he shakes his head, looking down at me.

"You're not there," I tell him. "You're here with me."

He leans forward, pressing his lips to the top of my head. I feel a tremble pass through his body, and I twist in his embrace, wrapping my arms around him.

He exhales and wipes at his eyes. "The three of them were facing me with damn big smiles, proud of themselves. They didn't see the man approaching behind them. They didn't see the grenade in his goddamn hand. But I did. I saw every fucking thing." He looks up at the ceiling. "I jumped out of the vehicle as fast as I could, aiming my rifle, but the three of them were in my line of fire. I couldn't… I couldn't make the damn shot, and so, at the exact moment I screamed at them to run, he dived for them. He activated the grenade and threw himself at them in a suicide mission…killing them."

His eyes water, but he doesn't shed a single tear. He fights it, even though he doesn't have to—especially not in front of me.

I reach up to cup his cheek. His glossy eyes meet mine, causing my own to well up with tears. "Let it out, Eli," I whisper. "It's eating you up inside when it's not your guilt to carry. Don't hold it in any longer."

One tear rolls down his cheek, and I catch it with my thumb, gently wiping it away.

"After that," he starts. "Everything happened so fast. I was ambushed by three men and taken to a warehouse. That's where they kept me tied up. They…" He looks down at me, fighting with himself to continue, unsure if I can handle the truth.

"I can handle it," I tell him, not sure if I actually can, but I need to be here for him however he needs me to be, even if it's just to listen to him tell his story.

"You saw my back that first night I moved in here, and well, that was from them. They would torture me when they were bored, usually by burning me. The pain was so bad I would pass out. Maybe for minutes or maybe hours. I lost track of time."

They burned him.

Fury swirls inside me. Anger like I've never felt before clouds my vision. "Who did this to you?" I ask, unable to hide the tremor in my voice. "Who fucking hurt you?"

"I don't know," he replies, tucking my hair behind my ear. "They never spoke English around me. I couldn't understand what they were saying. After spending so much time in Iraq, I became familiar with many of their words in Arabic and Kurdish, but they weren't speaking either of those languages."

A realization hits me, and my eyebrows furrow. "Were they Russian?"

His hand freezes against my face. "Why would you think that?"

"When I came in here tonight, you mumbled something against your pillow. It sounded like '*szhech' yego*,' but my Russian is a little rusty, so I'm not positive."

"What does that mean?"

I pause before answering, "It means *burn him*."

He shows no emotion as he processes this information, his mind deep in thought.

"If they were Russian, why would they take you?" I ask. "Why would they do this to you? What did they want?" I shake my head, my heart racing, my mind working into overdrive. "It doesn't make sense. I don't understand—"

"Shh," he whispers, tightening his hold around me. "It's okay."

"It's not okay." Tears spill out of my eyes. "They hurt you, and they got away with it. They hurt you, and I want to know why."

He gently wipes his thumb beneath my eyes. "Some questions I'll never have answers to, and I have to learn to live with that, or it will only fester inside me. It will hinder me from moving forward." He shrugs. "At least that's what my therapist tells me."

His words take me by surprise. "You saw a therapist?"

He nods. "Still do. It was recommended by my doctors when I came home. They diagnosed me with PTSD." He looks away from me, his fingers gliding over the sheet. "I displayed all the signs: flashbacks, nightmares, avoidance—you name it. Eventually, insomnia set in because I was too scared to fall asleep, fearing the dreams that would follow." He glances down at me with a sad smile. "Bet I don't seem so tough now, huh?"

I shake my head. "You're the bravest man I know. Nothing will ever change the way I see you." I press my lips to his chest, right over his heart. "What happened to you was something no one should ever have to endure. And it breaks my heart that you have."

I wish he had told me all of this sooner.

I wish he had felt safe enough to trust me with his story.

But I know why he didn't.

Because when he came home, I was engaged to another man.

And it was in his best interest that I kept my distance from him, which is exactly what I tried to do for so long.

Even if it broke my heart every damn day.

I glance up at him, the man who holds my heart in his hands. "Eli, I..." *Love you.* I close my lips because I have to. Because if I say those three words, then I risk his safety.

I risk everything.

And I won't do that.

He must see the sorrow in my eyes because he leans forward and softly presses his lips to mine. It's gentle and slow—everything we both need.

"I know," he whispers, brushing his lips over my temple. I press my face into his chest, listening to his heartbeat beneath my ear.

A moment of silence passes between us before I say, "Eli?"

"Yes, love?"

"How did you get out of there?" I ask, already knowing the answer.

He rubs a hand up and down my arm. "They got a call. I don't know who it was, but after that call, I was freed. Dropped off at a local hospital where I was treated and eventually reunited with my commanding officer."

I know who it was, I think as my heart pounds painfully beneath my chest.

"That was my last day in the military. I was honorably discharged afterward. They claimed my back injuries were too severe for me to perform my job satisfactorily any longer." He shrugs, pretending it isn't a big deal.

But I know how much being in the military meant to Eli.

I know how much it pained him to lose what he loved doing so deeply.

He brushes his hand over my hair, then pulls up the blanket. "Will you stay with me tonight?" he asks, his voice tinged with vulnerability.

I nod, peering up at him. "I'll keep the nightmares away. I won't let anyone hurt you ever again."

He kisses me one last time before sliding down the bed and tugging me against his chest. His arms wrap around me as I settle my head on his bicep, inhaling his comforting scent and wishing every night could be spent like this—safe in Eli's arms.

Chapter Eighteen

Eli

"I really fucking hate coming here," Vin gripes, gripping the steering wheel of the SUV with white knuckles.

"Stay calm," Leo advises him.

"I'm always calm," he responds as he approaches a roundabout.

Leo scoffs. "You remember how things went last time we were here, right?"

"Yes, I ensured the old bastard knew who he was dealing with."

Leo shakes his head, laughing. "Just remember, Mikhail and his brothers are bigger and stronger than their father was. If you piss them off, we might not make it out of here alive."

"Stop worrying," Vin remarks, peering in the rearview mirror at me and Mauro. "We have more muscle with us this time."

Mauro grunts, rolling his eyes.

As we navigate the city streets of Chicago, approaching the Vasiliev building, I can't help but recall what Madeleine told me the night before.

When I came in here tonight, you mumbled something against your pillow. It sounded like szhech' yego, but my Russian is a little rusty, so I'm not positive ... It means burn him.

Could my subconscious have remembered hearing those words from the people who tortured me?

"Everything okay?" Leo asks, eyeing me in the rearview mirror.

I lean forward. "What are the chances that the Vasilievs were involved in my kidnapping last year? Or, at least, that their men had something to do with it?"

Vin and Leo exchange glances.

"What makes you think they were involved?" Vin asks.

I drag my hand through my hair. "I had a nightmare last night. Always the same one." I stare out the window, watching people pass by while they gaze at their phones. "But apparently, I was speaking Russian in my sleep."

"How do you know you were speaking Russian in your sleep?" Vin asks, his voice suddenly turning a little colder.

Shit.

"I..." I clear my throat. "I guess I screamed out, waking Madeleine, who was sound asleep in her room." I shrug, trying to appear casual. "She came in to check on me, and that's when she heard me say, '*szhech'yego.*'"

The vehicle comes to a stop, and Vin turns to face me, narrowing his eyes. "Which means?"

"Burn him," I answer.

He nods before facing forward and accelerating the vehicle.

"Do you think they were involved with it?" Leo asks.

Vin sighs. "At this point, I wouldn't put anything past them. But I don't see what benefit it would have been for them to capture Eli and then release him just days later without gaining anything in return."

"That's the part I can't figure out," I say.

"Well, if it was them, then we have your back, Eli," Vin asserts. "And they will be dealt with accordingly."

Mauro grips my shoulder and nods in agreement.

The vehicle pulls over to the side of the road, and I look out the window to see armed men approaching.

"But Eli." I stare at Vin's cold blue eyes in the mirror. "If we find out you're fucking our sister, then the Vasilievs will be the least of your problems."

I don't let him see the fear in my eyes, nor do I have a chance to react as my door suddenly opens.

The four of us step out of the vehicle, and I stare up at the name "Vasiliev" displayed in giant gold letters across the building. Fucking tacky.

I scoff. "You think they're overcompensating for something?"

"Just wait until you see the rest of the place," Leo tells me.

"If it isn't my favorite guard," Vin declares with a wide grin, directing his gaze at a bulky, short man standing before him.

The guard scowls. "Fuck off."

Vin clicks his tongue in disapproval. "I thought you would have worked on your manners by now."

"Why you fucking—"

"Enough!" a deep, throaty voice snaps. I look past the guards to see a large man standing with his hands clasped behind his back. I'm not as familiar with the Vasilievs as the Alaries are, but it doesn't take a genius to recognize that this man is one of the infamous brothers.

"Kazimir." Vin greets him with a mask of indifference. "You should try to teach your fucking guards to have some respect toward your guests."

Kazimir's lips curve into a calculating smile. "Apologies. We're still in the process of weeding out any invaluable members during our transition," he replies, his dark gaze resting on the guard, who visibly swallows. "But if you'll follow me, my brothers are eager for your visit."

"I'm sure they are." Leo strides forward, and I follow closely behind, my senses heightened as we enter the building.

Kazimir points toward the front desk. "Check in your weapons."

I quickly glance toward Vin, who nods.

Fuck, I don't like this.

It feels like we're walking right into a goddamn trap, unarmed.

After depositing our guns, we enter the elevator, easily filling in the small space.

Once the doors close, we ascend to the top floor.

Mauro tugs at the collar of his shirt.

"Don't tell me the deadly Mauro Alarie is claustrophobic?" Kazimir mocks.

Mauro drops his hand and glares at him.

The doors slide open, and we step off directly into the gaudiest room I've ever seen. Gold covers everything, from the chandelier to the picture frames and even the wallpaper.

"Told you," Leo remarks quietly as we follow our host toward the end of the hall.

Kazimir pushes open the double-wide doors. "Brothers, our guests have arrived."

We step into the room, where the other four brothers are waiting for us with eager expressions.

The largest among them sits behind a desk, standing up as we enter, appearing emotionless. Tattoos cover every inch of his arms and peek out beneath the collar of his shirt, spreading up his neck. "The Alaries," he says.

"Mikhail," Vin acknowledges.

"It has been quite some time," Mikhail responds.

"Some might argue it hasn't been long enough." Vin crosses his arms over his chest.

Mikhail studies him for a moment before looking at the rest of us and sitting down. "Please, take a seat."

We do, the four of us positioning ourselves on one side of the desk while the five Vasiliev brothers occupy the other side, whether sitting or standing.

Mikhail steeples his fingers in front of him. "I heard you were here just a few months ago, visiting our father."

"We were," Leo confirms.

"What was the purpose of your visit?"

"Why don't you ask him?" Leo asks. "Oh wait…"

One of the brothers abruptly stands. "Sit, Emil," Mikhail orders, narrowing his eyes at Leo. "He didn't mean anything by his words." He leans forward. "Speaking of our father, you wouldn't have had anything to do with his death, correct?"

"Heard he was killed in an explosion," Vin says. "At an illegal sex club, if my memory serves me right." Vin *tsks*. "Nasty business to be involved in."

"Women were made for our pleasure," Kazimir answers. "Their only purpose in life is to provide a hole for fucking and heirs. Nothing more. Wouldn't you agree?"

"No, we don't," Leo quickly answers. "Your father was under the impression that it was okay to kidnap innocent women and then auction them off to work as sex slaves, all to make a quick buck. We had heard rumors that your views differed, but perhaps we were wrong."

"Not wrong," Mikhail offers, casting a sharp look at Kazimir. "But it's not entirely accurate either."

"Heard your wife was supposed to star in one of those auctions," Kazimir notes with a grin. "Is it too late to bid?"

Vin's hand slaps down on Leo's chest before he can rise from his seat. Leo's hands tighten around the arms of his chair as he tries to rein in his fury, his shoulders tightening by the second.

"The next time you bring Scarlett into this, I won't stop him from defending her honor," Vin warns, his authority clear.

Kazimir raises his hands in mock surrender. "Noted."

"We've heard rumors as well—that it was you who killed our father," another brother voices as he points an accusatory finger directly at Leo. "You, specifically."

Leo grins, relaxing in his seat. "Got any proof?"

The brother steps away from the wall, scowling at Leo. "I don't need any proof to kill you, motherfucker."

Vin stands. "Make one more threat against my brother, Alik, and it will be your last words."

One of the brothers laughs. "Jeez, you can cut the tension with a knife in here." He crosses his arms over his chest and leans back in his seat. "Maybe you four should just get to the point and tell us why you're here."

"Yes, Luka, I agree," Mikhail says, his tone laced with boredom. "Why have you requested such an urgent visit with us?"

"Alastor is not marrying Madeleine," I blurt out, causing every pair of eyes in the room to land on me.

For the first time since we arrived, Mikhail grins. "And why is that? Is the bride having cold feet?"

"We know you're involved in this," Vin accuses, taking his seat. "And we won't be idly sitting back while you fuck with our sister."

Kazimir grins wickedly. "Maybe we can just fuck her instead, then?"

I jump from my seat, repercussions be damned, as I lunge for his throat. "You fucking bastard!"

But before I have a chance to touch him, two pairs of hands grasp my shoulders. I look to see Mauro and Leo pulling me back.

Kazimir laughs. "This one's a little temperamental."

My chest heaves as I rock my neck from side to side, my fingers curling into fists.

"You say one more thing about my sister, and I will cover your atrociously decorated rooms with your blood," Vin threatens, somehow keeping his cool. "In the five minutes we've been here, you've insulted my sister-in-law, threatened my brother, and now you dare to offend my sister." He bangs his fist on the desk. "I consider myself to be a calm man, but you are testing my patience, and I advise you to stop."

The temperature in the room drops a few degrees.

Mikhail taps a finger on his desk, his gaze fixed on Vin. "The wedding is between Alastor and Madeleine. So, tell me, why have you come to us about it?"

"We believe there is a contract between them," Leo answers. "Something that Alastor is using to hold over Madeleine's head, forcing her hand in this marriage. And we believe you are involved."

Mikhail's hand freezes. "Where is your proof?"

"On New Year's Day, you met with Alastor just hours before he met with Madeleine," Vin states as he leans forward.

Mikhail's expression darkens. "How do you know this?"

"We have our ways." Silence ensues, and Vin leans back in his chair. "The next day, their engagement was announced." He clasps his hands together, his eyes sending an ominous message to each brother. "I don't claim to be the brains of my family, but it's not too difficult to put the two pieces together. So, it's time for you to tell us what game you're playing."

Kazimir pulls a knife from his pocket and taps the blade against his knee. "You think you can come into our home and tell us what the fuck to do?" He waves the knife animatedly. "That's not how this fucking works." He points the tip of the blade directly at Vin. "I should kill you right now for insulting us."

Vin grins. "Ah, but you can't."

"Yeah?" Emil asks. "Why the fuck not?"

"Because then you would be violating your contract with my dear cousins, the Marchettis," he explains. "And trust me, you do not want to make enemies of them."

Kazimir turns to Mikhail. "What the hell is he talking about?"

Mikhail sighs, lowering his head. "Well played, Vincenzo."

I glance between the Alarie men, feeling confused about what Vin is referring to.

"Mikhail..." Luka steps toward his brother and looks down at him. "The only active contract we have with the Marchettis is regarding Liliya." He then turns his gaze to Vin. "You don't mean to tell me that this asshole—"

"Yes," Mikhail clips. "This asshole is going to be your future brother-in-law."

Well, shit.

Kazimir doubles over in laughter. "How the fuck did Marco get out of that?"

"We needed a favor, and the Marchetti family never just does anything out of the goodness of their hearts," Vin clarifies. "He wanted out of the marriage contract. I took his place. Simple."

"Yeah, there's just one problem," Luka says seriously, crossing his arms over his chest. "She ran away months ago, and we can't fucking find her."

"That's not my problem," Vin responds, waving his hand dismissively. "The contract is still valid. So, it's in your best interest not to kill me so that when your sister decides to return home, we can marry. Considering, of course, that she even wants to. If she doesn't, you'll have to find someone to replace me because I won't be forcing her hand."

"Oh, Jesus Christ, Vincenzo Alarie has a fucking heart after all," Kazimir says with mock laughter.

"Having a heart in this world only makes you soft," Mikhail adds. "Have you gone soft, Vincenzo?"

Leo slams his hand down on the desk. "You're clearly well-versed in contracts, so whatever the agreement is between Alastor and Madeleine, we want it to be immediately nullified."

Mikhail shakes his head. "We have nothing to do with the contract. We're only the contingency should she decide not to walk down that aisle."

"What the fuck does that mean?" I demand.

"It means." Amusement spreads across Kazimir's face. "If the wedding doesn't happen, Madeleine loses. Game over for her."

Vin's chair crashes back as he stands, towering over Kazimir, his last bit of restraint vanishing. "If you lay a finger on her head, I will annihilate you!" Vin roars. "I will use your fucking knife to shred you into pieces and feed you to my dogs! Capisce?"

Kazimir does the one thing you don't do after a man threatens your life. He smiles. "It's not her head you should be worried about."

Vin gets within inches of his face. "I am going to be your worst fucking nightmare. Mark my words, Kazimir, you will regret ever getting on my bad side." Mauro places a hand on his shoulder, reining him in. Vin's gaze travels over the room, landing on each of the Vasiliev brothers. "I will tell you the same thing I told your worthless father. If you ever threaten one of my family members again, you risk a war with the Alaries, and believe me when I tell you, you won't fucking win!"

"I'm afraid you've wasted your time coming here today as we have no information to provide you," Mikhail informs him calmly. "Perhaps you should call next time to save yourself the trip."

"This wedding is not happening. Not over my dead body," Vin declares, his chest heaving.

Mikhail shrugs. "I can arrange that." The door opens, and three guards step inside with their guns raised. "Please escort our guests out. Our meeting is concluded."

As I stand, Kazimir stares at me intently while speaking in a hushed whisper to his brother.

I glare at him before following the others onto the elevator in silence, the guards trailing behind us. It isn't until we're safely inside our vehicle that we finally speak.

"Well, at least now we know for certain that there is a contact behind this marriage and that the Vasilievs are involved." Leo rubs his hand over his temple. "I think it's time we ask Madeleine what the fuck is going on."

"We can't." Vin shakes his head. "With our luck, it will only make her move the wedding up." He pinches the bridge of his nose. "Fucking Kazimir always gets under my skin."

"But, hey," Leo says, smiling. "At least you stayed calm."

"Vin's right," I add, dragging my fingers through my hair. "Madeleine needs to be the one who calls this wedding off. For whatever reason, she hasn't felt like she could come to any of us for help, and that doesn't sit right with me."

"But what if she doesn't call it off?" Leo asks. "She's pretty fucking stubborn."

I look out the window. "We give her until two days before to come to us. But we can't wait any longer than that. If she doesn't come to us by then, we handle things our way."

"Agreed," Vin responds, accelerating onto the highway.

I lean back in my seat. "So, speaking of stopping a wedding, when were you going to let me in on the fact that you're currently in an arranged marriage contract?"

"When the time was right," Vin responds.

"And back there, that was when the time was right?"

He nods. "Exactly."

"So when is this happening?"

"It's not," he states matter-of-factly.

My brows furrow in confusion. "But the contract with the Marchettis—"

"You heard Liliya's brothers. They can't find her. She ran away, and with any luck, she won't return, which means I'm in the clear and can continue living out my single life while honoring the contract."

Leo glances at me in the rearview mirror and rolls his eyes.

I grin. "Do you even know what she looks like?"

"No, and I don't care to find out."

Mauro grunts, shaking his head.

"Apparently, no one does," Leo answers. "Well, besides her brothers since she's never been seen in public. Who knows? Maybe she doesn't even exist."

I drag my fingers through my hair as I look out the window, trying but failing to understand how everything is connected. *Why would Madeleine agree to this? Why would she be okay with spending the rest of her life stuck by Alastor's side? And why the fuck would she go to him for help and not me?* Suddenly, Kazimir's words echo in my mind: *"It's not her head you should be worried about."*

What the hell did he mean by that?

Dread coils tightly in my stomach as I grip the ends of my hair. Frustration and fury swirl together within me, seizing my chest. I feel on the verge of—

"What time's your flight?" Leo's voice interrupts my thoughts.

I rub a hand over my sternum as I let out a heavy breath. "At two. Should land right around nine."

"What is it they say over there? Happy Christmas?" Vin asks, grinning.

"Yeah," I mutter, my chest tightening at the thought of leaving Madeleine here while I'm thousands of miles away. "You're sure you guys don't need me to stay?"

"No," Leo replies. "Go see your family. You haven't been home since the summer. We've got everything handled here."

"Yeah. Right. Okay."

He arches a brow. "Everything okay?"

I nod. "Of course. Just not looking forward to a crowded flight," I lie.

Because everything is not okay. Not by a long fucking shot.

Not until I put an end to this goddamn wedding once and for all.

May 22nd

Princess,

I can't stop thinking about that kiss.

And no, I'm not talking about our kiss from years ago during spin the bottle as children. I'm talking about the kiss of all kisses.

I'll forever remember the way you looked beneath the light of the moon as we stood on the dock. I'll forever remember how perfectly you fit in my arms. And I'll forever remember that goddamn kiss.

I hope you don't regret it. I don't. Not when it was the best night of my life.

Yours,
Eli

CHAPTER NINETEEN

Madeleine

I stare at the black tank in my mother's front yard, positioned next to three camouflage-colored ones, my mouth agape in disbelief.

"You're insane," I mutter, still trying to process what I'm seeing.

"You don't like it?" Vin asks, his expression shifting to a slight frown.

"I..." My eyelashes flutter as I glance around at my brothers, searching for backup.

Leo scratches the top of his head. "Where are we supposed to store them?"

Vin grins proudly. "I had one of the warehouses enlarged specifically for this reason."

"You bought us official military tanks...for Christmas," I state, walking up to the black one and placing my hand on the smooth exterior to ensure it's real.

"Well," Vin begins, clearing his throat, "after our home was attacked, I thought this would be an appropriate gift. But now that I'm standing here, taking it all in, I realize it might seem a little extreme."

"A little?" Alex interjects. "I could maybe understand one, but four?"

"Five," Vin corrects.

"Come again?" Alex arches a brow.

"Well, obviously, I had to get one for myself," Vin says matter-of-fact-ly.

"Oh, Jesus." Alex removes his glasses and drags a hand down his face.

Mauro bends over, gripping his knees as a strangled sound escapes him.

"Oh my God. Is he choking?" I ask, patting his back.

But when he stands up straight, there's a giant smile on his face and tears in his eyes. He's laughing, and for some reason, it makes me start laughing uncontrollably, too.

A chain reaction occurs as Leo and Alex join in. The four of us are in such high spirits, reveling in the absurdity of our Christmas gifts—gifts that only Vin would ever think to get us.

"You four don't deserve these. I'll have to return them," Vin mumbles as he spins on his heels and strides toward the front door of our mother's house.

"Aw, come back, Vin!" I wipe away a few stray tears. "We love them!"

"Yeah." Leo grins, shoving his hands in his pockets. "Maybe we can have weekly races."

That gets us all cackling, especially when the front door slams shut behind Vin.

"Do you think he's really going to return them?" Scarlett asks, trudging through the snow in her boots.

"No," Leo answers. "He has too much pride to do that. Just be thankful he got you those first editions you were looking for."

She smiles softly. "I've already added them to my library."

I interlock my arm with hers. "Let's go inside. Every part of me is frozen!"

Once we enter the house, Scarlett and I head to the kitchen, where we're greeted by the mouthwatering scent of all my Christmas Eve favorites.

"So," my mother says, standing beside the chef with a glass of wine, "what did you think of your gift?"

"You knew he was getting those for us?" I ask. "I would have preferred some new slippers."

She lifts a shoulder. "You know how stubborn he is. Once he sets his mind on something he wants, there's no stopping him."

"Isn't that the truth," I respond.

"I do blame your cousin, Caine, though. He's the one who put this idea in his head." She takes a sip of her wine and glances between me and Scarlett. "Do you both have everything you need for the party tonight?"

Every Christmas Eve, my family hosts an annual party for all the workers and their families on the Alarie Estate. Aside from our Halloween party, this is the biggest event of the year, with hundreds of people in attendance.

It was my dad's favorite day of the year. He always enjoyed giving back to his employees in any way he could, and after his passing, it became a tradition that we knew we would always uphold.

"Of course. We'll be there early to help set up," I tell her as I grab two wineglasses, and Scarlett steals a bottle of wine from the wire rack.

"The pantry?" Scarlett asks.

"The pantry," I repeat, heading straight for the chef's pantry—a place where the two of us used to hide out when we were kids.

Some things never change.

I turn on the light and shut the door behind us before we both plop our asses on the tiled floor. Scarlett pours us each a generous serving as I reach overhead for a bag of chips.

"Cheers," we say in unison as we clink our glasses and take a sip, the hints of cherry hitting my taste buds.

"I wish Alina could be here." I stretch my legs out and cross one ankle over the other.

"I know," Scarlett replies as she places her glass beside her and unbuttons her coat. "But she said she'll try to stop by at the party. She wanted to spend the day with her dad."

I nod and lean against the wall behind me. Scarlett digs into her coat pocket and pulls out a small, neatly wrapped rectangular box, then tosses it to me. I watch as it lands softly in my lap.

"I thought we weren't exchanging gifts until tomorrow?" I ask, eyeing the box with suspicion.

"It's not from me," she answers, a smile tugging at her lips.

That piques my curiosity.

Furrowing my brows, I finish my wine and set the glass aside. Warily, I unwrap the red plaid wrapping paper, revealing a white jewelry box. "Who's it from?"

"You'll find out as soon as you open it." She nudges my shoulder playfully before refilling my glass.

Opening the lid, I find a note lying on top of white tissue paper that reads...

This was my special item.

-Eli

My heart flutters as butterflies freely fall inside my stomach.

For a moment, I completely forget where I am or what I'm doing.

"What is it?" Scarlett asks.

"I—I don't know," I reply, my hands trembling as I carefully peel away a thin layer of tissue paper. Beneath it, I find a silver necklace. My fingers wrap around the sturdy beaded chain, holding it steady in front of me. A worn-looking dog tag hangs from the center, noticeably thicker than I would expect. The engraved name, Eli Lyon, stands out against the scratches and dents on the metal. I run my thumb across it, feeling my throat go dry.

"I think..." Scarlett leans closer for a better look. "I think it opens."

I run my finger along the edge and feel an indent. With two fingers, I gently pull on each side until it clicks open.

Everything freezes.

My heart.

Earth.

Time.

Everything.

Nothing else in the world matters as I stare at what's inside the locket.

"It's me," I whisper, completely overwhelmed.

On one side, there is a simple engraving that reads, "My Princess." And on the opposite side is a picture of...me. A photo that Eli took of me years ago.

"Why?" I ask, looking up at Scarlett as tears stream down my cheeks, and I don't bother to stop them. "Why would he give me this?"

She smiles warmly. "I think you know the answer to that."

I swallow hard, clutching his dog tag in my hand. "But I... But we can't... I mean, I'm—"

She reaches for my hand, intertwining our fingers. "He asked me to give this to you before he left. Said it was important that you knew what he always kept over his heart when he was on the other side of the world."

Me.

He kept a picture of me over his heart.

Tears tumble down my cheeks one by one like an overflowing river rushing down my skin.

"I have to see him," I whisper, every part of me urging me to get up and move. To run to him. To kiss him. To tell him how I feel—how I've always felt. I reach for the shelf above me to pull myself up. "I need to tell him—" I freeze as my heart shatters, my engagement ring staring back at me, reminding me why I can't go to the only man I've ever loved. "I can't." My voice breaks as I drop back to the floor. "I'm engaged." I wrap my arms around myself, the necklace pressed against my chest.

Scarlett slides closer, her eyes filled with genuine concern. "But you love him," she states as if it should be obvious.

I look down, brushing away my tears. "That's exactly why I can't go to him."

"I don't understand," she says softly.

"I know." I hide my face in my hands. "You just have to trust me on this. It's the right thing to do."

"I do trust you. You know I do," she responds. She reaches for one of my hands, taking it in her own. "I just wish you knew you could talk to me about whatever it is that's going on."

"I wish I could," I breathe. "You have no idea how much I wish I could."

She reaches out, gently tucking my hair behind my ear. "You've always been there for me. I just want to be there for you now." I nod, unable to find my voice. "Which is why, as your best friend, I'm not letting you spend Christmas here."

I let out a deep breath. "Scarlett—"

"No." She shakes her head firmly. "You deserve to be happy, Maddy. And right now, you're so far from it that it's not even funny."

I shrug. "Can't argue with that."

"So." She stands and holds her hands out for me, which I take. "It's time to get your butt moving. The pilot is waiting for you."

"What?"

She brushes her fingers across my cheeks, wiping away the rest of my tears. "I talked with the pilot and arranged a flight for you to England. Think of it as my Christmas present."

I shake my head. "But what—"

"No buts," she interjects firmly. "You're going to get your ass on your family's plane and fly across the damn ocean to get to your man."

I laugh at her attempt at being bossy. "But what about my family? My brothers will notice pretty quickly if I'm gone."

"Alina is ready to play the part of a sick friend who needs you by her side. And the pilot knows not to utter a word if he wants to keep his job." She winks. "We thought of everything."

"You guys really are the best friends I could ever ask for."

"I know, I know." She laughs. "Now go! They're about five hours ahead over there, and the flight is about seven hours. If you leave now, you'll make it in time for Christmas morning."

I wrap my arms around her, feeling so thankful for her. "Thank you."

"We all deserve to be with the one we love, even if it's just for a few days, right?" she asks.

"A few days is more than I could ask for," I tell her.

She tightens her hold around me. "I know you'll tell me everything when you're ready. But I just want you to know that I'm here whenever that day comes. Okay?"

I nod. "Thank you, Scarlett. For everything."

She pulls back to look at me with a smile on her face. "Go get him, Maddy."

***

As I walk up the snow-covered cobblestone steps, I smooth out my jacket, wishing I had a chance to change before the flight or even pack a bag, for that matter. But for now, what I'm wearing will have to do.

I raise my hand to the giant black door, ready to knock, but freeze when I catch sight of my engagement ring gleaming in the light.

Shit. I twist it off and shove it into my pocket, ensuring it remains out of sight. I raise my hand again but hesitate when I hear laughter coming from the other side of the door.

What am I doing?

What if he doesn't want me here?

What if his gift means more to me than it does to him?

What if—

Suddenly, the door opens, revealing a young girl—maybe seven or eight years old. I've never been very good at guessing ages.

"Who are you?" she asks, tilting her head to the side. Her long brown hair sways over the shoulder of her red sweater. "I saw you walking up the driveway."

"Oh, well, I'm a...friend of—"

"Angel, what are you doing?" Eli's deep voice carries from behind the door.

Angel?

"We're about to start opening—" Eli appears behind the girl, his eyes darting to me and widening in surprise. "Madeleine?" He steps around her, standing directly in front of me with concern carved on his face. "Is everything okay?"

"I...umm." I pull on the collar of my jacket, suddenly feeling too hot. "I needed to see you."

His eyes soften, and he looks at the young girl over his shoulder. "Angel, can you give us a minute?"

She crosses her arms over her chest defiantly.

Eli leans down and whispers, "Inside one of the boxes is your very own ice cream machine, but you didn't hear that from me."

"Really?" she squeals before turning and dashing down a hallway.

Eli steps outside, closing the door behind him. He shoves his hands in his pockets. "That's my cousin, Ava. More like a little sister, though."

"A girl after my own heart," I remark with a smile, relief washing over me. I guess this solves the mystery of who Angel is.

He shuffles his foot, kicking a rock to the side. "She moved in with my parents a few years ago after my aunt and uncle died in a car accident. And ever since my kidnapping last year, she's been worried about me when she doesn't hear from me, so we try to have daily calls, even if it's only for five minutes, so that she can hear my voice."

I bite my bottom lip. "Well, now I feel bad for stealing you away from her."

He laughs. "Don't worry. She doesn't know it yet, but my gift to her is a trip to Disney, so I'm sure I'll be forgiven after that."

I grin. "That will definitely put you back in her good graces."

He glances to the side before looking back at me. "So, are you going to tell me why you came here? Or were you just in the neighborhood?"

I reach inside my pocket and pull out the necklace, letting it dangle between us. "Why did you give me this?"

"I would think it would be obvious," he answers.

"Not to me." Silence hangs between us, my breaths escaping in puffs of smoke as the cold nips at my skin. "Why, Eli?"

He takes a step, eliminating the distance between us. I look down, suddenly too nervous to be this close to him.

He gently hooks two fingers under my chin, tilting my head up until our eyes meet. I'm lost in his orbit, surrendering to his dark gaze as he leans in, barely brushing his lips against mine.

"Because I wanted you to know that you were with me every day I was gone, whether you knew it or not. In my heart. In my mind. In my goddamn soul. And, love, I'm tired of pretending otherwise."

My eyes water, with tears threatening to spill over. I place my palms on his chest, feeling his heart racing beneath my touch. "This doesn't change anything," I whisper, defeat echoing in my words. "It can't. I don't want to give you false hope by being here, which I probably am, and I'm sorry. I'm so sorry." He swallows hard, his big brown eyes locked onto mine. "But while I'm here, and only while I'm here, I want to pretend the wedding isn't happening. I want to be yours. I just...I don't want to fight this anymore," I admit softly. "I'm so tired of fighting it."

His lips crash down on mine as my fingers dig into his navy button-down shirt. His tongue slides between my lips, waiting for me to open, and I do, eagerly tasting him.

His hand cups my cheek while the other snakes around my waist, pulling me against him.

He's the only one who has truly seen every part of me—the good and the bad.

And as much as I should stop this, knowing it will only give me a taste of a life I can never have with him, I can't. Because my heart has only ever beaten for one man in my life. And for the next few days only, I want to pretend that I can have him for the rest of my life.

"Eww. Aunt Audrey! Eli's kissing a girl!"

Eli and I quickly separate, both of us panting heavily as we turn to see Ava standing in the now-open doorway, her face twisted in disgust.

"Bloody hell, Ava." Eli's lips curve into a smirk, a small laugh escaping between his teeth.

"You need to put a pound in the swear jar," she tells him.

A woman with shoulder-length brown hair appears in the doorway behind Ava, wearing a warm smile. "What's all the commotion? It's Christmas—Oh." Her eyes flit between me and Eli. "Excuse me. I didn't know Eli had company."

"Mom." Eli clears his throat, brushing back his hair before looking at me. A soft shade of pink creeps up his neck, and I have to bite down on my lip to keep from laughing. "This is Madeleine Alarie."

I extend my hand. "It's nice to meet you, Mrs. Lyon."

She takes my hand in hers, her smile widening. "It's lovely to meet you. Please, call me Audrey."

I smile back, suddenly feeling self-conscious. It's a sensation I'm not used to, but this is Eli's mom—a woman whose approval actually matters to me.

"Well, we'll give you two some privacy," she says. "But please come in and join us when you're ready. We have plenty of food."

"Oh." I look at Eli and then back at his mom. "I don't want to impose. I was just stopping by—"

"Stopping by from New York?" Eli quips.

I tuck my hair behind my ear. "Well, when you put it like that…"

"I insist," Audrey says, taking Ava by the shoulders and directing her into the house.

"You're just going to let them stand out there and kiss?" Ava asks incredulously before the door shuts behind her.

We both laugh, and I can't help but look up at the sky, snowflakes floating around us.

For the first time in a while, I feel weightless.

Eli's arms wrap around me, and I look into his eyes.

"Happy Christmas, Madeleine."

"Happy Christmas, Eli."

"You must be exhausted," he notes with worry. "Want to rest first?"

I shake my head. "I'm good. I slept a little on the flight over."

He sighs. "I hope you know what you're in for. My dad was a general for most of his life and is going to interrogate the hell out of you, wanting to know everything about you."

I chuckle. "Bring it on."

He takes my hand and suddenly glances down, noticing the absence of a ring.

He doesn't say anything.

He doesn't remark on its whereabouts.

Instead, he merely intertwines our fingers, presses a kiss to my temple, and then leads me into his home.

CHAPTER TWENTY

Eli

"Jack, leave the poor girl alone. She's barely had a chance to take a breath between each one of your questions." Mom playfully shoves my dad's shoulder, shaking her head.

"What?" Dad exclaims. "It's the first time our son has ever brought someone home, and I'm not allowed to find out a little about her?"

"I'm the first one?" Madeleine asks with a pleased smile, sliding her arms into her coat that I'm holding out for her.

"The only one," Dad responds with a wink.

"For fuck's sake." I drag a hand down my face. "Don't you have a game to watch?"

"Ah. You're right. I think it's time for a little American football." He regards Madeleine with warmth. "It was lovely to meet you, dear."

"Lovely to meet you, sir," she responds politely.

"Sir?" Dad looks at me and points at her. "I like this one."

"Yeah, I'm pretty partial myself," I say, noting the blush that spreads over her cheeks. "You ready to go?" I ask her.

"I will be if you tell me where we're going."

"And where is the fun in that?"

Dad walks off, heading toward the living room, where I'm guessing he'll spend the rest of the night in his favorite recliner. Mom will eventually join him after she feels the house is put back together properly. All my aunts and uncles will meander through the house with full stomachs and drinks in their hands before deciding to call it a night, while Ava will take all her new toys to her room to inspect.

The typical Christmas day at my family's home.

Mom laughs at the two of us, a speculative gleam in her eyes. "You know, when Eli was just a little boy, he came home from school on winter break and told me story after story of all the exciting things he learned in the States. But one story always stood out to me the most."

"Oh? Was it about the time he screamed like a little girl when he spotted a spider on his shirt?" Madeleine teases.

"I didn't scream." I roll my eyes but smirk, remembering that day. Unfortunately, I did, in fact, scream like a little girl.

"No." Mom chuckles, appearing so at ease. "He told me about a princess he met and how he was going to be her knight in shining armor. He never called her by her first name; he just kept referring to her as his princess. Told us she had hair as dark as the night with big, beautiful blue eyes and that she lived in a castle." She smiles. "I always wondered if I was going to meet you."

Madeleine momentarily stills beside me, her lips parting and closing in surprise. "I didn't..." She turns toward me, her eyes wide. "You did?"

Fuck, she's cute when she's uncomfortable.

"Well, thank you, Mom. Can always count on you to make things awkward." I lean into my mom to place a kiss on her cheek.

"That's what I'm here for," she responds.

I shake my head, the corners of my lips lifting with ease. "We'll be back later. Don't wait up."

"Oh, to be young again," she muses.

I place my hand on Madeleine's lower back as I guide her toward my Land Rover and open the passenger door for her before making my way to the driver's side. The engine purrs to life as I accelerate, and heat quickly fills the space.

Madeleine sits quietly as I back out of the narrow driveway and turn onto the calm road. Streets that are usually bustling at this time of night are subdued, twinkling with strings of white lights.

It's my favorite time of year.

And the fact that I get to spend today with her...well, this might be the best Christmas yet. One I'll have to ensure she never forgets.

After driving for some time with only a soft hum of Christmas music in the background, Madeleine says softly, "I've never been to London before." Her curious eyes remain glued to the window as she takes in everything that the city has to offer.

I know she hasn't been, which is precisely why I'm taking her to the most prominent tourist attraction. Looking at my watch, I see we have just enough time to make it before they close for the evening.

I pull the car over to the side of the road and park.

"Where are we?" she asks.

"Do you trust me?"

"Of course."

There's no hesitation in her answer.

Only resounding confidence.

And it sends warmth through my chest.

After getting out of the car, I grab her hand and lead her around a building where we're met with a view of—

"Oh my God." Madeleine's eyes widen. "It's the London Eye." She swallows hard, her eyes never leaving the attraction. "Are we... Are we going on that?"

"You better believe it." I pull her along with me, wrapping an arm over her shoulder as we approach the ticket office. A moment later, we're next in line, waiting for an available capsule. I look at Madeleine and find her quietly nibbling on her thumbnail as she peers up to the top of the structure.

It's an old habit she's had since childhood—one that always signaled her nervousness or fear.

I nudge her shoulder. "Don't tell me you're scared of heights?"

She drops her hand and juts her chin out, holding her head high as she carries herself like royalty. "I'm not scared of anything."

There's a slight pull at one side of my lips as I say, "All right then." A capsule stops before us, and the man opens the door. I gesture with my arm, letting Madeleine go first. "Prove it."

She purses her lips and takes a few confident steps toward our awaiting pod, but the minute she places one foot inside, she turns toward me and grips my shirt.

"You won't let anything happen to me, right?" she asks, her voice growing soft.

My brows furrow as I grasp her chin between my fingers. "I would never let anything happen to you." Relief floats over her bright blue eyes. "But if you don't want to do this, we don't have to."

She shakes her head, a smile tugging at her lips. "No. I mean, I came all this way. I might as well give it a try."

I lean forward, brushing my lips over her ear. "That's my girl."

A soft blush spreads over her cheeks as she turns and steps into the capsule, walking to the other end, where she places both hands against the glass and gazes out at the view. After thanking the attendant and giving him a few bills for some extra time at the top, I follow behind her, entering the warm space. The door closes, locking us in together.

She doesn't notice as I scope out the discreet camera in the corner.

And she definitely doesn't notice as I reach inside my pocket and pull out a small roll of duct tape to cover the lens.

No, she's too lost in the beauty that is London.

"How long does it take to go fully around?" she asks, still mesmerized by everything before her.

"About thirty minutes."

I catch her smiling in the reflection. "I bet you take all the girls here."

I come up behind her, letting my hands skim over the fabric of her coat. I rest my palms against her stomach, wishing there was no material between us. The opening of my jacket drapes around her as I rest my chin on the top of her head.

"What girls?"

"The ones who've kept you company over the years. Probably fallen head over heels for your sexy accent and charm, not knowing any better," she teases.

I chuckle, pushing her hair aside and grazing my lips against the side of her neck. It's funny if she thinks I've ever been with anyone but her. "And what about you?"

"What about me?"

"Do you find my accent sexy?"

"Depends on what you say."

A motor churns beneath us, and the capsule begins to move. Madeleine lets out a soft gasp at the slight jerk, but I tighten my grip around her, not letting her go anywhere. She reaches in front of her, untying her coat. The material falls open, and she's ready to slide her arms out of it until I tell her, "Leave it on."

She arches an eyebrow but slides the material back over her shoulders. I inhale her enticing scent. "What do you want me to say?"

She glances over her shoulder, her eyelids appearing heavy, her chest heaving a little faster. "Tell me what you want to do to me...right now."

Fuck.

I groan, my cock hardening uncomfortably against the zipper of my pants.

"You want to hear about all the ways I want to fuck you, Princess? Is that what you want to hear?"

"Yes," she breathes, pushing her ass against me.

"Fuck, Madeleine." I grip her hips, spinning her around to face me as I press my body against hers. "I want to sink inside your tight pussy, thrusting so hard you come apart on my cock, screaming my name." I snake one hand between us, scrunching up the fabric of her dress so that I can sneak my way inside her panties. She bucks forward as I slowly slide two fingers through her wet center, dragging out the inevitable.

"Someone outside might see," she pants, her legs parting wider.

"No, they won't." I dip one finger inside, using my palm to grind against her clit. "We're facing the water, love. Besides, our coats are hiding all the good parts."

"What about cameras?" She begins to ride my hand, seeking the pleasure she so desperately needs.

"I covered it." My tongue trails up the side of her neck, stopping right below her ear. "But that won't stop them from hearing everything I'm about to do to you." Her eyes widen, and I smirk as I slip a second finger inside her. "Don't get shy on me, Princess. Let them know who this pussy belongs to."

She bites down on her bottom lip, fighting a grin. She motions zipping her lips shut, and I laugh.

"Is that a challenge?"

I'm about to pick up the speed when her hand shoots out, wrapping around my wrist.

"If you want them to hear who I belong to, then you need to earn it," she says mischievously, licking her bottom lip.

I pull my hand from her pussy, shoving my fingers between my lips to taste. I groan in appreciation as her arousal coats my tongue. She watches me with rapt fascination. I bend forward, brushing my lips over hers. "And how should I do that?"

I'd do anything this woman asked of me.

I'd scorch the world until there was nothing left if that's what she needed.

But it's the next word out of her luscious lips that takes me by surprise, sending a rush of blood to my hardening cock.

"Kneel."

The command slips between her plush lips like a seductive caress, sounding like something she's wanted to voice her whole goddamn life.

She just needed the right man for the job.

And I'll happily oblige.

My lips press softly against hers as I whisper, "As you wish, Princess."

As I kneel before her, she widens her stance and I settle myself between her legs, tilting my head forward. Her panties are soaked, and one inhale has me feeling like a feral beast.

"You better hold on to my shoulders," I advise. "I'm not stopping until you come on my tongue, screaming my name."

Her fingers grip me the moment my tongue makes contact. A delicious whimper escapes her lips, filling the entire space.

Fuck, her sweet noises send heat coursing through my entire length.

I press my tongue flat, dragging it over her slit before focusing on her clit where I roll my tongue faster and faster. My fingers swirl alongside her entrance, pushing against her walls before plunging deep inside. I thrust them in rhythm with my tongue, worshiping her body the way it was always meant to be.

"Oh, Eli," she moans so beautifully.

Her taste is like my own personal aphrodisiac; I can't get enough of it. Sweet mixed with a bit of sin.

She tastes like mine.

I feast on her like a starving man, lapping up every ounce of her delicious nectar.

"Right there... Yes... Faster..." Her voice drifts off as I give her exactly what she needs for her body to unravel.

Soon, her thighs begin to quiver as her fingers dig into my shoulders. Her head tilts back against the glass as her lips part, her breathing quickening by the second.

She's ready.

"Come for me, Madeleine."

"Eli," she cries out in a scream as her body arches off the glass. Her thighs tighten around my head while I pull every last ounce of the orgasm from her, savoring every drop.

"Oh my God," she breathes, growing slack against the glass. "That was…" A content smile spreads over her face, her eyes appearing heavy. "Wow."

"You're not done yet," I tell her as I stand, towering over her. I reach inside my pocket with one hand while I unzip my pants with the other.

"What do you mean?" Her eyes watch spellbound as I produce my hard cock, fisting it between my hand.

I rip the foil with my teeth and slide the condom over the tip, rolling the latex to the base. I may not particularly enjoy having a barrier between us, but her body, her rules. "You're going to give me one more, love."

Without giving her a chance to protest, I grip her ass, keeping the coat around her as a shield from prying eyes as I lift her in the air. Her legs promptly spread for me, wrapping tightly around my hips just as I plunge inside her wet center.

"Oh, fuck," she moans while adjusting to my size. Her nails drag down the back of my neck with each desperate thrust.

"That's it, love. You can take it." The palm of my hand smacks the glass as my other hand grips her tighter. Her core clenches as she throws her head back, her eyes pinching shut. Glancing down, I become lost in the sight of my cock sliding in and out of her. "Look at how well your pussy takes me."

Her eyes open, her head tilting forward to get a better view. She bites down on her bottom lip before her gaze lands back on me. There are so many thoughts swirling beneath those clear blue irises. Thoughts I wish I could unravel.

Angling my head beside her ear, I press my lips to her hair. "Tell them who you belong to."

Her body shakes, mimicking mine as a tremble like nothing I've ever felt before rushes between us. Tethering us together.

Making us one.

"I'm yours," she lets out a hoarse cry, her chest panting heavily as she goes limp in my arms, her fingers gripping me like I'm her only lifeline in this world.

My own orgasm washes over me like a tidal wave I can't escape. And I drown beneath it willingly, holding Madeleine securely to my chest. Never letting go.

We stand in silence.

Saying nothing.

Yet everything at the same time.

I am hers.

And she is mine.

"Was it true?" she asks.

"Was what true?"

She rolls in her bottom lip, her eyes glossing.

"Hey." I palm her cheek, my thumb gliding over her skin. "Talk to me."

There's so much anguish in her beautiful eyes. So much pain. So much suffering. So much goddamn fear.

And I know why.

But does she truly believe I'll let this wedding happen? That I would ever allow her to be with another man when she is mine and I am hers?

"The story your mom told me." She swallows hard. "I didn't know..." Her voice cracks, her chin wobbling. "I didn't know." She shakes in my arms as tears escape.

"Oh, love." I hold her tightly to my chest. "You've been my princess since the first moment I laid eyes on you. Nothing will ever change that." I press my lips to her head. "It's only ever been you for me. Only you."

CHAPTER TWENTY-ONE

Madeleine

G od, I don't think I've ever been this exhausted in my life.

Every second in England, after spending time with Eli's family, we would sneak off to spend together wrapped around one another, fucking until the sun shone bright, or at least as brightly as it could behind the dreary clouds. We took advantage of the time we had alone together. No prying brothers. No asshole fiancé.

And it was perfect.

But, in a way, it was also torture.

Because these past few days have shown me what I can never truly have.

And now, it's time to face reality.

Reluctantly taking the last step up the stairs, I position my palm against the scanner, waiting for the front door to open.

All I want to do is soak in the tub with a glass of wine and not get out until every inch of my body is pruned.

Eli stands behind me, his presence a constant comfort. Just his scent—cedar with a hint of spice—instantly calms my anxieties, which seem to be mounting exponentially high, especially with the wedding just days away.

The thought of that makes me immediately nauseous.

"Are you okay?" Eli asks, his voice laced with concern.

No.

"Yes."

"You don't seem okay."

I impatiently slap my hand against the scanner again, wanting this conversation to be over. Why the fuck won't this open? "I'm fine," I groan, frustrated. "What is wrong with this stupid thing?" My hand smacks it a few more times.

"Let me help." Eli steps behind me, his chest pressing against my back. My breath catches as his arm reaches around me, his hand covering my own on the scanner. He pushes lightly, his fingers meshing with mine. I swallow, glancing up at him over my shoulder just as a chime alerts me to the door unlocking itself.

"Thank you," I whisper.

"You know," he starts. "We don't have to pretend that—

"We do," I cut him off, my gaze shifting away. "England was amazing. One of the best memories I'll ever have. But I'm home now. And I'm getting married in...just a few days." It's a struggle to get the last part out, the reality of the situation hitting me harder than it should. I mean, I've had a year to prepare for this day, but now that it's almost here, I feel like I'm counting down the hours until my funeral instead of what is supposed to be the happiest day of my life.

However, as I look back up, my eyes meeting Eli's, I know I have to do this. I don't have a choice.

He nods. "Well, why don't we at least order some takeout and find a movie to watch?" I start to shake my head, opening my mouth to protest, knowing I have too much to get done, but he presses a finger to my lips. "I think you could use a night off. You barely got any sleep on the flight home."

I let out a heavy breath, my shoulders falling just a fraction. "You're right. I guess I could use a night to get over the jet lag." I turn away from him and step into my house, the foyer engulfed in darkness. My heels clack on the floor as I walk across the marble. I pause to kick them off before reaching for the light switch. "I could go for some—"

"Surprise!"

Boom! Boom! Boom!

One moment, I'm standing barefoot in my entryway, and the next, I'm slammed against the wall with Eli's body protectively in front of me and...confetti falling all around us.

"What the fuck?" My chest pants as Eli takes a step away, allowing me to see what's behind him.

Scarlett and Alina stand before me with nervous smiles as Cressida stands between them, a massive grin across her face.

"Jesus." I place my palm against my chest and laugh. "What the hell are you doing here?" I look back at my door. "And how did you get in here without my security system notifying me?"

"We're stealing you for your bachelorette party!" Cressida exclaims, tossing more confetti in the air.

A bachelorette party... *Fuck my life.*

Scarlett steps forward, wrapping her arms around me. "Please don't be mad. I know you didn't want to do this," she quickly whispers. "This was all Cressida. We couldn't stop her."

Ahh. I feign a smile as I drop my arms, looking between them. "What a surprise?"

"Well, you wouldn't pick a date, so we picked one for you," Cressida remarks.

"Alex helped us with sneaking in." Alina steps forward, placing a white sash over my head and letting it rest against my shoulder as it crosses over my torso. I look down to see the word bride and cringe internally. *Sorry,* she mouths as she steps back.

For as far as the eye can see, there are hundreds, if not thousands, of balloons, streamers, and bachelorette party signs.

Bach that ass up

Same wiener forever

Big bach energy

Miss to Mrs.

Lead fills my stomach, weighing down every part of me.

"We might have gone a little overboard." Scarlett surveys the space, crinkling her nose.

"No." I shake my head. "No, it's perfect. A nice, quiet girls' night in is exactly what I need."

Alina and Scarlett avoid making eye contact with me.

"What?" I ask, unease building inside me.

"We're going out!" Cressida struts over to me in her short, sparkly gold dress. But right before she reaches me, she turns toward Eli and places a hand on his shoulder. The sight of her touching him makes me see red. "You have confetti on you," she says with a smile as she pulls a piece from his shirt, letting her hand trail down his bicep.

He wipes a hand across his other shoulder as he takes a not-so-subtle step back.

"Well..." Cressida notices his movement and frowns before quickly masking her expression. Her pearly whites shine as she announces, "We're going to Red Eleven, and then you three will spend the night at your family's home in the Hamptons while I have a suite waiting for me at the Reform Club."

I don't even question why she wouldn't just stay at my family's house; honestly, I'd prefer that she doesn't.

I turn toward Scarlett. "Leo's okay with you going to a club?"

"Not exactly." She twirls a strand of hair around her finger, staring off to the side. "Which is why they're all coming with us."

"What?" I rub my ear. "I don't think I heard you correctly because, to me, it sounded like you said my brothers are coming to my bachelorette party?"

Alina pulls a piece of confetti off her glasses, letting it slip between her fingers to the floor. "Please don't be mad. It was the only way they would let us do this for you." She wraps her arms around me and whispers, "We figured if we were forced to do this, at least we could get a night of fun out of it."

I feel the beginnings of a headache forming behind my eyes.

"Oh, please say you'll come." Cressida frowns. "I feel like we haven't had a chance to spend a lot of time together before the wedding, so I thought we could make up for that tonight."

Her eyes begin to glisten, and any chance I had at saying no to this whole thing instantly vanishes.

I smile. "All right. Yeah, sure. This will be great."

Who knows? Maybe tonight will actually be fun.

Doubtful, but here's hoping.

They cheer in unison; only Cressida's is of pure excitement while Alina and Scarlett feign their enthusiasm.

"I'll umm..." Eli clears his throat and hooks a thumb over his shoulder before strolling toward the stairs.

"I'll be right back." I watch as Eli ascends the stairs, running a hand through his hair. "Let me just change real quick."

Cressida's eyes trail after Eli, lost in a trance, but I don't have time to decipher that look as I quickly chase after him. Before he enters his room, I place my hand on his bicep, wrapping my fingers around it to stop him.

"Hey." I step in front of him, his muscles tense beneath my touch as he closes his eyes. "What's wrong?"

"Nothing." He drags a shaking hand down his face and takes a deep breath. His eyes open, but they look lost and vacant, the rich brown hues of his irises appearing dull and muted.

"Talk to me." I try to piece together everything that just happened, wondering what triggered this...

The *booms* from the confetti cannons.

"It was the confetti," I say softly.

He gazes up at the ceiling. "Yeah. Stupid, I know."

"That's not stupid at all."

"For a few seconds, I wasn't here, but..."

"Overseas," I finish for him.

His eyes meet mine. "Sometimes I hear a loud noise, and I'm fine. Other times, I'm not. It's like it triggers a flashback that I have no control over. I can't make it stop."

I nod, taking a step closer. "I can't even imagine how tough that is on you."

"I'm fine," he replies quickly. Too quickly.

And my heart hurts for him. For all of the invisible pain he never allows anyone to see.

"Eli." I place my hand on his chest, looking up at him. "You're strong, and you're brave. Having PTSD doesn't change that one bit. It doesn't change the way I look at you. And it's okay to not always be okay."

He sighs. "I know. Or at least I'm trying to. But it's taking longer than I thought to feel any semblance of normalcy."

As if it were the most natural thing in the world for me to do, I wrap my arms around his waist, resting my head against his chest. "Why don't you stay home tonight? One of us should get some of that rest we were talking about earlier."

He slides two fingers under my chin, lifting my face until our eyes connect. "If you think you're going into the city without me, you clearly don't know me at all." He runs his hand over my hair, twirling the ends. "Where you go, I go, Princess. Don't ever forget that."

———

"My feet are killing me," Alina complains as she limps beside me, her poor feet suffering in her high heels after nearly two hours on the dance floor.

Red Eleven is a vibrant hotspot filled with partygoers, dancers, socialites, influencers, and everyone in between who come to see and be seen. It offers some of the most expensive alcohol available, including Ley .925 tequila, Henri IV Dudognon Héritage Cognac, and Macallan Exceptional Single Cask. It's a venue where individuals willingly pay more than the average mortgage for a membership in the VIP lounge. This establishment caters not only to the mega-wealthy but also to royalty and members of discreet organizations who prefer to remain anonymous.

And it just so happens to be one of my family's establishments. Specifically, one that generates a substantial amount of revenue every year, helping to finance some of my family's less scrupulous ventures. The ones I withhold from the books.

Scarlett pushes her hair back, her face flushed as she fans herself. "I think it's time for a break. How about we sit at the bar and order some drinks?"

"Lead the way," I tell her, adjusting the top of my strapless dress.

After finding free seats at the bar, the bartender quickly takes our order and, only a moment later, has four pink tropical-looking drinks placed before us.

Raising my drink in the air, I say, "Cheers to having the best friends I could ever ask for." I look over at Cressida, feeling slightly bad for how I've behaved toward her when she's only tried to welcome me into her horrible family, unbeknownst to her. "And here's to having a future sister."

Cressida's eyes water as she raises her glass. "To finally having a sister."

Scarlett wraps an arm around my shoulder and kisses my cheek. "To best friends."

"Best friends," Alina adds.

We all clink our glasses together, taking hearty sips. I twirl my straw through the pink slush and say, "Is it just me, or does anyone else feel their eyes on us?"

Alina peeks over her shoulder. "That's because five sets of eyes *are* on us." She chuckles. "Alex looks ready to pull out a bottle of disinfectant any second, and Mauro looks...uncomfortable." Her lips curve downward as her gaze focuses on him.

"At least they're giving us some space," Scarlett offers. "Leo promised me they wouldn't bother us tonight and that we'd hardly notice them."

I arch a brow. How can I not notice them?

Five of the most ruthless men I know are all sitting at a table with their eyes on us, appearing ready for an imminent attack.

"It's kind of hard to miss them." I give a slight shrug. "Nothing like having your big brothers and your bodyguard at your bachelorette party." I feign a smile, taking another sip.

"Eli looks so good." Cressida rests her chin on her hand as she sips her drink and gazes dreamily at him.

My knuckles tighten around my glass as I take a sip of my drink, pretending not to care.

She shakes her head and presses her fingers to her temple. "This drink is a little stronger than I'm used to." She laughs, pushing it away, and then looks at me. "So, do you and Alastor have any plans for the honeymoon?"

I nearly choke on my drink at the thought. The idea of a honeymoon with Alastor is ridiculous, especially since I would knee him in the balls if he even considered making a move on me.

That's not part of our agreement.

And never will be.

I've already given enough of myself as it is.

"You guys should visit our estate in Russia!" Cressida exclaims. "It's so beautiful in the winter with all the snow."

"Your family has a home in Russia?" Alina asks, surprised.

"Yes. Although the word *home* is putting it mildly. I think it was a former palace." She gives a slight shrug. "Alastor and Father are there all the time for business, so it made sense to have a place over there."

"What kind of business?" Scarlett asks.

Cressida pulls her drink back toward her and takes another sip. "I'm not sure of the logistics, but they work closely with my cousins, the Vasilievs."

"The Vasilievs?" Scarlett's bright blue eyes widen, appearing uneasy.

My stomach recoils as I take in Scarlett's pale complexion.

I never wanted her to know this bit of public information.

Everyone in our dark corner of the world is well aware of familial connections and long-standing alliances. Unfortunately for me, my future husband is related to one of the most powerful families in the world.

Second only to mine, of course.

"Yes!" She smiles. "Do you know them?"

Scarlett's lips part, but I speak for her. "We've had dealings with them in the past." Aka, Leo shot and killed the head of the family a couple of months ago after discovering his involvement in Scarlett's kidnapping. I wave a dismissive hand in the air. "Anyway, I don't think we'll have time for a honeymoon, which is fine. I'll be so busy with moving overseas, and he'll be busy with work."

Scarlett's eyes soften, her lips turning down. "I can't believe you're leaving the Alarie Estate. It won't feel the same without you."

I roll in my bottom lip, fighting back tears.

I will not cry.

I will not cry.

I will not cry.

"I know," I manage to get out. "But it'll be fine. I'll visit all the time."

Lie.

Alina glances over her shoulder and then looks back at me. "You know, Eli hasn't been able to take his eyes off of you all night."

I scoff. "It's literally his job."

Scarlett lifts her shoulder. "I don't know. He never looked at me that way when he was my bodyguard."

"That's because Leo would have severed his dick and made him choke on it if he did."

The three of us laugh.

"Madeleine," Cressida utters, her brows drawn together as she glares down at the countertop. "Is there something going on between you and Eli?" She looks up, her eyes boring into mine. "Alastor is my brother, and I won't—"

"What? No." I anxiously run my fingers through my hair. *Shit.* "Alina and Scarlett were just kidding. They didn't mean—"

"Hey, beautiful."

I twist to my side, finding a man standing a little too close for comfort. His green eyes roam over my body, not concealing his intentions, while his hand lands on my back, his thumb stroking my bare skin.

Oh, this should be good.

I smile and flutter my eyelashes. "You have five seconds."

He chuckles. "Five seconds until what?"

"Now, two."

His brows furrow in confusion. "Until—*Ahhhhh!*"

"Until I break your arm for touching what isn't yours!"

The man howls in pain as Eli suddenly pins him to the bar top and forcefully twists his arm behind his back.

"Who the fuck do you think you are putting your hands on her?" Eli roars, his body lined with tension.

"I wasn't... I didn't... *Ahhh!* I was just saying...hi!" The man screams out in agony as Eli bends his arm harder.

"Do you have any idea who the fuck she is?"

The man looks at me as if expecting me to give him the magical answer.

"Madeleine fucking Alarie," Eli answers roughly. "And you will never look at her, think about her, or even breathe the same goddamn air as her again because you are unworthy of such a thing." He releases the man's arm and yanks him by the back of his shirt, pushing him into the crowd. "Get the fuck out of here! And if I ever see you near her again, then a broken arm will be the least of your problems."

Eli's chest heaves with intensity, and his shoulder muscles tighten as he runs a hand through his hair. His dark eyes catch mine as he turns, taking in every part of me to ensure I'm okay.

Everyone around us fades away as he gently grips my chin, tilting my face upward toward his. I swallow hard as his lips part, every fiber of my being wishing I could melt into his embrace.

"Are you okay, Princess?"

I blink a few times before I register what he just asked. Quickly, I nod. "Y-yes," comes out of my throat in just barely a whisper. "You didn't need to—"

"I did." He brushes a tendril of hair out of my face. "I will always protect you."

My heart hammers beneath my chest as I lift on my tiptoes, eager for his taste, when a throat clears behind Eli, bursting our private bubble.

With a little too much force, I extract myself out of Eli's hold, backing against a bar stool. Disappointment flashes across Eli's eyes as his shoulders drop, his body turning away from mine. And just as he moves, I spot my four brothers watching our exchange, their expressions filled with so much wrath as they shift their gaze between me and Eli.

The tension in the air is thick, and none of us say a word. Cressida stands off to the side, arms crossed and glaring at me with accusations in her eyes.

Fuck. Fuck. Fuck.

A crowd begins to gather around us, fascinated by the current scandal unfolding.

Thank God this is an Alarie establishment.

"A round of drinks on the house," Vin announces with a smile to the crowd, who cheer at this bit of news and then quickly return their attention elsewhere, forgetting about what they just witnessed.

My brothers approach slowly like lions preparing to attack. But I'm not ready for them to ruin this for me.

Not yet.

Not when I only have a few days left of freedom.

"Well." I push myself away from the bar, adjusting my dress. "It's been fun, but I think I'm ready to call it a night." I quickly step away from everyone, knowing Eli will follow close behind.

I turn to Scarlett and Alina, who stare at the two of us, unsure of what to say or do to defuse the situation. "I'll see you guys later. Thanks for"—I gesture around—"this." I turn to say something to Cressida but find she's already gone.

Dread pools in my stomach, knowing she'll most likely go directly to Alastor about what she saw.

Marching toward the exit, I don't look back.

I'll deal with my brothers tomorrow.

But not tonight.

Upon arriving at my family's home in the Hamptons, I head straight to my room, walk over to the balcony doors, and gaze out at the ocean illuminated by the full moon.

I hear Eli enter my room and softly close the door behind him.

"I just wanted a quiet night with you," I say, wrapping my arms around myself.

"I know." His arms enclose me, tugging me against his chest. His lips glide across the side of my neck, his mouth peppering my skin with soft kisses. "There's a warm bath waiting for you with a glass of your favorite wine sitting on the ledge."

"What?" I pull back to look at him.

His lips press softly against mine in a tender kiss, one currently making me melt into his arms.

He pulls away, ghosting his lips over mine. "I called ahead and asked one of the butlers to prepare it."

My eyes lock with his, my breath catching in my throat.

How is it that he always seems to know what I need?

Tears build behind my eyes, but I don't let them fall.

"My brothers know," I whisper.

He nods and looks straight ahead out the window. "I'll deal with them when we get back to the estate tomorrow."

"They won't be happy."

He grins, pulling me closer to him until my head rests on his chest. "Are you worried about me, Princess?"

Yes.

"No. I would just hate to have to go through the trouble of finding a new bodyguard."

CHAPTER TWENTY-TWO

Eli

"You lied to me," Vin states as I enter his office, his tone carrying a heavy undercurrent of fury. "To us." He gestures toward his brothers, who look at me like wolves eyeing their prey. "I asked you if anything happened between you and Madeleine, and you told me, and I quote, 'No, nothing happened between us.'" He steeples his fingers before him. "Were those not your exact words?"

I let out a heavy sigh and take another step into the room, bracing myself for what's coming. "Let me explain—"

In one swift moment, Vin snaps his fingers, and Mauro has me pinned to the wall in a bone-crushing grip, his fingers digging into my throat.

If these men were anyone else, I would give them hell and fight back.

But I know I deserve this.

Because they're my brothers.

And I let them down.

So, I don't struggle beneath Mauro's hold.

I simply comply.

"So, it is true." The disappointment in Leo's voice slices through my chest. As my best friend, he's probably taking this the hardest, especially since he welcomed me into his family all those years ago. But now, he just looks ready to cause bloodshed. "You're fucking our sister?"

I quickly shake my head, and Mauro loosens his grip.

"So, you aren't fucking?" Alex questions, arching a brow as he leans forward in his seat, his jacket parting to reveal the gun tucked inside.

My eyes jump between each of them. "I promise it's not what you think."

"Enlighten us then." Vin leans back in his seat, appearing calm when I know he's far from it. In the face of danger, Madeleine has always been his top priority. And I expect no man will ever be good enough for her in his eyes—even me.

"Madeleine and I..." What should I say? Do I tell them everything? Do I start from the beginning? *No.* What's happened between us over the years isn't any of their goddamn business, but they at least deserve to know the truth behind our actions.

"You what?" Leo roars, losing all his patience.

Fuck it. "I love her!"

If someone dropped a bullet in this room right now, the sound would echo throughout the space tenfold.

Mauro's hands fall away from my neck as he takes a step back, his eyes fixed on my face.

After years spent learning how to interpret an enemy's tell, whether through facial changes, body language, eye contact, tone of voice, and so on, I consider myself an expert at reading faces. But at this very moment, I start questioning everything I thought I knew, as the four of them appear more stone-faced than an actual rock. And I'm not sure whether I should chance it and bolt from the room or stand here and await my punishment.

Clearing my throat, I say, "I know this probably comes as a shock to—"

"Pay up, brothers." My eyes dart to Vin, who holds his hand out with the palm facing up, his fingers gesturing for something.

Leo mirrors his actions. "That's five hundred for each of us."

Mauro lets out a deep grunt as he pulls out his wallet from his back pocket, counting out a stack of bills.

"Sorry, big guy." Vin displays a mock frown as Mauro places the money in his hand. "I know you hate to lose."

Alex sighs, slapping money onto Vin's hand and then Leo's. "I really hate when you two are right. It makes me question my intelligence."

I blink a few times, processing their reaction. Or, I guess I should say, lack of a reaction. "Wait a damn minute." The four of them look at me, cracking a hint of a smile on their smug faces. I rest my hands on my hips. "You knew? And you...you bet on this?"

Leo grips my shoulder. "We've known all along. We were just waiting for you to admit it to us." He laughs, adding, "Are you questioning our intellect?" He nods toward Alex and continues, "This one caught you sneaking onto our property on our surveillance system at least ten times over the years."

Alex adjusts his glasses. "Guess we never said anything because there's no one more worthy of our sister than you."

I face Vin. "You threatened my life when we arrived at the Vasiliev tower." I arch a brow, waiting for his response.

"Merely testing you." He gives a slight shrug. "It was fun watching you squirm."

"I didn't squirm," I murmur, rolling my eyes.

Leo gives me an *Oh, yes, you did face.*

"Fine!" I raise my hands to the ceiling, exasperated. "I squirmed. But can you blame me? I was fucking outnumbered in a confined space with nowhere to go." I rest my hands on my hips, glaring at each of them. "If I had known you wankers were betting on my love life, then I never would have admitted to this."

Vin laughs, shaking his head. "Sooner or later, everything reveals itself. It always does." His smile falls as he rubs his hand over his jaw. "The moment I told her you were missing in action, I witnessed my sister on the verge of breaking. I witnessed…her heart splitting down the middle, and that is not a sight I ever want to see again. It was the only confirmation I needed to know what was going on between you two." He clears his throat, slightly shaking his head as he pulls his gun out of his holster and uses a piece of cloth to polish the sides. "But back to the bigger problem at hand. It's time to put an end to this wedding tonight." He glances over his shoulder. "Madeleine has until"—he points his finger at the old gold clock—"midnight to make this decision for herself, but not a minute longer."

"Understood." I squeeze the back of my neck. "And if she doesn't?"

"Then we handle the issue ourselves," he replies coolly. "No more games." He places his gun on the desk in front of him and sits up straight, gliding the palm of his hand across his jawline. "After midnight, bring Madeleine to me. It's my fault for allowing this to go on for so long. I need to speak to her alone." He sighs. "Sometimes I forget how similar we are, which is why it finally occurred to me that she's doing all of this to protect someone else, not herself. It was never about her." He offers a sad smile. "Madeleine has a heart of gold. Unfortunately, the world tends to judge her harshly because she's a strong woman, but we all know who she truly is. I'm just disappointed in myself for not realizing it sooner."

My phone vibrates in my pocket, and I retrieve it to see Alastor's name on the screen. I sigh. "This should be good." Placing the call on speaker, I say, "What the hell do you want?"

"If I find out you had anything to do with Tony's death, I'm going to kill you."

Ha! I'd like to see him try.

"Tony?" I hum. "The name isn't ringing a bell."

"You know exactly who the fuck he is! He was my right-hand man for ten years!"

"Ah, that Tony. I heard it was a suicide." I *tsk*. "What a shame. My condolences, of course."

"You think you can get away with it? First, you steal my car and don't even try to fucking deny it, and now this?" he seethes, his fury practically palpable through the phone. "You have no idea what game you're playing here!"

Vin motions for me to move the phone closer to him, and I do. "Then why don't you explain it to us better so we know the rules," Vin states, his deep voice laced with power.

"Who the hell is this?"

"Vincenzo Alarie." Vin cracks his neck, his eyes darkening as he rubs his temple. "To be quite blunt, Alastor, I don't like you. Not even a little bit. And I don't like your parents. And I especially don't like your fucking cousins. In fact, I've had enough of all of you. You're all giving me a colossal motherfucking headache. So, I advise you to tread very carefully. Because when I find out what game you're playing with my sister, I will be sure that you lose and she wins. Because Alaries always win."

He motions for me to end the call, which I do before giving Alastor a chance to counter.

Vin sighs as he pours himself a glass of whiskey and takes a long sip before saying, "I can't wait for that prick to die."

A few minutes later, as I walk out Vin's front door, I'm surprised to find Reginald waiting outside.

"Hey, Reg, you drive for Vin, too?" I ask, heading toward my car.

He shakes his head, his brows furrowing as he peers up at me. "No. I actually came here to see you." His words stop me in my tracks as he steps closer, rubbing his salt-and-pepper scruff. "With Miss Alarie's wedding occurring in only a matter of days, I needed to talk to you."

I cross my arms over my chest and raise a brow. "I'm listening."

He removes his hat and drags a hand over his face. I notice dark circles under his eyes, and his expression looks downcast. "I've been torn about whether to say something or not since it's not my place, and I shouldn't interfere, but..." He lets out a heavy breath. "Madeleine has always been like a daughter to me." The corners of his lips slightly tug up. "She's good to me and my family. When she found out my wife was sick last year, she stopped everything she was doing to ensure my wife was seen by the best doctors in the world, receiving the best treatments available. Without her, I don't know if my wife would even be here right now." He swallows, his eyes glistening. "She's always looked out for me, which is why I've come to you. I can't let this wedding happen." He stares off to the side. "She asked me not to tell anyone, and I've always respected her wishes, but I can't hold my tongue anymore. Not when it's in regards to her safety."

"Hold your tongue about what?"

"Almost a year ago, on New Year's Day, she needed a ride into the city. Said it was urgent. I didn't think anything of it until she told me where she needed to go."

"Where?" I ask, already knowing damn well where.

"Manacorda Enterprises," he answers solemnly. "When we got there, she was a woman on a mission. Her head held high, her confidence soaring. But an hour later, when she left..." He shakes his head. "I had never seen her so downcast before. She looked like...well, to be frank, she looked like a woman who—"

"Just signed her life away," I finish for him, unease sweeping over me.

"Well, yes." He nods, deep in thought. "Before that day, she had never had any meetups with Alastor. And I would know, seeing that I'm her driver and all."

I nod, dragging my fingers through my hair. "Thank you for—"

"There's more."

I wait for him to continue.

He squeezes the back of his neck, seeming distressed. "On the way home, something happened."

"What?"

"She was in pain. A lot of pain. She asked me to drive her to the nearest hospital, and I did without question."

"Why didn't she call for the family doctor?"

"She didn't want anyone knowing," he answers. "She was released the next day, and she asked me to promise not to say anything to her brothers or mother. I promised her I wouldn't, but...I'm worried for her. I just can't shake the feeling that it's all connected."

My stomach twists into thousands of knots.

This isn't fucking good.

"Do you know what she was there for?"

"No." He shakes his head. "I never asked. And she never said."

I nod. "Is that everything?" I ask, praying there's nothing else that will send me over the edge.

"Yes." He clasps his hands behind his back. "That's everything."

"Thank you, Reginald." I grasp his shoulder. "We won't let this wedding happen."

He lets out a deep breath. "That's a relief. Truly. I'm on my way over there now. She would like to head to the casino."

Interesting. Only a couple of days before her wedding, and she wants to work?

"I'll meet you there." I step away, my mind surging into overdrive as I try to connect all the bloody pieces. "Everything ends tonight. You have my word." Reginald appears relieved as I turn and head for my car.

As I accelerate down the driveway, relief coasts over me, knowing that we're finally going to put an end to all of this tonight.

Once and for all.

July 28th

Princess,

I've rewritten this letter at least a dozen times, unsure of how to say what I need to. But I've decided that I should just come out with it because I can't hold it in any longer.

There was an accident in the field today. One of my mates wasn't paying attention, and he got in the line of fire. In just a single second, he was gone. Just like that. You could say it put the fear of God in me, but it also reminded me that tomorrow is not promised.

I've wanted to say these words to you in person for as long as I can remember, but I just can't wait another goddamn minute.

I love you, Madeleine. I'm pretty sure I've loved you since the first moment I laid eyes on you, and I know I will spend the rest of my life hopelessly in love with you.

I'll see soon, love.

Yours,
Eli

CHAPTER TWENTY-THREE

Madeleine

Numbers stare back at me from my laptop screen as I try to make sense of this quarter's profits from the casino.

"It says we're almost two million short from what was predicted, but how?" I ask aloud, tapping the tip of my pen against my chin in frustration.

It's not like me to make such a massive error.

But maybe with the stress of my upcoming wedding, I let things slip by unnoticed. Or maybe I just wasn't on my A-game.

Maybe if you had spent more time in your casino and less time fucking your bodyguard, you wouldn't be having this issue...

I groan in frustration, slamming my laptop closed. I need to go to the casino and have a word with Angelo, our manager. If anyone knows what's going on, it would be him. But he sees the numbers, too, so why hasn't he called to inform me of this situation?

I quickly send Reginald a text to let him know my schedule for today before sliding my phone into my back pocket. As I walk up the stairs, I take the printed reports with me to skim through them.

"Eli," I call out as I approach his doorway. "I need to go to the casino." There's no answer. "Eli?" I knock and wait for a response, but there's no sound or movement on the other side of the door. Hesitantly, I push it open and step inside. I'm immediately hit with the familiar smell of cedar and spice. A scent that wraps around every part of my soul, tantalizing my senses.

"Eli? Are you—" *Right.* I forgot he went to talk with my brothers. I rub my temple as stress builds behind my eyes.

It's not as if he's going to confess to them that he loves me or something... *Right?* No. No. Definitely not. I assume he's just going to explain that it was all one big misunderstanding and that he was only being slightly overprotective because another man had put his hands on me.

And I'm certain they aren't going to kill him.

Well, *almost* certain.

Curiosity piques my interest, and I step closer to the bed, running my fingers across the smooth comforter that's perfectly fitted to the mattress. But, of course, it is.

Eli would never leave his bed unmade.

I'm sure that's a bit of the military life that will forever be instilled into him.

I stop in front of the nightstand, drop my reports, and pick up the book that lies on top of it. I flip through the worn pages, noticing words like *life after the military, relearning civilian life,* and *PTSD.*

My chest constricts, and I absent-mindedly rub a hand over my sternum. The unknown of what he's had to face over all these years makes my heart feel too heavy.

And just thinking about the burns on his back makes me see red. It fills my veins with a need for violence and vengeance. It makes me want to find the men who tortured him and kill them all with my bare hands. I want to make them suffer. I want them to feel every ounce of pain that Eli had to endure. I want to—

I close my eyes and take a deep breath as I place the book down.

Eli will get his revenge.

Maybe not today or tomorrow.

But he will. I can feel it.

Opening my eyes, I look down at the drawer and grin as I begin to open it. "What secret sex toys are you hiding in—?" My words die on the tip of my tongue as the solo object that sits before me causes my heart to race faster than it should.

I pick up the black square box, holding it protectively in my hand as if it might jump and make a break for it.

This can't be what I think it is...right?

I swallow hard as my fingers tuck between the opening and lift the cover to reveal...

My heart stops beating.

Everything around me blurs as I stare at an engagement ring.

A beautiful, delicate oval ring with a thin band covered in evenly spaced-out diamonds.

"It's stunning," I whisper in awe, envisioning this ring on my finger instead of the ghastly one currently residing in its place.

And then it hits me...

This ring is for someone.

Someone who *isn't* me.

Swiftly, I drop the ring back in the drawer and slam it shut, my chest heaving as if I had just run a full-on marathon.

My knees shake, and a tremor travels through me, forcing me to sit on the side of the bed before I collapse to the floor.

As much as I would like to convince myself Eli got this for me, there's just no way that he did. It's not possible, and it wouldn't make any sense. He wouldn't get me an engagement ring, not when he knew I was engaged to someone else.

My heart feels as if it's cracking, splitting forcefully in two.

He loves someone else.

I lie back on the bed, my palms pressing against my chest. My heart is beating so loudly that it drowns out everything else around me. I turn to my side, burying my face into his pillow. His familiar scent only makes my eyes blur with an onslaught of tears as my hand rubs over the ache in the center of my chest.

What did I expect?

For him to remain single for the rest of his life while I marry Alastor? *Yes,* I admit to myself selfishly.

I grip the pillow, curling into a fetal position.

But if he's in love with someone else, why would he be sleeping with me? Was everything he said to me a bunch of lies to get what he wanted—revenge for me being engaged to another man? Why would he play with my heart and make me think there was ever a chance for us when there never was?

Because you've been doing the same thing to him.

"But I didn't mean to," I breathe out through tears, fighting back a sob that takes over my whole body from my head to my toes.

Anger begins to swirl with the sadness inside me, creating a ball of anxiety I can't control.

How could he do this to me?

I signed over my life for his, even after that damn letter he sent me, the one I've been purposely trying so hard to forget about these past few weeks, the one with four words that were burned into my soul, and he does—

He doesn't know what you did to save him.

"He doesn't know, and he can never know," I whisper, wiping away the tears that crawl down my cheeks.

I hide my face in my hands, feeling the weight of the world on my shoulders becoming unbearable.

The only person I have a right to be mad at is myself.

But I wouldn't change anything I did.

In fact, I'd do it all over again if it meant he gets to spend the rest of his life living while I spend the rest of mine surviving.

Because that's what you do when you love someone: you sign your life over to the devil to save them from hell.

September 18th

Dear Eli,

I miss you.
I need you.
I love you.

Come home to me and remind me who I
belong to.

Forever yours,
Madeleine

CHAPTER TWENTY-FOUR

Eli

"**W**e need to go to the casino."

That's the greeting I receive as I enter Madeleine's house. Cold and void of any emotion. Her eyes are darker than I'm used to as they stare straight ahead. Her slender arms are wrapped around her waist as if shielding herself from something or someone. Her right foot taps anxiously in her fuck-me heels.

What the fuck happened since I left her two hours ago?

As I walked through the front door, I intended to confront her with the information Reginald had just presented to me before giving her until the clock struck midnight and letting her know that Vin would like to speak with her.

However, the anguish in her blue eyes forces me to reconsider my approach, at least for the time being.

"Of course." I look down at my watch, noting seven hours until midnight. Plenty of time left for her to call off the wedding and tell me what the hell has been going on. "Something wrong?"

"It feels like something always is," she says in a cross tone.

She opens the closet door and pulls out her black peacoat, aggressively tying a knot around her midsection, I might add, before stepping past me and toward the waiting car with Reginald standing outside.

After sliding onto the seat beside her, she holds out her phone, taps a few times on the screen, and then a ring fills the space.

"What's wrong?" Alex asks.

"Jeez, can't a sister just call her brother to say hello?"

"Is that what you called for?"

"Not entirely…"

"Out with it then. I'm in the middle of something pretty important."

She tilts her head back, staring at the ceiling. "Can you do some digging for me?"

"Digging on what?"

"I want to see a record of every single transaction in and out of the casino, and I also want all of Angelo's bank records." She sighs. "It may be nothing, but my gut is telling me it's something."

"Angelo? Why? Is he stealing?" he asks with anger in his voice. "If he is, just tell me, and I'll—"

"He's not," she rushes out. "Or at least, it's not confirmed." She pinches the bridge of her nose. "The numbers I have projected for this quarter seem to be off. I've triple-checked them, but they're not equating anywhere close to the profit I had anticipated, even with a dip during the holidays. Could you please just send me that information? I'm heading to the casino now."

"Madeleine, if there's an issue, you should let me or Vin or—"

"I don't need you guys to fix this!" she states firmly. After closing her eyes and taking a deep breath, she adds, "I can take care of the problem myself. Now, can you provide me with those records or not?"

There's a moment of silence before Alex responds. "Fine." There's typing in the background. "I'll take a peek now and send you anything I can find. Just call me if you need me."

"Thank you." She ends the call and presses her fingers into her temple, rubbing small circles.

My hand reaches out, gently gripping her chin and turning her face toward me. "When are you going to let someone help you? You don't need to take care of everything yourself. Not when we're here for you."

For a brief moment, her glossy eyes are locked with mine, but then, with a single blink, her expression becomes unfazed and unaffected by my words. She shifts in her seat, pulling away from my grip. "I don't need anyone's help. Least of all yours."

The lashing of her words whips at me with anger, catching me by surprise. I rub my palm across my sternum, trying to soothe the sudden ache blooming across my chest as I face forward, giving her space.

The remainder of the drive passes by in silence until the car comes to a stop. She opens the door before Reginald even has a chance to assist her and quickly strides toward the entrance, her shoulders straight, her chin held high, but I can't help but notice a slight tremor in each step she takes.

"Miss Alarie, what an unexpected pleasure," Angelo remarks as he enters her office on the top floor of the casino. A room surrounded by privacy glass that allows anyone inside it to observe the floors below while allowing no one the privilege to see inside.

"Please take a seat." She gestures to the chair before her desk and leans forward, her elbows bracing the hard surface.

Angelo looks between me and her before taking a seat and tugging on the collar of his shirt like a kid who just got caught with his hand in the cookie jar.

Only the cookie jar, in this case, is a shit ton of money that's missing from the Alaries' bank accounts.

Madeleine displays one of her infamous deadly smiles. The one that says, "You're fucked," and not in a good way.

"What can I help you with?" he asks as a bead of sweat rolls down his temple, which he quickly wipes away.

"How much did you take?" she asks, cutting straight to the point of this meeting.

"Take?" His eyes widen as he swallows, shaking his head. "I don't believe I know what you're referring to."

She leans back, clasping her hands before her. "Are you sure about that?"

"Perhaps if you told me more specifically what you're looking for, I'd be more helpful to you."

A moment of silence passes as she stares down the man. "Fine. Since you want to play games, I'll play one with you. How about a riddle?" Her lips curve into a dangerous smile as she takes pleasure in seeing Angelo squirm in his seat. And I can't deny that I'm pretty fucking turned on watching her revel in her throne. "Who has the brain of a rat, the personality of a snake, and has stolen close to two million dollars from my family's business?"

"I...I don't know." He shakes his head adamantly. "I've never stolen a penny from your family."

I'll give it to the man; he won't back down without a fight.

And I'm guessing from the look on Madeleine's face that that is exactly what he is going to get.

Her hands slam down on the desk, her eyes narrowing on him as she leans forward. "You would dare to lie to me?"

"I would never," he rushes out, appalled.

"Eli." She jerks her chin toward him.

"You got it," I respond, stepping toward Angelo.

The man cowers in his seat, waving his hands before him. "Wait! Wait, this is just a misunderstanding!"

I yank the man from his seat and force him against the glass wall, holding him up by his neck. "Speak!"

"I didn't take any money!" he gasps, his cheeks turning crimson as he struggles for breath.

Madeleine swivels in her chair, scrolling through her phone. "I thought you might say that. That's why I asked Alex to look into you."

His eyes nearly bulge out of their sockets as he realizes how fucked he is.

There's almost nothing Alex can't uncover.

"It seems on November first, you had a seven-hundred-and-fifty-thousand-dollar transaction sent to an anonymous account in the Cayman Islands directly from the casino funds." She looks up at the man. "Probably assumed we'd be a little too busy that day to notice, huh?"

November first.

The day after, the Alaries almost lost everything to a couple of psychopaths.

The day after, I jumped in front of Madeleine, taking a bullet for her.

My grip tightens around the man's thick neck.

"You son of a bitch," I growl, my face only inches from his.

"Then, on November twenty-fourth, the day the whole family celebrated Leo and Scarlett's engagement, there was, conveniently, another transaction wired to the same account—this time for eight hundred and fifty thousand dollars." She scrolls through her phone. "There were several smaller transactions after that, and oh look." She turns her phone to face him. "My brother was even nice enough to send me a video from our security cameras showing you stealing portions of players' winnings under the table in cold hard cash. You probably thought we wouldn't be able to trace that money, right?"

The man's face pales.

"All together, I'd say that equals the two million I've been searching for." She *tsks*. "This amount is just a small fraction of the hundreds of millions this casino generates yearly. I assume that's why you thought no one would notice and that you could get away with it. But here we are." Madeleine's chair stops moving as she leans forward, pressing a finger to her lip, appearing deep in thought. "Now, what to do?"

"I can... I can give it back!" He struggles in my grip. "I just need some time."

"And how do you plan on giving it back when you've spent it all on prostitutes and cocaine?"

"But...how? You couldn't possibly know—"

She abruptly stands, placing the palms of her hands on her desk. "I am an Alarie. We know everything. Because sooner or later, we always find out. And you are just a worthless piece of scum at the bottom of a feeding pond about to discover what happens when you fuck with my family."

The man appears aghast, his face turning redder by the second. "You think you're going to teach me a lesson? You?" A vein on the edge of his temple bulges as he squirms relentlessly beneath my hold. "You are nothing but a stupid woman who should be spending her days where she's useful... like in the kitchen. It took you this long to even realize money was missing because you were probably too busy getting your cunt fucked by your bodyguard over here, you miserable bitch!"

All I see is red as I begin to strangle the life from Angelo, enjoying the look of defeat crossing his eyes.

"You watch your fucking mouth!" I shout. "If you ever say a word about her or dare to look in her direction, I will personally end you. Piece by fucking piece. Until you're nothing but a corpse six feet beneath the ground! Do you understand me?"

Boom!

CHAPTER TWENTY-FIVE

Madeleine

I *hate men.*

Lowering my gun to my side, I watch as the misogynistic asshole holds his groin, screaming profanities that would make a sailor blush.

"You shot my dick!" he shouts as blood soaks through the front of his pants.

I smirk. "You seem to be under the impression that since I don't have a cock swinging between my legs, I should be in a kitchen and not here, behind my desk." I drop my gun in the drawer and place my palms on the smooth wood surface, straightening my spine. "But let me be clear about two things. First, the only thing you will ever find me doing in a kitchen is looking for a takeout menu. Second, you messed with the wrong Alarie."

Eli drops the man from his hold, letting him fall to the floor as he turns to face me. His eyes darken, grazing over every square inch of my body, inspecting me for any injuries. He approaches, not stopping until he's standing directly beside me, his rough hand gently cupping my cheek.

"You did good, Princess."

Okay, maybe I was wrong.

Maybe there's one man I don't hate.

Even if I should.

The office door swings open, and two guards step inside, guns drawn, their eyes scanning the room before settling on Angelo.

I stand tall, smoothing out my skirt. "Take him to our warehouse. My brothers can deal with him later."

They both nod and quickly escort Angelo out of the room, shutting the door behind them.

Eli steps away from me, positioning himself in front of the door where his hand lifts to turn the lock into place.

My heart thumps wildly beneath my chest as he turns to face me, licking his lips.

"You always keep a gun on you?" he asks, tilting his head to the side.

I nod. "I can't take any chances," I say in a ragged breath.

As he steps toward me, I move back until I'm directly against the glass wall. His hand braces the wall beside my head while his other hand grips my chin, his thumb tracing my bottom lip.

He lowers his head to mine, skimming his lips against my ear. "I'd never let anything happen to you. You know that, right?"

I swallow hard, my breath catching in my throat as his hand glides down my neck. "Like I said, can't take any chances."

His lips press slowly and softly against my cheek, sliding down to my collarbone. "Someday, you're going to realize that you don't have to do all of this alone." He scrapes his teeth up the column of my neck and then nips my earlobe. "But for now." He hovers his lips right over mine. "I'm going to fuck you against this glass wall until you're screaming my name while coming around my cock."

His lips fuse to mine, devouring me whole.

Body and soul.

As his tongue snakes between my lips, finding mine, I try to remind myself that I shouldn't be doing this. That only a few hours ago, I found a beautiful engagement ring in his nightstand meant for another woman.

Not to mention the letter... The goddamn letter that has tormented me for over a year.

But with his scent overwhelming my senses and his touch electrifying every nerve ending in my body, I turn into a puddle of need in his arms as every reason why I shouldn't be doing this evaporates into thin air.

Fuck it. I deserve one more orgasm before my wedding. But that's it. This is the last one for God knows how long.

I guess I better make it count.

I grasp his shirt, pulling him right up against me. With a carnal need, I tug the fabric up his chest as he reaches behind him to pull the collar up and over his head.

I run my hands down his contoured chest and chiseled abs, entranced by every muscle groove forged by hard work, as I try to memorize the feel of him beneath my touch.

Eli's fingers tug at the fabric of my white blouse until they reach the hem. With a swift motion, he removes it from my body and tosses it onto the floor beside us. His fingers wrap around my back, unfastening my bra and letting it fall from my shoulders. As his lips brush against my neck, he quickly unzips my skirt and then kneels before me, igniting a fire deep within me.

He yanks my black leather skirt down to my ankles and then, just as quickly, slips his thumbs under the lace fabric of my thong, sliding it painfully slowly down my thighs and letting it drop to my ankles. Placing my hands on his shoulders, I step out of my heels and then my clothes, standing naked in front of him.

He looks up at me, a smirk growing on his face. "Are you wet for me, Princess?"

I bite my bottom lip, spreading my legs. "You should probably check."

Eli's eyes stay on mine as his hands move up the inside of my thighs. He pushes my legs even farther apart before his fingers trail through my wet slit.

"Bloody fucking hell," he groans in appreciation, twirling his fingers above my entrance before plunging inside.

My back arches as my eyes shut, my fingers curling into his body.

I love the feeling of him taking control.

I love the feeling of being at his mercy.

I love the way he makes me feel.

Powerful. Beautiful. Wanted.

I love—

"You're soaked for me, love," he murmurs, pressing a kiss to the inside of my leg. "Just the way I like you."

I whimper in protest as he removes his fingers and rises before me, towering over me.

His eyes darken, taking on an almost onyx hue. "Turn around and place your hands on the glass," he orders, his voice husky with authority.

I look over my shoulder, seeing hundreds of men and women walking across the floors of the casino.

My stomach twists into tight knots. Nerves swarm around me, preventing me from moving. But there's something bigger blooming within me. *Excitement.* The thought of being caught... The idea of being seen being fucked by Eli...

I've never been this aroused before.

Slowly, I turn around and glide my hands up the glass, stopping at shoulder height. I hear Eli unzip his pants and let them fall to the floor. His chest bears down on my back, which in turn presses my whole naked body against the glass. I stare down at the patrons and even my security guards, who are gathered beneath us, utterly oblivious to what is going on three floors above them.

Holy fuck.

"You know." Eli's hands grip my waist as his lips graze my neck. "If the light hits just right, someone could see right through this piece of glass and witness you getting thoroughly fucked by me." A shiver runs over me as the pulse between my legs turns into a thunderous pounding. "But you'd like that, wouldn't you?"

I hesitantly nod, suddenly feeling embarrassed by this revelation. What is wrong with me that I would want this?

Eli grips my chin, turning my face toward him. "Don't be embarrassed with me. Not when I'll give you everything you desire." His lips mold to mine, his fingers tightening their hold over me. "But know this, if anyone ever saw you in this state, I would be forced to kill them."

With one quick move, Eli thrusts himself inside me. A moan escapes between my lips as he fills me, stilling inside me.

"So fucking tight," he groans, his lips ghosting over the back of my neck.

The floor below us is in a flurry of activity as people walk around, gambling, betting, and chatting.

They have no idea that I'm being fucked right above them.

There's something so entirely erotic about this.

Eli's hand slides up my rib cage, over my shoulder, and around my neck, where he squeezes. My pussy pulses with need as he begins to move in a steady rhythm, in and out. Every time he thrusts inside, he hits that special spot inside me. The one that's making my knees weak and my core throb.

"More," I breathe, meeting him for each thrust. "I need more."

His other hand slides between me and the glass, lowering until it ends up cupping my center. Two fingers glide over my clit in smooth circles, over and over again. Faster and faster.

"Yes." I rest the back of my head against his chest, and the palms of my hands begin to slide down the glass.

"God, you feel so good, love." His thrusts grow harder and rougher, just the way I like it, as his hand slides down my side and his fingers dig into my hip bone, securing me to him. He pushes my body to its limit, knowing what I can handle. Knowing my body better than me. Always giving me everything I need. "You're so fucking perfect for me."

His fingers move with precision over my clit, the orgasm on the precipice of appearing at any second.

"Oh my God." I reach behind me, gripping his bicep for support.

He hisses as my nails dig into his skin, leaving half-moons behind. His thrusts grow more frantic, his hand maneuvering up my waist, over the side of my breast, and around my neck, squeezing. Black dots begin to line the edge of my vision, amplifying the intensity of every sensation in my body.

"Come for me, Princess."

"Eli," I scream, lost in a state of unfiltered pleasure. I unravel against the glass as he loosens his grip around my throat. The orgasm rocks through my center, taking me to heights unknown. Lands never traveled.

This is better than anything I've ever experienced.

This is a moment I'll never forget.

He groans as he thrusts one more time, his body shuddering as he spills inside me.

And that's when reality hits me like a bucket of ice-cold water.

We didn't use protection.

Granted, I'm on birth control and have been for years.

But it's not foolproof.

And after everything that happened a year ago...

The fucking letter...

The ring meant for another woman...

My wedding...

I maneuver my way out from beneath his weight, quickly reaching for my discarded clothes. Eli stands, his chest heaving with so much force as he rests his hands on his hips, staring down at me.

"What's going on, Madeleine?" he questions, his eyes never leaving me.

I shake my head, zipping up my skirt with a tremble in my fingers, looking away from him. "We shouldn't have done that." I feel his cum slide down my leg, adding fuel to the fire.

I need to get out of here.

"Why?"

"You know why."

"Enlighten me."

"Because we didn't use protection!" I snap, giving up on tucking in my shirt as my hands go in the air. My chest heaves with each breath I take, fury growing inside me.

How could I be so stupid?

"Shit." He drags a hand down his face, remorse evident on his features. "I'm sorry, I wasn't thinking. I mean, that's not an excuse, but I lose my head when I'm around you. I...fuck." He lets out a deep breath, regarding me with so much concern in his eyes. "You're on birth control, though, right?"

My fingers clench into fists at my side. "And how, may I ask, do you know that?"

"Your health records," he says as if it should be obvious.

I pinch the bridge of my nose. "Who the fuck gave you permission to look at my health records?" The only semblance of relief I feel is knowing they don't include outside hospital visits and only pertain to information from our private doctors on the estate.

"As your bodyguard, it's my job to know everything about you. I need to be able to take care of you if a situation arises—"

"I don't need you to take care of me!" I shout, losing my patience.

I can't believe we just did that.

He bends down to pull up his pants. "I'm clean if that's the issue. I get tested at every physical. Besides, like I said to you in London, it's only ever been—"

"That's not what I'm concerned about!" I take a deep breath, trying but failing to rein in my anger.

"Then talk to me. Tell me what the problem is because we never used condoms before—"

"Forget it, Eli. You're not the one who has to deal with the conse-quences. You never are."

"What the hell does that mean?"

Without answering, I finally tuck my shirt back inside my skirt, slide my feet into my heels, and smooth down my hair. I quickly turn and make my way for the door, but just as I wrap my fingers around the handle, Eli's palm slams against the metal surface.

"This conversation isn't over," he states with force, his eyes drilling into me, tearing me apart from the inside out as he tries to read every thought passing through my head.

"Yes, it is." I shove past him, open the door, and walk out, leaving him behind as he scrambles to get the rest of his clothes on.

Striding down the stairs toward the back exit, I open the door to find Reginald waiting for me.

At the sight of me, a frown appears on his face. "Is everything okay?" he asks, concern tinged in his words.

I swallow hard and force a smile. "Everything is fine. I'd like to go home now."

"Will Mr. Lyon be joining us?" His eyes dart to the door as if he's expecting Eli to appear.

"No, he won't be."

After I slide into the back seat, Reginald pulls away from the curb. I glance out the back window and see the door crash open and Eli standing there with a thunderous storm brewing in his beautiful eyes.

CHAPTER TWENTY-SIX

Eli

Throwing open the front door, I charge inside, knowing exactly where I'll find her.

"We need to talk, right fucking now," I shout as I find her in the kitchen sitting on a counter stool with her hand wrapped around a spoon midair, prepared to dig into the pint of chocolate fudge ice cream before her.

"No, we don't," she answers calmly, thrusting the spoon into the container.

"Do you think ice cream is going to solve whatever the fuck is going on inside your head right now?"

She ignores me, shoving the spoon into her mouth while staring down into the container. Even from where I'm standing, I can see tears building in her eyes.

I don't know if I want to throttle her and shake her until the truth comes out of her lips or wrap her in my arms and tell her everything is going to be okay.

"Madeleine!"

She pauses and meets my gaze, a slight twitch in her cheek as she bites her lip, trying to suppress the emotions racing through her.

I take a deep breath, placing my palms on the cool counter. "You need to talk to me. You need to tell me what is going on. And I'm not just talking about tonight. I'm talking about everything." I drag my fingers through my hair. "I want to hear the truth, starting with why you've agreed to marry Alastor. I deserve the fucking truth!"

"No, that's where you're wrong. I don't need to do anything." She drops her spoon on the counter and slides off her seat, ready to storm away. But before she can, I grip her arm and pull her into my chest.

She maintains her posture, her back as straight as an iron rod, but I can see how her jaw tightens, trying to hold together the last thread of her composure before she breaks.

I stare into her tear-filled eyes. "You're scared," I say softly.

She scoffs. "Scared? Of what?"

Her chest rises a little faster, and I don't miss the deep swallow she takes.

I reach for a tendril of her dark hair, pushing it behind her shoulder. "Why don't you tell me?"

For a moment, I think the wall between us has come crashing down, and she might actually begin to share what's been going on. But in an instant, she blinks, and I watch as her hard exterior falls back into place.

"Nothing scares me," she says flatly. "I'm an Alarie."

"And clearly, a liar."

Anger lines her features. "Don't forget who you work for, Eli. You're in no position to undermine me."

I can't help but let out a deep, throaty laugh. "Oh, Princess. That's where you're wrong." Her brows cinch in confusion as she waits for me to elaborate. "You're in charge of managing your family's finances regarding the main account, correct?"

"Obviously."

"Then you know every transaction that comes in and goes out?"

"Of course."

"Every employee's salary?"

"Yes!"

"Then tell me this: how much am I getting paid to be your bodyguard?"

"Well, you get... You make... I think it's somewhere around..." Her whole body freezes in my grasp; her lips, after seconds of contemplating my question, part in shock.

"How much?" I ask again, speaking slowly to emphasize my point.

"Nothing," she breathes.

"That's right. Not one fucking penny. Because after I agreed to this assignment and transitioned from being Scarlett's bodyguard to yours, I had the direct deposit to my account cancelled. And do you know why?"

She shakes her head, a tremble taking over her body. Her beautiful blue eyes blink back tears that she's too afraid to let fall.

"Because I'm not here as your paid employee. I'm here as a man who loves you and will stop at nothing to protect you. I'm here because you're mine and always have been. I'm here because there's no fucking way in hell I will ever let you walk down the aisle to marry any other man but me."

The smooth skin on her palm connects with my cheek, taking me by surprise. Her eyes widen as she covers her mouth with her hand. She slips out of my grip and quickly turns away. I rub the spot on my cheek where a fresh sting warms my skin, watching her scurry off toward the stairs. Shaking my head in disbelief, I take a deep breath, trying with all my strength to control my anger—something I've always been able to do.

But not this goddamn time.

A volcano can only take so much pressure before it erupts.

And this beautiful fucking crazy woman just unleashed my wrath.

Striding across the marble flooring, I reach the stairs just as her bedroom door slams shut. I take two steps at a time, arriving in front of her door in seconds. With a forceful shove, I open it, the door slamming against the wall, nearly dislodging from its hinges.

She spins in shock at my arrival.

Probably assuming I wouldn't have followed her.

But she's wrong.

She's so goddamn wrong it makes my fingers curl into fists at my sides.

Because I'd follow her to the fucking ends of the earth and back.

Her hand pulls back, and before I have a chance to comprehend what's happening, she hurls a small object at my chest. The box containing the engagement ring bounces off me and lands at my feet, its lid snapping open to reveal the diamond ring inside.

"How dare you stand there and tell me you love me when you bought that ring for someone else!" Pain and agony lace her voice, emotions so intense that they seem out of place.

Emotions that wouldn't be there if she knew who this ring was always meant for.

I bend down and pick up the ring, closing the lid. I stare at the box as I say, "You think this ring is for someone else?" My gaze shifts up to meet hers.

She gestures with her hands wide open. "Obviously. You bought it for—"

"You," I interject.

She slowly drops her arms to her sides and blinks a few times in surprise. "W-what?"

"I bought this ring for you." I tuck the box into my pocket. "I planned on giving it to you when I got back from my last deployment, but…" My eyes drift to the ring on her left hand.

She instinctively covers her hand.

I take one step into the room, and she takes one back.

"You think I don't know what's going on here?" My voice comes out rough, filled with pent-up frustration. "You signed your soul over to the devil. And now, it's time for you to tell me why."

Panic flashes across her face, but she remains silent. With each step I take toward her, she takes another step back until I have her cornered against the wall, our chests brushing against each other.

I can feel her warm breath cascading across my neck as she looks up at me, her chest heaving a little faster.

But she doesn't cower.

No. My princess is too rebellious to cower, and right now, as she juts her chin out, arching a brow at my proximity, I watch her attempt to build the thick stone wall between us. The one she's maintained for the past year to protect her secrets and guard her heart.

But I'm about to tear it all down to the motherfucking ground.

Brick. By. Brick.

"A little over a year ago, you promised me you'd wait for me. Do you remember? It was the last time we saw each other before I left for Iraq." My eyes drop to her pulse point, noting how it beats erratically. "And after losing my comrades and after being kidnapped and tortured, the only person I wanted to see was you." I pause, letting my gaze drift back up to meet hers. "Just you."

She looks away, shame spreading over her features. But I refuse to let her hide from me any longer, so I grip her chin, forcing her to face me.

"So, imagine my fucking surprise when I heard the news that Madeleine Alarie was engaged to Alastor Manacorda. I thought there was no way, not after everything that had happened between us. So, in disbelief, I took a flight straight here instead of to my own home. I made it all the way to your front door with my hand raised, ready to knock, but I stopped when I saw you through a window." She rolls in her bottom lip, her eyes staring at the floor. "You reached your hand up to your hair." I grab her left hand, bringing it between us. The gaudy ring on her finger mocks me as it shines brighter than ever. "And you were wearing another man's goddamn ring on your finger!" I roar, my voice echoing across the room.

Silence fills the space between us, suffocating me.

I drop her hand as my breaths come out heavy and labored. I remember that moment as if it were yesterday. And all the anger I feel comes crashing down on me. "I have given you no reason to hate me, yet you have given me every reason in the goddamn world to feel that way about you, and still, I bloody can't!"

Defiance flashes across her eyes as rage washes over her. "You've given me no reason to hate you?" she asks incredulously, gritting her teeth.

"None." I lower my face, leaving only an inch of space between us. "You, love, are the one who betrayed me."

Her shoulders rise and fall, and her hands clench into shaking fists at her sides. She looks ready to hit me again, and I'll probably let her, knowing that whatever is happening between us right now is likely to reveal more than either of us can understand.

But I'm suddenly taken aback when a single tear crawls down her porcelain skin, her hard exterior melting.

I reach out, ready to wipe the tear from her face, but she shoves me away and moves around me. I turn, prepared to confront her again, only to find her reaching under her bed for something. Pulling out an old shoebox, I watch as she throws off the lid and digs through a pile of papers, tossing them to the floor until she finds what she's looking for, holding it before her.

Her wild eyes lock onto mine, and I realize that whatever is about to happen will change everything between us.

Forever.

Her bare feet march over to me, and she doesn't hesitate as she shoves the paper against my chest, her fingers trembling like leaves in the wind.

"You betrayed me!" she yells, her voice cracking. "When you wrote these words for me to read, you broke my fucking heart!"

My brows furrow as I grasp the paper and read what it says.

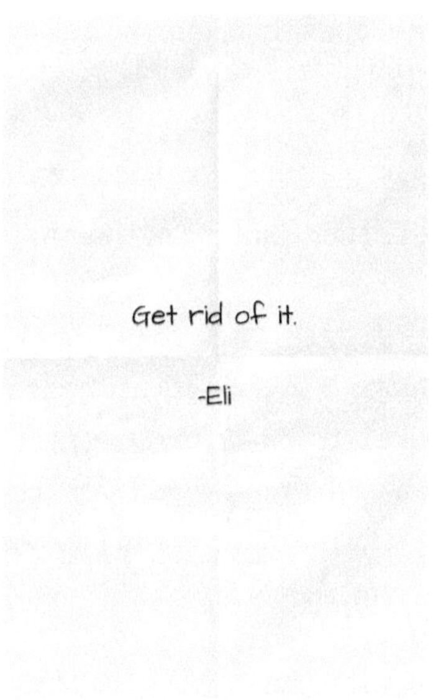

Four words.

One sentence.

And one signature—*my signature.*

The only problem is I have no idea what I'm looking at.

"What the hell is this?" I ask, lowering the paper so I can look at her face.

She scowls, shaking her head in frustration. "Don't play dumb with me; it doesn't suit you. You know exactly what that is. It's the last goddamn letter you sent me after I told you I was pregnant."

My world stops spinning.

The only sound I register is the thundering of my heart, pounding against my rib cage.

"It's the last goddamn letter you sent me after I told you I was pregnant."

"What?" I breathe, blinking violently as I try to clear my head. I must have misheard her. There's no way she just said what I think she said.

She turns away from me, staring out the window. Her shoulders slump as she lets out a defeated sigh. It feels like an eternity, though it's probably only a minute or two, before she quietly says, "Don't worry. You got what you asked for."

What I asked for?

What is she—

I glance down at the letter again, seeing those four words in an entirely new light.

Get rid of it.

Fear, unlike anything I've ever experienced, engulfs me.

"Madeleine..." I take a step closer, towering right behind her. Our eyes meet in the reflection of the window as I say, "This letter... This letter wasn't from me. I never wrote these words. I never received a letter from you saying that you were..."

Pregnant.

Oh God.

Everything spins as I grip the four-poster bed and close my eyes, taking a deep breath. Every emotion swirls around me like a vortex of agony. I sit on the edge of the mattress, placing the letter beside me and dragging a shaky hand through my hair. "You were pregnant...with our baby?" I look up at her, finding her completely at a loss for words as she slowly nods. I grip the sides of my head and lean forward, tugging at my hair.

She was pregnant.

She was pregnant with our baby.

And I had no fucking clue.

The center of my chest tightens painfully, and I feel like I can't get enough oxygen into my lungs.

"I don't... I don't understand what's going on." Her voice trembles as she wraps her arms around her waist, her eyes wide in disbelief. "You never... You never got my letter?"

I shake my head.

"Oh my God..." she breathes, her voice breaking as she reaches for the wall for support. "You really didn't know."

I swallow hard, trying to muster the courage within me for what I need to ask her. But even as a man who has seen the horrors of this world firsthand, I'll never be strong enough for the answer she'll give me.

"Princess," I say as softly and calmly as I can manage. Tears pour from her blue eyes, soaking her cheeks. *She knows.* She knows exactly what I'm about to ask her, and as much as I don't want to hurt her, I need to know. "What happened to our baby?"

CHAPTER TWENTY-SEVEN

Madeleine

"**I** ...lost...it."

My knees give out as I slowly fall to the ground, but before my legs touch the carpet, Eli's strong arms wrap around my waist, hauling me against his chest as he sits on the floor, leaning against the wall for support.

Tears fill my eyes, blurring my vision as they stream down my cheeks like raging rivers. An agonizing sob escapes my lips as every ounce of pain pierces my chest. It feels as if all the days I should have spent grieving the loss of my baby are crashing over me at once, and I don't know if I'm strong enough to survive it.

It hurts too much.

Eli's hold on me tightens as if he's scared I might get up and run out of his reach. But I won't. Not this time.

I cram my face into the crook of his neck, my tears soaking his shirt. I grip the fabric with shaking fingers, tethering him to me. His hands glide smoothly up and down my back, and I think it's his way of trying to calm himself as much as me.

It could be days, hours, or merely minutes that we sit like this, wrapped tightly around one another, but after I finally feel oxygen filling my lungs, I part my lips.

"All this time," I breathe against his chest. "I thought...you knew. I thought..." I look up at him, guilt slamming into me. His eyes are brimming with unshed tears he's holding back. He's trying to stay strong for me when he doesn't have to. "I'm so sorry." My hand reaches up, cupping his face. "I was cruel to you. And you've let me be with no consequences. You were my punching bag for months, and I'm so fucking sorry."

"You have not one damn thing to be sorry for." His lips press against my temple, lingering before gliding across my skin. "You thought... You thought I told you to abort our baby. As if I were a monster, giving you no option in the matter. You thought I was abandoning you because of this when, instead, I would have stepped up to the plate and been there for you in whatever way you needed me to be." He rolls our foreheads together. "I would hate me too if I were you."

"I should have known it wasn't you." I look down at my fingers curling into his shirt. "You would never have said those words to me. That's not who you are. But I was alone. I was so confused and hurt. I didn't know what to do. I'm so ashamed of myself." I shake my head, nausea invading my stomach.

So much time has been lost.

So much pain has been felt.

So much anger directed at a man who didn't deserve an ounce of it.

"I'm sorry you went through all of this alone." His hand slides around my neck, his thumb tracing back and forth. "But I'm here now, and you won't have to go through anything alone ever again."

I relax a fraction in his hold, wishing he was right.

He reaches behind me and brings the letter between us, staring at the words with so much vehemence.

"It's a perfect replica of my handwriting," he remarks.

"I know," I whisper.

"But I don't understand," he continues, running his hand around to the back of my head. "What does this have to do with you marrying Alastor? Did he know you were pregnant and try to blackmail you with it?"

"He didn't know," I whisper. "He had no idea."

"You're sure?"

"I'm positive. There's no way he could have known."

"But then, who did?" Eli asks, searching my gaze.

"I don't know." I release a deep exhale. "Besides my gynecologist, I never had a chance to tell anyone. Not a soul. I only put it on paper in my letter to you..." I freeze.

"What is it?" he asks.

"If you didn't get my letter, then someone else did. Someone who...most likely, sent the response letter to me. That letter was the only way anyone would have known I was pregnant."

I look at the letter lying on the floor.

The one that has haunted me for a year.

"I'll find out who did this. I promise you, I won't let them get away with it." His arms lock around me. "But I need you to do something for me, Madeleine."

"Anything."

"Tell me what Alastor is holding over you. If it's not this, then tell me why you would've agreed to marry him. Tell me everything, love."

I pinch my eyes closed, my breath coming out choppy. "I can't. Please don't make me."

"Whatever it is, I'll help you out of it. I'll take care of the problem. But I can't if you don't tell me what is going on."

"But that's just it... If I tell you, you'll try to do something about it. You'll try to stop the wedding. You'll try to save me, but you can't. Not this time, Eli."

He lowers his face to mine. "I will always save you, and there's nothing you will ever be able to do to stop me from putting an end to this wedding because I love you, Madeleine. So goddamn much. And it will be a cold day in hell before I ever let you marry that man. You are mine. And I am yours. That's how it's always been. And I won't let this monster interfere with our destiny."

I roll in my bottom trembling lip, shaking my head. "You don't know what you're saying."

"I do." He glides his lips over mine. Gently. Slowly. Softly. He pulls away, pressing his temple to mine. "Tell me everything from the beginning. Tell me your secret, Princess, and I'll guard it with my life. I'll save you from the villain in this story."

With a pleading look in his eyes that draws me into his orbit, I reluctantly give in.

I don't stop to consider the consequences of my words.

I don't give myself a moment to back down.

I just breathe and tell him my secret.

LAST NEW YEAR'S DAY

It's New Year's Day. A day meant for celebrating with loved ones or simply to start fresh. To start working on those damn resolutions everyone feels it's necessary to make.

But I don't feel much like celebrating.

It's been just over a week since I received my last letter from Eli, the one I'm currently rereading for the hundredth time. The four words repeat in my head over and over again as if on an endless loop, causing my heart to splinter with each repetition.

"Get rid of it."

Eli wants me to get rid of our baby.

My hand instinctively glides across my abdomen in a protective gesture.

When I wrote him to tell him that I was pregnant, I never expected this response. It's not like I purposely planned for my birth control to fail the ultimate test. I certainly didn't expect a letter from the man I love urging me to "get rid of it" with no further explanation.

It's not even like I can pick up a phone and scream at him for this heartache because he's in the middle of God knows where!

Sighing, I roll onto my side, tucking the letter beneath my pillow.

At this point, I'm almost ten weeks pregnant, and I need to talk to someone.

After getting ready for the day, I make my way to my mom's house and let myself in. Everyone was here last night for the festivities. But not me.

"Mom, are you here?" I walk through the living room and head to the kitchen but am met with silence. I know she's an early riser, so there's no way she's still sleeping. A dull chatter coming from her office catches my attention, and I immediately head that way.

I knock on the door, opening it simultaneously. "Hey, Mom, can I talk—"

I'm caught off guard to find my four brothers standing around, looking a little disheveled. Their gazes meet mine, and instantly, I feel it.

Something's wrong.

Stepping inside and looking around at everyone, I ask, "What's going on?" Alex is speaking on the phone in the corner of the room while the other four members of my family stand gathered around the desk.

My mother steps out from behind the desk and forces a smile—one that doesn't reach her eyes. "Dear, I wasn't expecting you. Is everything okay?"

"I don't know. Maybe you guys should tell me."

Leo, Alex, and Mauro all look at Vin, uncertainty clouding their expressions.

And if they're looking at the head of the family that way, then it's even worse than I thought.

Alex covers the speaker of his phone with his fingers. "You might as well tell her. She'll find out soon enough. It's all over the news. My team can't make this disappear. It's too late."

"Tell me what?" Silence. "Someone better start telling me what the hell is going on." Anxiety sweeps over me as I begin to lose my patience.

"Sit down, Madeleine," Vin orders, leaning against the desk.

I shake my head. "No." I cross my arms over my chest, bracing myself for whatever is coming my way.

His shoulders sag, and he taps his index finger on the smooth surface of the desk before suddenly stilling. "Eli's missing."

My world stops spinning.

My heart stops beating.

And the silence surrounding me becomes almost deafening.

I swallow hard. "What do you mean, missing? You mean to tell me the military just lost him?"

Vin shakes his head, looking down. "He was a part of a recon operation in Iraq that went sour. We don't have all of the details at the moment, but we do know the men in his unit...were killed, and Eli is now missing. It's assumed that the rebel group in the area took him and plans on using him as a hostage to obtain what they're looking for, but there has been no confirmation yet. No groups have taken responsibility for this."

"What do they want?" I ask, my throat tightening.

"We don't know. There haven't been any demands made yet, which is...unsettling."

I glance around the room. "Well, what are we doing? You can make a call, right? There must be someone you can contact to get him out of there and bring him home."

Mauro comes up to my side, placing a hand on my shoulder. When I look up into his eyes, I know I'm not about to hear the answer I want.

Leo approaches my other side. "It's not that simple, Mad—"

"What do you mean, it's not that simple? We are the Alaries." My eyes dart back to Vin, pleading with him. "Make the call, Vin."

"We don't have any connections in Iraq," he answers. "This is a level even we can't interfere with for fear of making the situation worse."

"Make the call!" I scream, barely recognizing my voice.

The room goes silent.

My brothers glance at each other as if my outburst has answered an age-old question. As if, after all this time, their suspicion regarding me and Eli has been confirmed.

And normally, I would deflect their accusatory glances. I would scoff at their insinuation. I would do everything in my power to protect our secret.

But I'm in too much pain to care.

I'm paralyzed by everything around me as I process Vin's words.

Eli's missing.

We don't have any connections in Iraq.

They watch me cautiously, waiting for me to shatter into a million pieces.

But I won't break in front of them.

My mom's arm wraps around my shoulders. "I know this must be difficult for you to understand, sweetheart. It's hard for all of us. Eli's a part of this family. He's one of us. But while we wait for an update, why don't we—"

I don't give her a chance to finish her thought as I remove myself from her hold and storm out of the room.

"Madeleine!"

"Let her go, Vin. She needs space," I hear Alex say.

I return to my house, throw open the door, and rush into the living room. My fingers shake as I grab the remote, pressing button after button until I find the channel I need.

"Breaking news," the woman reporter on the TV screen announces. "A soldier who was declared missing in action in Iraq is now believed to be a part of an ongoing hostage situation. Although the demands are not yet known, authorities are working to gather more information."

I drop to the floor, tears smearing my vision.

This can't be happening.

I let out a sob, my hands clutching my stomach.

This can't be real.

This is just a nightmare.

One fucked-up nightmare I can't escape from.

But it's not.

It's reality.

Reality being that Eli is kidnapped in the Middle East.

And there's not one goddamn thing that me or my family can do to save him.

"Iraq is currently one of the world's leading oil producers, generating over four million barrels per day. Manacorda Enterprises, primarily operated by Alastor Manacorda, his brother Enzio, and their father Adolfo, is responsible for producing nearly seventy-five percent of the total oil distributed to other countries. There has been no word yet from the oil tycoons regarding their plans for future involvement..."

The words from the news anchor blur in the background.

I look up at the screen as an idea flashes in my mind.

An idea that I may regret.

But at this point, I don't have any other option.

Pulling out my phone, I dial Reginald, who picks up immediately.

"Miss Alarie."

"I need to go into the city. Now."

"Of course. I'll be there in five minutes."

A few hours later, I find myself being escorted up to the top floor of Manacorda Enterprises headquarters.

The elevator opens, and my eyes find the man I need to speak with.

His guard, Tony, enters the room with me as I walk directly toward Alastor Manacorda.

He stands to his full six-foot-plus height, running a hand over his slicked-back blond hair before holding out a hand for me to shake.

The moment my hand is enveloped with his, it feels dirty.

This all feels wrong.

I've never had to seek help outside of the family before.

But I have no other choice.

"Madeleine Alarie." He motions toward the chair across from him. "I have to say, I was surprised when my secretary told me you requested a meeting."

I take my seat, smoothing out my dress. "Yes, well, it is quite imperative." I watch Tony take a free seat to the side, opening a magazine as if he's not here to listen to every word of our conversation.

Alastor steeples his fingers before him, leaning back in his chair. "How can I be of service?"

I glance at Tony and then back at Alastor. "Could we speak in private?"

Alastor flicks a wrist at Tony. "Give us the room."

Tony sighs, dropping the magazine on the chair as he gets up and then walks back to the elevator.

As soon as the doors close behind Tony, I get straight to the point. "Your family's responsible for exporting oil out of Iraq, correct?"

He leans forward. "Yes. We have an operation over there responsible for extracting crude oil and refining it. It's one of the many countries we work out of."

I nod. This is good. "I have a favor to ask of you." He waits for me to continue. "A...family friend, Eli Lyon, is currently being held hostage over there. My family would normally take care of a situation like this ourselves, but we don't—"

"Have any connections over there."

"Yes. And since this is now in the hands of the government, we need someone who can pull some strings to resolve this matter urgently."

"I see." He taps a finger on his desk while maintaining his unwavering gaze. "So, just to clarify, you want me to be the one to pull the strings by making some calls and getting your friend freed?"

"Yes," I answer matter-of-factly.

"Well, you've come to the right person, then. It shouldn't be a problem. I know exactly who to contact for this sort of situation. I can have Eli released by the end of the day."

Relief courses through me. "Thank you."

His head tilts to the side. "And what do I get in return?"

I swallow hard, aware that this moment was bound to arrive. Nobody in my world does anything out of the goodness of their hearts. "Name your price."

It'll probably be some astronomical figure he presents to me, but I'll do it. I'll do anything to get—

"Marriage."

My lips part, shock whirling through me. "Marriage?" I scoff, straightening my spine. "Be serious. I didn't come here to play games."

"Oh, Madeleine," he starts in a condescending tone. "I thought you were a smart girl. You came here because you know I can make one call and have Eli saved. But you also knew that I wouldn't be doing it without receiving something of value in return." He chuckles. "A marriage to you would open more doors for my family than I could ever imagine. It would form a powerful alliance that the world has never seen before."

My eyes narrow. "Why does it seem like the idea of marrying me isn't a new concept to you?"

He gives a slight shrug. "It's passed my mind once or twice. I'm not going to lie by not saying this situation doesn't make things more convenient for me."

I look out the side window, taking in the view of the city beneath us.

"It's up to you how fast I make that phone call," he muses. "I just hope it's in time before anything serious might happen..."

His words hang thick in the air between us.

Eli's life is on the line.

And there isn't any time for me to think this over.

But there's one thing he doesn't know—one thing that might cause him to change his mind about helping me if he found out.

So, instead of telling him that I'm pregnant and risking everything, I say, "I'll marry you."

I hate the weakness laced in my words.

A sly grin grows across his face. "See, you are a smart girl." He taps his chin. "But what's going to stop you from backing out of this deal once good old Eli is back home?"

My brows furrow. "I agreed to marry you. You have my word. What more—"

He laughs. "You've been a part of our world for long enough to know how it works."

I grind my back molars, feeling frustration bubble inside me. Why did I think coming to him would be a good idea?

"What are the stipulations?" I ask.

"Fairly simple. I'll be generous and give you one year to follow through on your end of the deal by marrying me. That way, we'll have time to make the announcement and plan a proper wedding—one that will be on the cover of every magazine and tabloid in the world." His smile drops. "But if you back out of the deal, I can promise you that Eli will be killed."

My heart thuds in my rib cage as I shake my head. This is ludicrous. "Do you know who my family is? You can't kill—"

"You won't make a fool out of me!" he snaps, his eyes burning into me. "Your family may hold power in the northeast, but their name means nothing in the Middle East, unlike mine." He exhales, rolling his neck. "I am offering to help you, and if you can't agree to the terms, then I'm left to wonder if you're even taking this seriously. So, if you can't agree to the stipulations set, then there's no deal to be made. Which would really be quite a shame for your...friend." He presses a button on the top of his desk, and a TV in the corner of the room lights up, displaying the newscaster I saw earlier, repeating the same breaking news. "Missing soldier in Iraq believed to be part of a hostage situation..."

"You knew," I say incredulously, glancing from the TV to him. "You already knew he was missing before I came in here."

"It's my job to know everything that goes on where my businesses are concerned. You coming to me for help was just a bonus." He shrugs. "I was

going to let the man die, seeing that he is of no importance to me, but you just made things a whole lot more interesting."

For the first time in my life, I feel powerless.

I've never not been able to take care of a problem myself.

I've never had to rely on an outside source.

But here I am. Ready to sign my life away.

Silence settles around us, thick and heavy, as I consider what I'm about to do.

"What's it going to be, Madeleine?" Alastor looks at his watch. "I have a flight to catch back to Italy shortly, so..."

I press two fingers to my temple. "If I agree to this, you promise Eli will be safe? That no harm will come to him? And that he will be returned to either his family in England or to us in New York?"

He sighs impatiently. "Yes. I promise no harm will come to him. He will be delivered in one piece."

A promise means nothing when a snake delivers it.

But right now, the snake is the only one who can help me.

"Fine," I grit out.

"Good. I'll have the call made before I leave, and Eli will be released soon after. I guarantee it."

"Great." I force a tight smile as I stand.

"We'll discuss the trivial matters concerning the wedding at another time. I'm sure my sister would love to help with the planning."

"Can't wait," I add as I turn to make my way toward the elevator. After Eli is returned safe and sound, I'm sure I can get out of this arrangement. Does he realize who my brothers are? I mean, I just have to tell them and—

"And Madeleine?"

I glance over my shoulder just as the elevator doors open, and I enter.

"It's in your best interest not to mention this to your brothers. I may not have the stomach to personally kill someone, but that doesn't stand true for everyone in my family. You see, my cousins, the Vasilievs, would not take kindly to them interfering with my family's business. They will view it as

an insult and personally see to it that Eli is killed should this wedding be canceled for any reason. Keep that in mind."

The Vasilievs. Fuck.

I swallow down the lump in my throat just as the doors close. How could I have forgotten who he's related to? They're cold and ruthless. Heartless monsters who rule over Chicago. And they will have no ounce of remorse in killing Eli if I don't follow through on my end of the deal.

Anxiety claws at my chest as I lean back against the wall, rubbing my hand over my temple.

A sudden and sharp pain pierces my stomach, and I place a hand over it, wincing. But just as quickly as it came, it disappeared.

What was that?

The elevator comes to a stop on the ground floor, and the doors open, allowing me to exit quickly as I stride through the lobby.

What the hell did I just do?

You signed a deal with the devil for the man you love.

For the man who broke your heart.

Did I just make the biggest mistake of my life?

And what will Alastor do when he finds out I'm pregnant?

Will he renege on our arrangement?

Fuck, I didn't think this through.

"Miss Alarie. Is everything okay?" I look up to see Reginald waiting by the car for me. I was so lost in my head that I didn't realize I ended up outside.

"Yes, everything is fine," I answer, lying through my teeth. He opens the door for me, and I slide across the seat.

A moment later, the car accelerates, and I look out the window, watching the imposing building slowly disappear from view.

I rest my hand protectively against my stomach.

Everything will be okay, *I think, closing my eyes.* All that matters is that Eli will be safe.

Abruptly, an intense cramp spreads over my stomach. I bite down hard as the pain radiates. I groan, catching the attention of Reginald.

"Is everything all right?" he asks.

"Yes. Yes. Fine." I wave him off as the pain starts to dissipate. "Must have just eaten something strange."

He nods in the rearview mirror, putting his eyes back on the road.

What the fuck was that?

I rub my stomach, which suddenly feels tight. It's not painful, just uncomfortable.

As we approach the highway, wetness coats the inside of my thighs. A cold dread settles over me. I swallow hard as I separate my legs and slightly pull up my dress, revealing blood on the inside of my thighs.

No. No. No.

"Reginald," I say in a shaky voice.

"Yes?"

"Take me to the nearest hospital."

His eyes dart up to the rearview mirror. "Miss?"

"Now," I state firmly. I clench my jaw as another shot of pain passes over me. "Please."

He nods, and I feel the car accelerate faster. "We'll be there in ten minutes."

"Thank you," I say as a tear rolls down my cheek. I wrap my arms around my stomach. "I'm sorry," I whisper. "I'm so sorry."

"I had a miscarriage," I tell him, looking away as shame overtakes me. "The doctors said there was nothing I could have done to prevent it, but I can't help feeling like…"

He brushes back my hair. "Feeling like what?"

"Like I'm to blame," I admit, the weight of my words hanging heavy between us.

"Madeleine, no," he says softly but firmly. "That's not true."

"But it is," I reply, my voice cracking as I wipe my eyes. "I wasn't even sure if I wanted it. I was so confused and upset. The stress of the situation, on top of what I just did, was eating away at me. But..." I take a deep breath. "The moment I lost it, that was when I realized how much I wanted it. How much I wanted to be a mom," I whisper. "But it was too late."

"This wasn't your fault, love. None of this was your fault," Eli reassures me, his hold feeling like everything I've ever needed. He's the one constant in my life, keeping me standing strong, even when I feel completely lost.

I look up at him, desperate for answers. "What are we going to do?"

He presses his lips gently to the top of my head. "I will take care of that son of a bitch. I don't want you to worry about him."

"But you heard what I said. If I don't marry him, he'll have you killed—"

He presses his lips to mine, my words dying on the tip of my tongue.

Rolling our temples together, he says, "You just went through all of this alone, keeping this secret for so long. You never had the chance to grieve this loss properly. So, let me hold you a little while longer. Let me take all the tears and pain and hold on to it for you so you don't have to bear the weight of the world on your shoulders anymore. You're not alone, love. I'm here."

"I've really missed you," I breathe. "I've needed to fall apart in your arms for so long."

"I know." He brushes his hand down the back of my head. "Tonight is for us. But tomorrow..." His muscles tense beneath me. "Tomorrow, I'm going to take care of everything."

I swallow hard. "You're going to tell my brothers, aren't you?"

"They need to know. At least," he continues, "they need to know about your deal with Alastor. They need to know what they're up against. Especially since it pertains to the Vasilievs." He nods, deep in thought, to himself.

"The Vasilievs are not good people. They make my brothers look like saints."

He chuckles softly. "No, they're not. But your brothers and I will handle whatever comes our way." He looks down, his eyes dark yet lost as he processes everything I've just revealed. "You signed away your life for me," he whispers in disbelief.

"I would do anything for you."

"But you should never be in a position where you have to. I'm the one who is supposed to be taking care of you."

I shake my head. "Sometimes the princess has to save her knight in shining armor."

He touches his lips to mine before I pull away and rest my head against his chest, exhaustion suddenly taking over me.

"I never stopped loving you," I whisper.

He presses his lips to the top of my head. "My heart has only ever beat for you. Only you."

It's not until every tear has dried that he kisses my temple and lifts me into his arms. Gently, he places me in the center of my bed and then slides under the covers beside me. I snuggle into his embrace as his arms engulf me, keeping me close.

Keeping me safe.

"You are mine," he says softly, his lips brushing over my hair. "Always have been and always will be. And I protect what is mine, no matter the price."

CHAPTER TWENTY-EIGHT

Eli

Four pairs of eyes stare back at us.

Shock.

Disbelief.

Anger. Fury. Vengeance.

It's all right there on their faces.

"I know." Madeleine twists her hands together and clears her throat. "I know you're probably very disappointed in me for seeking help from an outside source, but please know that I was desperate, and it was the only way I could think of to save Eli. I didn't know what else to do. I panicked, and I just hope—"

Vin's chair slams against the wall as he stands, his eyes locked on Madeleine as he strides around it, heading straight for her.

I step between them, placing her behind me. "I will not let you hurt her," I bite out. "She did what she thought was right. It's because of her that I'm even standing here right now."

Vin gives me a disbelieving look and inches closer to me. "Let. Me. See. My. Sister."

Hesitantly, I step aside, keeping one hand over the gun tucked in the back of my pants.

Vin approaches Madeleine, staring down at her, making her appear even smaller than usual.

"I'm so sorry, Vin." She sniffles, struggling to hold back tears. "I didn't mean to get the family involved in all of this. I just wanted to save Eli." She pauses before continuing, "I know I've let you down, but please don't look at me like that. I can't bear disappointing—"

Vin's bulky arms wrap around her, cutting off her words as he pulls her against his chest.

"Dammit, Madeleine," he says firmly. "Why didn't you come to me? I'm your big brother. I'm supposed to take care of shit like this. I'm supposed to take care of you, and I failed you."

She softens in his hold, her armor breaking as tears slide down her cheeks. Throwing her arms around him, she says, "I couldn't tell you. Not any of you. I wanted to. So many times, I came close to it, but I couldn't risk it. I'm so sorry."

"Shh." He rubs his hand in soft circles against her back. "You have nothing to be sorry for. You took care of one of our own, and you did it knowing what that would mean for you. You're so fucking selfless. I just, I wish I had figured out what was going on sooner."

Leo, Mauro, and Alex approach her as Vin releases her.

"We're family," Leo says. "There is nothing we wouldn't do for you."

Mauro's hand lands on her shoulder, and her eyes look up to meet his. "Fam... Family," he manages to say in a gravelly whisper.

"You're the glue that holds us together," Alex tells her with a slight smile. "Besides, we're the Alaries. We'll take care of this in the same manner we always take care of things."

Madeleine glances between all of them. "With guns, blood, and violence?"

"But, of course," Vin answers, flashing a wide, white-toothed grin. "Would you expect anything less?"

She shakes her head, a small smile briefly appearing before just as quickly fading away. "What are we going to do?"

"Well." He rubs his palm over his cheek, scratching at his facial hair, appearing deep in thought before turning to Alex. "If I get you Alastor's phone, how long will it take you to decode the calls and find what we need?"

Alex shrugs. "If I preprogram my system with the correct code words to flag, I can have the information ready in a matter of minutes."

"Good," Vin replies as he rolls up his shirt sleeves.

"What are you thinking?" My hand reaches for Madeleine's. Our fingers interlock, and all four brothers notice, their eyes fixated on our connected hands until Vin speaks.

"We act as if this wedding is still happening," he affirms.

"And why would we do that?" I ask, not liking this idea one bit.

"Because tonight, at the rehearsal dinner, we'll take Alastor's phone, and then Alex will do what he does best. I want physical proof that the Vasiliev brothers are involved with this. And once we have it, I'll call a meeting with them and the Manacordas. Tonight, after the dinner." He sighs, rubbing his temple. "We may be a powerful family, but the Vasilievs are just as powerful. We can't afford to make any mistakes, and we need hard evidence to back up our claims before taking action. Because when we do, this will, no doubt, start a war between our families. We need to approach them tactfully."

"And how do you expect to get your hands on Alastor's phone?" Madeleine asks. "He keeps it securely on himself at all times, never letting it out of his sight."

"I have my ways," Vin answers.

"I don't like this idea," I tell him. "No offense, but it feels like we'll be outnumbered by too many of our enemies with no escape route and no backup if we need it."

"Oh, we'll have backup," he affirms with a firm grip on my shoulder. "Just trust me. My plan will work. And after tonight, this whole nightmare will be over." He motions between me and Madeleine. "Then, you two lovebirds will be free to do whatever the hell you want."

Madeleine looks up at me with a mischievous glint in her eyes. "Like we haven't been doing that already."

Vin quickly covers his ears. "I'm going to pretend I didn't hear that." He walks around his desk and takes a seat, leaning back in his chair. He steeples his fingers before him, his eyes darkening. "It's time to remind everyone who the Alaries are and what happens when you mess with one of our own."

I reach for Madeleine's hand, intertwining our fingers as I bring her hand up to my mouth, brushing my lips over her knuckles. "I won't let you be anywhere alone with Alastor tonight. Someone will always be with you, understand?"

She looks up at me, smiling. "Yes, hu—"

"Where have you two been?" Vin's deep voice cuts off her words as he appears by her side, fastening the buttons on his jacket sleeve.

I offer a casual shrug. "We had something we needed to take care of." Madeleine looks up at me under her dark lashes, her eyes bright, her face glowing. "Something that couldn't wait," I add.

"If that's code for a quickie, I don't want to know about it."

Madeleine pats Vin on the chest. "Don't worry, dear brother. There's nothing quick about the way we do it."

He grimaces before dragging a hand down his face. "Alex!"

Alex strolls up casually. "Are we ready?" We all nod, and he gestures for us to follow him inside.

Madeleine steps after him, glancing over her shoulder at me. Her long, dark hair caresses her bare shoulders. The strapless black velvet dress hugs her figure, accentuating every part of her body that I just ran my lips over merely hours ago.

Vin and I follow closely as we walk through a sea of people.

We enter the main room of the venue, where the rehearsal dinner is being held, bypassing the gold curtains when Alex mentions, "By the way, the family just arrived."

"The family?" Madeleine regards Vin with wide eyes. "You don't mean our—"

"Cousins." A gravelly voice comes from behind me, and I quickly turn to find five intimidating figures standing before us: Marco, Caine, Romeo, Cassio, and Marcello Marchetti. They're cousins of the Alaries and currently reside in Italy when they're not in the States for business.

"Family." Vin takes a step forward, straightening his jacket. "We're honored you could be here."

Madeleine glances at Vin, arching a brow.

"They know the wedding is off, but they're not here to witness your vows; they're here as our backup, should we need it." Vin clasps my shoulder. "I told you to trust me."

"Anything for family," Marco declares coolly, running his fingers through his dark hair. "Especially when someone tries to hurt one of our own."

Alex takes a step toward Caine, eyeing his tactical gear. "You look ready for battle. Not a wedding."

"From what I've been told, I dressed appropriately," Caine responds with a shrug. He turns to Vin and adds, "I heard you got everyone tanks for Christmas." A sly grin pulls at his lips. "They must have loved that."

Vin rolls his eyes, crossing his arms over his chest. "Some more than others."

Leo walks up to Madeleine's side and leans down to place a kiss on her cheek. "Scarlett and I thought it would be best for her to stay home today. Being in close proximity to the Vasiliev brothers might trigger old memories for her, given her knowledge of who their father was. Alina is keeping her company."

"Of course," Madeleine responds. She looks around the room. "Where's Mauro?"

Alex adjusts his glasses. "Don't know. He was here a few minutes ago. Maybe he went to get some air. You know Mauro has a hard time in crowds."

Madeleine frowns. "With everything going on, I didn't even think of that. He should go home if he wants. It's not like this is real, anyway."

"He wanted to be here for you," Vin states. "Besides, we'll need the numbers."

"Oh, boys, there you are." Mrs. Alarie appears, stepping around Vin and opening her arms to the Marchetti men, embracing each one in a hug. Vin had informed her earlier about the unfolding situation, and to say that she was upset with Alastor would be an understatement. Despite Vin's objections, she insisted on being here at least for the start of the evening to present a united front for the Alarie family. Reluctantly, he agreed. "We're always so happy to see you."

"Some more than others," Leo mutters under his breath. She gently smacks his shoulder and narrows her eyes at him.

"And how is my dear brother doing?" she asks.

"Enjoying retirement," Romeo responds with a grin.

"Mrs. Alarie." A woman in a chef's coat appears. "Sorry to interrupt, but we need you in the kitchen. It seems there was a mix-up with the proteins; there's too much fish and not enough steak."

Mrs. Alarie sighs. "Of course." She glances around at everyone before adding, "Well, if you'll excuse me."

"Mother," Vin voices, stopping her. "Don't forget our deal and to meet your driver outside in twenty minutes. I'd rather you weren't here for the remainder of the evening in case things don't go well." He leans over and kisses her cheek. "I had the chef prepare a bag for you to take home."

She pats his bicep and shows a small smile. "Always looking out for me."

Everyone bids her farewell as she walks away.

Romeo turns toward the group. "So, what's the plan?"

"You want us to light things up as soon as they walk through the door?" Marcello asks with a mischievous grin.

"No," Vin answers firmly.

Caine pouts. "Where's the fun in that?"

Vin pinches the bridge of his nose. "The plan is—"

"They're here," Marco says smoothly, bringing a glass of amber liquid to his lips.

All at once, we turn to watch as the Vasilievs and the Manacordas enter the room: Adolfo, Alastor, Mila, Cressida, and Enzio, followed by Mikhail, Kazimir, Emil, Alik, and Luka.

Their arrival results in a sudden hushed silence among the crowd of guests.

My eyes rake over Alastor, and I start imagining all of the ways I'm going to kill him for what he's put my princess through. My hands, at my sides, curl into fists unknowingly as the muscles in my body tighten. I rock my neck from side to side and exhale.

"God, they're an ugly bunch," Cassio remarks. "Especially that one in the middle with the slicked-back blond hair. Is that Alastor?"

"Yes," Madeleine replies, swallowing hard as she wraps her arms around herself. "That's him."

"Don't worry, cuz." Caine winks. "We wouldn't let you marry someone that ugly. It would ruin our family's good genes."

She smiles at his teasing.

"How would you like for this to be handled, Vincenzo?" Marco asks.

"Once Alex retrieves what we need, I'll arrange a meeting with them after dinner to discuss the matter privately. But not until then. I want this matter to be handled as discreetly as possible," he states, straightening his tie. His eyes darken as Alastor and his cousins turn in our direction. "Follow my lead."

We wait as Alastor and the Vasilievs approach, stopping a few feet away. The rest of the Manacorda family moves to their seats at the other end of the room. Enzio glances at me and nods in greeting, which I return. As Cressida takes her seat, I notice that her eyes look darker than usual as she stares straight ahead...directly at Madeleine.

"Darling." Alastor's slimy smile widens, and it takes everything in me not to punch him in his smug face before choking all the life from his eyes. "There you are. I've been looking for you."

"I'm right here," Madeleine responds. "I was just catching up with my family."

Alastor's eye twitches. "Yes, I see." He looks to the Marchettis. "I wasn't aware you would be joining us from Italy for this special occasion."

"La famiglia è la nostra priorità," Marco says, a sinister grin tugging at his lips. "Wouldn't you agree, Mikhail?"

Mikhail's cold expression remains stoic. "Of course. Family is all that matters."

"Glad to see we agree," Vin remarks, his eyes narrowing in on Alastor. Tensions brew amongst the group as each of us sizes up the other. "Maybe we should all take our seats so we can get this night started."

"Agreed." Alastor holds his hand out for Madeleine. She smiles and avoids his touch, walking around him to take a seat at the Alarie table. Alastor appears ready to combust from the insult. "Dear, we're sitting with my parents and cousins."

Madeleine looks up from her seat, unfolding her napkin. "I'll join you shortly."

A vein pulses in his neck. "Of course." He looks at me with murder in his eyes. *The feeling is mutual, mate.* And then turns toward his cousins. "Let's take our places." The six of them walk away, heading to their seats.

"We'll take our seats too," Romeo says. "Just let us know when we're needed." The Marchetti men take their seats at the table closest to ours.

As the five of us sit, Mauro appears, taking the free seat beside Leo.

"Everything okay?" Alex asks.

He nods, tugging at his white collar. Madeleine shows him a sympathetic smile.

"Glad you could make it, cousin," Caine offers as he clasps a hand on his shoulder. "Wouldn't want you to miss out on all the fun we're going to have."

Mauro rolls his eyes, but the hint of a smile appears on his face.

Leo turns toward Vin. "How much longer?"

My brows cinch together. "How much longer until what?"

"Be patient," Vin answers, examining his watch. "He'll be here any minute."

I glance between all of them. "Who will be here—"

"Mr. Alarie, sir," a boy who looks no older than twelve says as he approaches Vin. "I've got it."

"Good work, kid." Vin reaches into his pocket for a roll of bills, which he hands to the boy. The child's eyes light up with excitement. "Now, hand over the goods." The boy pulls a phone from his back pocket and hands it to Vin. "And remember, if your father asks, you got that money from mowing my lawn. Capisce?"

The boy nods eagerly. "Yes, sir."

He turns and quickly leaves, walking through the exit.

We all stare at Vin.

Vin shrugs and explains, "He's the son of one of my guards. A few months ago, he stole my watch, but his father made him return it. The kid has quick hands." We continue to wait for a more detailed explanation. "So, I asked him to steal this." He holds out a phone, ensuring that only we can see it. "Alastor's phone."

He slides it across the table to Alex, who immediately grabs it and gets up from his seat, striding toward a back hallway.

"You're sure this will work?" I ask. "You really think he'll be able to find something on there to show that the Vasilievs were involved?"

Vin simply nods as plates are placed in front of us, revealing tonight's salad choice. A few minutes pass before someone taps a glass, drawing our attention to the other side of the room, where Alastor stands, waiting for everyone to look at him.

He smiles as he surveys the room. "I just wanted to take a moment to thank each and every one of you for joining us tonight. Madeleine and I are so delighted to share such a special occasion with so many of our dearest friends and family members."

A hand grips my shoulder, and I quickly turn to find Alex while Alastor's ramblings blur in the background. He leans down and whispers, "Come with me." He glances at Leo, Mauro, and Vin. "You too."

I shake my head. "I can't leave Madeleine."

He turns and motions toward his cousins, who all stand and take the extra seats around our table.

"Better?" he asks.

"That will do." As I stand, I lower my face toward Madeleine. "I'll be right back."

She nods, her attention still on Alastor as she plays the part of the doting fiancée that everyone thinks she is.

We follow Alex down a back hallway into a small room set up with computers.

Once the door shuts behind us, I ask, "What did you find? Are they involved?"

"Yeah. They're involved, all right. But it's a little more complicated than any of us could have realized." He sighs, his eyes focused on me. "You're going to need to listen to what I found for yourself."

My brows furrow as he presses play. Suddenly, familiar voices sound from the speaker.

"I have a job for you," Alastor states clearly. "One that will benefit not only my family but yours as well."

"I'll be the one who decides that," Mikhail responds. "Why are you coming to me about this and not my father?"

"Because I need to know that discretion will be a factor," Alastor answers. "Your father leaves too many loose ends."

Mikhail pauses before saying, "Understood. So, tell me, what does this job entail?"

"What, dear cousin, could provide our family with more power than we can possibly imagine?"

"An alliance with an even more powerful family," Mikhail answers, sounding bored. "What exactly are you getting at?"

"Madeleine Alarie."

Dread coils within me. I look at Leo, whose anger in his eyes reflects my own.

A moment passes before Mikhail says, "I'm listening."

"I have it on good authority that she has her heart set on a soldier overseas. One named Eli Lyon. And after some digging, I found that he's currently deployed in Iraq. Specifically, in our territory."

"How interesting... And your good authority?"

"My other half, of course."

"Hmm, and what do you want us to do with him?"

"I want him kidnapped."

My heart thunders so loudly I can barely hear the rest of their words. *I want him kidnapped.* This fucking cocksucker is the reason why I was taken. The reason why my friends died. The reason I was forced into an early retirement from what I loved doing. The reason for my nightmares and flashbacks. He orchestrated the whole fucking thing. But why?

"And why would we do that?" Mikhail asks. "I know that name. He's practically one of the Alaries. Are you trying to make an enemy out of them?"

"No," Alastor answers. "I'm trying to do just the opposite. If I marry Madeleine, then I become one of them."

"I see."

"If he goes missing, Madeleine will do whatever it takes to get him back. And when she realizes her family has no pull in that territory, but that mine does, well..."

"She'll come crawling to you for help."

"Exactly."

"And you'll offer her a marriage in order to save this man?"

"If everything goes according to plan, then yes."

Silence stretches between them before Mikhail voices, "We'll do it. I'll have my men take him, but what would you like for us to do to him?"

"It's no concern to me what they do with him. Torture him, for all I care, but just keep him alive. He'll be the only chess piece I have to play with to keep Madeleine in line for this deal to work. I'll reach out when it's time to release him. But if Madeleine backs out of the deal for any reason, you may kill him." He laughs. "Think of it as a contingency plan."

"That can be easily arranged. But what do my brothers and I get out of this?"

"If this plan works, my father has agreed to name me the rightful CEO of Manacorda Enterprises instead of Enzio. And I will personally grant you a fifty percent share of the company stocks."

Mikhail hums. "You have yourself a deal."

The call ends, and everything around me transforms into a deep shade of red.

"I'm going to fucking kill him," I breathe, a fire of vengeance scorching its way through my body from the tips of my toes to the top of my head. "All of them."

"We need to put a plan in place," Vin notes as he removes his jacket, leaning against the wall. "This is more than we thought them capable of. This changes everything." He drags his fingers through his hair, exhaling. "I understand what you might be feeling, but there's a room full of people between us and them, and we can't just walk out there and—"

"Watch me," I snap before turning and stepping out the door. I charge down the hall, hearing distant footsteps rushing after me, but I don't stop.

Nothing and no one can stop me.

Entering the main room, my eyes land on Alastor as he sits contently with his family, oblivious to the murderous undertone in the air.

I'm going to kill you.

I march toward him, catching his attention.

He feigns a half grin as his eyes regard me with disdain. "Well, if it isn't the body—"

His words die as I wrap my fingers around his neck. I haul him out of his seat and hold him before me like a shield, pressing my gun to the side of his head. The guests' screams blur in the background as I turn just in time to see the Vasiliev men stand, pointing their guns at me.

But no bullet pierces the air because they don't have a clean shot. They know it. And I know it.

Fortunately for me, the Marchetti brothers, along with the Alarie brothers, stand with their guns aimed at them, making the Vasilievs vastly outnumbered.

"Everyone out," Vin roars, sending the guests scurrying out of the room to leave us to finish this without witnesses.

"Not you, pops." Vin latches an arm around Adolfo's neck, stopping him. "You're not going anywhere." Vin presses his gun into his back.

"Whatever he told you, I'm not involved. I know nothing about the kidnapping. That's all on him."

"Who said anything about that?" Vin questions.

Adolfo pales as he realizes his mistake.

"Drop your gun," Mikhail demands, his eyes unnervingly calm.

I shake my head. "You motherfuckers staged everything. You kidnapped me to lead Madeleine right into your clammy hands. You tortured me for days!" I shout, my eyes moving to Alastor. "But your biggest mistake was thinking that when I came home, I would just let you marry her." My fingers dig harder into Alastor's neck, feeling his pulse beat wildly beneath my touch.

"It...was...just....business," he manages to get out.

"Business?" I laugh darkly. "This is just business." I shoot him in the thigh. He screams out curses as he sags against me. "This is also just business." I smash his head against the table, splitting his skin open. Blood flows down his temple, staining his perfectly white shirt.

"Okay," Kazimir says. "You've made your point. Now, what do you want? A goddamn war on your hands?"

"I want the mastermind behind this whole fucking scheme! I'm taking Alastor, and I'm going to torture him just like you fuckers did to me, and then when I'm good and ready to, I'll kill him."

Alastor laughs manically, clutching his head and leg. "Mastermind? You think I'm the one behind all of this?"

"Of course you are! I heard the whole bloody phone call you made to Mikhail, asking for his help. Asking them to kidnap me!"

He hums, either from losing too much blood or just because he's a smug prick. "If you heard the call and still think it was me behind all of this, then clearly you weren't paying attention."

"What the fuck are you talking about?" Alex demands. "We all heard it!"

He shakes his head, laughing even harder.

I look to Vin, dread building in my stomach.

"Then who is?" Vin asks with vehemence. He thumps his gun against the top of Adolfo's head and lets him drop to the floor before stepping toward Alastor's other side. He presses his gun into Alastor's temple. "Talk!"

My eyes dart to Madeleine's seat.

Madeleine's very *empty* seat.

"Where's Madeleine?" I yell, my wide eyes scanning the room in a panic.

"Some petite girl came over and asked if they could talk," Caine says. "They headed toward the bathroom about…" He looks at his watch. "Fifteen minutes ago."

I shake Alastor. "Who has her?"

"I'm not the only villain in this story," he murmurs, his lips tugging up into a grin.

"…And your good authority?"

"My other half, of course."

How did we miss it?

Fury. Wrath. Vengeance.

I become all three as I undergo an out-of-body experience.

My lips part, and a roar like only a murderous God could produce echoes off the walls.

"Where is my wife?"

CHAPTER TWENTY-NINE

Madeleine

My eyelids feel heavy as I let them slowly blink open. The room around me is engulfed in darkness, everything appearing blurry as I sit up. A groan escapes my throat as I clutch the back of my head, feeling a throbbing pain in one specific spot.

Suddenly, a light casts over the space, illuminating Cressida sitting on a worn, stained sofa in a long, baby blue satin gown; her right gold heel peeks out through the slit, bouncing impatiently in the air.

Everything looks out of place.

"Finally, you're up." Cressida smiles, her intent clear as she looks at me with a cruel glint in her eyes.

My eyes catch on a bright red substance coating my fingertips. Blood. Shit. I rub the back of my head again, realizing it's wet and sticky. *That's not good.*

"That's not my fault," she says. "You did that to yourself when you hit your head on the floor." She tilts her head to the side, observing me like a predator. "Don't you remember?"

The last thing I remember was Cressida asking if we could talk. Caine got up to follow me, but I told him I would be right back as I turned to follow Cressida toward the bathroom. Once we were inside, she lunged at me, catching me off guard as she jabbed a syringe into the side of my neck. Whatever was in it instantly took hold of me as my words slurred and my knees gave out, my body falling to the floor. Hence, my aching head.

But how did I get here?

And where the hell is here?

"Why the fuck did you take me here?" I ask, sitting up straighter against the cold, damp wall, trying to ignore the pain. As a chill skates across my shoulders, I adjust the top of my dress, wishing I had worn something with sleeves.

She uncrosses her legs and leans forward. "Isn't it obvious?"

My brow arches. "Enlighten me."

"Well, Eli, of course," she states matter-of-factly.

My heart stills.

Eli, as in *my* Eli?

I remain silent as she stands.

"I'm not stupid, Madeleine. Although many probably presume I am, simply because I'm a woman." Her arm comes forward, and I notice her knuckles wrapped around a gun. *My gun.* The one that was previously strapped to my thigh holster, hidden beneath my dress. "I know you're not marrying my brother for love. In fact, I know more than you about everything going on here."

She crouches down before me, a sympathetic smile playing on her lips. "You see, I love Eli. In fact, I've been in love with him for years." Her head tilts to the side, her smile growing wider. "And I have your dad to thank for that."

My nails dig into the palms of my hands. "What the hell are you talking about?"

"Well, if he hadn't gotten himself killed, I never would have bumped into Eli at his funeral."

Every muscle in my body tenses at her words, my blood boiling with fury as my knuckles shake.

"I have to admit, I found the funeral service quite boring. I mean, it's not like I knew the man. So, while everyone else was engaged in small talk, I wandered aimlessly through your family's house. And just as I was entering the living room, a man bumped into me." She looks off into the distance with a dreamy smile on her face. "It was Eli." She laughs softly. "I had no idea who he was until I heard one of your brothers call out to him." A slight flush spreads across her cheeks. "His deep brown eyes locked onto mine as his hands gripped my arms, steadying me to ensure I was okay. The deep timbre of his voice sent a pleasant shiver over my body as he apologized for not seeing me." She chuckles, her eyes glazing over as if lost in a memory. "I never believed in love at first sight until that moment." She stands to her full height, smoothing down the fabric of her dress. "And I just remember thinking, I would do anything to make him mine."

Her no-nonsense declaration causes my eyes to widen as alarm bells ring in my mind, warning me.

"It was simple for me to obtain all his basic information. Quite convenient for me that he spent most of his time here, in New York. I would make it a point to be at the same events as him. To ensure I was always in his line of sight. But did he ever notice me? Did he ever look my way? No, because"—she casually points the gun at me—"he was too busy looking at you. Never understood why, either. Let's be honest; between the two of us, I'm the real prize." She sneers at me in disgust, pausing before saying, "You probably don't even remember seeing me at the hospital."

"The hospital?" I ask, my brows cinching together in confusion.

"Yes, I was at my doctor's office for a routine visit, sitting in the corner of the waiting room, reading a magazine. Just minding my business. When you came traipsing out of the room with the nurse congratulating you and handing you pamphlets for expecting mothers." She looks down at the ground, shaking her head. "I just knew." A dark laugh escapes her lips. "So I decided to skip my appointment and follow you. I watched as you pulled over at a nearby park and walked over to a picnic table, brushing off the snow before you took out a pen and a piece of paper from your bag. You scribbled across it for a while, crossing things out and adding more until you finally held it up, smiling proudly at your work. Then you walked over to the nearby mailbox and dropped it inside, leaving it there." Her expression shifts to one of disapproval. "You just left such an important letter in a mailbox unprotected for anyone to take."

I shake my head, fury ensnaring me. After all this time, it was her behind that awful letter. It was her who wanted to see to my demise. *This fucking bitch.* "You took the letter."

"Of course. I had to see for myself what you wrote to my dear Eli. Although I must admit, it was rather upsetting to digest. I mean, the idea of you pregnant with Eli's baby... Well, it gave me nightmares." She grimaces, her brows knitting together as her features contort in disgust. "So, I responded as I thought Eli should in this situation. Or, I suppose, in a way that would ensure you would no longer want anything to do with him. I even replicated his signature for you, which I admit was quite a challenge given that I had never seen it before. That is, until I obtained a copy of his enlistment forms. It's quite convenient to have so many connections in high places, like the government, for instance." A smug smile appears on her face. "I'm guessing from the lack of a child that you took my advice."

"You psychotic bitch!" I shout, no longer able to contain my emotions, my fingers digging into the dirt, ready to pounce. "You are going to regret everything when I'm done with you!"

She swiftly jerks the gun toward me, causing me to refrain from unleashing upon her. "I don't think you're in any position to be threatening me."

I seethe through my teeth, fighting the violent tremble that races through me.

"Easy." She smiles wickedly, taking a step toward me. "We haven't even gotten to the best part yet."

I grind my back molars, my heart beating erratically beneath my rib cage. *I'm going to kill her.*

"You see, my letter to you was the key to breaking your heart, but I needed a way to break Eli's as well. So, I went to my dearest brother for help with that part, but I needed to ensure my plan would give him what he's always wanted in return to secure a deal."

I swallow hard, and against my better judgment, I ask, "What did you do?"

She brushes a hand across the couch cushion before taking a seat. "Oh, come on, Madeleine. You're smart. That's one of the things I like about you." She leans against the back of the couch with amusement in her eyes. "What do all men want?"

I grin, unable to help myself. "A good blow job after a long day? Don't tell me you and Alastor are that close?"

She scowls, her eyes narrowing in on me. "They want power, you cunt." She presses her fingers into her temple, briefly closing her eyes. "In order to achieve that, I merely suggested that he marry you, accomplishing two goals at once: you would no longer be available for Eli, and it would also establish a powerful alliance for my brother. But I explained that there was a slight dilemma in that you were in love with another man. So, I simply advised Alastor to use Eli as his pawn in this little game to achieve our end goal."

My breath catches as I realize that everything that happened to Eli is because of this raging psychopath. "Why the fuck would you do that?"

"Because when you came running to my brother for help—and we knew you would, considering our family's power in that country—desperate with no options, you would say yes to his proposal." She stares at her manicured hand. "Having the Vasiliev brothers as cousins is quite advantageous," she adds with a slight shrug of her shoulder. "It certainly made it easier to have him kidnapped in a foreign country."

"The Vasilievs are the ones who took him?" I ask, rage like I've never experienced coursing through my veins.

"Well, not them, but their men who reside there. Alastor doesn't like to get his hands dirty, but the Vasilievs don't mind at all. Of course, it cost a pretty penny. I believe Alastor offered them half of our company's shares, but that was nothing compared to what he would be gaining once he married you."

"His unit was killed during their attack!" I yell. "Those men tortured him, and he has the burns to prove it." I shake my head, glaring down at my blood-covered hands. "He has fucking PTSD because of you!"

"It's not my fault that he was hurt," she responds, taken aback that I could even suggest such a thing. "I didn't tell them to torture him! Sometimes, men just take things too far."

I scoff. "Do you hear yourself? He could have died!"

She rolls her eyes in annoyance. "I never would have let that happen. I had planned to take care of him when he came home. However, his returning to the States and working for your family was never part of my plan. I had no way of getting into the Alarie Estate unless I hiked up the stone walls surrounding your property." She gestures to herself. "Do I look like someone who can climb walls?"

My lips part. She's actually delusional. "So, what now, Cressida?" I look around the deserted warehouse. "Do you plan on killing me? Is that why you've taken me here? Is that how your whole plan comes together?"

She frowns, tilting her head to the side. "Of course not. I didn't take you here to kill you. Well..." She waves the gun around. "Unless you put me in a position where I need to. No, I brought you here to have a little chat, woman to woman."

Oh, this will be good. "I'm all ears."

"You will follow through with marrying my brother, and then you will let me and Eli live out our happily ever after the way we were always meant to. You won't get in the way of our happiness."

I bite my bottom lip, trying to suppress a laugh.

Apparently, that doesn't make her too happy because she clicks back the safety of the gun, aiming it right at me. "Okay, I tried to play nice, but now you're really pissing me off. I'm giving you two choices here. You can either marry Alastor and stay the fuck away from Eli or if you can't agree to that, then I'll have to kill you and leave you here. And who knows how long it will take for someone to find you." She uses the tip of her heel to kick something that looks like it might have been alive at one point but is definitely not anymore. "The coyotes may find you before your brothers do," she warns.

"Gee, thanks for that lovely image." I roll my eyes and stare up at the ceiling.

"I don't think the choice is that hard. I mean, if you marry Alastor, you'll have me as a sister-in-law. Haven't you always wanted a sister?"

"Yeah, just not one who I would consider to be certifiably insane!"

Her expression freezes, and her eyes remain unblinking. "What did you just call me?"

"Insane!" I lean toward her, my chest heaving.

"Don't call me that!" She stands to her full height, pressing one hand into her scalp.

"But that's what you are, for thinking Eli would want anything to do with you." I laugh, leaning against the wall. "Do you have any idea what he's going to do to you when he finds me like this?"

"Eli loves me!" she screams, stomping a foot like a disobedient child. Her eyes widen, her chest heaving erratically. "Or, at least, he will when you're no longer in the picture." She raises the gun, tilting her head to the side. "I'm giving you to the count of ten. And if you don't choose by then, I'll decide for you. One..."

Shit. "Cressida, just put the gun down," I say calmly. "We can talk about this."

"No." She shakes her head. "There's nothing left to talk about. I love Eli, and he will love me. And we'll be happy together once you're gone. Two..."

"Cressida, please, you don't have to do this."

"Three..."

Maybe I can run? I look toward the door.

"Don't even think about it. My guards are waiting just on the other side. Do you think I lugged you here myself?" She scoffs. "Four, five, six, seven..."

Sweat rolls down my temple as my heart thrashes against my rib cage.

This is it.

I'm going to die.

In a fucking warehouse, wearing vintage Chanel.

The door bursts open, revealing the darkest pair of eyes I've ever seen. They lock onto me before shifting to the monster standing in front of me. "Drop the fucking gun, Cressida!"

CHAPTER THIRTY

Eli

"What did you say?" Vin questions, his eyes widening a fraction as he scratches his temple. "Did you just call Madeleine...your wife?"

"I did," I rush out, dropping Alastor to the ground. He rolls onto his side, whimpering in pain as he clutches his leg. A pool of blood soaks into the fabric of his pants before dripping to the floor beneath him. "We stopped at the courthouse on the way here."

Why the fuck would Cressida take her?

And where the fuck would she take her?

"And why," Vin voices, "may I ask, did you think you should—"

"Because I couldn't wait one more goddamn minute before I made her my wife!" I shout, my chest heaving.

A strong hand grips my shoulder, and I look to see Mauro standing beside me with a stoic expression. In the face of danger, he's always the calmest among us.

He lifts his phone to my eye level. **We're going to find her.**

I nod, my pulse quickening. I straighten my arm, pointing my gun right at Alastor's head. "Tell us where the fuck she is, or I swear to God, I will have this floor painted with your brains."

Alastor looks over his shoulder at his cousins and then back at me. "You wouldn't be stupid enough to do that. If you kill me, you'll never see that bitch again!"

I shoot and purposely miss his head by only an inch.

"You fucking bastard!"

"Next time you force my hand, I won't miss."

"Will one of you just fucking shoot him already?" Alastor screams at his cousins.

Kazimir raises his gun but stops the moment Mauro's gun presses into the back of his head.

"I wouldn't do that if I were you," Alex says calmly.

"You're going to fucking regret this," Kazimir threatens, dropping his gun to the floor.

Mikhail sighs and shakes his head. "You brought this on yourself, Alastor." He looks at Vin. "If we let you keep Alastor and his father, will you let us walk out of here unscathed? Or would you rather have a blood bath? Because if you think we traveled here without more guards waiting outside for us, you're sorely mistaken."

"Are you fucking kidding me?" Alastor cries. "We had a deal!"

Mikhail crouches down before him. "No one will kill my brothers. You should have already known where our loyalties lie. With each other. Not with you."

Vin steps toward me, his expression grave. "This is your call. Our men are waiting outside for my signal. We can stay here and fight with them by our side, so you may claim your revenge on the men who plotted your kidnapping. Or we can accept their offering of Alastor and Adolfo, the men responsible for Madeleine's suffering, and leave now to go find her before it's too late."

I stare at Mikhail, contemplating my options, but it doesn't take me long to decide what's most important. Sure, I may want to put a bullet in each of the Vasiliev brothers' heads for agreeing to this plan or the names of every last fucking Russian who took pleasure in torturing me, but finding Madeleine is more vital to me than seeking my own revenge. "We don't have time to waste. The Marchettis will take Alastor and Adolfo back to the Alaries' warehouse. But someone better fucking tell me where Cressida took Madeleine, or none of you will walk out of here alive—"

"I know where she is." Enzio's voice approaches as he wheels through the room. He holds out his phone, the screen facing me. "I have a tracking device on Cressida's car, a security feature that has come in handy."

"You worthless piece of shit!" Adolfo yells, holding the back of his head. "You'd give up your sister that easily? We're your family!"

Enzio shakes his head. "I don't have a family." He hands his phone over to me, and I locate the blue dot on the map.

Leo looks over my shoulder to pinpoint the location and then turns, striding urgently toward the exit.

I toss Enzio his phone. "Thank you. We won't forget this."

He dips his chin, displeasure crossing his features as he views his father and stepbrother. "I'll send the location to your phone so you have it."

Vin's deathly gaze scans each of the Vasiliev men. "I suggest the five of you get the fuck out of here before we change our minds," Vin orders. "Our hospitality only extends so far."

Kazimir grins wickedly. "Until we meet again. Is it too soon to call you brother?"

Vin's eyes darken, his knuckles curling into the palms of his hands. "Get the fuck out of here!"

Kazimir *tsks*. "Touchy subject."

Mikhail grabs his shoulder. "Let's go, brothers." He leads the five of them out of sight, leaving behind Alastor and his father for us to deal with.

"We can take it from here," Marco says.

Vin nods. "After we locate Madeleine, we'll meet you back at my house."

My mind races as we quickly head toward the exit, and I think of the best plan of action—the safest way to get Madeleine out of what could potentially become a hostage situation. "We'll take two cars. The location is situated in the middle of the woods, approximately fifteen minutes away. I'm certain her guards will be with her and have assisted her in this situation. Stay alert. Cressida will be unpredictable and very dangerous if she's willing to go to this length."

"Can't wait to find out why she thought taking our sister would be a good idea," Vin seethes with venom in his voice. "She's either stupid or crazy."

I worry it's the latter.

The five of us split into two cars: Leo and I get into my vehicle while Vin, Mauro, and Alex climb into Vin's SUV.

I grip the steering wheel tightly, my jaw clenched with anxiety as my foot presses down hard on the accelerator. *If we don't get to her on time—*

"She'll be okay," Leo insists, staring out the window before glancing my way. "She's a fighter. You know that. Not to mention stubborn as hell. She's always insisted on doing everything herself."

I shake my head. "But she shouldn't have to. Not anymore. Not when I'm here."

"I know." He grins, grabbing my shoulder. "And when she sees you coming to her rescue like a damn knight in shining armor, she might finally realize that too."

"I hope so," I say, lost in thought.

"By the way," Leo adds. "Welcome to the family."

A sense of pride swirls through my chest from his words.

However, the warmth is short-lived as we turn onto a dirt road, currently covered by a thick layer of snow, leading deeper into the woods. In the rearview mirror, I see Vin's SUV right behind us.

The location of Cressida's car becomes increasingly close on the screen, prompting me to pull to the side of the road. Vin parks his car beside mine.

"What's the plan?" Vin asks, stepping out of his car.

I unclick the safety on my gun and secure it in my holster. "We walk the rest of the way, using the woods as cover. We don't know how many guards she might have with her. We could be outnumbered, but if we use the element of surprise, it could work to our advantage."

"I agree," Alex replies. "We need to be ready for anything."

We continue our path on foot, trudging through the snow with the full moon as our only source of light, and after about five minutes, we spot an old, abandoned warehouse up ahead. Each of us conceals ourselves behind a tree or the thick brush as we peek around for a better view.

"They must be in there." Leo moves with stealth as he crouches close to the ground, his eyes narrowing on the warehouse's front. "There are three armed guards outside. There could be more inside, but we can't know for certain."

I scan the area. "Alex, do you think you can get up there undetected?" I point to the lower portion of the roof that has access to windows. "You have the best shot among us."

He takes off his glasses and rubs the lenses with his shirt as he looks up. "Yeah, I can go around to the back and see if I can find a ladder or something to use." A deep exhale escapes him while he puts his glasses back on. "I just really hope it doesn't come to that."

"I understand," I answer, knowing his hesitation. Our world is a dark place, one where killing men—evil men—has become a regular part of our daily lives. But we've never been in a situation involving a woman as our prime target. This is new for all of us. "It's not ideal, but we need to be ready in case it does come down to that."

He nods and starts walking around the thicker part of the woods, remaining hidden as he makes his way to the building.

I regard Vin and Mauro. "You two go in from the left, while Leo and I will go to the right." I secure the silencer on my gun, watching as the others do the same. "Keep your eyes open in case there are more guards we aren't aware of."

They nod in agreement before we all depart. Leo and I round the right side of the warehouse and quickly press our backs against the wall when we hear voices coming from the front.

"Do you think she'll kill her?" one of the guards asks. "She seemed a little high-strung today."

"I've learned to expect the unexpected from her," another guard responds with a chuckle.

"Maybe she'll let us have some fun with that Alarie girl," a third guard remarks.

And there goes the last of my restraint.

In one move, I have my gun held out before me as I turn the corner and shoot all three of them on the spot, none of them having a chance to raise their weapons in defense.

Vin and Mauro appear on the other side, dropping their guns as they view the three bodies on the ground. Disappointment flashes over their faces.

"Thanks for saving some for us," Vin notes dryly.

I shrug. "You were taking too long." I step over one of the men and stand before the sliding wood door. My fingers wrap around the edge as I carefully slide it open, unsure of what I might find on the other side. Vin, Mauro, and Leo stand behind me with their weapons drawn, prepared for an attack.

The moment the light from the moon shines through, illuminating the scene unfolding before me, my body freezes.

Cressida has her back toward me as she stands tall, pointing a gun directly at Madeleine.

My wife.

My *trembling* wife.

My trembling wife with blood dripping down her temple.

Madeleine's beautiful blue eyes lock onto mine, coated in terror.

All of my fury unleashes as I point my gun in Cressida's direction, pressing my finger firmly against the trigger.

"Drop the fucking gun, Cressida!"

She spins, throwing her free hand against her chest while still keeping her gun aimed at Madeleine. "Oh, Eli, you scared me." A smile grows on her face. One that would haunt children's nightmares. "You came for me!" she exclaims. "I guess I shouldn't be surprised. I mean, I knew you would one day, and now here you are. For me."

Oh, bloody hell. This isn't good.

Leo exchanges a glance with me, one that says, *We might have a problem.*

Yeah, I'd say we fucking do.

He cautiously steps toward my right side. "Step away from Madeleine," he orders. "We don't want to hurt you, but if we have to, we will."

Cressida frowns. "Eli wouldn't let you hurt me. Right, Eli?"

"That's where you're wrong, Cressida," I say firmly. "Because if you attempt to hurt my wife any further, I will be forced to stop you by any means necessary."

Cressida's body freezes, her skin paling. Her lips part as she repeatedly blinks, soaking in my words. "I think I misheard you." Her eyes jump to Madeleine as the gun in her hand begins to wobble, and she slowly lowers it to her side. "Did you..." Her eyes bounce back to me, throwing daggers my way. "Did you say, wife?"

I swallow hard, aware that one wrong move or word could set her off. She's like a firecracker with an extremely short fuse, one I don't want to ignite.

And *wife* was probably the worst word for her to hear.

The tension in the air becomes stifling. Vin and Mauro distance them-selves from me, blocking all escape routes. Their postures are rigid, and their eyes are unnerving as they watch their sister shiver on the ground.

"I did," I respond evenly. "Madeleine is my wife."

"But... But how?" Her eyes water, a single tear escaping, sliding down her cheek. "You were supposed to marry me." She shakes her head, disbelieving my words. "I did all of this so that you would end up with me!" she screams in frustration.

With reluctance, I lower my gun as I take a step forward. "I'm sorry, Cressida. Truly, I am. But Madeleine is the one my heart has always belonged to. There's nothing you or any other woman, for that matter, could have done to change that."

She blinks away her tears, her eyes pinching shut as she aggressively shakes her head. "You're... You're lying!"

I take another step toward her, causing her to swiftly raise her gun at Madeleine. Fuck. Not wanting to make matters worse, I decide to drop mine to the ground to show her I mean no harm. "I'm not," I answer softly.

She presses her free hand against her head, her fingers digging into her scalp, appearing to be in pain. "This wasn't how things were supposed to go."

This is more than good versus evil.

This is someone who's struggling.

Someone whose mind told her a different story than what reality presented her with.

Someone who needs help.

"We can get you help," I offer, taking another step. "I know it seems impossible now, but you don't always have to feel this way." I look down at Madeleine, her gaze holding mine. "I've been told it's okay not to be okay. And I'm here to tell you the same thing, too." One side of her lips lift slightly before my attention turns back toward Cressida. "There are people who can assist you. There are options we can explore to help you feel better. Medicines. Therapy."

Tears stream down her face. "I've tried everything," she murmurs quietly. "Nothing ever works." Her eyes flick down to the floor, and I think this is my chance to apprehend her. But just as I take another step, her head shakes violently as she looks up at me, her gaze rushing between each of the Alaries behind me. Her chest heaves, her arm straightens, and the gun gets closer to Madeleine. "I brought her here to give her a choice. To marry my brother and forget about you, or if she refused, I would be forced to kill her." Her features contort, defeat crossing her eyes. "But if she already married you, then she'll never forget you. And I can never forgive her for taking what was mine." She closes her eyes. "Please forgive me, Eli."

"Cressida, no!" I roar.

At the exact moment, two shots ring out into the air.

One, a bullet from Alex's gun.

The other, from Cressida's.

My eyes dart to Madeleine, who clutches her shoulder, blood exuding between her fingers as Cressida's body drops to the floor with a loud thud.

I run to Madeleine, dropping to my knees as I tear off the bottom half of my shirt and use it to wrap around her shoulder as a tourniquet. She groans out in agony as I tighten it.

"Eli," she sobs, reaching her trembling hands for me. "It hurts so much."

As someone who's been shot at least a handful of times, I know firsthand the burning pain she's experiencing.

And I wish there was a way I could carry it for her.

"I'm sorry, Princess." I scoop her up into my arms, cradling her to my chest. "I'm so fucking sorry, but you're going to be okay. I promise. I'm getting you out of here. I'm taking you home."

"Hurry," she says faintly, her face paling.

Leo looks down at her, fear coating his irises. "Alex and I will take care of Cressida. Get Madeleine to the house. Now."

I turn quickly, not waiting for further instructions.

"I need you to stay awake, love. Can you do that for me?"

She nods, but her eyes begin to flutter closed. From the red coating her pale skin, I know she's losing way too much damn blood.

"Madeleine!" I shout with force.

Her eyelids pop open, but only for a second.

"Fuck!"

"Dr. Rose, have everything ready for a gunshot wound to the shoulder. Extensive blood loss," Vin clips into his phone as we race through the woods for my SUV.

I approach the back, and Mauro opens the door so that I can slide her gently across the seat. She whimpers at the impact. "I know, love. I know," I say softly as I sit beside her, resting her head on my thigh.

Mauro jumps into the driver's seat while Vin takes the passenger seat. My heart races violently in my chest with each second the drive home takes. Mauro presses down on the gas pedal, accelerating the vehicle as fast as it will go, but it still doesn't feel fast enough.

Looking in the rearview mirror, I find pure, unfiltered fear in their eyes. Nothing like I've ever seen before.

Which only adds to my own alarm.

I stare down at Madeleine, gliding a trembling finger over her soft cheeks, pushing back her loose strands of hair.

I lean forward and press a soft kiss on her forehead. "I won't lose you, Princess. Not after I just got you back."

CHAPTER THIRTY-ONE

Madeleine

A rhythmic beeping is the first thing I hear, a strong antiseptic scent is the first thing I smell, and Eli, my husband, is the first thing I see as I force my heavy eyelids to flutter open.

I slowly raise my hand, feeling tension in my left shoulder. Ignoring the pain, I bring my palm to the top of his head, resting on the side of my bed. I run my fingers through his hair, watching as he begins to stir, his eyes blinking a few times.

The moment his eyes are fully open, meeting mine, he becomes an alert soldier, instantly standing, his hand reaching out to cup my cheek. I melt into his strong touch, closing my eyes, savoring the safety I feel in his embrace. He leans down and presses his forehead against mine, intertwining our fingers with his free hand.

There's a slight tremor in our touch, but I'm not sure if it's coming from me or him.

"I thought I lost you," he breathes. He cranes his neck back, his eyes shiny with unshed tears. So many thoughts swirl through his dark orbs.

Fear. Guilt. Love.

I place my hand on his cheek, grazing my palm against his stubble. "I'm right here."

He leans down, softly pressing his lips against mine. The familiar taste of him sends warmth coursing through my body, a feeling I never want to live without.

"How are you feeling, love?" he asks as his eyes scan over me.

I glance at my shoulder, unable to see the extent of the damage hidden beneath the gauze and tape. I attempt to lift it but wince from the pain. "Pretty damn sore."

He runs his fingers through his hair, visibly distressed. "I'm so sorry. You should have never been in a position where this happened to you. I shouldn't have left your side for one moment."

"It's not your fault," I tell him. "Cressida was clearly not...okay."

"No, she wasn't."

"Is she...?" I ask, remembering Cressida falling to the ground beside me, blood pouring out of her neck.

"She is," Eli says with displeasure. "You don't have to worry about her anymore."

"Who... Who did it?"

"Alex." He looks out the window. "He didn't want to kill her. None of us did. But the second she fired a shot, he fired one, too. He had no choice. If he didn't, she could have kept shooting. She would have..." He lets out a deep breath. "Killed you." He brings my hand to his lips, kissing my knuckles. "And that was never an option that any of us would have ever let happen."

I roll in my bottom lip, fighting tears.

Knowing Alex, this is going to be hard on him.

Hurting a woman goes against everything he stands for.

I can only imagine how he feels after taking her life.

But because of him, I'm alive.

"What about the Vasilievs? What did you do to them?" I ask.

He exhales, closing his eyes. "We let them go."

"What?" My eyes widen in shock. "But they... But Cressida told me that's who took you in Iraq. Their men are the ones who tortured you! You need to make them pay. You need to kill them. You need—"

"Shhh," he hums softly. "It's okay, love."

"It's not okay," I respond. "How can you stand there and say that? How can you let them live after what they did to you?"

"Because in a single moment, I had a choice to make. Either start a war in the middle of that ballroom, risking the lives of those closest to me, or find you." He grins softly, his knuckles stroking gently across my cheek. "I chose you, love. I'll always choose you."

A few tears escape, trailing down my cheeks. "I don't deserve you." I wipe my eyes. "You've always put me first. You've always been there. Always. Even thousands of miles away, you were there for me. I just..." I take a deep breath. "Cressida admitted to writing that letter to me. It was all her. Those were her words." I shake my head, more tears free falling down my cheeks. "How could I let even a small part of myself believe that you wrote that damn letter?"

He brushes my hair back. "That's all in the past. And the only thing I want to think about is the future—our future. One with you by my side." His eyes darken. "Besides, their time will come. One way or another, they will meet their maker. But I don't want you to waste a second thought on them."

He presses his lips to mine, and we savor each other for a few minutes until he pulls back and asks, "Are you ready for me to let your family know you're awake?"

I sigh, falling back against the pillow. "Are they here?"

"Are you kidding? They wouldn't leave your side. I finally got to be alone with you an hour ago when your mom kicked everyone out into the hallway so you didn't wake up with eight faces staring down at you."

I let out a soft laugh, but it quickly transforms into a grimace as pain shoots through my shoulder.

"I'll get the doctor, too," he adds, moving toward the door.

Seconds later, the room is filled with familiar faces: Mom, Vin, Alex, Mauro, Leo, Scarlett, and Alina. All of them tell me how thankful they are that I'm okay and how worried they've been.

"Seeing that you were just shot, I'll ignore the fact that you got married without your mother present," my mom says as she makes her way to my side. She reaches for my hand with a smile on her face. "I'm just so relieved you're okay."

"Always trying to be Mom's favorite when we both know that title belongs to me," Vin jokes with a wink as he makes his way to my other side.

"It's been my title since the day I was born," I respond, sticking out my tongue.

His expression softens, and his smile fades. "There aren't many things in this world that frighten me, but you somehow managed to give me one of the biggest scares of my life." He clears his throat and wipes his forearm across his eyes.

"We were so worried." Scarlett squeezes my hand, with Leo standing protectively behind her as Alina takes my other hand.

"Try not to let this happen again, okay?" Alina advises, smiling with tears forming in her eyes.

"I'll try not to." I squeeze their hands in assurance.

Mauro approaches Alina and stands beside her. His eyes scan every inch of me, searching for more injuries, but after not finding anything besides my shoulder injury, his eyes lock with mine, silently holding a conversation.

"I'm okay, I promise," I tell him, reaching out my hand for his.

His large hand envelops mine gently, squeezing it reassuringly. With his free hand, he points to his eye, then to his chest, and finally toward me. His eyes water, but he blinks the tears away before anyone else notices.

"I love you, too," I whisper.

"We all love you," Mom adds with tears forming in her eyes.

A knock sounds at the door, and Dr. Rose walks in with Eli.

"Looks like my patient is awake," Dr. Rose notes with a smile as she approaches. "I'd like to change your bandages and give you some medication for your pain."

"Of course," I reply, shifting slightly on the bed.

"Well, everyone," Mom begins, "let's give Madeleine some space. We can all take turns visiting her later."

Everyone says their goodbyes, leaving the room one after another, and that's when I notice Alex standing in the corner.

I turn to Eli and Dr. Rose and ask, "Can you please give me a minute with Alex first?" They both nod and step into the hall, with Eli closing the door behind him.

Alex stands at the foot of my bed, running a hand through his disheveled hair. His eyes are cast down, revealing dark bags beneath them. His shirt is wrinkled and unbuttoned at the top. This isn't the Alex I know, and it's killing me inside to see him like this.

"You saved me," I state.

He nods. "I did."

"Why do I feel like you regret it?"

His brows knit together as he shakes his head. "I would never regret saving you. You're my blood. My sister. I would do anything for you."

"I know. But I can't help but worry that you're going to take this harder than you should."

He turns away and walks to the window, glaring outside. "She needed help. She needed..." He shakes his head. "To be honest, I'm not a doctor, so I don't know exactly what she needed or if she was too far gone for treatment." He turns to me. "The world we live in isn't kind. It's cruel and dark to its core. Because of that, I've killed many men—men who deserved it." He shrugs slightly. "Maybe some who didn't, but I've never..." He shakes his head again. "I've never killed a woman. I've never even laid a hand on one."

I arch a brow, my lips curving up. "Oh, really?"

"You know what I mean." He rolls his eyes and flashes a fleeting smile before it quickly fades away. "Hurting women is not how we were raised. It's not who I am. And this is going to sit heavy on my shoulders for a while."

I sit up and clear my throat. "Cressida planted the seed for everything, orchestrating this entire situation. She wanted me to be as far away from Eli as possible, by any means necessary—even if that meant killing me. And she tried." I let out a breath. "I know you. And I know you're going to unnecessarily beat yourself up about this for a long time, and that's why I'm going to tell you what started this whole thing."

He furrows his brows in confusion.

I take a deep breath. "For years, Eli and I had been exchanging letters while he was in the military. It was just something we did. Something that turned our friendship into more. And last year, I wrote him a letter to tell him that I...that I was pregnant."

Alex's brows shoot up.

"And weeks later, I received a letter from Eli. Only it wasn't from Eli."

"Cressida?"

I nod. "She pretended to be Eli and told me to get rid of the baby." I roll in my bottom lip. "I was crushed. Devastated beyond words. I should have never believed Eli would say something like that to me, but at that moment, those words just bore themselves into my soul. It killed me. And I'll never forgive myself for thinking he had anything to do with that."

Alex sits in the chair closest to him. "Jesus."

"Yeah."

"But, what happened to—"

"I lost it," I answer. "The night I signed my soul over to the devil. I think the stress of everything happening around me was just too much for my body to handle."

He shakes his head in disbelief. "I'm so sorry, Madeleine."

"Me too." I run my hand under my eyes, catching the loose tears. "But I'm telling you this because I don't want you to punish yourself for what happened."

"Madeleine, I—"

"No." I cut him off, not giving him a chance to finish his thought, knowing he doesn't deserve this. "You saved me. You gave me and Eli a chance to start a family. And I'll be forever grateful for you. I just hope that someday, you'll see that you did the right thing with no remorse. You did what had to be done."

He shows a small smile, one I wish would grow bigger. But I know that won't happen today. It might not happen for a while.

He gives a slight nod. "I'm sure you're right."

I notice the tired look in his eyes, the one that tells me he wants to change the subject but is too polite to say so. "I always am."

He shakes his head, letting out a small laugh as he looks toward the door. "So, you're officially a married woman now? Just like that?"

"Just like that."

"Eli is certainly going to have his hands full with you."

I grin. "He can handle me."

"I know he can." He leans back in his seat. "I'm glad you two found your way to each other."

"Me too. But what about you?"

"What about me?"

"Is there anyone out there who's caught your eye?"

He swallows, looking away. "No."

"Someday," I offer.

"Someday," he repeats solemnly. Standing, he takes a step toward the door. "Well, I better let the doctor fix you up. And I'm sure Eli is chomping at the bit to get back by your side."

"Most likely... But, Alex, will you do one thing for me?"

He pauses, glancing over his shoulder. "Anything."

"Take a shower. Iron your shirt. Shave." I wave a hand at him. "I'm not used to this version of you, and it's scaring me."

He chuckles softly. "I think I can manage that."

Seconds after he walks out the door, Eli and Dr. Rose come inside.

"How's he doing?" Eli asks, taking my hand in his as Dr. Rose washes her hands at the sink.

I lift my good shoulder. "I think only time will tell."

"And how are you doing?"

"Feeling ready to go home."

He brushes the hair out of my face. "As soon as we get the all-clear, Princess, I'll take you back to your home."

I shake my head. "*Our* home."

His eyes lock onto mine, and a moment passes before he softly repeats, "Our home." He leans down to press a kiss to my lips and then pulls away to whisper in my ear, "I love you, wife."

The corners of my lips curve up.

I'll absolutely never tire of hearing him call me that.

"I love you, husband."

CHAPTER THIRTY-TWO

Eli

I use all my strength to force the warehouse doors open, the sunlight casting a glow directly over the two bodies hanging from the ceiling by their wrists.

Alastor and Adolfo.

Blood drips down their swollen faces and over the duct tape covering their lips. Their bodies sag, and their eyes appear heavy and hooded. They are two men who are moments away from meeting their demise.

"We were just warming them up for you." Caine grins proudly, admiring his work. He points a bloody finger at Alastor. "I'm pretty sure this one here already pissed his pants." As we approach, he clasps a hand on Mauro's shoulder. "Thanks for lending me the brass knuckles. Accidently left mine at home in my nightstand."

Marco stands next to Cassio and Marcello, glancing at his phone. "We need to get going. Romeo said the plane is about ready to take off."

"We appreciate your assistance," Vin says as he reaches out his hand to Marco, who accepts it with a firm grip.

"What is family for?" Marco replies, a smug grin on his face that quickly fades. "I'm sorry that you're now bound to the Vasiliev family, but if it's any consolation, I've heard she's not bad on the eyes." He shrugs. "If rumors are to be believed."

Vin squeezes the back of his neck. "Let's just hope she remains missing. It'll be better that way for both of us."

Caine gives a mock salute. "Later, cousins." He tilts his head, eyeing me. "I guess you're one of us now."

I nod. "I guess I am."

"Take care of her," he says. "If we find out otherwise..." He slides his index finger across his neck. "Capisce?"

"Crystal," I reply as I turn toward Marco. "Thank you for your assistance."

Marco looks me over before placing his hand on my shoulder, leaning in. *"Se tu fai del male a lei allora noi facciamo del male a te."* A ghost of a smile plays on his lips as he stands straight. "Until we meet again."

The four of them walk out of the warehouse just as the sun begins to set, the golden light casting them in dark shadows.

"Umm." I look at Vin, scratching my head. "Care to tell me what he just said?"

Vin chuckles, his eyes crinkling at the corners. "Nothing that you don't already know."

As I take a step toward the others, a black SUV pulls up outside. The driver exits the vehicle and presses a button on the side of the car. The whole door slowly slides open, revealing a ramp that extends to the ground. Enzio descends, making his way toward us.

"I hope you haven't changed your mind. We were just about to have some fun," Vin remarks with a slight frown.

Enzio shakes his head. "No, I just came by to thank you personally." He slants his head to the side, looking around Mauro at his father and brother. "Have they been up there long?"

I shake my head. "They've been chained to the corner of the room while they've been here, awaiting their endings, which we've decided is today. So, they were strung up like piñatas this morning in order for us to give them a proper farewell."

"Good," Enzio affirms. Mauro hands him a folder—the one containing all the key documents that Adolfo was forced to sign at gunpoint, transferring the rights of Manacorda Enterprises to Enzio. "Thank you." He flips through the pages, his eyes brightening. "You don't know what this means."

Alex approaches, looking better than he did a few days ago but still a bit somber. "I'm sorry about your sister."

Enzio lowers his chin. "Father never believed in mental health, and I fear over the years, with no treatment or care, she only became worse. I guess I never realized how bad it was, though. I blame myself for not checking in on her regularly." He regards Alex. "Did she suffer?"

"No," he answers firmly. "It was a clean shot."

"Then that's all I could have asked for."

Mumbling breaks out behind us, and we turn to see Alastor and Adolfo moving around. Mauro rips the tape off Alastor's face.

"Enzio!" he screams. "You have to help us. They're psychotic. All of them!"

Enzio merely watches them with boredom in his eyes. "I'm afraid everything they are about to do to you is rightfully deserved."

Alastor's eyes widen. "But you're my brother!"

"Let's get one thing straight," Enzio starts. "You were never a brother to me. Not in the way one should be. And when you leave this Earth, you will leave me as a stranger. Nothing more." He peers around at all of us. "I'll take my leave now. If you need anything in the future, I am in your debt." He returns to his vehicle, and we watch as it disappears past the gates.

We all turn toward the two monsters hanging in the center of the room, our eyes narrowing in on them.

"What do you want?" Alastor asks, with terror laced in his voice. "Money? I have lots of it! Just name a number!"

A laugh escapes me. Dark and consuming. It's always about money with him.

I take a few steps until I stand directly in front of him. Fury builds inside me like a forest fire that can't be extinguished. It only grows stronger and more deadly by the second. "You think I want money after everything you put Madeleine through? After everything you put me through?"

I hear metal grinding against the floor and look behind me to see Mauro dragging a baseball bat behind him—a special one designed with nails sticking out all over it.

We're not using it today.

But it's sure entertaining to let them think that we are.

"No. No. No!" Alastor wails. "Wait! Wait! We can talk about this!"

"You want to talk?" I ask while cracking my knuckles. "Then let's talk." I pace before him. "Your sister planted the seed in your tiny idiotic head about having me kidnapped. Once you did some digging and located where I was, you followed through with the plan by reaching out to your charming cousins, the Vasilievs, for assistance. Their men took me. Killed the men in my unit. Tortured me. And finally, you freed me only after Madeleine agreed to marry you. You then threatened to have me killed if Madeleine should renege on her verbal contract with you." I look around the room at the Alarie brothers. "Am I forgetting anything?"

Leo scrunches his face and shakes his head. "Nope, think that covers everything."

I face Alastor, watching as he swallows hard, sweat dribbling down his temple. "It was the only way." He trembles against the chains. "You have to understand, my father saw me as weak, and I needed Madeleine to gain—"

"She is not a pawn in your fucked-up family's chess game! She is my goddamn wife!" My words echo across the space, thundering between every floorboard and ceiling beam. "You meticulously planned everything like the snake you are, all to get what you wanted: power. You knew your sister struggled with mental health, yet you exploited that to your advantage, indifferent to the consequences, as long as it tore me and Madeleine apart."

"I-I never told her to—"

I get in his face, gripping him by the collar of his shirt. "You will pay for *everything* you did to her. Everything you put her through. And everything she *lost* because of you."

Adolfo mumbles into the tape, so Alex walks up to him and rips it off.

"I have nothing to do with any of this!" he yells.

"You're the one who told me to go through with this whole thing!" Alastor shouts. "You told me that if I married Madeleine, then you would make me CEO of the fucking company!"

"But I didn't know—"

"You knew, old man!" Alastor's face reddens, his neck veins bulging. "You knew everything. In fact, you wanted to have Eli killed after the wedding!"

I arch a brow. "That's news to me."

Adolfo visibly swallows. "We weren't going to follow through with it. It was merely an idea."

"An idea that has guaranteed your death," Leo tells him, crossing his arms over his chest.

"Can't we come to an arrangement?" Adolfo asks, looking frantically among us.

"The arrangement is," I start. "You two will die. And I will live out the rest of my life with Madeleine in peace, knowing you will never be able to hurt her again."

"But we can—"

"Put the tape back on their mouths," I tell Alex and Mauro, who do just that. "I've heard enough."

Walking behind Alastor, I rip his shirt right down the middle, exposing his bare back. "When I was taken, they used to burn my back for fun. They would rub an alcohol wipe across my skin and then light a match and drop it. My screams would echo against the walls. It was the kind of pain that no one should ever experience. But they didn't just do it once." I shake my head, my mind reliving those memories. "They would put the fire out and wait and then do it over again. It was a vicious cycle that never ended." I step toward the back of Adolfo and rip his shirt down the middle, too. "I was maybe only seconds away from dying when I was finally freed."

Mauro comes to my side with a bottle of Macallan in his hands, unscrewing the cap. I step back to look at the two sons of bitches hanging from their chains. They won't last long with what we're about to do to them.

But I'll enjoy every second of it.

For Madeleine.

For our unborn child.

For my comrades.

I will get our revenge.

"So, now, that's exactly what we're going to do to the two of you," I state matter-of-factly.

The two of them begin wriggling against the chains, futilely fighting to free themselves as Mauro douses their backs in the whiskey. Fear reeks in the air around them as they mumble pleas against the tape.

"Sorry, we don't have wipes to use, so the fire will probably be a little unmanageable," I tell them as Leo and I both light a match. "Say hi to the devil for me." I toss my match against Alastor's back and watch as flames engulf him. Out of the corner of my eye, I see Leo do the same to Adolfo.

The two of them scream out in agony against the tape as the smell of burning flesh fills the room. Alex stands by with a fire extinguisher in his hands, ready for us to repeat the process over and over again until, eventually, they take their last dying breaths.

And it brings me comfort to know that the villains of my wife's story will no longer walk this Earth.

Chapter Thirty-Three

Madeleine

ONE MONTH LATER

Everything feels right in the world.

It's as if I can breathe for the first time in over a year. To prove it to myself, I take a deep breath, inhaling the scents of all the delicious food before me.

Eli's arm drapes across the back of my chair, and he presses a kiss to my shoulder, right over the scar from my bullet wound.

Scarlett sits beside me, with Leo on her other side. The two of them are wrapped up in each other, appearing just as in love with one another as they were years ago.

My mom is at one end of the table, smiling with a gleam in her eye as she looks around at everyone.

Alex is sitting beside Vin, and the two of them are deep in conversation, probably discussing the impending war with the Vasiliev family that is looming over us.

And Mauro and Alina are sitting across from me, both of them appearing...well, I'm not exactly sure what to make of it. I've never seen

Mauro so anxious; his index finger keeps tugging at the collar of his shirt. Alina, on the other hand, simply stares at her plate of food, her fork swirling through the pasta but not picking up any of it.

Hmm...

Ding! Ding! Ding!

Vin stands, the edge of his knife tapping against the crystal glass in his hand. All eyes in the room turn to him as his gaze finds mine.

"Family is all that matters in this world," he begins, his eyes shifting to Eli. "And we are blessed that our family keeps growing." He raises his glass high. "Eli, you've always been like a brother to me, Leo, Alex, and Mauro. But now, you are officially one of us—an Alarie. I am honored to welcome you to our family. There is no one we would have thought more perfect for our sister than you. And we know..." He clears his throat. "We know our father would be incredibly happy for the two of you." My eyes water, my throat slightly tightening as I place a hand on Eli's thigh. His dark eyes meet mine as the corners of his mouth turn up, causing mine to do the same. "So, here's to family."

Everyone raises their glasses. "To family."

Eli caresses his lips against my cheek. "I'll be right back, love."

"Where are you going? Dessert will probably be out soon."

"Trust me, I won't miss it." He winks. "Besides." He lowers his head, placing his lips beside my ear. "You know you're my favorite dessert."

Heat creeps up my neck as I bite down on my bottom lip. "Hurry back."

I watch as he walks off, disappearing toward the kitchen.

"So." Scarlett leans toward me, smiling. "Need any help planning your wedding?"

Eli and I haven't discussed what kind of wedding we would like to have, but I have a funny feeling we both already know where it will take place.

"Yeah, starting with a redo of my bachelorette party," I tell her, making us both laugh. "I'm thinking of doing a girls' trip somewhere tropical. Maybe—"

"You can go to the family's island," Leo cuts in.

"But I've been there before."

"So? It has a private security team, twenty-four-seven surveillance, not to mention it's in a no-fly zone."

I roll my eyes. "I guess it could be a compromise."

"What's a compromise?" Eli asks, his voice behind me.

"For my bachelorette—" I turn in my chair, and all the air leaves my lungs as Eli pushes a cart toward me, topped with my wedding cake.

Or, well, it looks like it's supposed to be my former wedding cake. It has the same number of tiers I requested and the same wraparound floral design.

But it's...

"You really thought I was going to let you order a vanilla cake when you dream of and live for chocolate?" he asks, a playful grin spreading across his face.

"What?" I shake my head in confusion. "I don't understand... How did you do this?"

He sits next to me, wrapping his arm around my shoulders, tucking me into his side. "I was never going to let you marry Alastor or any other man, for that matter." He gently sweeps my hair over my shoulder. "And I definitely wasn't going to let a cake go to waste. So, that night, after we left the bakery, I made a call. Asked her to change some things and to push back on the date. Elena seemed easily convinced." I roll my eyes, which makes him chuckle.

"Thank you," I say, placing a kiss on his lips.

He grins, giving a quick shrug. "It was nothing."

I shake my head. "It was everything."

Ding! Ding! Ding!

My head swivels to the side, finding Mauro standing. I arch an eyebrow, looking at Vin, who merely shrugs, appearing just as confused as I am.

Mauro looks down at Alina. She bites her bottom lip and tucks her hair behind her ear before hesitantly standing beside him. His hand slides behind her back to her waist, gently pulling her to his side.

I turn to Scarlett, her shock mirroring my own.

What the hell is going on?

"Hi, everyone," Alina says softly before clearing her throat. She pushes up her glasses and then twists her hands together anxiously. "Mauro and I, well, we just wanted to share that..." She glances around the table, her lips opening and closing as she searches for the right words.

Mauro's brows knit together, concern evident in his eyes as he watches her. He places a hand against his chest, and then, with his right hand in the shape of a loose C, his thumb touches his lower cheek before moving down toward his left hand, which is also shaped in a loose C, and interlocks his hands.

Alina displays a soft smile as a slight blush creeps over her cheeks.

I look around the room. "What did he just—"

"He said." Alex smirks as he leans back in his seat. "*My wife.*"

Silence fills the room.

"We, umm..." Alina gives a slight shrug. "We got married."

***

"Why have you asked me to meet you out here, husband? It's freezing!" I zip up my down jacket and wrap my arms around myself as I trudge through the fluffy snow, approaching Eli, who is standing by the dock.

He smiles at me, amusement dancing in his eyes. "You look like a marshmallow."

I gasp, swatting at his chest. "Take that back."

He wraps an arm around my waist, pulling me close. "A sexy marshmallow.

I tilt my head, considering it. "I'll take it."

He gently presses a soft kiss to my lips before standing me up straight. I take a look around. A small snowstorm swept through last night, leaving everything coated in fresh white—from the tips of the pine trees to the frozen lake.

It's beautiful and serene.

But also, really fucking cold.

"So, are you going to tell me why I'm currently out here freezing my butt off?"

He nods thoughtfully before reaching into his pocket. "I thought you should know that you weren't the only one who sent me letters over the years." He pulls out a worn-looking envelope and holds it out to me.

I raise an eyebrow. "What bitch do I have to fight?"

He lets out a genuine laugh, pushing the letter into my hands.

"I think you should read this one," he says. "It was one of my favorites."

My brows furrow in confusion, but I remove my gloves and open the folded piece of paper. I quickly scan to the bottom of the page to see who wrote this damn letter, and I freeze.

Because the name Charles Alarie stares back at me.

I look at Eli, my throat tightening, my nose stinging, and my eyes blurring. "He wrote to you?"

He nods. "I think he'd want you to read this one."

I quickly glance back down at the paper, grasping it with trembling hands.

June 1st

Eli,

I hope you're doing well, son. Serving in the military is an honorable commitment that not many are brave or selfless enough to undertake. It's not for the faint of heart, and it's certainly not for those seeking recognition.

Being a soldier reveals a great deal about a man's character—about who he is and what he stands for. You, Eli, are an exemplary man; one I would be honored to someday welcome into my family.

I see the way you look at Madeleine like she's the only star in the whole galaxy. I know this because it's the same way I look at her mother.

As a man who has been loyal to my family over the years, you know that our world is ruthless and cruel. And that tomorrow is never guaranteed, which is why I'm writing to you now.

My little girl deserves the whole world and more. But most importantly, she deserves a man who will treat her right, keep her safe, protect her from the evils of this world, and, above all, love her.

I know you are that man for my daughter.

So, this is me giving you my blessing to marry her.

Not tomorrow, not next week, or the week after that.

But when the time is right, I want you to know that you have my permission to get down on one knee and ask her those four words.

Charles Alarie

A river of tears cascades down my cheeks, probably turning into tiny icicles.

My chest tightens as I stare at the words my father wrote to Eli. *He gave him his blessing.* A smile forms on my face as I reach up to brush away my tears. "I can't believe he—" The words fade in my throat as I turn around and see Eli kneeling in the snow, holding out a ring box that contains the same beautiful engagement ring I found in his nightstand drawer.

"Madeleine Alarie," he begins, his eyes bright with genuine happiness, making my heart thunder beneath my rib cage. "Most people aren't lucky enough to meet their soul mate until later on in life, if they meet them at all. But the world did me a kindness when it placed me in the home of the Alarie Estate, intertwining our lives and our stories." He pauses for a moment before continuing, "I've loved you from the moment I laid eyes on you, and I will love you even after the world stops spinning." He drags his fingers nervously through his hair. "I know, we technically already got married, but I wouldn't feel right if I didn't officially ask you." His eyes water, but he clears his throat and says, "Madeleine Alarie, will you marry me?"

I nod, my vision blurring as tears fill my eyes. "Yes, Eli Lyon, I will marry you."

He places the ring on my shaking finger, and the second it's secure, I jump into his arms, knocking him down onto the snowy ground. We laugh as our lips meet, both of our hearts beating as fast as one another's.

"I'm going to spend forever loving you," he promises me. His hands cradle my cheeks as he pulls me toward him, pressing his lips to mine. He pulls away, rolling our foreheads together. "Although, to tell you the truth, forever doesn't sound like enough time."

"You're right. It doesn't." I brush my lips over his, my fingers tangling in his hair. How did I get lucky enough to be able to call this man mine for the rest of my life? Softly, I place a kiss on his lips, lingering for a moment before pulling back and saying, "So, let's make the most of the time we have together, starting right now."

Epilogue

MADELEINE

Eight Months Later

A warm breeze flows through the open French doors, and the pink and gold sky reflects off the pristine lake, evoking a scene worthy of a museum painting.

It's a beautiful day—perhaps the most beautiful day of the year.

And it's time.

"You look so stunning," my mom says as she greets me, holding out my bouquet of white roses. She gazes at my ivory mermaid-style off-the-shoulder lace dress with admiration in her eyes. "This dress was made for you, sweetheart."

"Thank you." I bring the flowers up to my nose and inhale their perfume.

She reaches out, gently tucking a loose strand of hair back in place. "I know your father is watching over you. He's here right now. I can feel it." Her eyes glisten with tears, and mine follow suit. "And I know he's so proud of the woman you've become."

I nod, my throat tightening. "I can feel him here too."

She smiles, wiping carefully under her eyes. "Well, I better get out there."

"I'll be right there." I pull at the top of my dress; the bodice suddenly feels tighter than it did when I last tried it on a week ago. Or was it always this snug?

Just as she steps outside to head toward the dock and take her seat, Vin approaches, lost in thought, peering down at the grass.

With every step he takes, it becomes increasingly difficult to hold back my tears. I suddenly don't feel like a twenty-five-year-old woman, but rather like a little girl—one on the brink of having to say goodbye to the man who has been the missing father figure in her life for the past eight years.

Which is silly, of course, because I'm not going anywhere.

And neither is he.

But there's something about weddings that bring out the damn tears.

As he walks through the door, he looks up and smiles with tears in his eyes, and I can't hold back anymore.

"Ugh, Vin." I wave a hand over my eyes in a futile attempt to dry the tears.

He pinches the bridge of his nose. "Oh, fuck, Madeleine. Why is this so hard?"

"Because we love each other, idiot."

We both share a lighthearted laugh as he approaches my side.

"You're the most beautiful bride I've ever seen," he tells me with sincerity in his voice.

"You probably say that to all of the brides before you walk them down the aisle," I tease, knowing he walked Scarlett down the aisle only a couple of months ago.

He chuckles, rubbing his chin. "I guess it's turning into a new tradition, huh? Me walking the brides of this family down the aisle."

"I wouldn't want it to be anyone else."

He clears his throat. "I'm sorry that Dad's not here to do this part."

I roll in my bottom lip, holding back every emotion. "He may not be able to walk with me down the aisle, but he's here."

"You're probably right." He grins. "A bird shit on my jacket earlier. Do you think that was him?"

I press the palm of my hand over my mouth as a laugh bubbles out of me. "Most likely. Probably getting you back for wrecking his favorite car when you were a teenager."

Vin laughs and pats his pocket before retrieving a letter, which he holds out for me to take. "Eli asked me to give this to you to read before we meet him out there." I accept the letter, curiosity taking over. "I'll go make myself a drink and give you a minute," he adds as he walks away.

I place my bouquet on a side table and carefully tear open the envelope. Pulling out the folded piece of paper, I hold it in front of me.

September 12th

Princess,

Your letters over the years saved me in more ways than I can ever tell you. Every single one took away my fears and my doubts, giving me a reason to fight for each day. They gave me a reason to come home, and most importantly, they gave me a reason to stay alive.

It's because of you that I'm here today.

I will spend the rest of my life trying to be the man you deserve.

A man who will always put your needs before his own.

A man who will hold you when you cry on the bad days and smile with you on the good days.

And a man who will love you even after taking his last breath.

Your husband,
Eli
P.S. I know I haven't technically seen you yet, but you look beautiful.

"Oh my God," I say softly as tears steadily fall down both cheeks. I place a shaking hand over my wildly beating heart, overcome with so many emotions.

This man is the best thing that has ever happened to me.

How I ever doubted that... I shake my head.

There's no use in looking back on the past when my future is so clear.

It's one with Eli by my side.

"Thought you might need this." Vin hands over a tissue, which I take, carefully dabbing at my face.

"Thank God for waterproof mascara." I chuckle as I tuck the letter back into the envelope and replace it with my bouquet on the table.

"I'm so fucking happy for you, Madeleine," he tells me just as the quartet outside begins playing, signaling to me that it's time. "You ready to go get your happily ever after?"

"I've never been more ready for anything in my life."

With my heart racing, we step out the door, leading to the path of white flower petals that extend all the way to the dock. Lanterns hang in a row on each side of us, guiding our route.

To the left of the dock, Scarlett and Alina stand on the grass, both looking absolutely beautiful in their champagne satin dresses and dabbing at their eyes. On the right, Leo, Mauro, and Alex are dressed in matching black suits with champagne-colored ties.

As we get closer to the dock, all the guests stand, and Eli turns to face me, his eyes taking in every inch of me as if seeing me for the very first time.

That's my husband.

He fights back tears but loses the battle the moment I mouth, *I love you.*

I love you, he mouths back, his eyes crinkling at the corners as he quickly wipes at his face.

Vin leans closer to me, whispering so only I can hear, "If he hurts you, just give me the word, and I'll kill him."

I elbow him inconspicuously in the ribs, and he lets out a grunt as we take the final step.

Vin places my hand in Eli's, who gently tugs me to his side, intertwining our fingers.

The officiant speaks, but his words blur in the background as Eli presses our temples together.

"Why do I feel like you're going to make me cry again?" I ask, closing my eyes.

He grins. "I take it Vin gave you my letter."

"He did." I open my eyes. "Why didn't you tell me any of that before?"

"It didn't feel right. But I don't want anything between us anymore. No secrets. Big or small. I don't want to risk anything ever coming between us again."

"Nothing ever will," I promise him. "We found our way back to each other. And this time, I'm never letting you go."

"Good, because I have plans for us." The corners of his lips curve up. "Starting with creating a mini you."

My smile drops. "But what if—"

He cups my cheeks. "If it happens, it happens. If it doesn't, well, you've already made me the happiest man in the world just by being my wife. There's nothing I need more in my life than you, love. Anything beyond that is just a bonus. But this time, I'll be by your side through the whole journey. You won't ever have to go through anything alone again."

Tears crawl down my cheeks. "God, why can't I stop crying? I've never been this emotional in my life."

Eli's thumbs wipe away every tear before they have a chance to fall to the ground.

I've never been this emotional in my life.

...the bodice suddenly feels tighter than it did when I last tried it on a week ago...

My body goes still while my heart races in anticipation as I quickly do some mental math.

And then it hits me.

"I'm late," I whisper, the realization suddenly striking me.

Eli's brows furrow. "Late for what?"

I raise an eyebrow in response.

His eyes widen, his lips parting. "Late as in...*late?*"

I nod in disbelief, a smile taking over my face, one I find impossible to contain. Two months ago, I stopped taking my birth control, knowing that both of us dream of starting a family. I assumed it would take some time for the medication to leave my system, so I never imagined it would happen this quickly. "I think I might be—"

"And do you, Eli Lyon, take Madeleine Alarie to be your lawfully wedded spouse, to have and to hold from this day forward, in sickness and in health, in poverty and in wealth, for as long as you both shall live?"

"I do," Eli rushes out with a giant smile that reaches his eyes.

"And do you, Madeleine Alarie, take Eli Lyon to be your lawfully wedded spouse, to have and to hold from this day forward, in sickness and in health, in poverty and in wealth, for as long as you both—"

"I do," I interject, too impatient for the man to finish his words.

"Then, by the power vested in me, I now pronounce you husband and wife. You may kiss the bride."

Eli wraps an arm around my waist, dipping me as the audience cheers excitedly around us.

"I plan to. Every day. For the rest of my life," he says right before capturing my lips in the most tantalizing kiss of my entire life.

The end.

Thank you for reading *Betrayed in the Dark*!

If you enjoyed this love story, I would be forever grateful if you could leave a review on the platform of your choice. Your support means so much to me and helps spread the word to other readers!

Acknowledgments

To you, the person who decided to give my book a chance—Thank you! I am a relatively new author and hope to learn and grow with each book release, so thank you for your support.

To my twin sister, Amanda—I'll say it again and again, but thank you for always being my biggest fan. I love you!

To my mom and dad—Let me repeat my plea. I appreciate your love and support, but please don't read any of my books. I love you!

To my editor, Erica Russikoff—I absolutely could not do this without you! Thank you for looking after my story!

Thank you to all my readers who share their love for my books on social media! Your kind words help spread the word to more readers, and I am forever grateful for your support.

ABOUT THE AUTHOR

Ashley Elizabeth is an author of steamy contemporary romance. Her books will always tell a love story with just the right amount of spice and, most importantly, end with a happily ever after. When she's not reading a romance novel or overthinking everything, you can find her watching Jurassic Park for the thousandth time with her fur baby, Bailey.

ALSO BY ASHLEY ELIZABETH

The Before series
Book 1 - *Before I Tell You*
Book 2 - *Before I Saw You*
Book 3 - *Before I Loved You*

The Alarie Heirs
Book 1 – *Broken in the Dark*
Book 2 – *Betrayed in the Dark*
Book 3 – *Whispers in the Dark*

KEEP IN TOUCH WITH ASHLEY ELIZABETH

WEBSITE: ashleyelizabethauthor.com
INSTAGRAM: @ashleyelizabethauthor
TIKTOK: @ashleyelizabethauthor
GOODREADS: goodreads.com/ashleyelizabeth